Dylan Thomas was born in Swansea on 27 October 1914. After leaving school he worked briefly on the *South Wales Evening Post* before embarking on his literary career in London. Not only a poet, he wrote short stories, film scripts, features and radio plays, the most famous being *Under Milk Wood*. On 9 November 1953, shortly after his 39th birthday, he collapsed and died in New York City. In 1982 a memorial stone to commemorate him was unveiled in Poets' Corner in Westminster Abbey.

Also available from W&N

A Dylan Thomas Treasury
The Best of Dylan Thomas
I Think of You Always All the Time: Love Letters
The Loud Hill of Wales
Under Milk Wood
Selected Poems
Collected Letters
Collected Poems
Collected Stories

THE BEST OF DYLAN THOMAS

DYLAN THOMAS

Previously published as
Dylan Thomas Omnibus

W&N
WEIDENFELD & NICOLSON

First published as *Dylan Thomas Omnibus* in Great Britain in 1995
by Weidenfeld & Nicolson
This paperback edition published in 2026 by Weidenfeld & Nicolson,
an imprint of The Orion Publishing Group Ltd
Carmelite House, 50 Victoria Embankment
London EC4Y 0DZ

An Hachette UK Company

The authorised representative in the EEA is Hachette Ireland,
8 Castlecourt Centre, Dublin 15, D15 XTP3, Ireland
(email: info@hbgi.ie)

1 3 5 7 9 10 8 6 4 2

A CIP catalogue record for this book is
available from the British Library.

ISBN (Mass Market Paperback) 978 1 3996 3785 5

Printed in Great Britain by Clays Ltd, Elcograf, S.p.A.

MIX
Paper | Supporting
responsible forestry
FSC® C104740

www.weidenfeldandnicolson.co.uk
www.orionbooks.co.uk

CONTENTS

POEMS

STORIES

BROADCASTS

UNDER MILK WOOD 329

BRIEF CHRONOLOGY

27 Oct 1914	Dylan Marlais Thomas born in Swansea
Sept 1925	Enters Swansea Grammar School, where his father was Senior English Master
27 Apr 1930	Starts the first of the 'Notebooks' into which he copied his early poems. (The Notebooks continued until Apr 1934)
Aug 1931	Leaves school. Employed as Reporter on the *South Wales Daily Post* (until Dec 1932)
Mar 1933	First poem published in London ('And death shall have no dominion' in the *New English Weekly*)
Aug 1933	First visit to London
Sept 1933	First poem published in 'Poet's Corner' of the *Sunday Referee* ("That Sanity be Kept"). Correspondence with Pamela Hansford Johnson begins
22 Apr 1934	Wins Book Prize of the 'Poet's Corner' – i.e. the *Sunday Referee*'s sponsorship of his first collection of poems
Feb–Nov 1934	Several visits to London
10 Nov 1934	Moves to London
18 Dec 1934	*18 Poems* published
Apr 1936	Meets Caitlin Macnamara
10 Sept 1936	*Twenty-five Poems* published
21 Apr 1937	First radio broadcast ('Life and the Modern Poet')
11 July 1937	Marries Caitlin Macnamara
May 1938	First moved to live in Laugharne, Carmarthenshire
30 Jan 1939	First son (Llewelyn) born, in Hampshire
24 Aug 1939	*The Map of Love* (poems and stories) published
20 Dec 1939	*The World I Breathe* (a selection of his poetry and prose) – his first volume publication in America
4 Apr 1940	*Portrait of the Artist as a Young Dog* (short stories) published
July 1940	Leaves Laugharne for London
Sept 1940	Begins work as script-writer for films with the Strand Film Company

1940–2	Living partly in London, partly in Wales
Late 1942	Brings wife and son to live in Chelsea
Feb 1943	*New Poems* (USA)
3 Mar 1943	Daughter (Aeronwy) born
1943	Continuous work as broadcaster begins
Sept 1944–Summer 1945	Living at New Quay, Cardiganshire
Summer 1945–Spring 1946	Living in London
7 Feb 1946	*Deaths and Entrances* published
Mar 1946–May 1949	Living in or near Oxford
8 Nov 1946	*Selected Writings* (USA)
Apr–Aug 1947	Visits Italy
Sept 1947	Moves to live in South Leigh, Oxfordshire
1948	Writing feature films for Gainsborough
Mar 1949	Visits Prague as guest of Czechoslovak government
May 1949	Laugharne again becomes his main home (The Boat House)
24 July 1949	Second son (Colm) born
Feb–June 1950	First American tour
Jan 1951	In Iran, writing film script for the Anglo Iranian Oil Company
Jan–May 1952	Second American tour
Feb 1952	*In Country Sleep* (USA)
10 Nov 1952	*Collected Poems 1934–1952* published
16 Dec 1952	The poet's father dies
31 Mar 1953	*Collected Poems* (USA)
Apr–June 1953	Third American tour
14 May 1953	First performance of *Under Milk Wood* in New York
14 May 1953	*The Doctor and the Devils*. The first of the film scripts to be published
Oct 1953	Leaves on final American tour
9 Nov 1953	Dies in St Vincent's Hospital, New York City
1 Mar 1982	Memorial stone unveiled in 'Poets' Corner', Westminster Abbey

POEMS

Prologue

This day winding down now
At God speeded summer's end
In the torrent salmon sun,
In my seashaken house
On a breakneck of rocks
Tangled with chirrup and fruit,
Froth, flute, fin and quill
At a wood's dancing hoof,
By scummed, starfish sands
With their fishwife cross
Gulls, pipers, cockles, and sails,
Out there, crow black, men
Tackled with clouds, who kneel
To the sunset nets,
Geese nearly in heaven, boys
Stabbing, and herons, and shells
That speak seven seas,
Eternal waters away
From the cities of nine
Days' night whose towers will catch
In the religious wind
Like stalks of tall, dry straw,
At poor peace I sing
To you, strangers, (though song
Is a burning and crested act,
The fire of birds in
The world's turning wood,
For my sawn, splay sounds),
Out of these seathumbed leaves
That will fly and fall
Like leaves of trees and as soon
Crumble and undie

Into the dogdayed night.
Seaward the salmon, sucked sun slips,
And the dumb swans drub blue
My dabbed bay's dusk, as I hack
This rumpus of shapes
For you to know
How I, a spinning man,
Glory also this star, bird
Roared, sea born, man torn, blood blest.
Hark: I trumpet the place,
From fish to jumping hill! Look:
I build my bellowing ark
To the best of my love
As the flood begins,
Out of the fountainhead
Of fear, rage red, manalive,
Molten and mountainous to stream
Over the wound asleep
Sheep white hollow farms

To Wales in my arms.
Hoo, there, in castle keep,
You king singsong owls, who moonbeam
The flickering runs and dive
The dingle furred deer dead!
Huloo, on plumbed bryns,
O my ruffled ring dove
In the hooting, nearly dark
With Welsh and reverent rook,
Coo rooing the woods' praise,
Who moons her blue notes from her nest
Down to the curlew herd!
Ho, hullaballoing clan
Agape, with woe
In your beaks, on the gabbing capes!
Heigh, on horseback hill, jack
Whisking hare! who
Hears, there, this fox light, my flood ship's
Clangour as I hew and smite
(A clash of anvils for my

Hubbub and fiddle, this tune
On a tongued puffball)
But animals thick as thieves
On God's rough tumbling grounds
(Hail to His beasthood!).
Beasts who sleep good and thin,
Hist, in hogsback woods! The haystacked
Hollow farms in a throng
Of waters cluck and cling,
And barnroofs cockcrow war!
O kingdom of neighbours, finned
Felled and quilled, flash to my patch
Work ark and the moonshine
Drinking Noah of the bay,
With pelt, and scale, and fleece:
Only the drowned deep bells
Of sheep and churches noise
Poor peace as the sun sets
And dark shoals every holy field.
We shall ride out alone, and then,
Under the stars of Wales,
Cry, Multitudes of arks! Across
The water lidded lands,
Manned with their loves they'll move,
Like wooden islands, hill to hill.
Huloo, my prowed dove with a flute!
Ahoy, old, sea-legged fox,
Tom tit and Dai mouse!
My ark sings in the sun
At God speeded summer's end
And the flood flowers now.

18 POEMS

I see the boys of summer

I

I see the boys of summer in their ruin
Lay the gold tithings barren,
Setting no store by harvest, freeze the soils;
There in their heat the winter floods
Of frozen loves they fetch their girls,
And drown the cargoed apples in their tides.

These boys of light are curdlers in their folly,
Sour the boiling honey;
The jacks of frost they finger in the hives;
There in the sun the frigid threads
Of doubt and dark they feed their nerves;
The signal moon is zero in their voids.

I see the summer children in their mothers
Split up the brawned womb's weathers,
Divide the night and day with fairy thumbs;
There in the deep with quartered shades
Of sun and moon they paint their dams
As sunlight paints the shelling of their heads.

I see that from these boys shall men of nothing
Stature by seedy shifting,
Or lame the air with leaping from its heats;
There from their hearts the dogdayed pulse
Of love and light bursts in their throats,
O see the pulse of summer in the ice.

II

But seasons must be challenged or they totter
Into a chiming quarter
Where, punctual as death, we ring the stars;
There, in his night, the black-tongued bells
The sleepy man of winter pulls,
Nor blows back moon-and-midnight as she blows

We are the dark deniers, let us summon
Death from a summer woman,
A muscling life from lovers in their cramp,
From the fair dead who flush the sea
The bright-eyed worm on Davy's lamp,
And from the planted womb the man of straw.

We summer boys in this four-winded spinning,
Green of the seaweeds' iron,
Hold up the noisy sea and drop her birds,
Pick the world's ball of wave and froth
To choke the deserts with her tides,
And comb the county gardens for a wreath.

In spring we cross our foreheads with the holly,
Heigh ho the blood and berry,
And nail the merry squires to the trees;
Here love's damp muscle dries and dies,
Here break a kiss in no love's quarry.
O see the poles of promise in the boys.

III

I see you boys of summer in your ruin.
Man in his maggot's barren.
And boys are full and foreign in the pouch.
I am the man your father was.
We are the sons of flint and pitch.
O see the poles are kissing as they cross.

When once the twilight locks

When once the twilight locks no longer
Locked in the long worm of my finger
Nor dammed the sea that sped about my fist,
The mouth of time sucked, like a sponge,
The milky acid on each hinge,
And swallowed dry the waters of the breast.

When the galactic sea was sucked
And all the dry seabed unlocked,
I sent my creature scouting on the globe,
That globe itself of hair and bone
That, sewn to me by nerve and brain,
Had stringed my flask of matter to his rib.

My fuses timed to charge his heart,
He blew like powder to the light
And held a little sabbath with the sun,
But when the stars, assuming shape,
Drew in his eyes the straws of sleep,
He drowned his father's magics in a dream.

All issue armoured, of the grave,
The redhaired cancer still alive,
The cataracted eyes that filmed their cloth;
Some dead undid their bushy jaws,
And bags of blood let out their flies;
He had by heart the Christ-cross-row of death.

Sleep navigates the tides of time;
The dry Sargasso of the tomb
Gives up its dead to such a working sea;
And sleep rolls mute above the beds
Where fishes' food is fed the shades
Who periscope through flowers to the sky.

The hanged who lever from the limes
Ghostly propellers for their limbs,

The cypress lads who wither with the cock,
These, and the others in sleep's acres,
Of dreaming men make moony suckers,
And snipe the fools of vision in the back.

When once the twilight screws were turned,
And mother milk was stiff as sand,
I sent my own ambassador to light;
By trick or chance he fell asleep
And conjured up a carcase shape
To rob me of my fluids in his heart.

Awake, my sleeper, to the sun,
A worker in the morning town,
And leave the poppied pickthank where he lies;
The fences of the light are down,
All but the briskest riders thrown,
And worlds hang on the trees.

A process in the weather of the heart

A process in the weather of the heart
Turns damp to dry; the golden shot
Storms in the freezing tomb.
A weather in the quarter of the veins
Turns night to day; blood in their suns
Lights up the living worm.

A process in the eye forwarns
The bones of blindness; and the womb
Drives in a death as life leaks out.

A darkness in the weather of the eye
Is half its light; the fathomed sea
Breaks on unangled land.
The seed that makes a forest of the loin
Forks half its fruit; and half drops down,

Slow in a sleeping wind.

A weather in the flesh and bone
Is damp and dry; the quick and dead
Move like two ghosts before the eye.

A process in the weather of the world
Turns ghost to ghost; each mothered child
Sits in their double shade.
A process blows the moon into the sun,
Pulls down the shabby curtains of the skin;
And the heart gives up its dead.

Before I knocked

Before I knocked the flesh let enter,
With liquid hands tapped on the womb,
I who was shapeless as the water
That shaped the Jordan near my home
Was brother to Mnetha's daughter
And sister to the fathering worm.

I who was deaf to spring and summer,
Who knew not sun nor moon by name,
Felt thud beneath my flesh's armour,
As yet was in a molten form,
The leaden stars, the rainy hammer
Swung by my father from his dome.

I knew the message of the winter,
The darted hail, the childish snow,
And the wind was my sister suitor;
Wind in me leaped, the hellborn dew;
My veins flowed with the Eastern weather;
Ungotten I knew night and day.

As yet ungotten, I did suffer;

The rack of dreams my lily bones
Did twist into a living cipher,
And flesh was snipped to cross the lines
Of gallow crosses on the liver
And brambles in the wringing brains.

My throat knew thirst before the structure
Of skin and vein around the well
Where words and water make a mixture
Unfailing till the blood runs foul;
My heart knew love, my belly hunger;
I smelt the maggot in my stool.

And time cast forth my mortal creature
To drift or drown upon the seas
Acquainted with the salt adventure
Of tides that never touch the shores.
I who was rich was made the richer
By sipping at the vine of days.

I, born of flesh and ghost, was neither
A ghost nor man, but mortal ghost.
And I was struck down by death's feather.
I was mortal to the last
Long breath that carried to my father
The message of his dying christ.

You who bow down at cross and altar,
Remember me and pity Him
Who took my flesh and bone for armour
And doublecrossed my mother's womb.

The force that through the green fuse

The force that through the green fuse drives the flower
Drives my green age; that blasts the roots of trees
Is my destroyer.

And I am dumb to tell the crooked rose
My youth is bent by the same wintry fever.

The force that drives the water through the rocks
Drives my red blood; that dries the mouthing streams
Turns mine to wax.
And I am dumb to mouth unto my veins
How at the mountain spring the same mouth sucks.

The hand that whirls the water in the pool
Stirs the quicksand; that ropes the blowing wind
Hauls my shroud sail.
And I am dumb to tell the hanging man
How of my clay is made the hangman's lime.

The lips of time leech to the fountain head;
Love drips and gathers, but the fallen blood
Shall calm her sores.
And I am dumb to tell a weather's wind
How time has ticked a heaven round the stars.

And I am dumb to tell the lover's tomb
How at my sheet goes the same crooked worm.

My hero bares his nerves

My hero bares his nerves along my wrist
That rules from wrist to shoulder,
Unpacks the head that, like a sleepy ghost,
Leans on my mortal ruler,
The proud spine spurning turn and twist.

And these poor nerves so wired to the skull
Ache on the lovelorn paper
I hug to love with my unruly scrawl
That utters all love hunger
And tells the page the empty ill.

My hero bares my side and sees his heart
Tread, like a naked Venus,
The beach of flesh, and wind her bloodred plait;
Stripping my loin of promise,
He promises a secret heat.

He holds the wire from this box of nerves
Praising the mortal error
Of birth and death, the two sad knaves of thieves,
And the hunger's emperor;
He pulls the chain, the cistern moves.

Where once the waters of your face

Where once the waters of your face
Spun to my screws, your dry ghost blows,
The dead turns up its eye;
Where once the mermen through your ice
Pushed up their hair, the dry wind steers
Through salt and root and roe.

Where once your green knots sank their splice
Into the tided cord, there goes
The green unraveller,
His scissors oiled, his knife hung loose
To cut the channels at their source
And lay the wet fruits low.

Invisible, your clocking tides
Break on the lovebeds of the weeds;
The weed of love's left dry;
There round about your stones the shades
Of children go who, from their voids,
Cry to the dolphined sea.

Dry as a tomb, your coloured lids
Shall not be latched while magic glides

Sage on the earth and sky;
There shall be corals in your beds,
There shall be serpents in your tides,
Till all our sea-faiths die.

If I were tickled by the rub of love

If I were ticked by the rub of love,
A rooking girl who stole me for her side,
Broke through her straws, breaking my bandaged string,
If the red tickle as the cattle calve
Still set to scratch a laughter from my lung,
I would not fear the apple nor the flood
Nor the bad blood of spring.

Shall it be male or female? say the cells,
And drop the plum like fire from the flesh.
If I were tickled by the hatching hair,
The winging bone that sprouted in the heels,
The itch of man upon the baby's thigh,
I would not fear the gallows nor the axe
Nor the crossed sticks of war.

Shall it be male or female? say the fingers
That chalk the walls with green girls and their men.
I would not fear the muscling-in of love
If I were tickled by the urchin hungers
Rehearsing heat upon a raw-edged nerve.
I would not fear the devil in the loin
Nor the outspoken grave.

If I were tickled by the lovers' rub
That wipes away not crow's-foot nor the lock
Of sick old manhood on the fallen jaws,
Time and the crabs and the sweethearting crib
Would leave me cold as butter for the flies,

The sea of scums could drown me as it broke
Dead on the sweethearts' toes.

This world is half the devil's and my own,
Daft with the drug that's smoking in a girl
And curling round the bud that forks her eye.
An old man's shank one-marrowed with my bone,
And all the herrings smelling in the sea,
I sit and watch the worm beneath my nail
Wearing the quick away.

And that's the rub, the only rub that tickles.
The knobbly ape that swings along his sex
From damp love-darkness and the nurse's twist
Can never raise the midnight of a chuckle,
Nor when he finds a beauty in the breast
Of lover, mother, lovers, or his six
Feet in the rubbing dust.

And what's the rub? Death's feather on the nerve?
Your mouth, my love, the thistle in the kiss?
My Jack of Christ born thorny on the tree?
The words of death are dryer than his stiff,
My wordy wounds are printed with your hair.
I would be tickled by the rub that is:
Man be my metaphor.

Our eunuch dreams

I

Our eunuch dreams, all seedless in the light,
Of light and love, the tempers of the heart,
Whack their boys' limbs,
And, winding-footed in their shawl and sheet,
Groom the dark brides, the widows of the night
Fold in their arms.

The shades of girls, all flavoured from their shrouds,
When sunlight goes are sundered from the worm,
The bones of men, the broken in their beds,
By midnight pulleys that unhouse the tomb.

II

In this our age the gunman and his moll,
Two one-dimensioned ghosts, love on a reel,
Strange to our solid eye,
And speak their midnight nothings as they swell;
When cameras shut they hurry to their hole
Down in the yard of day.

They dance between their arclamps and our skull,
Impose their shots, throwing the nights away;
We watch the show of shadows kiss or kill,
Flavoured of celluloid give love the lie.

III

Which is the world? Of our two sleepings, which
Shall fall awake when cures and their itch
Raise up this red-eyed earth?
Pack off the shapes of daylight and their starch,
The sunny gentlemen, the Welshing rich,
Or drive the night-geared forth.

The photograph is married to the eye,
Grafts on its bride one-sided skins of truth;
The dream has sucked the sleeper of his faith
That shrouded men might marrow as they fly.

IV

This is the world: the lying likeness of
Our strips of stuff that tatter as we move
Loving and being loth;

The dream that kicks the buried from their sack
And lets their trash be honoured as the quick.
This is the world. Have faith.

For we shall be a shouter like the cock,
Blowing the old dead back; our shots shall smack
The image from the plates;
And we shall be fit fellows for a life,
And who remain shall flower as they love,
Praise to our faring hearts.

Especially when the October wind

Especially when the October wind
With frosty fingers punishes my hair,
Caught by the crabbing sun I walk on fire
And cast a shadow crab upon the land,
By the sea's side, hearing the noise of birds,
Hearing the raven cough in winter sticks,
My busy heart who shudders as she talks
Sheds the syllabic blood and drains her words.

Shut, too, in a tower of words, I mark
On the horizon walking like the trees
The wordy shapes of women, and the rows
Of the star-gestured children in the park.
Some let me make you of the vowelled beeches,
Some of the oaken voices, from the roots
Of many a thorny shire tell you notes,
Some let me make you of the water's speeches.

Behind a pot of ferns the wagging clock
Tells me the hour's word, the neural meaning
Flies on the shafted disc, declaims the morning
And tells the windy weather in the cock.
Some let me make you of the meadow's signs;
The signal grass that tells me all I know

Breaks with the wormy winter through the eye.
Some let me tell you of the raven's sins.

Especially when the October wind
(Some let me make you of autumnal spells,
The spider-tongued, and the loud hill of Wales)
With fist of turnips punishes the land,
Some let me make you of the heartless words.
The heart is drained that, spelling in the scurry
Of chemic blood, warned of the coming fury.
By the sea's side hear the dark-vowelled birds.

When, like a running grave

When, like a running grave, time tracks you down,
Your calm and cuddled is a scythe of hairs,
Love in her gear is slowly through the house,
Up naked stairs, a turtle in a hearse,
Hauled to the dome,

Comes, like a scissors stalking, tailor age,
Deliver me who, timid in my tribe,
Of love am barer than Cadaver's trap
Robbed of the foxy tongue, his footed tape
Of the bone inch,

Deliver me, my masters, head and heart,
Heart of Cadaver's candle waxes thin,
When blood, spade-handed, and the logic time
Drive children up like bruises to the thumb,
From maid and head,

For, sunday faced, with dusters in my glove,
Chaste and the chaser, man with the cockshut eye,
I, that time's jacket or the coat of ice
May fail to fasten with a virgin o
In the straight grave,

Stride through Cadaver's country in my force,
My pickbrain masters morsing on the stone
Despair of blood, faith in the maiden's slime,
Halt among eunuchs, and the nitric stain
On fork and face.

Time is a foolish fancy, time and fool.
No, no, you lover skull, descending hammer
Descends, my masters, on the entered honour.
You hero skull, Cadaver in the hangar
Tells the stick 'fail'.

Joy is no knocking nation, sir and madam,
The cancer's fusion, or the summer feather
Lit on the cuddled tree, the cross of fever,
Nor city tar and subway bored to foster
Man through macadam.

I damp the waxlights in your tower dome.
Joy is the knock of dust, Cadaver's shoot
Of bud of Adam through his boxy shift,
Love's twilit nation and the skull of state,
Sir, is your doom.

Everything ends, the tower ending and,
(Have with the house of wind) the leaning scene,
Ball of the foot depending from the sun,
(Give, summer, over) the cemented skin,
The actions' end.

All, men my madmen, the unwholesome wind
With whistler's cough contages, time on track
Shapes in a cinder death; love for his trick,
Happy Cadaver's hunger as you take
The kissproof world.

From love's first fever

From love's first fever to her plague, from the soft second
And to the hollow minute of the womb,
From the unfolding to the scissored caul,
The time for breast and the green apron age
When no mouth stirred about the hanging famine,
All world was one, one windy nothing,
My world was christened in a stream of milk.
And earth and sky were as one airy hill,
The sun and moon shed one white light.

From the first print of the unshodden foot, the lifting
Hand, the breaking of the hair,
And to the miracle of the first rounded word,
From the first secret of the heart, the warning ghost,
And to the first dumb wonder at the flesh,
The sun was red, the moon was grey,
The earth and sky were as two mountains meeting.

The body prospered, teeth in the marrowed gums,
The growing bones, the rumour of manseed
Within the hallowed gland, blood blessed the heart,
And the four winds, that had long blown as one,
Shone in my ears the light of sound,
Called in my eyes the sound of light.
And yellow was the multiplying sand,
Each golden grain spat life into its fellow,
Green was the singing house.

The plum my mother picked matured slowly,
The boy she dropped from darkness at her side
Into the sided lap of light grew strong,
Was muscled, matted, wise to the crying thigh
And to the voice that, like a voice of hunger,
Itched in the noise of wind and sun.

And from the first declension of the flesh
I learnt man's tongue, to twist the shapes of thoughts

Into the stony idiom of the brain,
To shade and knit anew the patch of words
Left by the dead who, in their moonless acre,
Need no word's warmth.
The root of tongues ends in a spentout cancer,
That but a name, where maggots have their X.

I learnt the verbs of will, and had my secret;
The code of night tapped on my tongue;
What had been one was many sounding minded.

One womb, one mind, spewed out the matter,
One breast gave suck the fever's issue;
From the divorcing sky I learnt the double,
The two-framed globe that spun into a score;
A million minds gave suck to such a bud
As forks my eye;
Youth did condense; the tears of spring
Dissolved in summer and the hundred seasons;
One sun, one manna, warmed and fed.

In the beginning

In the beginning was the three-pointed star,
One smile of light across the empty face;
One bough of bone across the rooting air,
The substance forked that marrowed the first sun;
And, burning cophers on the round of space,
Heaven and hell mixed as they spun.

In the beginning was the pale signature,
Three-syllabled and starry as the smile;
And after came the imprints on the water,
Stamp of the minted face upon the moon;
The blood that touched the crosstree and the grail
Touched the first cloud and left a sign.

In the beginning was the mounting fire
That set alight the weathers from a spark,
A three-eyed, red-eyed spark, blunt as a flower;
Life rose and spouted from the rolling seas,
Burst in the roots, pumped from the earth and rock
The secret oils that drive the grass.

In the beginning was the word, the word
That from the solid bases of the light
Abstracted all the letters of the void;
And from the cloudy bases of the breath
The word flowed up, translating to the heart
First characters of birth and death.

In the beginning was the secret brain.
The brain was celled and soldered in the thought
Before the pitch was forking to a sun;
Before the veins were shaking in their sieve,
Blood shot and scattered to the winds of light
The ribbed original of love.

Light breaks where no sun shines

Light breaks where no sun shines;
Where no sea runs, the waters of the heart
Push in their tides;
And, broken ghosts with glow-worms in their heads,
The things of light
File through the flesh where no flesh decks the bones.

A candle in the thighs
Warms youth and seed and burns the seeds of age;
Where no seed stirs,
The fruit of man unwrinkles in the stars,
Bright as a fig;
Where no wax is, the candle shows its hairs.

Dawn breaks behind the eyes;
From poles of skull and toe the windy blood
Slides like a sea;
Nor fenced, nor staked, the gushers of the sky
Spout to the rod
Divining in a smile the oil of tears.

Night in the sockets rounds,
Like some pitch moon, the limit of the globes;
Day lights the bone;
Where no cold is, the skinning gales unpin
The winter's robes;
The film of spring is hanging from the lids.

Light breaks on secret lots,
On tips of thought where thoughts smell in the rain;
When logics die,
The secret of the soil grows through the eye,
And blood jumps in the sun;
Above the waste allotments the dawn halts.

I fellowed sleep

I fellowed sleep who kissed me in the brain,
Let fall the tear of time; the sleeper's eye,
Shifting to light, turned on me like a moon.
So, 'planing-heeled, I flew along my man
And dropped on dreaming and the upward sky.

I fled the earth and, naked, climbed the weather,
Reaching a second ground far from the stars;
And there we wept, I and a ghostly other,
My mothers-eyed, upon the tops of trees;
I fled that ground as lightly as a feather.

'My fathers' globe knocks on its nave and sings.'
'This that we tread was, too, your fathers' land.'

'But this we tread bears the angelic gangs,
Sweet are their fathered faces in their wings.'
'These are but dreaming men. Breathe, and they fade.'

Faded my elbow ghost, the mothers-eyed,
As, blowing on the angels, I was lost
On that cloud coast to each grave-gabbing shade;
I blew the dreaming fellows to their bed
Where still they sleep unknowing of their ghost.

Then all the matter of the living air
Raised up a voice, and, climbing on the words,
I spelt my vision with a hand and hair,
How light the sleeping on this soily star,
How deep the waking in the worlded clouds.

There grows the hours' ladder to the sun,
Each rung a love or losing to the last,
The inches monkeyed by the blood of man.
An old, mad man still climbing in his ghost,
My fathers' ghost is climbing in the rain.

I dreamed my genesis

I dreamed my genesis in sweat of sleep, breaking
Through the rotating shell, strong
As motor muscle on the drill, driving
Through vision and the girdered nerve.

From limbs that had the measure of the worm, shuffled
Off from the creasing flesh, filed
Through all the irons in the grass, metal
Of suns in the man-melting night.

Heir to the scalding veins that hold love's drop, costly
A creature in my bones I

Rounded my globe of heritage, journey
In bottom gear through night-geared man.

I dreamed my genesis and died again, shrapnel
Rammed in the marching heart, hole
In the stitched wound and clotted wind, muzzled
Death on the mouth that ate the gas.

Sharp in my second death I marked the hills, harvest
Of hemlock and the blades, rust
My blood upon the tempered dead, forcing
My second struggling from the grass.

And power was contagious in my birth, second
Rise of the skeleton and
Rerobing of the naked ghost. Manhood
Spat up from the resuffered pain.

I dreamed my genesis in sweat of death, fallen
Twice in the feeding sea, grown
Stale of Adam's brine until, vision
Of new man strength, I seek the sun.

My world is pyramid

I

Half of the fellow father as he doubles
His sea-sucked Adam in the hollow hulk,
Half of the fellow mother as she dabbles
Tomorrow's diver in her horny milk,
Bisected shadows on the thunder's bone
Bolt for the salt unborn.

The fellow half was frozen as it bubbled
Corrosive spring out of the iceberg's crop,
The fellow seed and shadow as it babbled
The swing of milk was tufted in the pap,

For half of love was planted in the lost,
And the unplanted ghost.

The broken halves are fellowed in a cripple,
The crutch that marrow taps upon their sleep,
Limp in the street of sea, among the rabble
Of tide-tongued heads and bladders in the deep,
And stake the sleepers in the savage grave
That the vampire laugh.

The patchwork halves were cloven as they scudded
The wild pigs' wood, and slime upon the trees,
Sucking the dark, kissed on the cyanide,
And loosed the braiding adders from their hairs;
Rotating halves are horning as they drill
The arterial angel.

What colour is glory? death's feather? tremble
The halves that pierce the pin's point in the air,
And prick the thumb-stained heaven through the thimble.
The ghost is dumb that stammered in the straw,
The ghost that hatched his havoc as he flew
Blinds their cloud-tracking eye.

II

My world is pyramid. The padded mummer
Weeps on the desert ochre and the salt
Incising summer.
My Egypt's armour buckling in its sheet,
I scrape through resin to a starry bone
And a blood parhelion.

My world is cypress, and an English valley.
I piece my flesh that rattled on the yards
Red in an Austrian volley.
I hear, through dead men's drums, the riddled lads,
Strewing their bowels from a hill of bones,
Cry Eloi to the guns.

My grave is watered by the crossing Jordan.
The Arctic scut, and basin of the South,
Drip on my dead house garden.
Who seek me landward, marking in my mouth
The straws of Asia, lose me as I turn
Through the Atlantic corn.

The fellow halves that, cloven as they swivel
On casting tides, are tangled in the shells,
Bearding the unborn devil,
Bleed from my burning fork and smell my heels.
The tongues of heaven gossip as I glide
Binding my angel's hood.

Who blows death's feather? What glory is colour?
I blow the stammel feather in the vein.
The loin is glory in a working pallor.
My clay unsuckled and my salt unborn,
The secret child, I shift about the sea
Dry in the half-tracked thigh.

All all and all

I

All all and all the dry worlds lever,
Stage of the ice, the solid ocean,
All from the oil, the pound of lava.
City of spring, the governed flower,
Turns in the earth that turns the ashen
Towns around on a wheel of fire.

How now my flesh, my naked fellow,
Dug of the sea, the glanded morrow,
Worm in the scalp, the staked and fallow.
All all and all, the corpse's lover,

Skinny as sin, the foaming marrow,
All of the flesh, the dry worlds lever.

II

Fear not the working world, my mortal,
Fear not the flat, synthetic blood,
Nor the heart in the ribbing metal.
Fear not the tread, the seeded milling,
The trigger and scythe, the bridal blade,
Nor the flint in the lover's mauling.

Man of my flesh, the jawbone riven,
Know now the flesh's lock and vice,
And the cage for the scythe-eyed raven.
Know, O my bone, the jointed lever,
Fear not the screws that turn the voice,
And the face to the driven lover.

III

All all and all the dry worlds couple,
Ghost with her ghost, contagious man
With the womb of his shapeless people.
All that shapes from the caul and suckle,
Stroke of mechanical flesh on mine,
Square in these worlds the mortal circle.

Flower, flower the people's fusion,
O light in zenith, the coupled bud,
And the flame in the flesh's vision.
Out of the sea, the drive of oil,
Socket and grave, the brassy blood,
Flower, flower, all all and all.

TWENTY-FIVE POEMS

I, in my intricate image

I

I, in my intricate image, stride on two levels,
Forged in man's minerals, the brassy orator
Laying my ghost in metal,
The scales of this twin world tread on the double,
My half ghost in armour hold hard in death's corridor,
To my man-iron sidle.

Beginning with doom in the bulb, the spring unravels,
Bright as her spinning-wheels, the colic season
Worked on a world of petals;
She threads off the sap and needles, blood and bubble
Casts to the pine roots, raising man like a mountain
Out of the naked entrail.

Beginning with doom in the ghost, and the springing marvels,
Image of images, my metal phantom
Forcing forth through the harebell,
My man of leaves and the bronze root, mortal, unmortal,
I, in my fusion of rose and male motion,
Create this twin miracle.

This is the fortune of manhood: the natural peril,
A steeplejack tower, bonerailed and masterless,
No death more natural;
Thus the shadowless man or ox, and the pictured devil,
In seizure of silence commit the dead nuisance:
The natural parallel.

My images stalk the trees and the slant sap's tunnel,
No tread more perilous, the green steps and spire
Mount on man's footfall,

I with the wooden insect in the tree of nettles,
In the glass bed of grapes with snail and flower,
Hearing the weather fall.

Intricate manhood of ending, the invalid rivals,
Voyaging clockwise off the symboled harbour,
Finding the water final,
On the consumptives' terrace taking their two farewells,
Sail on the level, the departing adventure,
To the sea-blown arrival.

II

They climb the country pinnacle,
Twelve winds encounter by the white host at pasture,
Corner the mounted meadows in the hill corral;
They see the squirrel stumble,
The haring snail go giddily round the flower,
A quarrel of weathers and trees in the windy spiral.

As they dive, the dust settles,
The Cadaverous gravels, falls thick and steadily,
The highroad of water where the seabear and mackerel
Turn the long sea arterial
Turning a petrol face blind to the enemy
Turning the riderless dead by the channel wall.

(Death instrumental,
Splitting the long eye open, and the spiral turnkey,
Your corkscrew grave centred in navel and nipple,
The neck of the nostril,
Under the mask and the ether, they making bloody
The tray of knives, the antiseptic funeral;

Bring out the black patrol,
Your monstrous officers and the decaying army,
The sexton sentinel, garrisoned under thistles,
A cock-on-a-dunghill
Crowing to Lazarus the morning is vanity,
Dust be your saviour under the conjured soil.)

As they drown, the chime travels,
Sweetly the diver's bell in the steeple of spindrift
Rings out the Dead Sea scale;
And, clapped in water till the triton dangles,
Strung by the flaxen whale-weed, from the hangman's raft,
Hear they the salt glass breakers and the tongues of burial.

(Turn the sea-spindle lateral,
The grooved land rotating, that the stylus of lightning
Dazzle this face of voices on the moon-turned table,
Let the wax disc babble
Shames and the damp dishonours, the relic scraping.
These are your years' recorders. The circular world stands still.)

III

They suffer the undead water where the turtle nibbles,
Come unto sea-stuck towers, at the fibre scaling,
The flight of the carnal skull
And the cell-stepped thimble;
Suffer, my topsy-turvies, that a double angel
Sprout from the stony lockers like a tree on Aran.

Be by your one ghost pierced, his pointed ferrule,
Brass and the bodiless image, on a stick of folly
Star-set at Jacob's angle,
Smoke hill and hophead's valley,
And the five-fathomed Hamlet on his father's coral,
Thrusting the tom-thumb vision up the iron mile.

Suffer the slash of vision by the fin-green stubble,
Be by the ships' sea broken at the manstring anchored
The stoved bones' voyage downward
In the shipwreck of muscle;
Give over, lovers, locking, and the seawax struggle,
Love like a mist or fire through the bed of eels.

And in the pincers of the boiling circle,
The sea and instrument, nicked in the locks of time,
My great blood's iron single

In the pouring town,
I, in a wind on fire, from green Adam's cradle,
No man more magical, clawed out the crocodile.

Man was the scales, the death birds on enamel,
Tail, Nile, and snout, a saddler of the rushes,
Time in the hourless houses
Shaking the sea-hatched skull,
And, as for oils and ointments on the flying grail,
All-hallowed man wept for his white apparel.

Man was Cadaver's masker, the harnessing mantle,
Windily master of man was the rotten fathom,
My ghost in his metal neptune
Forged in man's mineral.
This was the god of beginning in the intricate seawhirl,
And my images roared and rose on heaven's hill.

This bread I break

This bread I break was once the oat,
This wine upon a foreign tree
Plunged in its fruit;
Man in the day or wind at night
Laid the crops low, broke the grape's joy.

Once in this wine the summer blood
Knocked in the flesh that decked the vine,
Once in this bread
The oat was merry in the wind;
Man broke the sun, pulled the wind down.

This flesh you break, this blood you let
Make desolation in the vein,
Were oat and grape
Born of the sensual root and sap;
My wine you drink, my bread you snap.

Incarnate devil

Incarnate devil in a talking snake,
The central plains of Asia in his garden,
In shaping-time the circle stung awake,
In shapes of sin forked out the bearded apple,
And God walked there who was a fiddling warden
And played down pardon from the heavens' hill.

When we were strangers to the guided seas,
A handmade moon half holy in a cloud,
The wisemen tell me that the garden gods
Twined good and evil on an eastern tree;
And when the moon rose windily it was
Black as the beast and paler than the cross.

We in our Eden knew the secret guardian
In sacred waters that no frost could harden,
And in the mighty mornings of the earth;
Hell in a horn of sulphur and the cloven myth,
All heaven in a midnight of the sun,
A serpent fiddled in the shaping-time.

Today, this insect

Today, this insect, and the world I breathe,
Now that my symbols have outelbowed space,
Time at the city spectacles, and half
The dear, daft time I take to nudge the sentence,
In trust and tale have I divided sense,
Slapped down the guillotine, the blood-red double
Of head and tail made witnesses to this
Murder of Eden and green genesis.

The insect certain is the plague of fables.
This story's monster has a serpent caul,

Blind in the coil scrams round the blazing outline,
Measures his own length on the garden wall
And breaks his shell in the last shocked beginning;
A crocodile before the chrysalis,
Before the fall from love the flying heartbone,
Winged like a sabbath ass this children's piece
Uncredited blows Jericho on Eden.

The insect fable is the certain promise.

Death: death of Hamlet and the nightmare madmen,
An air-drawn windmill on a wooden horse,
John's beast, Job's patience, and the fibs of vision,
Greek in the Irish sea the ageless voice:
'Adam I love, my madmen's love is endless,
No tell-tale lover has an end more certain,
All legends' sweethearts on a tree of stories,
My cross of tales behind the fabulous curtain.'

The seed-at-zero

The seed-at-zero shall not storm
That town of ghosts, the trodden womb
With her rampart to his tapping,
No god-in-hero tumble down
Like a tower on the town
Dumbly and divinely stumbling
Over the manwaging line.

The seed-at-zero shall not storm
That town of ghosts, the manwaged womb
With her rampart to his tapping,
No god-in-hero tumble down
Like a tower on the town
Dumbly and divinely leaping
Over the warbearing line.

Through the rampart of the sky
Shall the star-flanked seed be riddled,
Manna for the rumbling ground,
Quickening for the riddled sea;
Settled on a virgin stronghold
He shall grapple with the guard
And the keeper of the key.

Through the rampart of the sky
Shall the star-flanked seed be riddled,
Manna for the guarded ground,
Quickening for the virgin sea;
Settling on a riddled stronghold
He shall grapple with the guard
And the loser of the key.

May a humble village labour
And a continent deny?
A hemisphere may scold him
And a green inch be his bearer;
Let the hero seed find harbour,
Seaports by a drunken shore
Have their thirsty sailors hide him.

May a humble planet labour
And a continent deny?
A village green may scold him
And a high sphere be his bearer;
Let the hero seed find harbour,
Seaports by a thirsty shore
Have their drunken sailors hide him.

Man-in-seed, in seed-at-zero,
From the foreign fields of space,
Shall not thunder on the town
With a star-flanked garrison,
Nor the cannons of his kingdom
Shall the hero-in-tomorrow
Range on the sky-scraping place.

Man-in-seed, in seed-at-zero,

From the star-flanked fields of space,
Thunders on the foreign town
With a sand-bagged garrison,
Nor the cannons of his kingdom
Shall the hero-in-tomorrow
Range from the grave-groping place.

Shall gods be said

Shall gods be said to thump the clouds
When clouds are cursed by thunder,
Be said to weep when weather howls?
Shall rainbows be their tunics' colour?

When it is rain where are the gods?
Shall it be said they sprinkle water
From garden cans, or free the floods?

Shall it be said that, venuswise,
An old god's dugs are pressed and pricked,
The wet night scolds me like a nurse?

It shall be said that gods are stone.
Shall a dropped stone drum on the ground,
Flung gravel chime? Let the stones speak
With tonges that talk all tongues.

Here in this spring

Here in this spring, stars float along the void;
Here in this ornamental winter
Down pelts the naked weather;
This summer buries a spring bird.

Symbols are selected from the years'
Slow rounding of four seasons' coasts,
In autumn teach three seasons' fires
And four birds' notes.

I should tell summer from the trees, the worms
Tell, if at all, the winter's storms
Or the funeral of the sun;
I should learn spring by the cuckooing,
And the slug should teach me destruction.

A worm tells summer better than the clock,
The slug's a living calendar of days;
What shall it tell me if a timeless insect
Says the world wears away?

Do you not father me

Do you not father me, nor the erected arm
For my tall tower's sake cast in her stone?
Do you not mother me, nor, as I am,
The lovers' house, lie suffering my stain?
Do you not sister me, nor the erected crime
For my tall turrets carry as your sin?
Do you not brother me, nor, as you climb,
Adore my windows for their summer scene?

Am I not father, too, and the ascending boy,
The boy of woman and the wanton starer
Marking the flesh and summer in the bay?
Am I not sister, too, who is my saviour?
Am I not all of you by the directed sea
Where bird and shell are babbling in my tower?
Am I not you who front the tidy shore,
Nor roof of sand, nor yet the towering tiler?

You are all these, said she who gave me the long suck,

All these, he said who sacked the children's town,
Up rose the Abraham-man, mad for my sake,
They said, who hacked and humoured, they were mine.
I am, the tower told, felled by a timeless stroke,
Who razed my wooden folly stands aghast,
For man-begetters in the dry-as-paste,
The ringed-sea ghost, rise grimly from the wrack.

Do you not father me on the destroying sand?
You are your sisters' sire, said seaweedy,
The salt sucked dam and darlings of the land
Who play the proper gentleman and lady.
Shall I still be love's house on the widdershin earth,
Woe to the windy masons at my shelter?
Love's house, they answer, and the tower death
Lie all unknowing of the grave sin-eater.

Out of the sighs

Out of the sighs a little comes,
But not of grief, for I have knocked down that
Before the agony; the spirit grows,
Forgets, and cries;
A little comes, is tasted and found good;
All could not disappoint;
There must, be praised, some certainty,
If not of loving well, then not,
And that is true after perpetual defeat.

After such fighting as the weakest know,
There's more than dying;
Lose the great pains or stuff the wound,
He'll ache too long
Through no regret of leaving woman waiting
For her soldier stained with spilt words
That spill such acrid blood.

Were that enough, enough to ease the pain,
Feeling regret when this is wasted
That made me happy in the sun,
And, sleeping, made me dream
How much was happy while it lasted,
Were vaguenesses enough and the sweet lies plenty,
The hollow words could bear all suffering
And cure me of ills.

Were that enough, bone, blood, and sinew,
The twisted brain, the fair-formed loin,
Groping for matter under the dog's plate,
May should be cured of distemper.
For all there is to give I offer:
Crumbs, barn, and halter.

Hold hard, these ancient minutes

Hold hard, these ancient minutes in the cuckoo's month,
Under the lank, fourth folly on Glamorgan's hill,
As the green blooms ride upward, to the drive of time;
Time, in a folly's rider, like a county man
Over the vault of ridings with his hound at heel,
Drives forth my men, my children, from the hanging south.

Country, your sport is summer, and December's pools
By crane and water-tower by the seedy trees
Lie this fifth month unskated, and the birds have flown;
Hold hard, my country children in the world of tales,
The greenwood dying as the deer fall in their tracks,
This first and steepled season, to the summer's game.

And now the horns of England, in the sound of shape,
Summon your snowy horsemen, and the four-stringed hill,
Over the sea-gut loudening, sets a rock alive;
Hurdles and guns and railings, as the boulders heave,

Crack like a spring in a vice, bone breaking April,
Spill the lank folly's hunter and the hard-held hope.

Down fall four padding weathers on the scarlet lands,
Stalking my children's faces with a tail of blood,
Time, in a rider rising, from the harnessed valley;
Hold hard, my county darlings, for a hawk descends,
Golden Glamorgan straightens, to the falling birds.
Your sport is summer as the spring runs angrily.

Was there a time

Was there a time when dancers with their fiddles
In children's circuses could stay their troubles?
There was a time they could cry over books,
But time has set its maggot on their track.

Under the arc of the sky they are unsafe.
What's never known is safest in this life.
Under the skysigns they who have no arms
Have cleanest hands, and, as the heartless ghost
Alone's unhurt, so the blind man sees best.

Now

Now
Say nay,
Man dry man,
Dry lover mine
The deadrock base and blow the flowered anchor,
Should he, for centre sake, hope in the dust,
Foresake, the fool, the hardiness of anger.

Now
Say nay,

Sir no say,
Death to the yes,
The yes to death, the yesman and the answer,
Should he who split his children with a cure
Have brotherless his sister on the handsaw.

Now
Say nay,
No say sir
Yea the dead stir,
And this, nor this, is shade, the landed crow,
He lying low with ruin in his ear,
The cockerel's tide upcasting from the fire.

Now
Say nay,
So star fall,
So the ball fail,
So solve the mystic sun, the wife of light,
The sun that leaps on petals through a nought,
The come-a-cropper rider of the flower.

Now
Say nay
A fig for
The seal of fire,
Death hairy-heeled, and the tapped ghost in wood,
We make me mystic as the arm of air,
The two-a-vein, the foreskin, and the cloud.

Why east wind chills

Why east wind chills and south wind cools
Shall not be known till windwell dries
And west's no longer drowned
In winds that bring the fruit and rind
Of many a hundred falls;

Why silk is soft and the stone wounds
The child shall question all his days,
Why night-time rain and the breast's blood
Both quench his thirst he'll have a black reply.

When cometh Jack Frost? the children ask.
Shall they clasp a comet in their fists?
Not till, from high and low, their dust
Sprinkles in children's eyes a long-last sleep
And dusk is crowded with the children's ghosts,
Shall a white answer echo from the rooftops.

All things are known: the stars' advice
Calls some content to travel with the winds,
Though what the stars ask as they round
Time upon time the towers of the skies
Is heard but little till the stars go out.

I hear content, and 'Be content'
Ring like a handbell through the corridors,
And 'Know no answer,' and I know
No answer to the children's cry
Of echo's answer and the man of frost
And ghostly comets over the raised fists.

A grief ago

A grief ago,
She who was who I hold, the fats and flower,
Or, water-lammed, from the scythe-sided thorn,
Hell wind and sea,
A stem cementing, wrestled up the tower,
Rose maid and male,
Or, masted venus, through the paddler's bowl
Sailed up the sun;

Who is my grief,
A chrysalis unwrinkling on the iron,
Wrenched by my fingerman, the leaden bud
Shot through the leaf,
Was who was folded on the rod the aaron
Rose cast to plague,
The horn and ball of water on the frog
Housed in the side.

And she who lies,
Like exodus a chapter from the garden,
Brand of the lily's anger on her ring,
Tugged through the days
Her ropes of heritage, the wars of pardon,
On field and sand
The twelve triangles of the cherub wind
Engraving going.

Who then is she,
She holding me? The people's sea drives on her,
Drives out the father from the caesared camp;
The dens of shape
Shape all her whelps with the long voice of water,
That she I have,
The country-handed grave boxed into love,
Rise before dark.

The night is near,
A nitric shape that leaps her, time and acid;
I tell her this: before the suncock cast
Her bone to fire,
Let her inhale her dead, through seed and solid
Draw in their seas,
So cross her hand with their grave gipsy eyes,
And close her fist.

How soon the servant sun

How soon the servant sun
(Sir morrow mark)
Can time unriddle, and the cupboard stone
(Fog has a bone
He'll trumpet into meat)
Unshelve that all my gristles have a gown
And the naked egg stand straight,

Sir morrow at his sponge,
(The wound records)
The nurse of giants by the cut sea basin,
(Fog by his spring
Soaks up the sewing tides)
Tells you and you, my masters, as his strange
Man morrow blows through food.

All nerves to serve the sun,
The rite of light,
A claw I question from the mouse's bone,
The long-tailed stone
Trap I with coil and sheet,
Let the soil squeal I am the biting man
And the velvet dead inch out.

How soon my level, lord,
(Sir morrow stamps
Two heels of water on the floor of seed)
Shall raise a lamp
Or spirit up a cloud,
Erect a walking centre in the shroud,
Invisible on the stump.

A leg as long as trees,
This inward sir,
Mister and master, darkness for his eyes,
The womb-eyed, cries,

And all sweet hell, deaf as an hour's ear,
Blasts back the trumpet voice.

Ears in the turrets hear

Ears in the turrets hear
Hands grumble on the door,
Eyes in the gables see
The fingers at the locks.
Shall I unbolt or stay
Alone till the day I die
Unseen by stranger-eyes
In this white house?
Hands, hold you poison or grapes?

Beyond this island bound
By a thin sea of flesh
And a bone coast,
The land lies out of sound
And the hills out of mind.
No bird or flying fish
Disturbs this island's rest.

Ears in this island hear
The wind pass like a fire,
Eyes in this island see
Ships anchor off the bay.
Shall I run to the ships
With the wind in my hair,
Or stay till the day I die
And welcome no sailor?
Ships, hold you poison or grapes?

Hands grumble on the door,
Ships anchor off the bay,
Rain beats the sand and slates.
Shall I let in the stranger,

Shall I welcome the sailor,
Or stay till the day I die?

Hands of the stranger and holds of the ships,
Hold you poison or grapes?

Foster the light

Foster the light nor veil the manshaped moon,
Nor weather winds that blow not down the bone,
But strip the twelve-winded marrow from his circle;
Master the night nor serve the snowman's brain
That shapes each bushy item of the air
Into a polestar pointed on an icicle.

Murmur of spring nor crush the cockerel's eggs,
Nor hammer back a season in the figs,
But graft these four-fruited ridings on your country;
Farmer in time of frost the burning leagues,
By red-eyed orchards sow the seeds of snow,
In your young years the vegetable century.

And father all nor fail the fly-lord's acre,
Nor sprout on owl-seed like a goblin-sucker,
But rail with your wizard's ribs the heart-shaped planet;
Of mortal voices to the ninnies' choir,
High lord esquire, speak up the singing cloud,
And pluck a mandrake music from the marrowroot.

Roll unmanly over this turning tuft,
O ring of seas, nor sorrow as I shift
From all my mortal lovers with a starboard smile;
Nor when my love lies in the cross-boned drift
Naked among the bow-and-arrow birds
Shall you turn cockwise on a tufted axle.

Who gave these seas their colour in a shape
Shaped my clayfellow, and the heaven's ark

In time at flood filled with his coloured doubles;
O who is glory in the shapeless maps,
Now make the world of me as I have made
A merry manshape of your walking circle.

The hand that signed the paper

The hand that signed the paper felled a city;
Five sovereign fingers taxed the breath,
Doubled the globe of dead and halved a country;
These five kings did a king to death.

The mighty hand leads to a sloping shoulder,
The finger joints are cramped with chalk;
A goose's quill has put an end to murder
That put an end to talk.

The hand that signed the treaty bred a fever,
And famine grew, and locusts came;
Great is the hand that holds dominion over
Man by a scribbled name.

The five kings count the dead but do not soften
The crusted wound nor stroke the brow;
A hand rules pity as a hand rules heaven;
Hands have no tears to flow.

Should lanterns shine

Should lanterns shine, the holy face,
Caught in an octagon of unaccustomed light,
Would wither up, and any boy of love
Look twice before he fell from grace.
The features in their private dark

Are formed of flesh, but let the false day come
And from her lips the faded pigments fall,
The mummy cloths expose an ancient breast.

I have been told to reason by the heart,
But heart, like head, leads helplessly;
I have been told to reason by the pulse,
And, when it quickens, alter the actions' pace
Till field and roof lie level and the same
So fast I move defying time, the quiet gentleman
Whose beard wags in Egyptian wind.

I have heard many years of telling,
And many years should see some change.

The ball I threw while playing in the park
Has not yet reached the ground.

I have longed to move away

I have longed to move away
From the hissing of the spent lie
And the old terrors' continual cry
Growing more terrible as the day
Goes over the hill into the deep sea;
I have longed to move away
From the repetition of salutes,
For there are ghosts in the air
And ghostly echoes on paper,
And the thunder of calls and notes.

I have longed to move away but am afraid;
Some life, yet unspent, might explode
Out of the old lie burning on the ground,
And, crackling into the air, leave me half-blind.
Neither by night's ancient fear,
The parting of hat from hair,

Pursed lips at the receiver,
Shall I fall to death's feather.
By these I would not care to die,
Half convention and half lie.

Find meat on bones

'Find meat on bones that soon have none,
And drink in the two milked crags,
The merriest marrow and the dregs
Before the ladies' breasts are hags
And the limbs are torn.
Disturb no winding-sheets, my son,
But when the ladies are cold as stone
Then hang a ram rose over the rags.

Rebel against the binding moon
And the parliament of sky,
The kingcrafts of the wicked sea,
Autocracy of night and day,
Dictatorship of sun.
Rebel against the flesh and bone,
The word of the blood, the wily skin,
And the maggot no man can slay.'

'The thirst is quenched, the hunger gone,
And my heart is cracked across;
My face is haggard in the glass,
My lips are withered with a kiss,
My breasts are thin.
A merry girl took me for man,
I laid her down and told her sin,
And put beside her a ram rose.

The maggot that no man can kill
And the man no rope can hang
Rebel against my father's dream

That out of a bower of red swine
Howls the foul fiend to heel.
I cannot murder, like a fool,
Season and sunshine, grace and girl,
Nor can I smother the sweet waking.

Black night still ministers the moon,
And the sky lays down her laws,
The sea speaks in a kingly voice,
Light and dark are no enemies
But one companion.
"War on the spider and the wren!
War on the destiny of man!
Doom on the sun!"
Before death takes you, O take back this.'

Grief thief of time

Grief thief of time crawls off,
The moon-drawn grave, with the seafaring years,
The knave of pain steals off
The sea-halved faith that blew time to his knees,
The old forget the cries,
Lean time on tide and times the wind stood rough,
Call back the castaways
Riding the sea light on a sunken path,
The old forget the grief,
Hack of the cough, the hanging albatross,
Cast back the bone of youth
And salt-eyed stumble bedward where she lies
Who tossed the high tide in a time of stories
And timelessly lies loving with the thief.

Now Jack my fathers let the time-faced crook,
Death flashing from his sleeve,
With swag of bubbles in a seedy sack
Sneak down the stallion grave,

Bull's-eye the outlaw through a eunuch crack
And free the twin-boxed grief,
No silver whistles chase him down the weeks'
Dayed peaks to day to death,
These stolen bubbles have the bites of snakes
And the undead eye-teeth,
No third eye probe into a rainbow's sex
That bridged the human halves,
All shall remain and on the graveward gulf
Shape with my fathers' thieves.

And death shall have no dominion

And death shall have no dominion.
Dead men naked they shall be one
With the man in the wind and the west moon;
When their bones are picked clean and the clean bones gone,
They shall have stars at elbow and foot;
Though they go mad they shall be sane,
Though they sink through the sea they shall rise again;
Though lovers be lost love shall not;
And death shall have no dominion.

And death shall have no dominion.
Under the windings of the sea
They lying long shall not die windily;
Twisting on racks when sinews give way,
Strapped to a wheel, yet they shall not break;
Faith in their hands shall snap in two,
And the unicorn evils run them through;
Split all ends up they shan't crack;
And death shall have no dominion.

And death shall have no dominion.
No more may gulls cry at their ears
Or waves break loud on the seashores;
Where blew a flower may a flower no more

Lift its head to the blows of the rain;
Though they be mad and dead as nails,
Heads of the characters hammer through daisies;
Break in the sun till the sun breaks down,
And death shall have no dominion.

Then was my neophyte

Then was my neophyte,
Child in white blood bent on its knees
Under the bell of rocks,
Ducked in the twelve, disciple seas
The winder of the water-clocks
Calls a green day and night.
My sea hermaphrodite,
Snail of man in His ship of fires
That burn the bitten decks,
Knew all His horrible desires
The climber of the water sex
Calls the green rock of light.

Who in these labyrinths,
This tidethread and the lane of scales,
Twine in a moon-blown shell,
Escapes to the flat cities' sails
Furled on the fishes' house and hell,
Nor falls to His green myths?
Stretch the salt photographs,
The landscape grief, love in His oils
Mirror from man to whale
That the green child see like a grail
Through veil and fin and fire and coil
Time on the canvas paths.

He films my vanity.
Shot in the wind, by tilted arcs,
Over the water come

Children from homes and children's parks
Who speak on a finger and thumb,
And the masked, headless boy.
His reels and mystery
The winder of the clockwise scene
Wound like a ball of lakes
Then threw on that tide-hoisted screen
Love's image till my heartbone breaks
By a dramatic sea.

Who kills my history?
The year-hedged row is lame with flint,
Blunt scythe and water blade.
'Who could snap off the shapeless print
From your tomorrow-treading shade
With oracle for eye?'
Time kills me terribly.
'Time shall not murder you,' He said,
'Nor the green nought be hurt;
Who could hack out your unsucked heart,
O green and unborn and undead?'
I saw time murder me.

Altarwise by owl-light

I

Altarwise by owl-light in the halfway-house
The gentleman lay graveward with his furies;
Abaddon in the hang-nail cracked from Adam,
And, from his fork, a dog among the fairies,
The atlas-eater with a jaw for news,
Bit out the mandrake with tomorrow's scream.
Then, penny-eyed, that gentleman of wounds,
Old cock from nowheres and the heaven's egg,
With bones unbuttoned to the halfway winds,
Hatched from the windy salvage on one leg,

Scraped at my cradle in a walking word
That night of time under the Christward shelter,
I am the long world's gentleman, he said,
And share my bed with Capricorn and Cancer.

II

Death is all metaphors, shape in one history;
The child that sucketh long is shooting up,
the planet-ducted pelican of circles
Weans on an artery the gender's strip;
Child of the short spark in a shapeless country
Soon sets alight a long stick from the cradle;
The horizontal cross-bones of Abaddon.
You by the cavern over the black stairs,
Rung bone and blade, the verticals of Adam,
And, manned by midnight, Jacob to the stars;
Hairs of your head, then said the hollow agent,
Are but the roots of nettles and of feathers
Over these groundworks thrusting through a pavement
And hemlock-headed in the wood of weathers.

III

First there was the lamb on knocking knees
And three dead seasons on a climbing grave
That Adam's wether in the flock of horns,
Butt of the tree-tailed worm that mounted Eve,
Horned down with skullfoot and the skull of toes
On thunderous pavements in the garden time;
Rip of the vaults, I took my marrow-ladle
Out of the wrinkled undertaker's van,
And, Rip Van Winkle from a timeless cradle,
Dipped me breast-deep in the descended bone;
The black ram, shuffling of the year, old winter,
Alone alive among his mutton fold,
We rung our weathering changes on the ladder,
Said the antipodes, and twice spring chimed.

IV

What is the metre of the dictionary?
The size of genesis? the short spark's gender?
Shade without shape? the shape of Pharaoh's echo?
(My shape of age nagging the wounded whisper).
Which sixth of wind blew out the burning gentry?
(Questions are hunchbacks to the poker marrow).
What of a bamboo man among your acres?
Corset the boneyards for a crooked lad?
Button your bodice on a hump of splinters,
My camel's eye will needle through the shroud.
Love's a reflection of the mushroom features,
Stills snapped by night in the bread-sided field,
Once close-up smiling in the wall of pictures,
Ark-lamped thrown back upon the cutting flood.

V

And from the windy West came two-gunned Gabriel,
From Jesu's sleeve trumped up the king of spots,
The sheath-decked jacks, queen with a shuffled heart;
Said the fake gentleman in suit of spades,
Black-tongued and tipsy from salvation's bottle,
Rose my Byzantine Adam in the night;
For loss of blood I fell on Ishmael's plain,
Under the milky mushrooms slew my hunger,
A climbing sea from Asia had me down
And Jonah's Moby snatched me by the hair;
Cross-stroked salt Adam to the frozen angel
Pin-legged on pole-hills with a black medusa
By waste seas where the white bear quoted Virgil
And sirens singing from our lady's sea-straw.

VI

Cartoon of slashes on the tide-traced crater,
He in a book of water tallow-eyed
By lava's light split through the oyster vowels

And burned sea silence on a wick of words:
Pluck, cock, my sea eye, said medusa's scripture,
Lop, love, my fork tongue, said the pin-hilled nettle;
And love plucked out the stinging siren's eye,
Old cock from nowheres lopped the minstrel tongue
Till tallow I blew from the wax's tower
The fats of midnight when the salt was singing;
Adam, time's joker, on a witch of cardboard
Spelt out the seven seas, an evil index,
The bagpipe-breasted ladies in the deadweed
Blew out the blood gauze through the wound of manwax.

VII

Now stamp the Lord's Prayer on a grain of rice,
A Bible-leaved of all the written woods
Strip to this tree: a rocking alphabet,
Genesis in the root, the scarecrow word,
And one light's language in the book of trees;
Doom on deniers at the wind-turned statement.
Time's tune my ladies with the teats of music,
The scaled sea-sawers, fix in a naked sponge
Who sucks the bell-voiced Adam out of magic,
Time, milk, and magic, from the world beginning.
Time is the tune my ladies lend their heartbreak,
From bald pavilions and the house of bread
Time tracks the sound of shape on man and cloud,
On rose and icicle the ringing handprint.

VIII

This was the crucifixion on the mountain,
Time's nerve in vinegar, the gallow grave
As tarred with blood as the bright thorns I wept;
The world's my wound, God's Mary in her grief,
Bent like three trees and bird-papped through her shift,
With pins for teardrops is the long wound's woman.
This was the sky, Jack Christ, each minstrel angle
Drove in the heaven-driven of the nails
Till the three-coloured rainbow from my nipples

From pole to pole leapt round the snail-waked world.
I by the tree of thieves, all glory's sawbones
Unsex the skeleton this mountain minute,
And by this blowclock witness of the sun
Suffer the heaven's children through my heartbeat.

IX

From the oracular archives and the parchment,
Prophets and fibre kings in oil and letter,
The lamped calligrapher, the queen in splints,
Buckle to lint and cloth their natron footsteps,
Draw on the glove of prints, dead Cairo's henna
Pour like a halo on the caps and serpents.
This was the resurrection in the desert,
Death from a bandage, rants the mask of scholars
Gold on such features, and the linen spirit
Weds my long gentleman to dusts and furies;
With priest and pharaoh bed my gentle wound,
World in the sand, on the triangle landscape,
With stones of odyssey for ash and garland
And rivers of the dead around my neck.

X

Let the tale's sailor from a Christian voyage
Atlaswise hold halfway off the dummy bay
Time's ship-racked gospel on the globe I balance:
So shall winged harbours through the rockbirds' eyes
Spot the blown word, and on the seas I image
December's thorn screwed in a brow of holly.
Let the first Peter from a rainbow's quayrail
Ask the tall fish swept from the bible east,
What rhubarb man peeled in her foam-blue channel
Has sown a flying garden round that sea-ghost?
Green as beginning, let the garden diving
Soar, with its two bark towers, to that Day
When the worm builds with the gold straws of venom
My nest of mercies in the rude, red tree.

THE MAP OF LOVE

Because the pleasure-bird whistles

Because the pleasure-bird whistles after the hot wires,
Shall the blind horse sing sweeter?
Convenient bird and beast lie lodged to suffer
The supper and knives of a mood.
In the sniffed and poured snow on the tip of the tongue of the year
That clouts the spittle like bubbles with broken rooms,
An enamoured man alone by the twigs of his eyes, two fires,
Camped in the drug-white shower of nerves and food,
Savours the lick of the times through a deadly wood of hair
In a wind that plucked a goose,
Nor ever, as the wild tongue breaks its tombs,
Rounds to look at the red, wagged root.
Because there stands, one story out of the bum city,
That frozen wife whose juices drift like a fixed sea
Secretly in statuary,
Shall I, struck on the hot and rocking street,
Not spin to stare at an old year
Toppling and burning in the muddle of towers and galleries
Like the mauled pictures of boys?
The salt person and blasted place
I furnish with the meat of a fable;
If the dead starve, their stomachs turn to tumble
An upright man in the antipodes
Or spray-based and rock-chested sea:
Over the past table I repeat this present grace.

I make this in a warring absence

I make this in a warring absence when
Each ancient, stone-necked minute of love's season

Harbours my anchored tongue, slips the quaystone,
When, praise is blessed, her pride in mast and fountain
Sailed and set dazzling by the handshaped ocean,
In that proud sailing tree with branches driven
Through the last vault and vegetable groyne,
And this weak house to marrow-columned heaven.

Is corner-cast, breath's rag, scrawled weed, a vain
And opium head, crow stalk, puffed, cut, and blown,
Or like the tide-looped breastknot reefed again
Or rent ancestrally the roped sea-hymen,
And, pride is last, is like a child alone
By magnet winds to her blind mother drawn,
Bread and milk mansion in a toothless town.

She makes for me a nettle's innocence
And a silk pigeon's guilt in her proud absence,
In the molested rocks the shell of virgins,
The frank, closed pearl, the sea-girls' lineaments
Glint in the staved and siren-printed caverns,
Is maiden in the shameful oak, omens
Whalebed and bulldance, the gold bush of lions
Proud as a sucked stone and huge as sandgrains.

These are her contraries: the beast who follows
With priest's grave foot and hand of five assassins
Her molten flight up cinder-nesting columns,
Calls the starved fire herd, is cast in ice,
Lost in a limp-treed and uneating silence,
Who scales a hailing hill in her cold flintsteps
Falls on a ring of summers and locked noons.

I make a weapon of an ass's skeleton
And walk the warring sands by the dead town,
Cudgel great air, wreck east, and topple sundown,
Storm her sped heart, hang with beheaded veins
Its wringing shell, and let her eyelids fasten.
Destruction, picked by birds, brays through the jawbone,
And, for that murder's sake, dark with contagion
Like an approaching wave I sprawl to ruin.
Ruin, the room of errors, one rood dropped

Down the stacked sea and water-pillared shade,
Weighed in rock shroud, is my proud pyramid;
Where, wound in emerald linen and sharp wind,
The hero's head lies scraped of every legend,
Comes love's anatomist with sun-gloved hand
Who picks the live heart on a diamond.

'His mother's womb had a tongue that lapped up mud,'
Cried the topless, inchtaped lips from hank and hood
In that bright anchorground where I lay linened,
'A lizard darting with black venom's thread
Doubled, to fork him back, through the lockjaw bed
And the breath-white, curtained mouth of seed.'
'See,' drummed the taut masks, 'how the dead ascend:
In the groin's endless coil a man is tangled.'

These once-blind eyes have breathed a wind of visions,
The cauldron's root through this once-rindless hand
Fumed like a tree, and tossed a burning bird;
With loud, torn tooth and tail and cobweb drum
The crumpled packs fled past this ghost in bloom,
And, mild as pardon from a cloud of pride,
The terrible world my brother bares his skin.

Now in the cloud's big breast lie quiet countries,
Delivered seas my love from her proud place
Walks with no wound, nor lightning in her face,
A calm wind blows that raised the trees like hair
Once where the soft snow's blood was turned to ice.
And though my love pulls the pale, nippled air,
Prides of tomorrow suckling in her eyes,
Yet this I make in a forgiving presence.

When all my five and country senses

When all my five and country senses see,
The fingers will forget green thumbs and mark

How, through the halfmoon's vegetable eye,
Husk of young stars and handfull zodiac,
Love in the frost is pared and wintered by,
The whispering ears will watch love drummed away
Down breeze and shell to a discordant beach,
And, lashed to syllables, the lynx tongue cry
That her fond wounds are mended bitterly.
My nostrils see her breath burn like a bush.

My one and noble heart has witnesses
In all love's countries, that will grope awake;
And when blind sleep drops on the spying senses,
The heart is sensual, though five eyes break.

We lying by seasand

We lying by seasand, watching yellow
And the grave sea, mock who deride
Who follow the red rivers, hollow
Alcove of words out of cicada shade,
For in this yellow grave of sand and sea
A calling for colour calls with the wind
That's grave and gay as grave and sea
Sleeping on either hand.
The lunar silences, the silent tide
Lapping the still canals, the dry tide-master
Ribbed between desert and water storm,
Should cure our ills of the water
With a one-coloured calm;
The heavenly music over the sand
Sounds with the grains as they hurry
Hiding the golden mountains and mansions
Of the grave, gay, seaside land.
Bound by a sovereign strip, we lie,
Watch yellow, wish for wind to blow away
The strata of the shore and drown red rock;
But wishes breed not, neither

Can we fend off rock arrival,
Lie watching yellow until the golden weather
Breaks, O my heart's blood, like a heart and hill.

It is the sinners' dust-tongued bell

It is the sinners' dust-tongued bell claps me to churches
When, with his torch and hourglass, like a sulphur priest,
His beast heel cleft in a sandal,
Time marks a black aisle kindle from the brand of ashes,
Grief with dishevelled hands tear out the altar ghost
And a firewind kill the candle.

Over the choir minute I hear the hour chant:
Time's coral saint and the salt grief drown a foul sepulchre
And a whirlpool drives the prayerwheel;
Moonfall and sailing emperor, pale as their tideprint,
Hear by death's accident the clocked and dashed-down spire
Strike the sea hour through bellmetal.

There is loud and dark directly under the dumb flame,
Storm, snow, and fountain in the weather of fireworks,
Cathedral calm in the pulled house;
Grief with drenched book and candle christens the cherub time
From the emerald, still bell; and from the pacing weathercock
The voice of bird on coral prays.

Forever it is a white child in the dark-skinned summer
Out of the font of bone and plants at that stone tocsin
Scales the blue wall of spirits;
From blank and leaking winter sails the child in colour,
Shakes, in crabbed burial shawl, by sorcerer's insect woken,
Ding dong from the mute turrets.

I mean by time the cast and curfew rascal of our marriage,
At nightbreak born in the fat side, from an animal bed
In a holy room in a wave;

And all love's sinners in sweet cloth kneel to a hyleg image,
Nutmeg, civet, and sea-parsley serve the plagued groom and bride
Who have brought forth the urchin grief.

O make me a mask

O make me a mask and a wall to shut from your spies
Of the sharp, enamelled eyes and the spectacled claws
Rape and rebellion in the nurseries of my face,
Gag of a dumbstruck tree to block from bare enemies
The bayonet tongue in this undefended prayerpiece,
The present mouth, and the sweetly blown trumpet of lies,
Shaped in old armour and oak the countenance of a dunce
To shield the glistening brain and blunt the examiners,
And a tear-stained widower grief drooped from the lashes
To veil belladonna and let the dry eyes perceive
Others betray the lamenting lies of their losses
By the curve of the nude mouth or the laugh up the sleeve.

The spire cranes

The spire cranes. Its statue is an aviary.
From the stone nest it does not let the feathery
Carved birds blunt their striking throats on the salt gravel,
Pierce the spilt sky with diving wing in weed and heel
An inch in froth. Chimes cheat the prison spire, pelter
In time like outlaw rains on that priest, water,
Time for the swimmers' hands, music for silver lock
And mouth. Both note and plume plunge from the spire's hook.
Those craning birds are choice for you, songs that jump back
To the built voice, or fly with winter to the bells,
But do not travel down dumb wind like prodigals.

After the funeral

(In memory of Ann Jones)

After the funeral, mule praises, brays,
Windshake of sailshaped ears, muffle-toed tap
Tap happily of one peg in the thick
Grave's foot, blinds down the lids, the teeth in black,
The spittled eyes, the salt ponds in the sleeves,
Morning smack of the spade that wakes up sleep,
Shakes a desolate boy who slits his throat
In the dark of the coffin and sheds dry leaves,
That breaks one bone to light with a judgment clout,
After the feast of tear-stuffed time and thistles
In a room with a stuffed fox and a stale fern,
I stand, for this memorial's sake, alone
In the snivelling hours with dead, humped Ann
Whose hooded, fountain heart once fell in puddles
Round the parched worlds of Wales and drowned each sun
(Though this for her is a monstrous image blindly
Magnified out of praise; her death was a still drop;
She would not have me sinking in the holy
Flood of her heart's fame; she would lie dumb and deep
And need no druid of her broken body).
But I, Ann's bard on a raised hearth, call all
The seas to service that her wood-tongued virtue
Babble like a bellbuoy over the hymning heads,
Bow down the walls of the ferned and foxy woods
That her love sing and swing through a brown chapel,
Bless her bent spirit with four, crossing birds.
Her flesh was meek as milk, but this skyward statue
With the wild breast and blessed and giant skull
Is carved from her in a room with a wet window
In a fiercely mourning house in a crooked year.
I know her scrubbed and sour humble hands
Lie with religion in their cramp, her threadbare
Whisper in a damp word, her wits drilled hollow,
Her fist of a face died clenched on a round pain;
And sculptured Ann is seventy years of stone.
These cloud-sopped, marble hands, this monumental

Argument of the hewn voice, gesture and psalm
Storm me forever over her grave until
The stuffed lung of the fox twitch and cry Love
And the strutting fern lay seeds on the black sill.

Once it was the colour of saying

Once it was the colour of saying
Soaked my table the uglier side of a hill
With a capsized field where a school sat still
And a black and white patch of girls grew playing;
The gentle seaslides of saying I must undo
That all the charmingly drowned arise to cockcrow and kill.
When I whistled with mitching boys through a reservoir park
Where at night we stoned the cold and cuckoo
Lovers in the dirt of their leafy beds,
The shade of their trees was a word of many shades
And a lamp of lightning for the poor in the dark;
Now my saying shall be my undoing,
And every stone I wind off like a reel.

Not from this anger

Not from this anger, anticlimax after
Refusal struck her loin and the lame flower
Bent like a beast to lap the singular floods
In a land strapped by hunger
Shall she receive a bellyful of weeds
And bear those tendril hands I touch across
The agonized, two seas.

Behind my head a square of sky sags over
The circular smile tossed from lover to lover
And the golden ball spins out of the skies;

Not from this anger after
Refusal struck like a bell under water
Shall her smile breed that mouth, behind the mirror,
That burns along my eyes.

How shall my animal

How shall my animal
Whose wizard shape I trace in the cavernous skull,
Vessel of abscesses and exultation's shell,
Endure burial under the spelling wall,
The invoked, shrouding veil at the cap of the face,
Who should be furious,
Drunk as a vineyard snail, flailed like an octopus,
Roaring, crawling, quarrel
With the outside weathers,
The natural circle of the discovered skies
Draw down to its weird eyes?

How shall it magnetize,
Towards the studded male in a bent, midnight blaze
That melts the lionhead's heel and horseshoe of the heart,
A brute land in the cool top of the country days
To trot with a loud mate the haybeds of a mile,
Love and labour and kill
In quick, sweet, cruel light till the locked ground sprout out,
The black, burst sea rejoice,
The bowels turn turtle,
Claw of the crabbed veins squeeze from each red particle
The parched and raging voice?

Fishermen of mermen
Creep and harp on the tide, sinking their charmed, bent pin
With bridebait of gold bread, I with a living skein,
Tongue and ear in the thread, angle the temple-bound
Curl-locked and animal cavepools of spells and bone,
Trace out a tentacle,

Nailed with an open eye, in the bowl of wounds and weed
To clasp my fury on ground
And clap its great blood down;
Never shall beast be born to atlas the few seas
Or poise the day on a horn.

Sigh long, clay cold, lie shorn,
Cast high, stunned on gilled stone; sly scissors ground in frost
Clack through the thicket of strength, love hewn in pillars drops
With carved bird, saint, and sun, the wrackspiked maiden mouth
Lops, as a bush plumed with flames, the rant of the fierce eye,
Clips short the gesture of breath.
Die in red feathers when the flying heaven's cut,
And roll with the knocked earth:
Lie dry, rest robbed, my beast.
You have kicked from a dark den, leaped up the whinnying light,
And dug your grave in my breast.

The tombstone told

The tombstone told when she died.
Her two surnames stopped me still.
A virgin married at rest.
She married in this pouring place,
That I struck one day by luck,
Before I heard in my mother's side
Or saw in the looking-glass shell
The rain through her cold heart speak
And the sun killed in her face.
More the thick stone cannot tell.

Before she lay on a stranger's bed
With a hand plunged through her hair,
Or that rainy tongue beat back
Through the devilish years and innocent deaths
To the room of a secret child,
Among men later I heard it said

She cried her white-dressed limbs were bare
And her red lips were kissed black,
She wept in her pain and made mouths,
Talked and tore though her eyes smiled.

I who saw in a hurried film
Death and this mad heroine
Meet once on a mortal wall
Heard her speak through the chipped beak
Of the stone bird guarding her:
I died before bedtime came
But my womb was bellowing
And I felt with my bare fall
A blazing red harsh head tear up
And the dear floods of his hair.

On no work of words

On no work of words now for three lean months in the bloody
Belly of the rich year and the big purse of my body
I bitterly take to task my poverty and craft:

To take to give is all, return what is hungrily given
Puffing the pounds of manna up through the dew to heaven,
The lovely gift of the gab bangs back on a blind shaft.

To lift to leave from the treasures of man is pleasing death
That will rake at last all currencies of the marked breath
And count the taken, forsaken mysteries in a bad dark.

To surrender now is to pay the expensive ogre twice.
Ancient woods of my blood, dash down to the nut of the seas
If I take to burn or return this world which is each man's work.

A saint about to fall

A saint about to fall,
The stained flats of heaven hit and razed
To the kissed kite hems of his shawl,
On the last street wave praised
The unwinding, song by rock,
Of the woven wall
Of his father's house in the sands,
The vanishing of the musical ship-work and the chucked bells,
The wound-down cough of the blood-counting clock
Behind a face of hands,
On the angelic etna of the last whirring featherlands,
Wind-heeled foot in the hole of a fireball,
Hymned his shrivelling flock,
On the last rick's tip by spilled wine-wells
Sang heaven hungry and the quick
Cut Christbread spitting vinegar and all
The mazes of his praise and envious tongue were worked in flames and shells.

Glory cracked like a flea.
The sun-leaved holy candlewoods
Drivelled down to one singeing tree
With a stub of black buds,
The sweet, fish-gilled boats bringing blood
Lurched through a scuttled sea
With a hold of leeches and straws,
Heaven fell with his fall and one crocked bell beat the left air.
O wake in me in my house in the mud
Of the crotch of the squawking shores,
Flicked from the carbolic city puzzle in a bed of sores
The scudding base of the familiar sky,
The lofty roots of the clouds.
From an odd room in a split house stare,
Milk in your mouth, at the sour floods
That bury the sweet street slowly, see
The skull of the earth is barbed with a war of burning brains and hair.

Strike in the time-bomb town,
Raise the live rafters of the eardrum,
Throw your fear a parcel of stone
Through the dark asylum,
Lapped among herods wail
As their blade marches in
That the eyes are already murdered,
The stocked heart is forced, and agony has another mouth to feed.
O wake to see, after a noble fall,
The old mud hatch again, the horrid
Woe drip from the dishrag hands and the pressed sponge of the forehead,
The breath draw back like a bolt through white oil
And a stranger enter like iron.
Cry joy that this witchlike midwife second
Bullies into rough seas you so gentle
And makes with a flick of the thumb and sun
A thundering bullring of your silent and girl-circled island.

If my head hurt a hair's foot

'If my head hurt a hair's foot
Pack back the downed bone. If the unpricked ball of my breath
Bump on a spout let the bubbles jump out.
Sooner drop with the worm of the ropes round my throat
Than bully ill love in the clouted scene.

All game phrases fit your ring of a cockfight:
I'll comb the snared woods with a glove on a lamp,
Peck, sprint, dance on fountains and duck time
Before I rush in a crouch the ghost with a hammer, air,
Strike light, and bloody a loud room.

If my bunched, monkey coming is cruel
Rage me back to the making house. My hand unravel
When you sew the deep door. The bed is a cross place.
Bend, if my journey ache, direction like an arc or make

A limp and riderless shape to leap nine thinning months.'

'No. Not for Christ's dazzling bed
Or a nacreous sleep among soft particles and charms
My dear would I change my tears or your iron head.
Thrust, my daughter or son, to escape, there is none, none, none,
Nor when all ponderous heaven's host of waters breaks.

Now to awake husked of gestures and my joy like a cave
To the anguish and carrion, to the infant forever unfree,
O my lost love bounced from a good home;
The grain that hurries this way from the rim of the grave
Has a voice and a house, and there and here you must couch
and cry.

Rest beyond choice in the dust-appointed grain,
At the breast stored with seas. No return
Through the waves of the fat streets nor the skeleton's thin ways.
The grave and my calm body are shut to your coming as stone,
And the endless beginning of prodigies suffers open.'

Twenty-four years

Twenty-four years remind the tears of my eyes.
(Bury the dead for fear that they walk to the grave in labour.)
In the groin of the natural doorway I crouched like a tailor
Sewing a shroud for a journey
By the light of the meat-eating sun.
Dressed to die, the sensual strut begun,
With my red veins full of money,
In the final direction of the elementary town
I advance for as long as forever is.

DEATHS AND ENTRANCES

The conversation of prayers

The conversation of prayers about to be said
By the child going to bed and the man on the stairs
Who climbs to his dying love in her high room,
The one not caring to whom in his sleep he will move
And the other full of tears that she will be dead,

Turns in the dark on the sound they know will arise
Into the answering skies from the green ground,
From the man on the stairs and the child by his bed.
The sound about to be said in the two prayers
For the sleep in a safe land and the love who dies

Will be the same grief flying. Whom shall they calm?
Shall the child sleep unharmed or the man be crying?
The conversation of prayers about to be said
Turns on the quick and the dead, and the man on the stairs
Tonight shall find no dying but alive and warm

In the fire of his care his love in the high room.
And the child not caring to whom he climbs his prayer
Shall drown in a grief as deep as his true grave,
And mark the dark eyed wave, through the eyes of sleep,
Dragging him up the stairs to one who lies dead.

A Refusal to Mourn the Death, by Fire, of a Child in London

Never until the mankind making
Bird beast and flower

Fathering and all humbling darkness
Tells with silence the last light breaking
And the still hour
Is come of the sea tumbling in harness

And I must enter again the round
Zion of the water bead
And the synagogue of the ear of corn
Shall I let pray the shadow of a sound
Or sow my salt seed
In the least valley of sackcloth to mourn

The majesty and burning of the child's death.
I shall not murder
The mankind of her going with a grave truth
Nor blaspheme down the stations of the breath
With any further
Elegy of innocence and youth.

Deep with the first dead lies London's daughter,
Robed in the long friends,
The grains beyond age, the dark veins of her mother,
Secret by the unmourning water
Of the riding Thames.
After the first death, there is no other.

Poem in October

  It was my thirtieth year to heaven
Woke to my hearing from harbour and neighbour wood
  And the mussel pooled and the heron
        Priested shore
        The morning beckon
With water praying and call of seagull and rook
And the knock of sailing boats on the net webbed wall
      Myself to set foot
        That second

In the still sleeping town and set forth.

My birthday began with the water-
Birds and the birds of the winged trees flying my name
Above the farms and the white horses
And I rose
In rainy autumn
And walked abroad in a shower of all my days.
High tide and the heron dived when I took the road
Over the border
And the gates
Of the town closed as the town awoke.

A springful of larks in a rolling
Cloud and the roadside bushes brimming with whistling
Blackbirds and the sun of October
Summery
On the hill's shoulder,
Here were fond climates and sweet singers suddenly
Come in the morning where I wandered and listened
To the rain wringing
Wind blow cold
In the wood faraway under me.

Pale rain over the dwindling harbour
And over the sea wet church the size of a snail
With its horns through mist and the castle
Brown as owls
But all the gardens
Of spring and summer were blooming in the tall tales
Beyond the border and under the lark full cloud.
There could I marvel
My birthday
Away but the weather turned around.

It turned away from the blithe country
And down the other air and the blue altered sky
Streamed again a wonder of summer
With apples
Pears and red currants
And I saw in the turning so clearly a child's

Forgotten mornings when he walked with his mother
Through the parables
Of sun light
And the legends of the green chapels

And the twice told fields of infancy
That his tears burned my cheeks and his heart moved in mine.
These were the woods the river and sea
Where a boy
In the listening
Summertime of the dead whispered the truth of his joy
To the trees and the stones and the fish in the tide.
And the mystery
Sang alive
Still in the eater and singingbirds.

And there could I marvel my birthday
Away but the weather turned around. And the true
Joy of the long dead child sang burning
In the sun.
It was my thirtieth
Year to heaven stood there then in the summer noon
Though the town below lay leaved with October blood.
O may my heart's truth
Still be sung
On this high hill in a year's turning.

This side of the truth

(for Llewelyn)

This side of the truth,
You may not see, my son,
King of your blue eyes
In the blinding country of youth,
That all is undone,
Under the unminding skies,
Of innocence and guilt

Before you move to make
One gesture of the heart or head,
Is gathered and spilt
Into the winding dark
Like the dust of the dead.

Good and bad, two ways
Of moving about your death
By the grinding sea,
King of your heart in the blind days,
Blow away like breath,
Go crying through you and me
And the souls of all men
Into the innocent
Dark, and the guilty dark, and good
Death, and bad death, and then
In the last element
Fly like the stars' blood,

Like the sun's tears,
Like the moon's seed, rubbish
And fire, the flying rant
Of the sky, king of your six years.
And the wicked wish,
Down the beginning of plants
And animals and birds,
Water and light, the earth and sky,
Is cast before you move,
And all your deeds and words,
Each truth, each lie,
Die in unjudging love.

To Others than You

Friends by enemy I call you out.

You with a bad coin in your socket,

You my friend there with a winning air
Who palmed the lie on me when you looked
Brassily at my shyest secret,
Enticed with twinkling bits of the eye
Till the sweet tooth of my love bit dry,
Rasped at last, and I stumbled and sucked,
Whom now I conjure to stand as thief
In the memory worked by mirrors,
With unforgettably smiling act,
Quickness of hand in the velvet glove
And my whole heart under your hammer,
Were once such a creature, so gay and frank
A desireless familiar
I never thought to utter or think
While you displaced a truth in the air.

That though I loved them for their faults
As much as for their good,
My friends were enemies on stilts
With their heads in a cunning cloud.

Love in the Asylum

A stranger has come
To share my room in the house not right in the head,
A girl mad as birds

Bolting the night of the door with her arm her plume.
Strait in the mazed bed
She deludes the heaven-proof house with entering clouds

Yet she deludes with walking the nightmarish room,
At large as the dead,
Or rides the imagined oceans of the male wards.

She has come possessed
Who admits the delusive light through the bouncing wall,

Possessed by the skies

She sleeps in the narrow trough yet she walks the dust
Yet raves at her will
On the madhouse boards worn thin by my walking tears.

And taken by light in her arms at long and dear last
I may without fail
Suffer the first vision that set fire to the stars.

Unluckily for a death

Unluckily for a death
Waiting with phoenix under
The pyre yet to be lighted of my sins and days,
And for the woman in shades
Saint carved and sensual among the scudding
Dead and gone, dedicate forever to my self
Though the brawl of the kiss has not occurred,
On the clay cold mouth, on the fire
Branded forehead, that could bind
Her constant, nor the winds of love broken wide
To the wind the choir and cloister
Of the wintry nunnery of the order of lust
Beneath my life, that sighs for the seducer's coming
In the sun strokes of summer.

Loving on this sea banged guilt
My holy lucky body
Under the cloud against love is caught and held and kissed
In the mill of the midst
Of the descending day, the dark our folly,
Cut to the still star in the order of the quick
But blessed by such heroic hosts in your every
Inch and glance that the wound
Is certain god, and the ceremony of souls
Is celebrated there, and communion between suns.

Never shall my self chant
About the saint in shades while the endless breviary
Turns of your prayed flesh, nor shall I shoo the bird below me:
The death biding two lie lonely.

I see the tigron in tears
In the androgynous dark,
His striped and noon maned tribe striding to holocaust,
The she mules bear their minotaurs,
The duck-billed platypus broody in a milk of birds.
I see the wanting nun saint carved in a garb
Of shades, symbol of desire beyond my hours
And guilts, great crotch and giant
Continence. I see the unfired phoenix, herald
And heaven crier, arrow now of aspiring
And the renouncing of islands.
All love but for the full assemblage in flower
Of the living flesh is monstrous or immortal,
And the grave its daughters.

Love, my fate got luckily,
Teaches with no telling
That the phoenix' bid for heaven and the desire after
Death in the carved nunnery
Both shall fail if I bow not to your blessing
Nor walk in the cool of your mortal garden
With immortality at my side like Christ the sky.
This I know from the native
Tongue of your translating eyes. The young stars told me,
Hurling into beginning like Christ the child.
Lucklessly she must lie patient
And the vaulting bird be still. O my true love, hold me.
In your every inch and glance is the globe of genesis spun,
And the living earth your sons.

The hunchback in the park

The hunchback in the park
A solitary mister
Propped between trees and water
From the opening of the garden lock
That lets the trees and water enter
Until the Sunday sombre bell at dark

Eating bread from a newspaper
Drinking water from the chained cup
That the children filled with gravel
In the fountain basin where I sailed my ship
Slept at night in a dog kennel
But nobody chained him up.

Like the park birds he came early
Like the water he sat down
And Mister they called Hey mister
The truant boys from the town
Running when he had heard them clearly
On out of sound

Past lake and rockery
Laughing when he shook his paper
Hunchbacked in mockery
Through the loud zoo of the willow groves
Dodging the park keeper
With his stick that picked up leaves.

And the old dog sleeper
Alone between nurses and swans
While the boys among willows
Made the tigers jump out of their eyes
To roar on the rockery stones
And the groves were blue with sailors

Made all day until bell time
A woman figure without fault

Straight as a young elm
Straight and tall from his crooked bones
That she might stand in the night
After the locks and chains

All night in the unmade park
After the railings and shrubberies
The birds the grass the trees the lake
And the wild boys innocent as strawberries
Had followed the hunchback
To his kennel in the dark.

Into her lying down head

I

Into her lying down head
His enemies entered bed,
Under the encumbered eyelid,
Through the rippled drum of the hair-buried ear;
And Noah's rekindled now unkind dove
Flew man-bearing there.
Last night in a raping wave
Whales unreined from the green grave
In fountains of origin gave up their love,
Along her innocence glided
Juan aflame and savagely young King Lear,
Queen Catherine howling bare
And Samson drowned in his hair,
The colossal intimacies of silent
Once seen strangers or shades on a stair;
There the dark blade and wanton sighing her down
To a haycock couch and the scythes of his arms
Rode and whistled a hundred times
Before the crowing morning climbed;
Man was the burning England she was sleep-walking, and the enamouring island

Made her limbs blind by luminous charms,
Sleep to a newborn sleep in a swaddling loin-leaf stroked and sang
And his runaway beloved childlike laid in the acorned sand.

II

There where a numberless tongue
Wound their room with a male moan,
His faith around her flew undone
And darkness hung the walls with baskets of snakes,
A furnace-nostrilled column-membered
Super-or-near man
Resembling to her dulled sense
The thief of adolescence,
Early imaginary half remembered
Oceanic lover alone
Jealousy cannot forget for all her sakes,
Made his bad bed in her good
Night, and enjoyed as he would.
Crying, white gowned, from the middle moonlit stages
Out to the tiered and hearing tide,
Close and far she announced the theft of the heart
In the taken body at many ages,
Trespasser and broken bride
Celebrating at her side
All blood-signed assailings and vanished marriages in which he had no lovely part
Nor could share, for his pride, to the least
Mutter and foul wingbeat of the solemnizing nightpriest
Her holy unholy hours with the always anonymous beast.

III

Two sand grains together in bed,
Head to heaven-circling head,
Singly lie with the whole wide shore,
The covering sea their nightfall with no names;
And out of every domed and soil-based shell

One voice in chains declaims
The female, deadly, and male
Libidinous betrayal,
Golden dissolving under the water veil.
A she bird sleeping brittle by
Her lover's wings that fold tomorrow's flight,
Within the nested treefork
Sings to the treading hawk
Carrion, paradise, chirrup my bright yolk.
A blade of grass longs with the meadow,
A stone lies lost and locked in the lark-high hill.
Open as to the air to the naked shadow
O she lies alone and still,
Innocent between two wars,
With the incestuous secret brother in the seconds to perpetuate the stars,
A man torn up mourns in the sole night.
And the second comers, the severers, the enemies from the deep
Forgotten dark, rest their pulse and bury their dead in her faithless sleep.

Paper and sticks

Paper and sticks and shovel and match
Why won't the news of the old world catch
And the fire in a temper start

Once I had a rich boy for myself
I loved his body and his navy blue wealth
And I lived in his purse and his heart

When in our bed I was tossing and turning
All I could see were his brown eyes burning
By the green of a one pound note

I talk to him as I clean the grate
O my dear it's never too late

To take me away as you whispered and wrote

I had a handsome and well-off boy
I'll share my money and we'll run for joy
With a bouncing and silver spooned kid

Sharp and shrill my silly tongue scratches
Words on the air as the fire catches
You never did and *he* never did.

Deaths and Entrances

On almost the incendiary eve
  Of several near deaths,
When one at the great least of your best loved
  And always known must leave
Lions and fires of his flying breath,
  Of your immortal friends
Who'd raise the organs of the counted dust
  To shoot and sing your praise,
One who called deepest down shall hold his peace
  That cannot sink or cease
  Endlessly to his wound
In many married London's estranging grief.

On almost the incendiary eve
  When at your lips and keys,
Locking, unlocking, the murdered strangers weave,
  One who is most unknown,
Your polestar neighbour, sun of another street,
  Will dive up to his tears.
He'll bathe his raining blood in the male sea
  Who strode for your own dead
And wind his globe out of your water thread
  And load the throats of shells
  With every cry since light
Flashed first across his thunderclapping eyes.

On almost the incendiary eve
  Of deaths and entrances,
When near and strange wounded on London's waves
  Have sought your single grave,
One enemy, of many, who knows well
  Your heart is luminous
In the watched dark, quivering through locks and caves,
  Will pull the thunderbolts
To shut the sun, plunge, mount your darkened keys
  And sear just riders back,
  Until that one loved least
Looms the last Samson of your zodiac.

A Winter's Tale

    It is a winter's tale
That the snow blind twilight ferries over the lakes
And floating fields from the farm in the cup of the vales,
Gliding windless through the hand folded flakes,
The pale breath of cattle at the stealthy sail,

    And the stars falling cold,
And the smell of hay in the snow, and the far owl
Warning among the folds, and the frozen hold
Flocked with the sheep white smoke of the farm house cowl
In the river wended vales where the tale was told.

    Once when the world turned old
On a star of faith pure as the drifting bread,
As the food and flames of the snow, a man unrolled
The scrolls of fire that burned in his heart and head,
Torn and alone in a farm house in a fold

    Of fields. And burning then
In his firelit island ringed by the winged snow
And the dung hills white as wool and the hen
Roosts sleeping chill till the flame of the cock crow

Combs through the mantled yards and the morning men

Stumble out with their spades,
The cattle stirring, the mousing cat stepping shy,
The puffed birds hopping and hunting, the milk maids
Gentle in their clogs over the fallen sky,
And all the woken farm at its white trades,

He knelt, he wept, he prayed,
By the spit and the black pot in the log bright light
And the cup and the cut bread in the dancing shade,
In the muffled house, in the quick of night,
At the point of love, forsaken and afraid.

He knelt on the cold stones,
He wept from the crest of grief, he prayed to the veiled sky
May his hunger go howling on bare white bones
Past the statues of the stables and the sky roofed sties
And the duck pond glass and the blinding byres alone

Into the home of prayers
And fires where he should prowl down the cloud
Of his snow blind love and rush in the white lairs.
His naked need struck him howling and bowed
Though no sound flowed down the hand folded air

But only the wind strung
Hunger of birds in the fields of the bread of water, tossed
In high corn and the harvest melting on their tongues.
And his nameless need bound him burning and lost
When cold as snow he should run the wended vales among

The rivers mouthed in night,
And drown in the drifts of his need, and lie curled caught
In the always desiring centre of the white
Inhuman cradle and the bride bed forever sought
By the believer lost and the hurled outcast of light.

Deliver him, he cried,
By losing him all in love, and cast his need
Alone and naked in the engulfing bride,

Never to flourish in the fields of the white seed
Or flower under the time dying flesh astride.

Listen. The minstrels sing
In the departed villages. The nightingale,
Dust in the buried wood, flies on the grains of her wings
And spells on the winds of the dead his winter's tale.
The voice of the dust of water from the withered spring

Is telling. The wizened
Stream with bells and baying water bounds. The dew rings
On the gristed leaves and the long gone glistening
Parish of snow. The carved mouths in the rock are wind swept string
Time sings through the intricately dead snow drop. Listen.

It was a hand or sound
In the long ago land that glided the dark door wide
And there outside on the bread of the ground
A she bird rose and rayed like a burning bride.
A she bird dawned, and her breast with snow and scarlet downed.

Look. And the dancers move
On the departed, snow bushed green, wanton in moon light
As a dust of pigeons. Exulting, the grave hooved
Horses, centaur dead, turn and tread the drenched white
Paddocks in the farms of birds. The dead oak walks for love.

The carved limbs in the rock
Leap, as to trumpets. Calligraphy of the old
Leaves is dancing. Lines of age on the stones weave in a flock.
And the harp shaped voice of the water's dust plucks in a fold
Of fields. For love, the long ago she bird rises. Look.

And the wild wings were raised
Above her folded head, and the soft feathered voice
Was flying through the house as though the she bird praised
And all the elements of the slow fall rejoiced
That a man knelt alone in the cup of the vales,

In the mantle and calm,
By the spit and the black pot in the log bright light.

And the sky of birds in the plumed voice charmed
Him up and he ran like a wind after the kindling flight
Past the blind barns and byres of the windless farm.

In the poles of the year
When black birds died like priests in the cloaked hedge row
And over the cloth of counties the far hills rode near,
Under the one leaved trees ran a scarecrow of snow
And fast through the drifts of the thickets antlered like deer,

Rags and prayers down the knee-
Deep hillocks and loud on the numbed lakes,
All night lost and long wading in the wake of the she-
Bird through the times and lands and tribes of the slow flakes.
Listen and look where she sails the goose plucked sea,

The sky, the bird, the bride,
The cloud, the need, the planted stars, the joy beyond
The fields of seed and the time dying flesh astride,
The heavens, the heaven, the grave, the burning font.
In the far ago land the door of his death glided wide,

And the bird descended.
On a bread white hill over the cupped farm
And the lakes and floating fields and the river wended
Vales where he prayed to come to the last harm
And the home of prayers and fires, the tale ended.

The dancing perishes
On the white, no longer growing green, and, minstrel dead,
The singing breaks in the snow shoed villages of wishes
That once cut the figures of birds on the deep bread
And over the glazed lakes skated the shapes of fishes

Flying. The rite is shorn
Of nightingale and centaur dead horse. The springs wither
Back. Lines of age sleep on the stones till trumpeting dawn.
Exultation lies down. Time buries the spring weather
That belled and bounded with the fossil and the dew reborn.

For the bird lay bedded
In a choir of wings, as though she slept or died,
And the wings glided wide and he was hymned and wedded,
And through the thighs of the engulfing bride,
The woman breasted and the heaven headed

Bird, he was brought low,
Burning in the bride bed of love, in the whirl-
Pool at the wanting centre, in the folds
Of paradise, in the spun bud of the world.
And she rose with him flowering in her melting snow.

On a Wedding Anniversary

The sky is torn across
This ragged anniversary of two
Who moved for three years in tune
Down the long walks of their vows.

Now their love lies a loss
And Love and his patients roar on a chain;
From every true or crater
Carrying cloud, Death strikes their house.

Too late in the wrong rain
They come together whom their love parted:
The windows pour into their heart
And the doors burn in their brain.

There was a saviour

There was a saviour
Rarer than radium,
Commoner than water, crueller than truth;
Children kept from the sun

Assembled at his tongue
To hear the golden note turn in a groove,
Prisoners of wishes locked their eyes
In the jails and studies of his keyless smiles.

The voice of children says
From a lost wilderness
There was calm to be done in his safe unrest,
When hindering man hurt
Man, animal, or bird
We hid our fears in that murdering breath,
Silence, silence to do, when earth grew loud,
In lairs and asylums of the tremendous shout.

There was glory to hear
In the churches of his tears,
Under his downy arm you sighed as he struck,
O you who could not cry
On to the ground when a man died
Put a tear for joy in the unearthly flood
And laid your cheek against a cloud-formed shell:
Now in the dark there is only yourself and myself.

Two proud, blacked brothers cry,
Winter-locked side by side,
To this inhospitable hollow year,
O we who could not stir
One lean sigh when we heard
Greed on man beating near and fire neighbour
But wailed and nested in the sky-blue wall
Now break a giant tear for the little known fall,

For the drooping of homes
That did not nurse our bones,
Brave deaths of only ones but never found,
Now see, alone in us,
Our own true strangers' dust
Ride through the doors of our unentered house.
Exiled in us we arouse the soft,
Unclenched, armless, silk and rough love that breaks all rocks.

On the Marriage of a Virgin

Waking alone in a multitude of loves when morning's light
Surprised in the opening of her nightlong eyes
His golden yesterday asleep upon the iris
And this day's sun leapt up the sky out of her thighs
Was miraculous virginity old as loaves and fishes,
Though the moment of a miracle is unending lightning
And the shipyards of Galilee's footprints hide a navy of doves.

No longer will the vibrations of the sun desire on
Her deepsea pillow where once she married alone,
Her heart all ears and eyes, lips catching the avalanche
Of the golden ghost who ringed with his streams her mercury bone,
Who under the lids of her windows hoisted his golden luggage,
For a man sleeps where fire leapt down and she learns through his arm
That other sun, the jealous coursing of the unrivalled blood.

In my craft or sullen art

In my craft or sullen art
Exercised in the still night
When only the moon rages
And the lovers lie abed
With all their griefs in their arms,
I labour by singing light
Not for ambition or bread
Or the strut and trade of charms
On the ivory stages
But for the common wages
Of their most secret heart.

Not for the proud man apart
From the raging moon I write
On these spindrift pages

Nor for the towering dead
With their nightingales and psalms
But for the lovers, their arms
Round the griefs of the ages,
Who pay no praise or wages
Nor heed my craft or art.

Ceremony After a Fire Raid

I

Myselves
The grievers
Grieve
Among the street burned to tireless death
A child of a few hours
With its kneading mouth
Charred on the black breast of the grave
The mother dug, and its arms full of fires.

Begin
With singing
Sing
Darkness kindled back into beginning
When the caught tongue nodded blind,
A star was broken
Into the centuries of the child
Myselves grieve now, and miracles cannot atone.

Forgive
Us forgive
Give
Us your death that myselves the believers
May hold it in a great flood
Till the blood shall spurt,
And the dust shall sing like a bird
As the grains blow, as your death grows, through our heart.

Crying
Your dying
Cry,
Child beyond cockcrow, by the fire-dwarfed
Street we chant the flying sea
In the body bereft.
Love is the last light spoken. Oh
Seed of sons in the loin of the black husk left.

II

I know not whether
Adam or Eve, the adorned holy bullock
Or the white ewe lamb
Or the chosen virgin
Laid in her snow
On the altar of London,
Was the first to die
In the cinder of the little skull,
O bride and bride groom
O Adam and Eve together
Lying in the lull
Under the sad breast of the head stone
White as the skeleton
Of the garden of Eden.

I know the legend
Of Adam and Eve is never for a second
Silent in my service
Over the dead infants
Over the one
Child who was priest and servants,
Word, singers, and tongue
In the cinder of the little skull,
Who was the serpent's
Night fall and the fruit like a sun,
Man and woman undone,
Beginning crumbled back to darkness
Bare as the nurseries
Of the garden of wilderness.

III

Into the organpipes and steeples
Of the luminous cathedrals,
Into the weathercocks' molten mouths
Rippling in twelve-winded circles,
Into the dead clock burning the hour
Over the urn of sabbaths
Over the whirling ditch of daybreak
Over the sun's hovel and the slum of fire
And the golden pavements laid in requiems,
Into the cauldrons of the statuary,
Into the bread in a wheatfield of flames,
Into the wine burning like brandy,
The masses of the sea
The masses of the sea under
The masses of the infant-bearing sea
Erupt, fountain, and enter to utter for ever
Glory glory glory
The sundering ultimate kingdom of genesis' thunder.

Once below a time

I

Once below a time,
When my pinned-around-the-spirit
Cut-to-measure flesh bit,
Suit for a serial sum
On the first of each hardship,
My paid-for slaved-for own too late
In love torn breeches and blistered jacket
On the snapping rims of the ashpit,
In grottoes I worked with birds,
Spiked with a mastiff collar,
Tasselled in cellar and snipping shop
Or decked on a cloud swallower.

Then swift from a bursting sea with bottlecork boats
And out-of-perspective sailors,
In common clay clothes disguised as scales,
As a he-god's paddling water skirts,
I astounded the sitting tailors,
I set back the clock faced tailors,

Then, bushily swanked in bear wig and tails,
Hopping hot leaved and feathered
From the kangaroo foot of the earth,
From the chill, silent centre
Trailing the frost bitten cloth,
Up through the lubber crust of Wales
I rocketed to astonish
The flashing needle rock of squatters,
The criers of Shabby and Shorten,
The famous stitch droppers.

II

My silly suit, hardly yet suffered for,
Around some coffin carrying
Birdman or told ghost I hung.
And the owl hood, the heel hider,
Claw fold and hole for the rotten
Head, deceived, I believed, my maker,

The cloud perched tailors' master with nerves for cotton.
On the old seas from stories, thrashing my wings,
Combing with antlers, Columbus on fire,
I was pierced by the idol tailor's eyes,
Glared through shark mask and navigating head,
Cold Nansen's beak on a boat full of gongs,

To the boy of common thread,
The bright pretender, the ridiculous sea dandy
With dry flesh and earth for adorning and bed.
It was sweet to drown in the readymade handy water
With my cherry capped dangler green as seaweed

Summoning a child's voice from a webfoot stone,
Never never oh never to regret the bugle I wore
On my cleaving arm as I blasted in a wave.

Now shown and mostly bare I would lie down,
Lie down, lie down and live
As quiet as a bone.

When I woke

When I woke, the town spoke.
Birds and clocks and cross bells
Dinned aside the coiling crowd,
The reptile profligates in a flame,
Spoilers and pokers of sleep,
The next-door sea dispelled
Frogs and satans and woman-luck,
While a man outside with a billhook,
Up to his head in his blood,
Cutting the morning off,
The warm-veined double of Time
And his scarving beard from a book,
Slashed down the last snake as though
It were a wand or subtle bough,
Its tongue peeled in the wrap of a leaf.

Every morning I make,
God in bed, good and bad,
After a water-face walk,
The death-stagged scatter-breath
Mammoth and sparrowfall
Everybody's earth.
Where birds ride like leaves and boats like ducks
I heard, this morning, waking,
Crossly out of the town noises
A voice in the erected air,
No prophet-progeny of mine,

Cry my sea town was breaking.
No Time, spoke the clocks, No God, rang the bells,
I drew the white sheet over the islands
And the coins on my eyelids sang like shells.

Among those Killed in the Dawn Raid was a Man Aged a Hundred

When the morning was waking over the war
He put on his clothes and stepped out and he died,
The locks yawned loose and a blast blew them wide,
He dropped where he loved on the burst pavement stone
And the funeral grains of the slaughtered floor.
Tell his street on its back he stopped a sun
And the craters of his eyes grew springshoots and fire
When all the keys shot from the locks, and rang.
Dig no more for the chains of his grey-haired heart.
The heavenly ambulance drawn by a wound
Assembling waits for the spade's ring on the cage.
O keep his bones away from that common cart,
The morning is flying on the wings of his age
And a hundred storks perch on the sun's right hand.

Lie still, sleep becalmed

Lie still, sleep becalmed, sufferer with the wound
In the throat, burning and turning. All night afloat
On the silent sea we have heard the sound
That came from the wound wrapped in the salt sheet.

Under the mile off moon we trembled listening
To the sea sound flowing like blood from the loud wound
And when the salt sheet broke in a storm of singing
The voices of all the drowned swam on the wind.

Open a pathway through the slow sad sail,
Throw wide to the wind the gates of the wandering boat
For my voyage to begin to the end of my wound,
We heard the sea sound sing, we saw the salt sheet tell.
Lie still, sleep becalmed, hide the mouth in the throat,
Or we shall obey, and ride with you through the drowned.

Vision and Prayer

I

Who
Are you
Who is born
In the next room
So loud to my own
That I can hear the womb
Opening and the dark run
Over the ghost and the dropped son
Behind the wall thin as a wren's bone?
In the birth bloody room unknown
To the burn and turn of time
And the heart print of man
Bows no baptism
But dark alone
Blessing on
The wild
Child.

I
Must lie
Still as stone
By the wren bone
Wall hearing the moan
Of the mother hidden
And the shadowed head of pain
Casting tomorrow like a thorn
And the midwives of miracle sing
Until the turbulent new born
Burns me his name and his flame
And the winged wall is torn
By his torrid crown
And the dark thrown
From his loin
To bright
Light.

When
The wren
Bone writhes down
And the first dawn
Furied by his stream
Swarms on the kingdom come
Of the dazzler of heaven
And the splashed mothering maiden
Who bore him with a bonfire in
His mouth and rocked him like a storm
I shall run lost in sudden
Terror and shining from
The once hooded room
Crying in vain
In the caldron
Of his
Kiss

In
The spin
Of the sun
In the spuming
Cyclone of his wing
For I was lost who am
Crying at the man drenched throne
In the first fury of his stream
And the lightnings of adoration
Back to the black silence melt and mourn
For I was lost who have come
To dumbfounding haven
And the finding one
And the high noon
Of his wound
Blinds my
Cry

There
Crouched bare
In the shrine
Of his blazing
Breast I shall waken
To the judge blown bedlam
Of the uncaged sea bottom
The cloud climb of the exhaling tomb
And the bidden dust upsailing
With his flame in every grain.
O spiral of ascension
From the vultured urn
Of the morning
Of man when
The land
And

The
Born sea
Praised the sun
The finding one
And upright Adam
Sang upon origin
O the wings of the children!
The woundward flight of the ancient
Young from the canyons of oblivion!
The sky stride of the always slain
In battle! the happening
Of saints to their vision!
The world winding home!
And the whole pain
Flows open
And I
Die.

II

In the name of the lost who glory in
The swinish plains of carrion
Under the burial song
Of the birds of burden
Heavy with the drowned
And the green dust
And bearing
The ghost
From
The ground
Like pollen
On the black plume
And the beak of slime
I pray though I belong
Not wholly to that lamenting
Brethren for joy has moved within
The inmost marrow of my heart bone

That he who learns now the sun and moon
Of his mother's milk may return
Before the lips blaze and bloom
To the birth bloody room
Behind the wall's wren
Bone and be dumb
And the womb
That bore
For
All men
The adored
Infant light or
The dazzling prison
Yawn to his upcoming.
In the name of the wanton
Lost on the unchristened mountain
In the centre of dark I pray him

That he let the dead lie though they moan
For his briared hands to hoist them
To the shrine of his world's wound
And the blood drop's garden
Endure the stone
Blind host to sleep
In the dark
And deep
Rock
Awake
No heart bone
But let it break
On the mountain crown
Unbidden by the sun
And the beating dust be blown
Down to the river rooting plain
Under the night forever falling.

Forever falling night is a known
Star and country to the legion
Of sleepers whose tongue I toil
To mourn his deluging
Light through sea and soil
And we have come
To know all
P l a c e s
W a y s
M a z e s
P a s s a g e s
Quarters and graves
Of the endless fall.
Now common lazarus
Of the charting sleepers prays
Never to awake and arise
For the country of death is the heart's size

And the star of the lost the shape of the eyes.
In the name of the fatherless
In the name of the unborn
And the undesirers
Of midwiving morning's
Hands or instruments
O in the name
Of no one
Now or
No
One to
Be I pray
May the crimson
Sun spin a grave grey
And the colour of clay
Stream upon his martyrdom
In the interpreted evening
And the known dark of the earth amen.

I turn the corner of prayer and burn
In a blessing of the sudden
Sun. In the name of the damned
I would turn back and run
To the hidden land
But the loud sun
Christens down
The sky.
I
Am found.
O let him
Scald me and drown
Me in his world's wound.
His lightning answers my
Cry. My voice burns in his hand.
Now I am lost in the blinding
One. The sun roars at the prayer's end.

Ballad of the Long-legged Bait

The bows glided down, and the coast
Blackened with birds took a last look
At his thrashing hair and whale-blue eye;
The trodden town rang its cobbles for luck.

Then goodbye to the fishermanned
Boat with its anchor free and fast
As a bird hooking over the sea,
High and dry by the top of the mast,

Whispered the affectionate sand
And the bulwarks of the dazzled quay.
For my sake sail, and never look back,
Said the looking land.

Sails drank the wind, and white as milk
He sped into the drinking dark;
The sun shipwrecked west on a pearl
And the moon swam out of its hulk.

Funnels and masts went by in a whirl.
Goodbye to the man on the sea-legged deck
To the gold gut that sings on his reel
To the bait that stalked out of the sack,

For we saw him throw to the swift flood
A girl alive with his hooks through her lips;
All the fishes were rayed in blood,
Said the dwindling ships.

Goodbye to chimneys and funnels,
Old wives that spin in the smoke,
He was blind to the eyes of candles
In the praying windows of waves

But heard his bait buck in the wake
And tussle in a shoal of loves.

Now cast down your rod, for the whole
Of the sea is hilly with whales.

She longs among horses and angels,
The rainbow-fish bend in her joys,
Floated the lost cathedral
Chimes of the rocked buoys.

Where the anchor rode like a gull
Miles over the moonstruck boat
A squall of birds bellowed and fell,
A cloud blew the rain from its throat;

He saw the storm smoke out to kill
With fuming bows and ram of ice,
Fire on starlight, rake Jesu's stream;
And nothing shone on the water's face

But the oil and bubble of the moon,
Plunging and piercing in his course
The lured fish under the foam
Witnessed with a kiss.

Whales in the wake like capes and Alps
Quaked the sick sea and snouted deep,
Deep the great bushed bait with raining lips
Slipped the fins of those humpbacked tons

And fled their love in a weaving dip.
Oh, Jericho was falling in their lungs!
She nipped and dived in the nick of love,
Spun on a spout like a long-legged ball

Till every beast blared down in a swerve
Till every turtle crushed from his shell
Till every bone in the rushing grave
Rose and crowed and fell!

Good luck to the hand on the rod,
There is thunder under its thumbs;
Gold gut is a lightning thread,

His fiery reel sings off its flames,

The whirled boat in the burn of his blood
Is crying from nets to knives,
Oh the shearwater birds and their boatsized brood
Oh the bulls of Biscay and their calves

Are making under the green, laid veil
The long-legged beautiful bait their wives.
Break the black news and paint on a sail
Huge weddings in the waves,

Over the wakeward-flashing spray
Over the gardens of the floor
Clash out the mounting dolphin's day,
My mast is a bell-spire,

Strike and smoothe, for my decks are drums,
Sing through the water-spoken prow
The octopus walking into her limbs
The polar eagle with his tread of snow.

From salt-lipped beak to the kick of the stern
Sing how the seal has kissed her dead!
The long, laid minute's bride drifts on
Old in her cruel bed.

Over the graveyard in the water
Mountains and galleries beneath
Nightingale and hyena
Rejoicing for that drifting death

Sing and howl through sand and anemone
Valley and sahara in a shell,
Oh all the wanting flesh his enemy
Thrown to the sea in the shell of a girl

Is old as water and plain as an eel;
Always goodbye to the long-legged bread
Scattered in the paths of his heels
For the salty birds fluttered and fed

And the tall grains foamed in their bills;
Always goodbye to the fires of the face,
For the crab-backed dead on the sea-bed rose
And scuttled over her eyes,

The blind, clawed stare is cold as sleet.
The tempter under the eyelid
Who shows to the selves asleep
Mast-high moon-white women naked

Walking in wishes and lovely for shame
Is dumb and gone with his flame of brides.
Susanna's drowned in the bearded stream
And no-one stirs at Sheba's side

But the hungry kings of the tides;
Sin who had a woman's shape
Sleeps till Silence blows on a cloud
And all the lifted waters walk and leap.

Lucifer that bird's dropping
Out of the sides of the north
Has melted away and is lost
Is always lost in her vaulted breath,

Venus lies star-struck in her wound
And the sensual ruins make
Seasons over the liquid world,
White springs in the dark.

Always goodbye, cried the voices through the shell,
Goodbye always for the flesh is cast
And the fisherman winds his reel
With no more desire than a ghost.

Always good luck, praised the finned in the feather
Bird after dark and the laughing fish
As the sails drank up the hail of thunder
And the long-tailed lightning lit his catch.

The boat swims into the six-year weather,

A wind throws a shadow and it freezes fast.
See what the gold gut drags from under
Mountains and galleries to the crest!

See what clings to hair and skull
As the boat skims on with drinking wings!
The statues of great rain stand still,
And the flakes fall like hills.

Sing and strike his heavy haul
Toppling up the boatside in a snow of light!
His decks are drenched with miracles.
Oh miracle of fishes! The long dead bite!

Out of the urn the size of a man
Out of the room the weight of his trouble
Out of the house that holds a town
In the continent of a fossil

One by one in dust and shawl,
Dry as echoes and insect-faced,
His fathers cling to the hand of the girl
And the dead hand leads the past,

Leads them as children and as air
On to the blindly tossing tops;
The centuries throw back their hair
And the old men sing from newborn lips:

Time is bearing another son.
Kill Time! She turns in her pain!
The oak is felled in the acorn
And the hawk in the egg kills the wren.

He who blew the great fire in
And died on a hiss of flames
Or walked on the earth in the evening
Counting the denials of the grains

Clings to her drifting hair, and climbs;
And he who taught their lips to sing

Weeps like the risen sun among
The liquid choirs of his tribes.

The rod bends low, divining land,
And through the sundered water crawls
A garden holding to her hand
With birds and animals

With men and women and waterfalls
Trees cool and dry in the whirlpool of ships
And stunned and still on the green, laid veil
Sand with legends in its virgin laps

And prophets loud on the burned dunes;
Insects and valleys hold her thighs hard,
Time and places grip her breast bone,
She is breaking with seasons and clouds;

Round her trailed wrist fresh water weaves,
With moving fish and rounded stones
Up and down the greater waves
A separate river breathes and runs;

Strike and sing his catch of fields
For the surge is sown with barley,
The cattle graze on the covered foam,
The hills have footed the waves away,

With wild sea fillies and soaking bridles
With salty colts and gales in their limbs
All the horses of his haul of miracles
Gallop through the arched, green farms,

Trot and gallop with gulls upon them
And thunderbolts in their manes.
O Rome and Sodom Tomorrow and London
The country tide is cobbled with towns,

And steeples pierce the cloud on her shoulder
And the streets that the fisherman combed
When his long-legged flesh was a wind on fire

And his loin was a hunting flame

Coil from the thoroughfares of her hair
And terribly lead him home alive
Lead her prodigal home to his terror,
The furious ox-killing house of love.

Down, down, down, under the ground,
Under the floating villages,
Turns the moon-chained and water-wound
Metropolis of fishes,

There is nothing left of the sea but its sound,
Under the earth the loud sea walks,
In deathbeds of orchards the boat dies down
And the bait is drowned among hayricks,

Land, land, land, nothing remains
Of the pacing, famous sea but its speech,
And into its talkative seven tombs
The anchor dives through the floors of a church.

Goodbye, good luck, struck the sun and the moon,
To the fisherman lost on the land.
He stands alone at the door of his home,
With his long-legged heart in his hand.

Holy Spring

O

Out of a bed of love
When that immortal hospital made one more move to soothe
The cureless counted body,
and ruin and his causes
Over the barbed and shooting sea assumed an army
And swept into our wounds and houses,
I climb to greet the war in which I have no heart but only

That one dark I owe my light,
Call for confessor and wiser mirror but there is none
To glow after the god stoning night
And I am struck as lonely as a holy maker by the sun.

No
Praise that the spring time is all
Gabriel and radiant shrubbery as the morning grows joyful
Out of the woebegone pyre
And the multitude's sultry tear turns cool on the weeping wall,
My arising prodigal
Sun the father his quiver full of the infants of pure fire,
But blessed be hail and upheaval
That uncalm still it is sure alone to stand and sing
Alone in the husk of man's home
And the mother and toppling house of the holy spring,
If only for a last time.

Fern Hill

Now as I was young and easy under the apple boughs
About the lilting house and happy as the grass was green,
The night above the dingle starry,
Time let me hail and climb
Golden in the heydays of his eyes,
And honoured among wagons I was prince of the apple towns
And once below a time I lordly had the trees and leaves
Trail with daisies and barley
Down the rivers of the windfall light.

And as I was green and carefree, famous among the barns
About the happy yard and singing as the farm was home,
In the sun that is young once only,
Time let me play and be
Golden in the mercy of his means,
And green and golden I was huntsman and herdsman, the calves
Sang to my horn, the foxes on the hills barked clear and cold,
And the sabbath rang slowly
In the pebbles of the holy streams.

All the sun long it was running, it was lovely, the hay
Fields high as the house, the tunes from the chimneys, it was air
    And playing, lovely and watery
        And fire green as grass.
    And nightly under the simple stars
As I rode to sleep the owls were bearing the farm away,
All the moon long I heard, blessed among stables, the nightjars
    Flying with the ricks, and the horses
        Flashing into the dark.

And then to awake, and the farm, like a wanderer white
With the dew, come back, the cock on his shoulder: it was all
    Shining, it was Adam and maiden,
        The sky gathered again
    And the sun grew round that very day.
So it must have been after the birth of the simple light
In the first, spinning place, the spellbound horses walking warm
    Out of the whinnying green stable
        On to the fields of praise.

And honoured among foxes and pheasants by the gay house
Under the new made clouds and happy as the heart was long,
    In the sun born over and over,
        I ran my heedless ways,
    My wishes raced through the house high hay
And nothing I cared, at my sky blue trades, that time allows
In all his tuneful turning so few and such morning songs
    Before the children green and golden
        Follow him out of grace,

Nothing I cared, in the lamb white days, that time would take me
Up to the swallow thronged loft by the shadow of my hand,
    In the moon that is always rising,
        Nor that riding to sleep
    I should hear him fly with the high fields
And wake to the farm forever fled from the childless land.
Oh as I was young and easy in the mercy of his means,
        Time held me green and dying
    Though I sang in my chains like the sea.

IN COUNTRY SLEEP

In Country Sleep

I

Never and never, my girl riding far and near
In the land of the hearthstone tales, and spelled asleep,
Fear or believe that the wolf in a sheepwhite hood
Loping and bleating roughly and blithely shall leap,
                    My dear, my dear,
Out of a lair in the flocked leaves in the dew dipped year
To eat your heart in the house in the rosy wood.

Sleep, good, for ever, slow and deep, spelled rare and wise,
My girl ranging the night in the rose and shire
Of the hobnail tales: no gooseherd or swine will turn
Into a homestall king or hamlet of fire
                    And prince of ice
To court the honeyed heart from your side before sunrise
In a spinney of ringed boys and ganders, spike and burn,

Nor the innocent lie in the rooting dingle wooed
And staved, and riven among plumes my rider weep.
From the broomed witch's spume you are shielded by fern
And flower of country sleep and the greenwood keep.
                    Lie fast and soothed,
Safe be and smooth from the bellows of the rushy brood.
Never, my girl, until tolled to sleep by the stern

Bell believe or fear that the rustic shade or spell
Shall harrow and snow the blood while you ride wide and near,
For who unmanningly haunts the mountain ravened eaves
Or skulks in the dell moon but moonshine echoing clear
                    From the starred well?
A hill touches an angel. Out of a saint's cell
The nightbird lauds through nunneries and domes of leaves

Her robin breasted tree, three Marys in the rays.
Sanctum sanctorum the animal eye of the wood
In the rain telling its beads, and the gravest ghost
The owl at its kneeling. Fox and holt kneel before blood.
Now the tales praise
The star rise at pasture and nightlong the fables graze
On the lord's table of the bowing grass. Fear most

For ever of all not the wolf in his baaing hood
Nor the tusked prince, in the ruttish farm, at the rind
And mire of love, but the Thief as meek as the dew.
The country is holy: O bide in that country kind,
Know the green good,
Under the prayer wheeling moon in the rosy wood
Be shielded by chant and flower and gay may you

Lie in grace. Sleep spelled at rest in the lowly house
In the squirrel nimble grove, under linen and thatch
And star: held and blessed, though you scour the high four
Winds, from the dousing shade and the roarer at the latch,
Cool in your vows.
Yet out of the beaked, web dark and the pouncing boughs
Be you sure the Thief will seek a way sly and sure

And sly as snow and meek as dew blown to the thorn,
This night and each vast night until the stern bell talks
In the tower and tolls to sleep over the stalls
Of the hearthstone tales my own, last love; and the soul walks
The waters shorn.
This night and each night since the falling star you were born,
Ever and ever he finds a way, as the snow falls,

As the rain falls, hail on the fleece, as the vale mist rides
Through the haygold stalls, as the dew falls on the wind-
Milled dust of the apple tree and the pounded islands
Of the morning leaves, as the star falls, as the winged
Apple seed glides,
And falls, and flowers in the yawning wound at our sides,
As the world falls, silent as the cyclone of silence.

II

Night and the reindeer on the clouds above the haycocks
And the wings of the great roc ribboned for the fair!
The leaping saga of prayer! And high, there, on the hare-
Heeled winds the rooks
Cawing from their black bethels soaring, the holy books
Of birds! Among the cocks like fire the red fox

Burning! Night and the vein of birds in the winged, sloe wrist
Of the wood! Pastoral beat of blood through the laced leaves!
The stream from the priest black wristed spinney and sleeves
Of thistling frost
Of the nightingale's din and tale! The upgiven ghost
Of the dingle torn to singing and the surpliced

Hill of cypresses! The din and tale in the skimmed
Yard of the buttermilk rain on the pail! The sermon
Of blood! The bird loud vein! The saga from mermen
To seraphim
Leaping! The gospel rooks! All tell, this night, of him
Who comes as red as the fox and sly as the heeled wind.

Illumination of music! the lulled black backed
Gull, on the wave with sand in its eyes! And the foal moves
Through the shaken greensward lake, silent, on moonshod hooves,
In the winds' wakes.
Music of elements, that a miracle makes!
Earth, air, water, fire, singing into the white act,

The haygold haired, my love asleep, and the rift blue
Eyed, in the haloed house, in her rareness and hilly
High riding, held and blessed and true, and so stilly
Lying the sky
Might cross its planets, the bell weep, night gather her eyes,
The Thief fall on the dead like the willynilly dew,

Only for the turning of the earth in her holy
Heart! Slyly, slowly, hearing the wound in her side go
Round the sun, he comes to my love like the designed snow,

And truly he
Flows to the strand of flowers like the dew's ruly sea,
And surely he sails like the ship shape clouds. Oh he

Comes designed to my love to steal nor her tide raking
Wound, nor her riding high, nor her eyes, nor kindled hair,
But her faith that each vast night and the saga of prayer
He comes to take
Her faith that this last night for his unsacred sake
He comes to leave her in the lawless sun awaking

Naked and forsaken to grieve he will not come.
Ever and ever by all your vows believe and fear
My dear this night he comes and night without end my dear
Since you were born:
And you shall wake, from country sleep, this dawn and each
first dawn,
Your faith as deathless as the outcry of the ruled sun.

Over Sir John's hill

Over Sir John's hill,
The hawk on fire hangs still;
In a hoisted cloud, at drop of dusk, he pulls to his claws
And gallows, up the rays of his eyes the small birds of the bay
And the shrill child's play
Wars
Of the sparrows and such who swansing, dusk, in wrangling hedges
And blithely they squawk
To fiery tyburn over the wrestle of elms until
The flash the noosed hawk
Crashes, and slowly the fishing holy stalking heron
In the river Towy below bows his tilted headstone.

Flash, and the plumes crack,
And a black cap of jack-

Daws Sir John's just hill dons, and again the gulled birds hare
To the hawk on fire, the halter height, over Towy's fins,
In a whack of wind.
There
Where the elegiac fisherbird stabs and paddles
In the pebbly dab filled
Shallow and sedge, and 'dilly dilly,' calls the loft hawk,
'Come and be killed,'
I open the leaves of the water at a passage
Of psalms and shadows among the pincered sandcrabs prancing

And read, in a shell,
Death clear as a buoy's bell:
All praise of the hawk on fire in hawk-eyed dusk be sung,
When his viperish fuse hangs looped with flames under the brand
Wing, and blest shall
Young
Green chickens of the bay and bushes cluck, 'dilly dilly,
Come let us die.'
We grieve as the blithe birds, never again, leave shingle and elm,
The heron and I,
I young Aesop fabling to the near night by the dingle
Of eels, saint heron hymning in the shell-hung distant

Crystal harbour vale
Where the sea cobbles sail,
And wharves of water where the walls dance and the white cranes stilt.
It is the heron and I, under judging Sir John's elmed
Hill, tell-tale the knelled
Guilt
Of the led-astray birds whom God, for their breast of whistles,
Have mercy on,
God in his whirlwind silence save, who marks the sparrows hail,
For their souls' song.
Now the heron grieves in the weeded verge. Through windows
Of dusk and water I see the tilting whispering.

Heron, mirrored, go,
As the snapt feathers snow,
Fishing in the tear of the Towy. Only a hoot owl

Hollows, a grassblade blown in cupped hands, in the looted elms,
And no green cocks or hens
Shout
Now on Sir John's hill. The heron, ankling the scaly
Lowlands of the waves,
Makes all the music; and I who hear the tune of the slow,
Wear-willow river, grave,
Before the lunge of the night, the notes on this time-shaken
Stone for the sake of the souls of the slain birds sailing.

Poem on his Birthday

In the mustardseed sun,
By full tilt river and switchback sea
Where the cormorants scud,
In his house on stilts high among beaks
And palavers of birds
This sandgrain day in the bent bay's grave
He celebrates and spurns
His driftwood thirty-fifth wind turned age;
Herons spire and spear.

Under and round him go
Flounders, gulls, on their cold, dying trails,
Doing what they are told,
Curlews aloud in the congered waves
Work at their ways to death,
And the rhymer in the long tongued room,
Who tolls his birthday bell,
Toils towards the ambush of his wounds;
Herons, steeple stemmed, bless.

In the thistledown fall,
He sings towards anguish; finches fly
In the claw tracks of hawks
On a seizing sky; small fishes glide

Through wynds and shells of drowned
Ship towns to pastures of otters. He
In his slant, racking house
And the hewn coils of his trade perceives
Herons walk in their shroud,

The livelong river's robe
Of minnows wreathing around their prayer;
And far at sea he knows,
Who slaves to his crouched, eternal end
Under a serpent cloud,
Dolphins dive in their turnturtle dust,
The rippled seals streak down
To kill and their own tide daubing blood
Slides good in the sleek mouth.

In a cavernous, swung
Wave's silence, wept white angelus knells.
Thirty-five bells sing struck
On skull and scar where his loves lie wrecked,
Steered by the falling stars.
And tomorrow weeps in a blind cage
Terror will rage apart
Before chains break to a hammer flame
And love unbolts the dark

And freely he goes lost
In the unknown, famous light of great
And fabulous, dear God.
Dark is a way and light is a place,
Heaven that never was
Nor will be ever is always true,
And, in that brambled void,
Plenty as blackberries in the woods
The dead grow for His joy.

There he might wander bare
With the spirits of the horseshoe bay
Or the stars' seashore dead,
Marrow of eagles, the roots of whales
And wishbones of wild geese,

With blessed, unborn God and His Ghost,
   And every soul His priest,
Gulled and chanter in young Heaven's fold
   Be at cloud quaking peace,

   But dark is a long way.
He, on the earth of the night, alone
   With all the living, prays,
Who knows the rocketing wind will blow
   The bones out of the hills,
And the scythed boulders bleed, and the last
   Rage shattered waters kick
Masts and fishes to the still quick stars,
   Faithlessly unto Him

   Who is the light of old
And air shaped Heaven where souls grow wild
   As horses in the foam:
Oh, let me midlife mourn by the shrined
   And druid herons' vows
The voyage to ruin I must run,
   Dawn ships clouted aground,
Yet, though I cry with tumbledown tongue,
   Count my blessings aloud:

   Four elements and five
Senses, and man a spirit in love
   Tangling through this spun slime
To his nimbus bell cool kingdom come
   And the lost, moonshine domes,
And the sea that hides his secret selves
   Deep in its black, base bones,
Lulling of spheres in the seashell flesh,
   And this last blessing most,

   That the closer I move
To death, one man through his sundered hulks,
   The louder the sun blooms
And the tusked, ramshackling sea exults;
   And every wave of the way
And gale I tackle, the whole world then

With more triumphant faith
Than ever was since the world was said
Spins its morning of praise,

I hear the bouncing hills
Grow larked and greener at berry brown
Fall and the dew larks sing
Taller this thunderclap spring, and how
More spanned with angels ride
The mansouled fiery islands! Oh,
Holier then their eyes,
And my shining men no more alone
As I sail out to die.

Do not go gentle into that good night

Do not go gentle into that good night,
Old age should burn and rave at close of day;
Rage, rage against the dying of the light.

Though wise men at their end know dark is right,
Because their words had forked no lightning they
Do not go gentle into that good night.

Good men, the last wave by, crying how bright
Their frail deeds might have danced in a green bay,
Rage, rage against the dying of the light.

Wild men who caught and sang the sun in flight,
And learn, too late, they grieved it on its way,
Do not go gentle into that good night.

Grave men, near death, who see with blinding sight
Blind eyes could blaze like meteors and be gay,
Rage, rage against the dying of the light.

And you, my father, there on the sad height,

Curse, bless, me now with your fierce tears, I pray.
Do not go gentle into that good night.
Rage, rage against the dying of the light.

Lament

When I was a windy boy and a bit
And the black spit of the chapel fold,
(Sighed the old ram rod, dying of women),
I tiptoed shy in the gooseberry wood,
The rude owl cried like a telltale tit,
I skipped in a blush as the big girls rolled
Ninepin down on the donkeys' common,
And on seesaw sunday nights I wooed
Whoever I would with my wicked eyes,
The whole of the moon I could love and leave
All the green leaved little weddings' wives
In the coal black bush and let them grieve.

When I was a gusty man and a half
And the black beast of the beetles' pews,
(Sighed the old ram rod, dying of bitches),
Not a boy and a bit in the wick-
Dipping moon and drunk as a new dropped calf,
I whistled all night in the twisted flues,
Midwives grew in the midnight ditches,
And the sizzling beds of the town cried, Quick! –
Whenever I dove in a breast high shoal,
Wherever I ramped in the clover quilts,
Whatsoever I did in the coal-
Black night, I left my quivering prints.

When I was a man you could call a man
And the black cross of the holy house,
(Sighed the old ram rod, dying of welcome),
Brandy and ripe in my bright, bass prime,
No springtailed tom in the red hot town

With every simmering woman his mouse
But a hillocky bull in the swelter
Of summer come in his great good time
To the sultry, biding herds, I said,
Oh, time enough when the blood creeps cold,
And I lie down but to sleep in bed,
For my sulking, skulking, coal black soul!

When I was a half of the man I was
And served me right as the preachers warn,
(Sighed the old ram rod, dying of downfall),
No flailing calf or cat in a flame
Or hickory bull in milky grass
But a black sheep with a crumpled horn,
At last the soul from its foul mousehole
Slunk pouting out when the limp time came;
And I gave my soul a blind, slashed eye,
Gristle and rind, and a roarer's life,
And I shoved it into the coal black sky
To find a woman's soul for a wife.

Now I am a man no more no more
And a black reward for a roaring life,
(Sighed the old ram rod, dying of strangers),
Tidy and cursed in my dove cooed room
I lie down thin and hear the good bells jaw –
For, oh, my soul found a sunday wife
In the coal black sky and she bore angels!
Harpies around me out of her womb!
Chastity prays for me, piety sings,
Innocence sweetens my last black breath,
Modesty hides my thighs in her wings,
And all the deadly virtues plague my death!

In the White Giant's Thigh

Through throats where many rivers meet, the curlews cry,
Under the conceiving moon, on the high chalk hill,
And there this night I walk in the white giant's thigh
Where barren as boulders women lie longing still

To labour and love though they lay down long ago.

Through throats where many rivers meet, the women pray,
Pleading in the waded bay for the seed to flow
Though the names on their weed grown stones are rained away,

And alone in the night's eternal, curving act
They yearn with tongues of curlews for the unconceived
And immemorial sons of the cudgelling, hacked

Hill. Who once in gooseskin winter loved all ice leaved
In the courters' lanes, or twined in the ox roasting sun
In the wains tonned so high that the wisps of the hay
Clung to the pitching clouds, or gay with anyone
Young as they in the after milking moonlight lay

Under the lighted shapes of faith and their moonshade
Petticoats galed high, or shy with the rough riding boys,
Now clasp me to their grains in the gigantic glade,

Who once, green countries since, were a hedgerow of joys.

Time by, their dust was flesh the swineherd rooted sly,
Flared in the reek of the wiving sty with the rush
Light of his thighs, spreadeagle to the dunghill sky,
Or with their orchard man in the core of the sun's bush
Rough as cows' tongues and thrashed with brambles their buttermilk
Manes, under his quenchless summer barbed gold to the bone,

Or rippling soft in the spinney moon as the silk
And ducked and draked white lake that harps to a hail stone.

Who once were a bloom of wayside brides in the hawed house
And heard the lewd, wooed field flow to the coming frost,
The scurrying, furred small friars squeal, in the dowse
Of day, in the thistle aisles, till the white owl crossed

Their breast, the vaulting does roister, the horned bucks climb
Quick in the wood at love, where a torch of foxes foams,
All birds and beasts of the linked night uproar and chime

And the mole snout blunt under his pilgrimage of domes,

Or, butter fat goosegirls, bounced in a gambo bed,
Their breasts full of honey, under their gander king
Trounced by his wings in the hissing shippen, long dead
And gone that barley dark where their clogs danced in the spring,
And their firefly hairpins flew, and the ricks ran round –

(But nothing bore, no mouthing babe to the veined hives
Hugged, and barren and bare on Mother Goose's ground
They with the simple Jacks were a boulder of wives) –

Now curlew cry me down to kiss the mouths of their dust.

The dust of their kettles and clocks swings to and fro
Where the hay rides now or the bracken kitchens rust
As the arc of the billhooks that flashed the hedges low
And cut the birds' boughs that the minstrel sap ran red.
They from houses where the harvest kneels, hold me hard,
Who heard the tall bell sail down the Sundays of the dead
And the rain wring out its tongues on the faded yard,
Teach me the love that is evergreen after the fall leaved
Grave, after Beloved on the grass gulfed cross is scrubbed
Off by the sun and Daughters no longer grieved
Save by their long desirers in the fox cubbed
Streets or hungering in the crumbled wood: to these
Hale dead and deathless do the women of the hill
Love forever meridian through the courters' trees

And the daughters of darkness flame like Fawkes fires still.

STORIES

After the Fair

The fair was over, the lights in the coconut stalls were put out, and the wooden horses stood still in the darkness, waiting for the music and the hum of the machines that would set them trotting forward. One by one, in every booth, the naphtha jets were turned down and the canvases pulled over the little gaming tables. The crowd went home, and there were lights in the windows of the caravans.

Nobody had noticed the girl. In her black clothes she stood against the side of the roundabouts, hearing the last feet tread upon the sawdust and the last voices die in the distance. Then, all alone on the deserted ground, surrounded by the shapes of wooden horses and cheap fairy boats, she looked for a place to sleep. Now here and now there, she raised the canvas that shrouded the coconut stalls and peered into the warm darkness. She was frightened to step inside, and as a mouse scampered across the littered shavings on the floor, or as the canvas creaked and a rush of wind set it dancing, she ran away and hid again near the roundabouts. Once she stepped on the boards; the bells round a horse's throat jingled and were still; she did not dare breathe again until all was quiet and the darkness had forgotten the noise of the bells. Then here and there she went peeping for a bed, into each gondola, under each tent. But there was nowhere, nowhere in all the fair for her to sleep. One place was too silent, and in another was the noise of mice. There was straw in the corner of the Astrologer's tent, but it moved as she touched it; she knelt by its side and put out her hand; she felt a baby's hand upon her own.

Now there was nowhere, so slowly she turned towards the caravans on the outskirts of the field, and found all but two to be unlit. She waited, clutching her empty bag, and wondering which caravan she should disturb. At last she decided to knock upon the window of the little, shabby one near her, and, standing on tiptoes, she looked in. The fattest man she had ever seen was sitting in front of the stove, toasting a piece of bread. She tapped three times on the glass, then hid in the shadows. She heard him come to the top of the steps and call out 'Who? Who?' but she dare not answer. 'Who? Who?' he called again.

She laughed at his voice which was as thin as he was fat.

He heard her laughter and turned to where the darkness concealed her. 'First you tap,' he said, 'then you hide, then you laugh.'

She stepped into the circle of light, knowing she need no longer hide herself.

'A girl,' he said. 'Come in, and wipe your feet.' He did not wait but retreated into his caravan, and she could do nothing but follow him up the steps and into the crowded room. He was seated again, and toasting the same piece of bread. 'Have you come in?' he said, for his back was towards her.

'Shall I close the door?' she asked, and closed it before he replied.

She sat on the bed and watched him toast the bread until it burnt.

'I can toast better than you,' she said.

'I don't doubt it,' said the Fat Man.

She watched him put the charred toast upon a plate by his side, take another round of bread and hold that, too, in front of the stove. It burnt very quickly.

'Let me toast it for you,' she said. Ungraciously he handed her the fork and the loaf.

'Cut it,' he said, 'toast it, and eat it.'

She sat on the chair.

'See the dent you've made on my bed,' said the Fat Man. 'Who are you to come in and dent my bed?'

'My name is Annie,' she told him.

Soon all the bread was toasted and buttered, so she put it in the centre of the table and arranged two chairs.

'I'll have mine on the bed,' said the Fat Man. 'You'll have it here.'

When they had finished their supper, he pushed back his chair and stared at her across the table.

'I am the Fat Man,' he said. 'My home is Treorchy; the Fortune-Teller next door is Aberdare.'

'I am nothing to do with the fair,' she said, 'I am Cardiff.'

'There's a town,' agreed the Fat Man. He asked her why she had come away.

'Money,' said Annie.

Then he told her about the fair and the places he had been to and the people he had met. He told her his age and his weight and the names of his brothers and what he would call his son. He showed her a picture of Boston Harbour and the photograph of his mother who lifted weights. He told her how summer looked in Ireland.

'I've always been a fat man,' he said, 'and now I'm the Fat Man; there's nobody to touch me for fatness.' He told her of a heat-wave in Sicily and of the Mediterranean Sea. She told him of the baby in the Astrologer's tent.

'That's the stars again,' he said.

'The baby'll die,' said Annie.

He opened the door and walked out into the darkness. She looked about her but did not move, wondering if he had gone to fetch a policeman. It would never do to be caught by the policeman again. She stared through the open door into the inhospitable night and drew her chair closer to the stove.

'Better to be caught in the warmth,' she said. But she trembled at the sound of the Fat Man approaching, and pressed her hands upon her thin breast as he climbed up the steps like a walking mountain. She could see him smile through the darkness.

'See what the stars have done,' he said, and brought in the Astrologer's baby in his arms.

After she had nursed it against her and it had cried on the bosom of her dress, she told him how she had feared his going.

'What should I be doing with a policeman.'

She told him that the policeman wanted her. 'What have you done for a policeman to be wanting you?'

She did not answer but took the child nearer to her wasted breast. He saw her thinness.

'You must eat, Cardiff,' he said.

Then the child began to cry. From a little wail its voice rose into a tempest of despair. The girl rocked it to and fro on her lap, but nothing soothed it.

'Stop it! Stop it!' said the Fat Man, and the tears increased. Annie smothered it in kisses, but it howled again.

'We must do something,' she said.

'Sing it a lullaby.'

She sang, but the child did not like her singing.

'There's only one thing,' said Annie, 'we must take it on the roundabouts.' With the child's arm around her neck she stumbled down the steps and ran towards the deserted fair, the Fat Man panting behind her.

She found her way through the tents and stalls into the centre of the ground where the wooden horses stood waiting, and clambered up on a saddle. 'Start the engine,' she called out. In the distance the

Fat Man could be heard cranking up the antique machine that drove the horses all the day into a wooden gallop. She heard the spasmodic humming of the engines; the boards rattled under the horses' feet. She saw the Fat Man get up by her side, pull the central lever, and climb on to the saddle of the smallest horse of all. As the roundabout started, slowly at first and slowly gaining speed, the child at the girl's breast stopped crying and clapped its hands. The night wind tore through its hair, the music jangled in its ears. Round and round the wooden horses sped, drowning the cries of the wind with the beating of their hooves.

And so the men from the caravans found them, the Fat Man and the girl in black with a baby in her arms, racing round and round on their mechanical steeds to the ever-increasing music of the organ.

The Tree

Rising from the house that faced the Jarvis hills in the long distance, there was a tower for the day-birds to build in and for the owls to fly around at night. From the village the light in the tower window shone like a glow-worm through the panes; but the room under the sparrows' nests was rarely lit; webs were spun over its unwashed ceilings; it stared over twenty miles of the up-and-down county, and the corners kept their secrets where there were claw marks in the dust.

The child knew the house from roof to cellar; he knew the irregular lawns and the gardener's shed where flowers burst out of their jars; but he could not find the key that opened the door of the tower.

The house changed to his moods, and a lawn was the sea or the shore or the sky or whatever he wished it. When a lawn was a sad mile of water, and he was sailing on a broken flower down the waves, the gardener would come out of his shed near the island of bushes. He too would take a stalk, and sail. Straddling a garden broom, he would fly wherever the child wished. He knew every story from the beginning of the world.

'In the beginning,' he would say, 'there was a tree.'

'What kind of a tree?'

'The tree where that blackbird's whistling.'

'A hawk, a hawk,' cried the child.

The gardener would look up at the tree, seeing a monstrous hawk perched on a bough or an eagle swinging in the wind.

The gardener loved the Bible. When the sun sank and the garden was full of people, he would sit with a candle in his shed, reading of the first love and the legend of apples and serpents. But the death of Christ on a tree he loved most. Trees made a fence around him, and he knew of the changing of the seasons by the hues on the bark and the rushing of sap through the covered roots. His world moved and changed as spring moved along the branches, changing their nakedness; his God grew up like a tree from the apple-shaped earth, giving bud to His children and letting His children be blown from their places by the breezes of winter; winter and death moved in one wind. He would sit in his shed and read of the crucifixion, looking over the jars on his window-shelf into the winter nights. He would think that love fails on such nights, and that many of its children are cut down.

The child transfigured the blowsy lawns with his playing. The gardener called him by his mother's name, and seated him on his knee, and talked to him of the wonders of Jerusalem and the birth in the manger.

'In the beginning was the village of Bethlehem,' he whispered to the child before the bell rang for tea out of the growing darkness.

'Where is Bethlehem?'

'Far away,' said the gardener, 'in the East.'

To the east stood the Jarvis hills, hiding the sun, their trees drawing up the moon out of the grass.

The child lay in bed. He watched the rocking-horse and wished that it would grow wings so that he could mount it and ride into the Arabian sky. But the winds of Wales blew at the curtains, and crickets made a noise in the untidy plot under the window. His toys were dead. He started to cry and then stopped, knowing no reason for tears. The night was windy and cold, he was warm under the sheets; the night was as big as a hill, he was a boy in bed.

Closing his eyes, he stared into a spinning cavern deeper than the darkness of the garden where the first tree on which the unreal birds had fastened stood alone and bright as fire. The tears ran back under his lids as he thought of the first tree that was planted so near him, like a friend in the garden. He crept out of bed and tiptoed to the door. The rocking-horse bounded forward on its springs, startling the child into a noiseless scamper back to bed. The child looked at the horse and the horse was quiet; he tiptoed again along the carpet, and reached the door, and turned the knob around, and ran on to the landing. Feeling blindly in front of him, he made his way to the top of the stairs; he looked down the dark stairs into the hall, seeing a host of shadows curve in and out of the corners, hearing their sinuous voices, imagining the pits of their eyes and their lean arms. But they would be little and secret and bloodless, not cased in invisible armour but wound around with cloths as thin as a web; they would whisper as he walked, touch him on the shoulder, and say S in his ear. He went down the stairs; not a shadow moved in the hall, the corners were empty. He put out his hand and patted the darkness, thinking to feel some dry and velvet head creep under the fingers and edge, like a mist, into the nails. But there was nothing. He opened the front door, and the shadows swept into the garden.

Once on the path, his fears left him. The moon had lain down on the unweeded beds, and her frosts were spread on the grass. At last he came to the illuminated tree at the long gravel end, older even than the marvel of light, with the woodlice asleep under the bark, with the boughs standing out from the body like the frozen arms of a woman. The child touched the tree; it bent as to his touch. He saw a star, brighter than any in the sky, burn steadily above the first birds' tower, and shine on nowhere but on the leafless boughs and the trunk and the travelling roots.

The child had not doubted the tree. He said his prayers to it, with knees bent on the blackened twigs the night wind fetched to the ground. Then, trembling with love and cold, he ran back over the lawns towards the house.

There was an idiot to the east of the county who walked the land like a beggar. Now at a farmhouse and now at a widow's cottage he begged for his bread. A parson gave him a suit, and it lopped round his hungry ribs and shoulders and waved in the wind as he shambled over the fields. But his eyes were so wide and his neck so clear of the country dirt that no one refused him what he asked. And asking for water, he was given milk.

'Where do you come from?'

'From the east,' he said.

So they knew he was an idiot, and gave him a meal to clean the yards.

As he bent with a rake over the dung and the trodden grain, he heard a voice rise in his heart. He put his hand into the cattle's hay, caught a mouse, rubbed his hand over its muzzle, and let it go away.

All day the thought of the tree was with the child; all night it stood up in his dreams as the star stood above its plot. One morning towards the middle of December, when the wind from the farthest hills was rushing around the house, and the snow of the dark hours had not dissolved from lawns and roofs, he ran to the gardener's shed. The gardener was repairing a rake he had found broken. Without a word, the child sat on a seedbox at his feet, and watched him tie the teeth, and knew that the wire would not keep them together. He looked at the gardener's boots, wet with snow, at the patched knees of his trousers, at the undone buttons of his coat, and the folds of his belly under the patched flannel shirt. He looked at his hands as they busied themselves over the golden knots of wire; they were hard, brown hands, with the stains of the soil under the broken nails and the stains of tobacco on the tips of the fingers. Now the lines of the gardener's face were set in determination as time upon time he knotted the iron teeth only to feel them shake insecurely from the handle. The child was frightened of the strength and the uncleanliness of the old man; but, looking at the long, thick beard, unstained and white as fleece, he soon became reassured. The beard was the beard of an apostle.

'I prayed to the tree,' said the child.

'Always pray to a tree,' said the gardener, thinking of Calvary and Eden.

'I pray to the tree every night.'

'Pray to a tree.'

The wire slid over the teeth.

'I pray to that tree.'

The wire snapped.

The child was pointing over the glasshouse flowers to the tree that, alone of all the trees in the garden, had no sign of snow.

'An elder,' said the gardener, but the child stood up from his box and shouted so loud that the unmended rake fell with a clatter on the floor.

'The first tree. The first tree you told me of. In the beginning was the tree, you said. I heard you,' the child shouted.

'The elder is as good as another,' said the gardener, lowering his voice to humour the child.

'The first tree of all,' said the child in a whisper.

Reassured again by the gardener's voice, he smiled through the window at the tree, and again the wire crept over the broken rake.

'God grows in strange trees,' said the old man. 'His trees come to rest in strange places.'

As he unfolded the story of the twelve stages of the cross, the tree waved its boughs to the child. An apostle's voice rose out of the tarred lungs.

So they hoisted him up on a tree, and drove nails through his belly and his feet.

There was the blood of the noon sun on the trunk of the elder, staining the bark.

*

The idiot stood on the Jarvis hills, looking down into the immaculate valley from whose waters and grasses the mists of morning rose and were lost. He saw the dew dissolving, the cattle staring into the stream, and the dark clouds flying away at the rumour of the sun. The sun turned at the edges of the thin and watery sky like a sweet in a glass of water. He was hungry for light as the first and almost invisible rain fell on his lips; he plucked at the grass, and, tasting it, felt it lie green on his tongue. So there was light in his mouth, and light was a sound at his ears, and the whole dominion of light in the valley that had such a curious name. He had known of the Jarvis Hills; their shapes rose over the slopes of the county to be seen for miles around, but no one had told him of the valley lying under the hills. Bethlehem, said the idiot to the valley, turning over the sounds of the word and giving it all the glory of the Welsh morning. He brothered the world around him, sipped at the air, as a child newly born sips and brothers the light. The life of the Jarvis valley, steaming up from the body of the grass and the trees and the long hand of the stream, lent him a new blood. Night had emptied the idiot's veins, and dawn in the valley filled them again.

'Bethlehem,' said the idiot to the valley.

The gardener had no present to give the child, so he took out a key from his pocket and said: 'This is the key to the tower. On Christmas Eve I will unlock the door for you.'

Before it was dark, he and the child climbed the stairs to the tower, the key turned in the lock, and the door, like the lid of a secret box, opened and let them in. The room was empty. 'Where are the secrets?' asked the child, staring up at the matted rafters and into the spider's corners and along the leaden panes of the window.

'It is enough that I have given you the key,' said the gardener, who believed the key of the universe to be hidden in his pocket along with the feathers of birds and the seeds of flowers.

The child began to cry because there were no secrets. Over and over again he explored the empty room, kicking up the dust to look for a colourless trap-door, tapping the unpanelled walls for the hollow voice of a room beyond the tower. He brushed the webs from the window, and looked out through the dust into the snowing Christmas Eve. A world of hills stretched far away into the measured sky, and the tops of hills he had never seen climbed up to meet the falling flakes. Woods and rocks, wide seas of barren land, and a new tide of mountain sky sweeping through the black beeches, lay before him.

To the east were the outlines of nameless hill creatures and a den of trees.

'Who are they? Who are they?'

'They are the Jarvis hills,' said the gardener, 'which have been from the beginning.'

He took the child by the hand and led him away from the window. The key turned in the lock.

That night the child slept well; there was power in snow and darkness; there was unalterable music in the silence of the stars; there was a silence in the hurrying wind. And Bethlehem had been nearer than he expected.

*

On Christmas morning the idiot walked into the garden. His hair was wet and his flaked and ragged shoes were thick with the dirt of the fields. Tired with the long journey from the Jarvis hills, and weak for the want of food, he sat down under the elder-tree where the gardener had rolled a log. Clasping his hands in front of him, he saw the desolation of the flower-beds and the weeds that grew in profusion on the edges of the paths. The tower stood up like a tree of stone and glass over the red eaves. He pulled his coat-collar round his neck as a fresh wind sprang up and struck the tree; he looked down at his hands and saw that they were praying. Then a fear of the garden came over him, the shrubs were his enemies, and the trees that made an avenue down to the gate lifted their arms in horror. The place was too high, peering down on to the tall hills; the place was too low, shivering up at the plumed shoulders of a new mountain. Here the wind was too wild, fuming about the silence, raising a Jewish voice out of the elder boughs; here the silence beat like a human heart. And as he sat under the cruel hills, he heard a voice that was in him cry out: 'Why did you bring me here?'

He could not tell why he had come; they had told him to come and had guided him, but he did not know who they were. The voice of a people rose out of the garden beds, and rain swooped down from heaven.

'Let me be,' said the idiot, and made a little gesture against the sky. There is rain on my face, there is wind on my cheeks. He brothered the rain.

So the child found him under the shelter of the tree, bearing the torture of the weather with a divine patience, letting his long hair blow where it would, with his mouth set in a sad smile.

Who was this stranger? He had fires in his eyes, the flesh of his neck under the gathered coat was bare. Yet he smiled as he sat in his rags under a tree on Christmas Day.

'Where do you come from?' asked the child.

'From the east,' answered the idiot.

The gardener had not lied, and the secret of the tower was true; this dark and shabby tree, that glistened only in the night, was the first tree of all.

But he asked again:

'Where do you come from?'

'From the Jarvis hills.'

'Stand up against the tree.'

The idiot, still smiling, stood up with his back to the elder.

'Put out your arms like this.'

The idiot put out his arms.

The child ran as fast as he could to the gardener's shed, and, returning over the sodden lawns, saw that the idiot had not moved but stood, straight and smiling, with his back to the tree and his arms stretched out.

'Let me tie your hands.'

The idiot felt the wire that had not mended the rake close round his wrists. It cut into the flesh, and the blood from the cuts fell shining on to the tree.

'Brother,' he said. He saw that the child held silver nails in the palm of his hand.

The Dress

They had followed him for two days over the length of the county, but he had lost them at the foot of the hills, and hidden in a golden bush, had heard them shouting as they stumbled down the valley. Behind a tree on the ridge of the hills he had peeped down on to the fields where they hurried about like dogs, where they poked the hedges with their sticks and set up a faint howling as a mist came suddenly from the spring sky and hid them from his eyes. But the mist was a mother to him, putting a coat around his shoulders where the shirt was torn and the blood dry on his blades. The mist made him warm; he had the food and the drink of the mist on his lips; and he smiled through her mantle like a cat. He worked away from the valleywards side of the hill into the denser trees that might lead him to light and fire and a basin of soup. He thought of the coals that might be hissing in the grate, and of the young mother standing alone. He thought of her hair. Such a nest it would make for his hands. He ran through the trees, and found himself on a narrow road. Which way should he walk: towards or away from the moon? The mist had made a secret of the position of the moon, but, in a corner of the sky, where the mist had fallen apart, he could see the angles of the stars. He walked towards the north where the stars were, mumbling a song with no tune, hearing his feet suck in and out of the spongy earth.

Now there was time to collect his thoughts, but no sooner had he started to set them in order than an owl made a cry in the trees that hung over the road, and he stopped and winked up at her, finding a mutual melancholy in her sounds. Soon she would swoop and fasten on a mouse. He saw her for a moment as she sat screeching on her bough. Then, frightened of her, he hurried on, and had not gone more than a few yards into the darkness when, with a fresh cry, she flew away. Pity the hare, he thought, for the weasel will drink her. The road sloped to the stars, and the trees and the valley and the memory of the guns faded behind.

He heard footsteps. An old man, radiant with rain, stepped out of the mist.

'Good night, sir,' said the old man.

'No night for the son of woman,' said the madman.

The old man whistled, and hurried, half running, in the direction of the roadside trees.

Let the hounds know, the madman chuckled as he climbed up the hill, let the hounds know. And, crafty as a fox, he doubled back to where the misty road branched off three ways. Hell on the stars, he said, and walked towards the dark.

The world was a ball under his feet; it kicked as he ran; it dropped; up came the trees. In the distance a poacher's dog yelled at the trap on its foot, and he heard it and ran the faster, thinking the enemy was on his heels. 'Duck, boys, duck,' he called out, but with the voice of one who might have pointed to a falling star.

Remembering of a sudden that he had not slept since the escape, he left off running. Now the waters of the rain, too tired to strike the earth, broke up as they fell and blew about in the wind like the sandman's grains. If he met sleep, sleep would be a girl. For the last two nights, while walking or running over the empty county, he had dreamed of their meeting. 'Lie down,' she would say, and would give him her dress to lie on, stretching herself out by his side. Even as he had dreamed, and the twigs under his running feet had made a noise like the rustle of her dress, the enemy had shouted in the fields. He had run on and on, leaving sleep farther behind him. Sometimes there was a sun, a moon, and sometimes under a black sky he had tossed and thrown the wind before he could be off.

'Where is Jack?' they asked in the gardens of the place he had left. 'Up on the hills with a butcher's knife,' they said, smiling. But the knife was gone, thrown at a tree and quivering there still. There was no heat in his head. He ran on and on, howling for sleep.

And she, alone in the house, was sewing her new dress. It was a bright country dress with flowers on the bodice. Only a few more stitches were needed before it would be ready to wear. It would lie neat on her shoulders, and two of the flowers would be growing out of her breasts.

When she walked with her husband on Sunday mornings over the fields and down into the village, the boys would smile at her behind their hands, and the shaping of the dress round her belly would set all the widow women talking. She slipped into her new dress, and, looking into the mirror over the fire-place, saw that it was prettier than she had imagined. It made her face paler and her long hair darker. She had cut it low.

A dog out in the night lifted its head up and howled. She turned away hurriedly from her reflection, and pulled the curtains closer.

Out in the night they were searching for a madman. He had green eyes, they said, and had married a lady. They said he had cut off her lips because she smiled at men. They took him away, but he stole a knife from the kitchen and slashed his keeper and broke out into the wild valleys.

From afar he saw the light in the house, and stumbled up to the edge of the garden. He felt, he did not see, the little fence around it. The rusting wire scraped on his hands, and the wet, abominable grass crept over his knees. And once he was through the fence, the hosts of the garden came rushing to meet him, the flower-headed, and the bodying frosts. He had torn his fingers while the old wounds were still wet. Like a man of blood he came out of the enemy's darkness on to the steps. He said in a whisper: 'Let them not shoot me.' And he opened the door.

She was in the middle of the room. Her hair had fallen untidily, and three of the buttons at the neck of her dress were undone. What made the dog howl as it did? Frightened of the howling, and thinking of the tales she had heard, she rocked in her chair. What became of the woman? she wondered as she rocked. She could not think of a woman without any lips. What became of women without any lips? she wondered.

The door made no noise. He stepped into the room, trying to smile, and holding out his hands.

'Oh, you've come back,' she said.

Then she turned in her chair and saw him. There was blood even by his green eyes. She put her fingers to her mouth. 'Not shoot,' he said.

But the moving of her arm drew the neck of her dress apart, and he stared in wonder at her wide, white forehead, her frightened eyes and mouth, and down on to the flowers on her dress. With the moving of her arm, her dress danced in the light. She sat before him, covered in flowers. 'Sleep,' said the madman. And, kneeling down, he put his bewildered head upon her lap.

The Visitor

His hands were weary, though all night they had lain over the sheets of his bed and he had moved them only to his mouth and his wild heart. The veins ran, unhealthily blue streams, into the white sea. Milk at his side steamed out of a chipped cup. He smelt the morning, and knew that cocks in the yard were putting back their heads and crowing at the sun. What were the sheets around him if not the covering sheets of the dead? What was the busy-voiced clock, sounding between photographs of mother and dead wife, if not the voice of an old enemy? Time was merciful enough to let the sun shine on his bed, and merciless to chime the sun away when night came over and even more he needed the red light and the clear heat.

Rhianon was attendant on a dead man, and put the chipped edge of the cup to a dead lip. It could not be heart that beat under the ribs. Hearts do not beat in the dead. While he had lain ready for the inch-tape and the acid, Rhianon had cut open his chest with a book-knife, torn out the heart, put in the clock. He heard her say, for the third time, Drink the lovely milk. And, feeling it run sour over his tongue, and her hand caress his forehead, he knew he was not dead. He was a living man. For many miles the months flowed into the years, rounding the dry days.

Callaghan today would sit and talk with him. He heard in his brain the voices of Callaghan and Rhianon battle until he slept, and tasted the blood of words. His hands were weary. He brooded over his long, white body, marking the ribs stick through the sides. The hands had held other hands and thrown a ball high into the air. Now they were dead hands. He could wind them about his hair and let them rest untingling on his belly or lose them in the valley between Rhianon's breasts. It did not matter what he did with them. They were as dead as the hands of the clock, and moved to clockwork.

Shall I close the windows until the sun's warmer? said Rhianon.

I'm not cold.

He would tell her that the dead feel neither cold nor warmth, sun and wind could never penetrate his cloths. But she would laugh in her kind way and kiss him on the forehead and say to him, Peter, what's getting you down? You'll be out and about one day. One day he would walk on the Jarvis hills like a boy's ghost, and hear the people say, There walks the ghost of Peter, a poet, who was dead for years before they buried him.

Rhianon tucked the sheets around his shoulders, gave him a morning kiss, and carried the chipped cup away.

A man with a brush had drawn a rib of colour under the sun and painted many circles around the circle of the sun. Death was a man with a scythe, but that summer day no living stalk was to be cut down.

The invalid waited for his visitor. Peter waited for Callaghan. His room was a world within a world. A world in him went round and round, and a sun rose in him and a moon fell. Callaghan was the west wind, and Rhianon blew away the chills of the west wind like a wind from Tahiti.

He let his hand rest on his head, stone on stone. Never had the voice of Rhianon been so remote as when it told him that the sour milk was lovely. What was she but a sweetheart talking madly to her sweetheart under a coffin of garments? Somebody in the night had turned him up and emptied him of all but a false heart. That under the ribs' armour was not his, not his the beating of a vein in the foot. His arms could no longer make their movements nor a circle around a girl to shield her from winds and robbers. There was nothing more remote under the sun than his own name, and poetry was a string of words stringed on a beanstick. With his lips he rounded a little ball of sound into some shape, and spoke a word.

There was no to-morrow for dead men. He could not think that after the next night and its sleeping, life would sprout up again like a flower through a coffin's cracks.

His room around him was a vast place. From their frames the lying likenesses of women looked down on him. That was the face of his mother, that nearly yellow oval in its frame of old gold and thinning hair. And, next to her, dead Mary. Though Callaghan blew hard, the walls around Mary would never fall down. He thought of her as she had been, remembered her Peter, darling, Peter, and her smiling eyes.

He remembered he had not smiled since that night, seven years ago, when his heart had trembled so violently within him that he had fallen to the ground. There had been strengthening in the unbelievable setting of the sun. Over the hills and the roof went the broad moons, and summer came after spring. How had he lived at all when Callaghan had not blown away the webs of the world with a great shout, and Rhianon spread her loveliness about him? But the dead need no friends. He peered over the turned coffin-lid. Stiff and straight, a man of wax stared back. Taking away the pennies from those dead eyes, he looked on his own face.

Breed, cardboard on cardboard, he had cried, before I blow down your paste huts with one bellow out of my lungs. When Mary came, there was nothing between the changing of the days but the divinity he had built around her. His child killed Mary in her womb. He felt his body turn to vapour, and men who had been light as air walked, metal-hooved, through and beyond him.

He started to cry, Rhianon, Rhianon, someone has upped and kicked me in the side. Drip, drip, goes my blood in me. Rhianon, he cried.

She hurried upstairs, and time and time over again wiped away the tears from his cheeks with the sleeve of her dress.

He lay still as the morning matured and grew up into a noble noon. Rhianon passed in and out, her dress, he smelt as she bent over him, smelling of clover and milk. With a new surprise he followed her cool movements around the room, the sweep of her hands as she brushed the dead Mary in her frame. With such surprise, he thought, do the dead follow the movements of the quick, seeing the bloom under the living skin. She should be singing as she moved from mantelpiece to window, putting things right, or should be humming like a bee about her work. But if she had spoken, or laughed, or struck her nails against the thin metal of the candlesticks, drawing forth a bellnote, or if the room had been suddenly crowded with the noises of birds, he would have wept again. It pleased him to look upon the unmoving waves of the bedclothes, and think himself an island set somewhere in the south sea. Upon this island of rich and miraculous plants, the seeds grown fruits hung from the trees and, smaller than apples, dropped with the pacific winds on to the ground to lie there and be the harbourers of the summer slugs.

And thinking of the island set somewhere in the south caverns, he thought of water and longed for water. Rhianon's dress, rustling about her, made the soft noise of water. He called her over to him and touched the bosom of her dress, feeling the water on his hands. Water, he told her, and told her how, as a boy, he had lain on the rocks, his fingers tracing cool shapes on the surfaces of the pools. She brought him water in a glass, and held the glass up level with his eyes so that he could see the room through a wall of water. He did not drink, and she set the glass aside. He imagined the coolness under the sea. Now on a summer day soon after noon, he wished again for water to close utterly around him, to be no island set above the water but a green place under, staring around a dizzy cavern. He thought of some cool words, and made a line about an olive-tree that grew under a lake. But the tree was a tree of words, and the lake rhymed with another word.

Sit and read to me, Rhianon.

After you have eaten, she said, and brought him food.

He could not think that she had gone down into the kitchen and, with her own hands, prepared his meal. She had gone and had returned with food, as simply as a maiden out of the Old Testament. Her name meant nothing. It was a cool sound. She had a strange name out of the Bible. Such a woman had washed the body after it had been taken off the tree, with cool and competent fingers that touched on the holes like ten blessings. He could cry out to her, Put a sweet herb under my arm. With your spittle make me fragrant.

What shall I read you? she asked when at last she sat by his side.

He shook his head, not caring what she read so long as he could hear her speak and think of nothing but the inflections of her voice.

Ah! gentle may I lay me down, and gentle rest my head,
And gentle sleep the sleep of death, and gentle hear the voice
Of Him that walketh in the garden in the evening time.

She read on until the Worm sat on the Lily's leaf.

Death lay over his limbs again, and he closed his eyes. There was no ease from pain nor from the figures of death that went about their familiar business even in the darkness of the heavy lids.

Shall I kiss you awake? said Callaghan. His hand was cold on Peter's hand.

And all the lepers kissed, said Peter, and fell to wondering what he had meant.

Rhianon saw that he was no longer listening to her, and went on tiptoes away.

Callaghan, left alone, leant over the bed and spread the soft ends of his fingers on Peter's eyes. Now it is night, he said. Where shall we go to-night?

Peter opened his eyes again, saw the spreading fingers and the candles glowing like the heads of poppies. A fear and a blessing were on the room.

The candles must not be blown out, he thought. There must be light, light, light. Wick and wax must never be low. All day and all night the three candles, like three girls, must blush over my bed. These three girls must shelter me.

The first flame danced and then went out. Over the second and the third flame Callaghan pursed his grey mouth. The room was dark. Where shall we go to-night? he said, but waited for no answer, pulling the sheets back from the bed and lifting Peter in his arms. His coat was damp and sweet on Peter's face.

Oh, Callaghan, Callaghan, said Peter with his mouth pressed on the black cloth. He felt the movements of Callaghan's body, the tense, the relaxing, muscles, the curving of the shoulders, the impact of the feet on the racing earth. A wind from under the clay and the limes of the earth swept up to his hidden face. Only when the boughs of trees scraped on his back did he know that he was naked. So that he might not cry aloud, he shut his lips firmly together over a damp fold of flesh. Callaghan, too, was naked as a baby.

Are we naked? We have our bones and our organs, our skin and our flesh. There is a ribbon of blood tied in your hair. Do not be frightened. You have a cloth of veins around your thighs. The world charged past them, the wind dropped to nothing, blowing the fruits of battle under the moon. Peter heard the songs of birds, but no such songs as he had heard the birds, on his bedroom sill, fetch out of their throats. The birds were blind.

Are they blind? said Callaghan. They have worlds in their eyes. There is white and black in their whistling. Do not be frightened. There are bright eyes under the shells of their eggs.

He came suddenly to a stop, Peter light as a feather in his arms, and set him gently down on a green globe of soil. Below there was a valley journeying far away with its burden of lame trees and grass into the distance where the moon hung on a navelstring from the dark. From the woods on either side came the sharp cracks of guns and the pheasants falling like a rain. But soon the night was silent, softening the triggers of the fallen twigs that had snapped out under Callaghan's feet.

Peter, conscious of his sick heart, put a hand to his side but felt none of the protecting flesh. The tips of his fingers tingled around the driving blood, but the veins were invisible. He was dead. Now he knew he was dead. The ghost of Peter, wound invisible about the ghost of the blood, stood on his globe and wondered at the corrupting night.

What is this valley? said Peter's voice.

The Jarvis valley, said Callaghan. Callaghan, too, was dead. Not a bone or a hair stood up under the steadily falling frost.

This is no Jarvis valley.

This is the naked valley.

The moon, doubling and redoubling the strength of her beams, lit up the barks and the roots and the branches of the Jarvis trees, the busy lice in the wood, the shapes of the stones and the black ants travelling under them, the pebbles in the streams, the secret grass, the untiring death-worms under the blades. From their holes in the flanks of the hills came the rats and weasels, hairs white in the moon, breeding and struggling as they rushed downward to set their teeth in the cattle's throats. No sooner did the cattle fall sucked on to the earth and the weasels race away, then all the flies, rising from the dung of the fields, came up like a fog and settled on the sides. There from the stripped valley rose the smell of death, widening the mountainous nostrils on the face of the moon. Now the sheep fell and the flies were at them. The rats and the weasels, fighting over the flesh, dropped one by one with a wound for the sheep's fleas staring out of their hair. It was to Peter but a little time before the dead, picked to the symmetrical bone, were huddled in under the soil by the wind that blew louder and harder as the fat flies dropped on to the grass. Now the worm and the death-beetle undid the fibres of the animal bones, worked at them brightly and minutely, and the weeds through the sockets and the flowers on the vanished breasts sprouted up with the colours of the dead life fresh on their leaves. And the blood that had flowed flowed over the ground, strengthening the blades of the grass, fulfilling the wind-planted seeds in its course, into the mouth of the spring. Suddenly all the streams were red with blood, a score of winding veins all over the twenty fields, thick with their clotted pebbles.

Peter, in his ghost, cried out with joy. There was life in the naked valley, life in his nakedness. He saw the streams and the beating water, how the flowers shot out of the dead, and the blades and roots were doubled in their power under the stride of the spilt blood.

And the streams stopped. Dust of the dead blew over the spring, and the mouth was choked. Dust lay over the waters like a dark ice. Light, that had been all-eyed and moving, froze in the beams of the moon.

Life in this nakedness, mocked Callaghan at his side, and Peter knew that he was pointing, with the ghost of a finger, down on to the dead streams. But as he spoke, and the shape that Peter's heart had taken in the time of the tangible flesh was aware of the knocks of terror, a life burst out of the pebbles like the thousand lives, wrapped in a boy's body, out of the womb. The streams again went on their way, and the light of the moon, in a new splendour, shone on the valley and magnified the shadows of the valley and pulled the moles and the badgers out of their winter into the deathless midnight season of the world.

Light breaks over the hill, said Callaghan, and lifted the invisible Peter in his arms. Dawn, indeed, was breaking far over the Jarvis wilderness still naked under the descending moon.

As Callaghan raced along the rim of the hills and into the woods and over an exultant country where the trees raced with him, Peter cried out joyfully.

He heard Callaghan's laughter like a rattle of thunder that the wind took and doubled. There was a shouting in the wind, a commotion under the surface of the earth. Now under the roots and now on the tops of the wild trees, he and his stranger were racing against the cock. Over and under the falling fences of the light they climbed and shouted.

Listen to the cock, cried Peter, and the sheets of the bed rolled up to his chin.

A man with a brush had drawn a red rib down the east. The ghost of a circle around the circle of the moon spun through a cloud. He passed his tongue over his lips that had miraculously clothed themselves with skin and flesh. In his mouth was a strange taste, as if last night, three hundred nights ago, he had squeezed the head of a poppy and drunk and slept. There was the old rumour of Callaghan down his brain. From dawn to dark he had talked of death, had seen a moth caught in the candle, had heard the laughter that could not have been his ring in his ears. The cock cried again, and a bird whistled like a scythe through wheat.

Rhianon, with a sweet, naked throat, stepped into the room.

Rhianon, he said, hold my hand, Rhianon.

She did not hear him, but stood over his bed and fixed him with an unbreakable sorrow.

Hold my hand, he said. And then: Why are you putting the sheet over my face?

The Vest

He rang the bell. There was no answer. She was out. He turned the key.

The hall in the late afternoon light was full of shadows. They made one almost solid shape. He took off his hat and coat, looking sideways, so that he might not see the shape, at the light through the sitting-room door.

'Is anybody in?'

The shadows bewildered him. She would have swept them up as she swept the invading dust.

In the drawing-room the fire was low. He crossed over to it and sat down. His hands were cold. He needed the flames of the fire to light up the corners of the room. On the way home he had seen a dog run over by a motorcar. The sight of the blood had confused him. He had wanted to go down on his knees and finger the blood that made a round pool in the middle of the road. Someone had plucked at his sleeve, asking him if he was ill. He remembered that the sound and strength of his voice had drowned the first desire. He had walked away from the blood, with the stained wheels of the car and the soaking blackness under the bonnet going round and round before his eyes. He needed the warmth. The wind outside had cut between his fingers and thumbs.

She had left her sewing on the carpet near the coal-scuttle. She had been making a petticoat. He picked it up and touched it, feeling where her breasts would sit under the yellow cotton. That morning he had seen her head enveloped in a frock. He saw her, thin in her nakedness, as a bag of skin and henna drifting out of the light. He let the petticoat drop on to the floor again.

Why, he wondered, was there this image of the red and broken dog? It was the first time he had seen the brains of a living creature burst out of the skull. He had been sick at the last yelp and the sudden caving of the dog's chest. He could have killed and shouted, like a child cracking a blackbeetle between its fingers.

A thousand nights ago, she had lain by his side. In her arms, he thought of the bones of her arms. He lay quietly by her skeleton. But she rose next morning in the corrupted flesh.

When he hurt her, it was to hide his pain. When he struck her cheek until the skin blushed, it was to break the agony of his own head. She told him of her mother's death. Her mother had worn a mask to hide the illness at her face. He felt the locust of that illness on his own face, in the mouth and the fluttering eyelid.

The room was darkening. He was too tired to shovel the fire into life, and saw the last flame die. A new coldness blew in with the early night. He tasted the sickness of the death of the flame as it rose to the tip of his tongue, and swallowed it down. It ran around the pulse of the heart, and beat until it was the only sound. And all the pain of the damned. The pain of a man with a bottle breaking across his face, the pain of a cow with a calf dancing out of her, the pain of the dog, moved through him from his aching hair to the flogged soles of his feet.

His strength returned. He and the dripping calf, the man with the torn face, and the dog on giddy legs, rose up as one, in one red brain and body, challenging the beast in the air. He heard the challenge in his snapping thumb and finger, as she came in.

He saw that she was wearing her yellow hat and frock.

'Why are you sitting in the dark?' she said.

She went into the kitchen to light the stove. He stood up from his chair. Holding his hands out in front of him as though they were blind, he followed her. She had a box of matches in her hand. As she took out a dead match and rubbed it on the box, he closed the door behind him. 'Take off your frock,' he said.

She did not hear him, and smiled.

'Take off your frock,' he said.

She stopped smiling, took out a live match and lit it.

'Take off your frock,' he said.

He stepped towards her, his hands still blind. She bent over the stove. He blew the match out.

'What is it?' she said.

His lips moved, but he did not speak.

'Why?' she said.

He slapped her cheek quite lightly with his open hand.

'Take off your frock,' he said.

He heard her frock rustle over her head, and her frightened sob as he touched her. Methodically his blind hands made her naked.

He walked out of the kitchen, and closed the door.

In the hall, the one married shadow had broken up. He could not see his own face in the mirror as he tied his scarf and stroked the brim of his hat. There were too many faces. Each had a section of his features, and each a stiffened lock of his hair. He pulled up the collar of his coat. It was a wet winter night. As he walked, he counted the lamps. He pushed a door open and stepped into the warmth. The room was empty. The woman behind the bar smiled as she rubbed two coins together. 'It's a cold night,' she said.

He drank up the whisky and went out.

He walked on through the increasing rain. He counted the lamps again, but they reached no number.

The corner bar was empty. He took his drink into the saloon, but the saloon was empty.

The Rising Sun was empty.

Outside, he heard no traffic. He remembered that he had seen nobody in the streets. He cried aloud in a panic of loneliness:

'Where are you, where are you?'

Then there was traffic, and the windows were blazing. He heard singing from the house on the corner.

The bar was crowded. Women were laughing and shouting. They spilt their drinks over their dresses and lifted their dresses up. Girls were dancing on the sawdust. A woman caught him by the arm, and rubbed his face on her sleeve, and took his hand in hers and put it on her throat. He could hear nothing but the voices of the laughing women and the shouting of the girls as they danced. Then the ungainly women from the seats and the corners rocked towards him. He saw that the room was full of women. Slowly, still laughing, they gathered close to him.

He whispered a word under his breath, and felt the old sickness turn sour in his belly. There was blood before his eyes.

Then he, too, burst into laughter. He stuck his hands deep in the pockets of his coat, and laughed into their faces.

His hand clutched around a softness in his pocket. He drew out his hand, the softness in it.

The laughter died. The room was still. Quiet and still, the women stood watching him.

He raised his hand up level with his eyes. It held a piece of soft cloth.

'Who'll buy a lady's vest,' he said, 'Going, going, ladies, who'll buy a lady's vest.'

The meek and ordinary women in the bar stood still, their glasses in their hands, as he leant with his back to the counter and shouted with laughter and waved the bloody cloth in front of them.

PORTRAIT OF THE ARTIST AS A YOUNG DOG

The Peaches

The grass-green cart, with 'J. Jones, Gorsehill' painted shakily on it, stopped in the cobblestone passage between 'The Hare's Foot' and 'The Pure Drop'. It was late on an April evening. Uncle Jim, in his black market suit with a stiff white shirt and no collar, loud new boots, and a plaid cap, creaked and climbed down. He dragged out a thick wicker basket from a heap of straw in the corner of the cart and swung it over his shoulder. I heard a squeal from the basket and saw the tip of a pink tail curling out as Uncle Jim opened the public door of 'The Pure Drop'.

'I won't be two minutes,' he said to me. The bar was full; two fat women in bright dresses sat near the door, one with a small dark child on her knee; they saw Uncle Jim and nudged up on the bench.

'I'll be out straight away,' he said fiercely, as though I had contradicted him, 'you stay there quiet.'

The woman without the child raised up her hands. 'Oh, Mr Jones,' she said in a high laughing voice. She shook like a jelly.

Then the door closed and the voices were muffled.

I sat alone on the shaft of the cart in the narrow passage, staring through a side window of 'The Hare's Foot'. A stained blind was drawn half over it. I could see into half of a smoky, secret room, where four men were playing cards. One man was huge and swarthy, with a handlebar moustache and a love-curl on his forehead; seated by his side was a thin, bald, pale old man, with his cheeks in his mouth; the faces of the other two were in shadow. They all drank out of brown pint tankards and never spoke, laying the cards down with a smack, scraping at their match-boxes, puffing at their pipes, swallowing unhappily, ringing the brass bell, ordering more, by a sign of the fingers, from a sour woman with a flowered blouse and a man's cap.

The passage grew dark too suddenly, the walls crowded in, and the roofs crouched down. To me, staring timidly there in the dark passage in a strange town, the swarthy man appeared like a giant in a cage surrounded by clouds, and the bald old man withered into a black hump with a white top; two white hands darted out of the corner with invisible cards. A man with spring-heeled boots and a two-edged knife might be bouncing towards me from Union Street.

I called, 'Uncle Jim, Uncle Jim,' softly so that he should not hear.

I began to whistle between my teeth, but when I stopped I thought the sound went hissing on behind me. I climbed down from the shaft and stepped close to the half-blind window; a hand clawed up the pane to the tassel of the blind; in the little, packed space between me on the cobbles and the card-players at the table, I could not tell which side of the glass was the hand that dragged the blind down slowly. I was cut from the night by a stained square. A story I had made in the warm, safe island of my bed, with sleepy midnight Swansea flowing and rolling round outside the house, came blowing down to me then with a noise on the cobbles. I remembered the demon in the story, with his wings and hooks, who clung like a bat to my hair as I battled up and down Wales after a tall, wise, golden, royal girl from Swansea convent. I tried to remember her true name, her proper, long, black-stockinged legs, her giggle and paper curls, but the hooked wings tore at me and the colour of her hair and eyes faded and vanished like the grass-green of the cart that was a dark, grey mountain now standing between the passage walls.

And all this time the old, broad, patient, nameless mare stood without stirring, not stamping once on the cobbles or shaking her reins. I called her a good girl and stood on tiptoe to try to stroke her ears as the door of 'The Pure Drop' swung open and the warm lamplight from the bar dazzled me and burned my story up. I felt frightened no longer, only angry and hungry. The two fat women near the door giggled 'Good night, Mr Jones' out of the rich noise and the comfortable smells. The child lay curled asleep under the bench. Uncle Jim kissed the two women on the lips.

'Good night.'

'Good night.'

'Good night.'

Then the passage was dark again.

He backed the mare into Union Street, lurching against her side, cursing her patience and patting her nose, and we both climbed into the cart.

'There are too many drunken gipsies,' he said as we rolled and rattled through the flickering lamp-lit town.

He sang hymns all the way to Gorsehill in an affectionate bass voice, and conducted the wind with his whip. He did not need to touch the reins. Once on the rough road, between hedges twisting out to twig the mare by the bridle and poke our caps, we stopped at a whispered 'Whoa,' for uncle to light his pipe and set the darkness on fire and show his long, red, drunken fox's face to me, with its bristling side-bushes and wet, sensitive nose. A white house with a light in one bedroom window shone in a field on a short hill beyond the road.

Uncle whispered, 'Easy, easy, girl,' to the mare, though she was standing calmly, and said to me over his shoulder in a suddenly loud voice: 'A hangman lived there.'

He stamped on the shaft, and we rattled on through a cutting wind. Uncle shivered, pulling down his cap to hide his ears; but the mare was like a clumsy statue trotting, and all the demons of my stories, if they trotted by her side or crowded together and grinned into her eyes, would not make her shake her head or hurry.

'I wish he'd have hung Mrs Jesus,' uncle said.

Between hymns he cursed the mare in Welsh. The white house was left behind, the light and the hill were swallowed up.

'Nobody lives there now,' he said.

We drove into the farm-yard of Gorsehill, where the cobbles rang and the black, empty stables took up the ringing and hollowed it so that we drew up in a hollow circle of darkness and the mare was a hollow animal and nothing lived in the hollow house at the end of the yard but two sticks with faces scooped out of turnips.

'You run and see Annie,' said uncle. 'There'll be hot broth and potatoes.'

He led the hollow, shappy statue towards the stable; clop, clop to the mice-house. I heard locks rattle as I ran to the farm-house door.

The front of the house was the single side of a black shell, and the arched door was the listening ear. I pushed the door open and walked into the passage out of the wind. I might have been walking into the hollow night and the wind, passing through a tall vertical shell on an island sea-shore. Then a door at the end of the passage opened; I saw the plates on the shelves, the lighted lamp on the long, oil-clothed table, 'Prepare to Meet Thy God' knitted over the fire-place, the smiling china dogs, the brown-stained settle, the grandmother clock, and I ran into the kitchen and into Annie's arms.

There was a welcome, then. The clock struck twelve as she kissed me, and I stood among the shining and striking like a prince taking off his disguise. One minute I was small and cold, skulking dead-scared down a black passage in my stiff, best suit, with my hollow belly thumping and my heart like a time bomb, clutching my grammar school cap, unfamiliar to myself, a snub-nosed story-teller lost in his own adventures and longing to be home; the next I was a royal nephew in smart town clothes, embraced and welcomed, standing in the snug centre of my stories and listening to the clock announcing me. She hurried me to the seat in the side of the cavernous fireplace and took off my shoes. The bright lamps and the ceremonial gongs blazed and rang for me.

She made a mustard bath and strong tea, told me to put on a pair of my cousin Gwilym's socks and an old coat of uncle's that smelt of rabbit and tobacco. She fussed and clucked and nodded and told me, as she cut bread and butter, how Gwilym was still studying to be a minister, and how Aunt Rach Morgan, who was ninety years old, had fallen on her belly on a scythe.

Then Uncle Jim came in like the devil with a red face and a wet nose and trembling, hairy hands. His walk was thick. He stumbled against the dresser and shook the coronation plates, and a lean cat shot booted out from the settle corner. Uncle looked nearly twice as tall as Annie. He could have carried her about under his coat and brought her out suddenly, a little, brown-skinned, toothless, hunch-backed woman with a cracked sing-song voice.

'You shouldn't have kept him out so long,' she said, angry and timid.

He sat down in his special chair, which was the broken throne of a bankrupt bard, and lit his pipe and stretched his legs and puffed clouds at the ceiling.

'He might catch his death of cold,' she said.

She talked at the back of his head while he wrapped himself in clouds. The cat slunk back. I sat at the table with my supper finished, and found a little empty bottle and a white balloon in the pockets of my coat.

'Run off to bed, there's a dear,' Annie whispered.

'Can I go and look at the pigs?'

'In the morning, dear,' she said.

So I said good night to Uncle Jim, who turned and smiled at me and winked through the smoke, and I kissed Annie and lit my candle.

'Good night.'

'Good night.'

'Good night.'

I climbed the stairs; each had a different voice. The house smelt of rotten wood and damp and animals. I thought that I had been walking long, damp passages all my life, and climbing stairs in the dark, alone. I stopped outside Gwilym's door on the draughty landing.

'Good night.'

The candle flame jumped in my bedroom where a lamp was burning very low, and the curtains waved; the water in a glass on a round table by the bed stirred, I thought, as the door closed, and lapped against the sides. There was a stream below the window; I thought it lapped against the house all night until I slept.

'Can I go and see the pigs?' I asked Gwilym next morning. The hollow fear of the house was gone, and, running downstairs to my breakfast, I smelt the sweetness of wood and the fresh spring grass and the quiet untidy farm-yard, with its tumbledown dirty-white cow-house and empty stables open.

Gwilym was a tall young man aged nearly twenty, with a thin stick of a body and spade-shaped face. You could dig the garden with him. He had a deep voice that cracked in half when he was excited, and he sang songs to himself, treble and bass, with the same sad hymn tune, and wrote hymns in the barn. He told me stories about girls who died for love. 'And she put a rope round the tree but it was too short,' he said; 'she stuck a pen-knife in her bosoms but it was too blunt.' We were sitting together on the straw heaps that day in the half-dark of the shuttered stable. He twisted and leaned near to me, raising his big finger, and the straw creaked.

'She jumped in the cold river, she jumped,' he said, his mouth against my ear, 'arse over tip and Diu, she was dead.' He squeaked like a bat.

The pigsties were at the far end of the yard. We walked towards them, Gwilym dressed in minister's black, though it was a weekday morning, and me in a serge suit with a darned bottom, past three hens scrabbling the muddy cobbles and a collie with one eye, sleeping with it open. The ramshackle outhouses had tumbling, rotten roofs, jagged holes in their sides, broken shutters, and peeling whitewash; rusty screws ripped out from the dangling, crooked boards; the lean cat of the night before sat snugly between the splintered jaws of bottles cleaning its face, on the tip of the rubbish pile that rose triangular and smelling sweet and strong to the level of the riddled cart-house roof. There was nowhere like that farm-yard in all the slapdash county, nowhere so poor and grand and dirty as that square of mud and rubbish and bad wood and falling stone, where a bucketful of old and bedraggled hens scratched and laid small eggs. A duck quacked out of the trough in one deserted sty. Now a young man and a curly boy stood staring and sniffing over a wall at a sow, with its tits on the mud, giving suck.

'How many pigs are there?'

'Five. The bitch ate one,' said Gwilym.

We counted them as they squirmed and wriggled, rolled on their backs and bellies, edged and pinched and pushed and squealed about their mother. There were four. We counted again. Four pigs, four naked pink tails curling up as their mouths guzzled down and the sow grunted with pain and joy.

'She must have ate another,' I said, and picked up a scratching stick and prodded the grunting sow and rubbed her crusted bristles backwards. 'Or a fox jumped over the wall,' I said.

'It wasn't the sow or the fox,' said Gwilym. 'It was father.'

I could see uncle, tall and sly and red, holding the writhing pig in his two hairy hands, sinking his teeth in its thigh, crunching its trotters up: I could see him leaning over the wall of the sty with the pig's legs sticking out of his mouth. 'Did Uncle Jim eat the pig?'

Now, at this minute, behind the rotting sheds, he was standing, knee-deep in feathers, chewing off the live heads of the poultry.

'He sold it to go on the drink,' said Gwilym in his deepest rebuking whisper, his eyes fixed on the sty. 'Last Christmas he took a sheep over his shoulder, and he was pissed for ten days.'

The sow rolled nearer the scratching stick, and the small pigs sucking at her, lost and squealing in the sudden darkness, struggled under her folds and pouches.

'Come and see my chapel,' said Gwilym. He forgot the lost pig at once and began to talk about the towns he had visited on a religious tour, Neath and Bridgend and Bristol and Newport, with their lakes and luxury gardens, their bright, coloured streets roaring with temptation. We walked away from the sty and the disappointed sow.

'I met actress after actress,' he said.

Gwilym's chapel was the last old barn before the field that led down to the river; it stood well above the farm-yard, on a mucky hill. There was one whole door with a heavy padlock, but you could get in easily through the holes on either side of it. He took out a ring of keys and shook them gently and tried each one in the lock. 'Very posh,' he said; 'I bought them from the junk-shop in Carmarthen.' We climbed into the chapel through a hole.

A dusty wagon with the name painted out and a white-wash cross on its side stood in the middle. 'My pulpit cart,' he said, and walked solemnly into it up the broken shaft. 'You sit on the hay; mind the mice,' he said. Then he brought out his deepest voice again, and cried to the heavens and the bat-lined rafters and the hanging webs: 'Bless us this holy day, O Lord, bless me and Dylan and this Thy little chapel for ever and ever, Amen. I've done a lot of improvements to this place.'

I sat on the hay and stared at Gwilym preaching, and heard his voice rise and crack and sink to a whisper and break into singing and Welsh and ring triumphantly and be wild and meek. The sun through a hole, shone on his praying shoulders, and he said: 'O God, Thou art everywhere all the time, in the dew of the morning, in the frost of the evening, in the field and the town, in the preacher and the sinner, in the sparrow and the big buzzard. Thou canst see everything, right down deep in our hearts; Thou canst see us when the sun is gone; Thou canst see us when there aren't any stars, in the gravy blackness, in the deep, deep, deep, deep pit; Thou canst see and spy and watch us all the time, in the little black corners, in the big cowboys' prairies, under the blankets when we're snoring fast, in the terrible shadows; pitch black, pitch black; Thou canst see everything we do, in the night and day, in the day and the night, everything, everything; Thou canst see all the time. O God, mun, you're like a bloody cat.'

He let his clasped hands fall. The chapel in the barn was still, and shafted with sunlight. There was nobody to cry Hallelujah or God-bless; I was too small and enamoured in the silence. The one duck quacked outside.

'Now I take a collection,' Gwilym said.

He stepped down from the cart and groped about in the hay beneath it and held out a battered tin to me.

'I haven't got a proper box,' he said.

I put two pennies in the tin.

'It's time for dinner,' he said, and we went back to the house without a word.

Annie said, when we had finished dinner: 'Put on your nice suit for this afternoon. The one with stripes.'

It was to be a special afternoon, for my best friend, Jack Williams, from Swansea, was coming down with his rich mother in a motor car, and Jack was to spend a fortnight's holiday with me.

'Where's Uncle Jim?'

'He's gone to market,' said Annie.

Gwilym made a small pig's noise. We knew where uncle was; he was sitting in a public house with a heifer over his shoulder and two pigs nosing out of his pockets, and his lips wet with bull's blood.

'Is Mrs Williams very rich?' asked Gwilym.

I told him she had three motor cars and two houses, which was a lie. 'She's the richest woman in Wales, and once she was a mayoress,' I said. 'Are we going to have tea in the best room?'

Annie nodded. 'And a large tin of peaches,' she said.

'That old tin's been in the cupboard since Christmas,' said Gwilym, 'mother's been keeping it for a day like this.'

'They're lovely peaches,' Annie said. She went upstairs to dress like Sunday.

The best room smelt of moth balls and fur and damp and dead plants and stale, sour air. Two glass cases on wooden coffin-boxes lined the window wall. You looked at the weed-grown vegetable garden through a stuffed fox's legs, over a partridge's head, along the red-paint-stained breast of a stiff wild duck. A case of china and pewter, trinkets, teeth, family brooches, stood beyond the bandy table; there was a large oil lamp on the patchwork table-cloth, a Bible with a clasp, a tall vase with a draped woman about to bathe on it, and a framed photograph of Annie, Uncle Jim, and Gwilym smiling in front of a fern-pot. On the mantelpiece were two clocks, some dogs, brass candlesticks, a shepherdess, a man in a kilt, and a tinted photograph of Annie, with high hair and her breasts coming out. There were chairs around the table and in each corner, straight, curved, stained, padded, all with lace cloths hanging over their backs. A patched white sheet shrouded the harmonium. The fireplace was full of brass tongs, shovels, and pokers. The best room was rarely used. Annie dusted and brushed and polished there once a week, but the carpet still sent up a grey cloud when you trod on it, and dust lay evenly on the seats of the chairs, and balls of cotton and dirt and black stuffing and long black horse hairs were wedged in the cracks of the sofa. I blew on the glass to see the pictures. Gwilym and castles and cattle.

'Change your suit now,' said Gwilym.

I wanted to wear my old suit, to look like a proper farm boy and have manure in my shoes and hear it squelch as I walked, to see a cow have calves and a bull on top of a cow, to run down in the dingle and wet my stockings, to go out and shout, 'Come on, you b—,' and pelt the hens and talk in a proper voice. But I went upstairs to put my striped suit on.

From my bedroom I heard the noise of a motor car drawing up the yard. It was Jack Williams and his mother.

Gwilym shouted, 'They're here, in a Daimler!' from the foot of the stairs, and I ran down to meet them with my tie undone and my hair uncombed.

Annie was saying at the door: 'Good afternoon, Mrs Williams, good afternoon. Come right in, it's a lovely day, Mrs Williams. Did you have a nice journey then? This way, Mrs Williams, mind the step.'

Annie wore a black, shining dress that smelt of moth balls, like the chair covers in the best room; she had forgotten to change her gym-shoes, which were caked with mud and all holes. She fussed on before Mrs Williams down the stone passage, darting her head round, clucking, fidgeting, excusing the small house, anxiously tidying her hair with one rough, stubby hand.

Mrs Williams was tall and stout, with a jutting bosom and thick legs, her ankles swollen over her pointed shoes; she was fitted out like a mayoress or a ship, and she swayed after Annie into the best room.

She said: 'Please don't put yourself out for me, Mrs Jones, there's a dear.' She dusted the seat of a chair with a lace handkerchief from her bag before sitting down.

'I can't stop, you know,' she said.

'Oh, you must stay for a cup of tea,' said Annie, shifting and scraping the chairs away from the table so that nobody could move and Mrs Williams was hemmed in fast with her bosom and her rings and her bag, opening the china cupboard, upsetting the Bible on the floor, picking it up, dusting it hurriedly with her sleeve.

'And peaches,' Gwilym said. He was standing in the passage with his hat on.

Annie said, 'Take your hat off, Gwilym, make Mrs Williams comfortable,' and she put the lamp on the shrouded harmonium and spread out a white table-cloth that had a tea stain in the centre, and brought out the china and laid knives and cups for five.

'Don't bother about me, there's a dear,' said Mrs Williams. 'There's a lovely fox!' She flashed a finger of rings at the glass case.

'It's real blood,' I told Jack, and we climbed over the sofa to the table.

'No, it isn't,' he said, 'it's red ink.'

'Oh, your shoes!' said Annie.

'Don't tread on the sofa, Jack, there's a dear.'

'If it isn't ink it's paint then.'

Gwilym said, 'Shall I get you a bit of cake, Mrs Williams?'

Annie rattled the tea-cups. 'There isn't a single bit of cake in the house,' said she; 'we forgot to order it from the shop; not a single bit. Oh, Mrs Williams!'

Mrs Williams said: 'Just a cup of tea thanks.' She was still sweating because she had walked all the way from the car. It spoiled her powder. She sparkled her rings and dabbed at her face.

'Three lumps,' she said. 'And I'm sure Jack will be very happy here.'

'Happy as sandboys,' Gwilym sat down.

'Now you must have some peaches, Mrs Williams, they're lovely.'

'They should be, they've been here long enough,' said Gwilym.

Annie rattled the tea-cups at him again.

'No peaches, thanks,' Mrs Williams said.

'Oh, you must, Mrs Williams, just one. With cream.'

'No, no, Mrs Jones, thanks the same,' she said. 'I don't mind pears or chunks, but I can't bear peaches.'

Jack and I had stopped talking. Annie stared down at her gym-shoes. One of the clocks on the mantelpiece coughed, and struck. Mrs Williams struggled from her chair.

'There, time flies!' she said.

She pushed her way past the furniture, jostled against the sideboard, rattled the trinkets and brooches, and kissed Jack on the forehead.

'You've got scent on,' he said.

She patted my head.

'Now behave yourselves.'

To Annie, she said in a whisper: 'And remember, Mrs Jones, just good plain food. No spoiling his appetite.'

Annie followed her out of the room. She moved slowly now. 'I'll do my very best, Mrs Williams.'

We heard her say, 'Goodbye then, Mrs Williams,' and go down the steps of the kitchen and close the door. The motor car roared in the yard, then the noise grew softer and died.

Down the thick dingle Jack and I ran shouting, scalping the brambles with our thin stick-hatchets, dancing, hallooing. We skidded to a stop and prowled on the bushy banks of the stream. Up above, sat one-eyed, dead-eyed, sinister, slim, ten-notched Gwilym, loading his guns in Gallows Farm. We crawled and rat-tatted through the bushes, hid, at a whistled signal, in the deep grass, and crouched there, waiting for the crack of a twig or the secret breaking of boughs.

On my haunches, eager and alone, casting an ebony shadow, with the Gorsehill jungle swarming, the violent, impossible birds and fishes leaping, hidden under four-stemmed flowers the height of horses, in the early evening in a dingle near Carmarthen, my friend Jack Williams invisibly near me, I felt all my young body like an excited animal surrounding me, the torn knees bent, the bumping heart, the long heat and depth between the legs, the sweat prickling in the hands, the tunnels down to the eardrums, the little balls of dirt between the toes, the eyes in the sockets, the tucked-up voice, the blood racing, the memory around and within flying, jumping, swimming, and waiting to pounce. There, playing Indians in the evening, I was aware of me myself in the exact middle of a living story, and my body was my adventure and my name. I sprang with excitement and scrambled up through the scratching brambles again.

Jack cried: 'I see you! I see you!' He scampered after me. 'Bang! bang! you're dead!'

But I was young and loud and alive, though I lay down obediently.

'Now you try and kill me,' said Jack. 'Count a hundred.'

I closed one eye, saw him rush and stamp towards the upper field, then tiptoe back and begin to climb a tree, and I counted fifty and ran to the foot of the tree and killed him as he climbed. 'You fall down,' I said.

He refused to fall, so I climbed too, and we clung to the top branches and stared down at the lavatory in the corner of the field. Gwilym was sitting on the seat with his trousers down. He looked small and black. He was reading a book and moving his hands.

'We can see you!' we shouted.

He snatched his trousers up and put the book in his pocket.

'We can see you, Gwilym!'

He came out into the field. 'Where are you, then?'

We waved our caps at him.

'In the sky!' Jack shouted.

'Flying!' I shouted.

We stretched our arms out like wings.

'Fly down here.'

We swung and laughed on the branches.

'There's birds!' cried Gwilym.

Our jackets were torn and our stockings were wet and our shoes were sticky; we had green moss and brown bark on our hands and faces when we went in for supper and a scolding. Annie was quiet that night, though she called me a ragamuffin and said she didn't know what Mrs Williams would think and told Gwilym he should know better. We made faces at Gwilym and put salt in his tea, but after supper he said: 'You can come to the chapel if you like. Just before bed.'

He lit a candle on the top of the pulpit cart. It was a small light in the big barn. The bats were gone. Shadows still clung upside down along the roof. Gwilym was no longer my cousin in a Sunday suit, but a tall stranger shaped like a spade in a cloak, and his voice grew too deep. The straw heaps were lively. I thought of the sermon on the cart: we were watched, Jack's heart was watched, Gwilym's tongue was marked down, my whisper, 'Look at the little eyes,' was remembered always.

'Now I take confessions,' said Gwilym from the cart.

Jack and I stood bareheaded in the circle of the candle, and I could feel the trembling of Jack's body.

'You first.' Gwilym's finger, as bright as though he had held it in the candle flame until it burned, pointed me out, and I took a step towards the pulpit cart, raising my head.

'Now you confess,' said Gwilym.

'What have I got to confess?'

'The worst thing you've done.'

I let Edgar Reynolds be whipped because I had taken his homework; I stole from my mother's bag; I stole from Gwyneth's bag; I stole twelve books in three visits from the library, and threw them away in the park; I drank a cup of my water to see what it tasted like; I beat a dog with a stick so that it would roll over and lick my hand afterwards; I looked with Dan Jones through the keyhole while his maid had a bath; I cut my knee with a penknife, and put the blood on my handkerchief and said it had come out of my ears so that I could pretend I was ill and frighten my mother; I pulled my trousers down and showed Jack Williams; I saw Billy Jones beat a pigeon to death with a fire-shovel, and laughed and got sick; Cedric Williams and I broke into Mrs Samuels' house and poured ink over the bedclothes.

I said: 'I haven't done anything bad.'

'Go on, confess,' said Gwilym. He was frowning down at me.

'I can't! I can't!' I said. 'I haven't done anything bad.'

'Go on, confess!'

'I won't! I won't!'

Jack began to cry. 'I want to go home,' he said.

Gwilym opened the chapel door and we followed him into the yard, down past the black, humped sheds, towards the house, and Jack sobbed all the way.

In bed together, Jack and I confessed our sins.

'I steal from my mother's bag, too; there are pounds and pounds.'

'How much do you steal?'

'Threepence.'

'I killed a man once.'

'No you didn't then.'

'Honest to Christ, I shot him through the heart.'

'What was his name?'

'Williams.'

'Did he bleed?'

I thought the stream was lapping against the house.

'Like a bloody pig,' I said.

Jack's tears had dried. 'I don't like Gwilym, he's barmy.'

'No he isn't. I found a lot of poems in his bedroom once. They were all written to girls. And he showed them to me afterwards, and he'd changed all the girls' names to God.'

'He's religious.'

'No, he isn't, he goes with actresses. He knows Corinne Griffith.'

Our door was open. I liked the door locked at night, because I would rather have a ghost in the bedroom than think of one coming in; but Jack liked it open, and we tossed and he won. We heard the front door rattle and footsteps in the kitchen passage.

'That's Uncle Jim.'

'What's he like?'

'He's like a fox, he eats pigs and chickens.'

The ceiling was thin and we heard every sound, the creaking of the bard's chair, the clatter of plates, Annie's voice saying: 'Midnight!'

'He's drunk,' I said. We lay quite still, hoping to hear a quarrel.

'Perhaps he'll throw plates,' I said.

But Annie scolded him softly. 'There's a fine state, Jim.'

He murmured to her.

'There's one pig gone,' she said. 'Oh, why do you have to do it, Jim? There's nothing left now. We'll never be able to carry on.'

'Money! money! money!' he said. I knew he would be lighting his pipe.

Then Annie's voice grew so soft we could not hear the words, and uncle said: 'Did she pay you the thirty shillings?'

'They're talking about your mother,' I told Jack.

For a long time Annie spoke in a low voice, and we waited for words. 'Mrs Williams,' she said, and 'motor car,' and 'Jack,' and 'peaches.' I thought she was crying for her voice broke on the last word.

Uncle Jim's chair creaked again, he might have struck his fist on the table, and we heard him shout: 'I'll give her peaches! Peaches, peaches! Who does she think she is? Aren't peaches good enough for her? To hell with her bloody motor car and her bloody son! Making us small.'

'Don't, don't Jim!' Annie said, 'you'll wake the boys.'

'I'll wake them and whip the hell out of them, too!'

'Please, please, Jim!'

'You send the boy away,' he said, 'or I'll do it myself. Back to his three bloody houses.'

Jack pulled the bedclothes over his head and sobbed into the pillow: 'I don't want to hear, I don't want to hear, I'll write to my mother. She'll take me away.'

I climbed out to close the door. Jack would not talk to me again, and I fell asleep to the noise of the voices below, which soon grew gentle.

Uncle Jim was not at breakfast. When we came down, Jack's shoes were cleaned for him and his jacket was darned and pressed. Annie gave two boiled eggs to Jack and one to me. She forgave me when I drank tea from the saucer.

After breakfast, Jack walked to the post office. I took the one-eyed collie to chase rabbits in the upper fields, but it barked at ducks and brought me a tramp's shoe from a hedge, and lay down with its tail wagging in a rabbit hole. I threw stones at the deserted duck pond, and the collie ambled back with sticks.

Jack went skulking into the damp dingle, his hands in his pockets, his cap over one eye. I left the collie sniffing at a molehill, and climbed to the tree-top in the corner of the lavatory field. Below me, Jack was playing Indians all alone, scalping through the bushes, surprising himself round a tree, hiding from himself in the grass. I called to him once, but he pretended not to hear. He played alone, silently and savagely. I saw him standing with his hands in his pockets, swaying like a Kelly, on the mudbank by the stream at the foot of the dingle. My bough lurched, the heads of the dingle bushes spun up towards me like green tops, 'I'm falling!' I cried, my trousers saved me, I swung and grasped, this was one minute of wild adventure, but Jack did not look up and the minute was lost. I climbed, without dignity, to the ground.

Early in the afternoon, after a silent meal, when Gwilym was reading the scriptures or writing hymns to girls or sleeping in his chapel, Annie was baking bread, and I was cutting a wooden whistle in the loft over the stable, the motor car drove up in the yard again.

Out of the house Jack, in his best suit, ran to meet his mother, and I heard him say as she stepped, raising her short skirts, on to the cobbles: 'And he called you a bloody cow, and he said he'd whip the hell out of me, and Gwilym took me to the barn in the dark and let the mice run over me, and Dylan's a thief, and that old woman's spoilt my jacket.'

Mrs Williams sent the chauffeur for Jack's luggage. Annie came to the door, trying to smile and curtsy, tidying her hair, wiping her hands on her pinafore.

Mrs Williams said, 'Good afternoon,' and sat with Jack in the back of the car and stared at the ruin of Gorsehill.

The chauffeur came back. The car drove off, scattering the hens. I ran out of the stable to wave to Jack. He sat still and stiff by his mother's side. I waved my handkerchief.

A Visit to Grandpa's

In the middle of the night I woke from a dream full of whips and lariats as long as serpents, and runaway coaches on mountain passes, and wide, windy gallops over cactus fields, and I heard the man in the next room crying, 'Gee-up!' and 'Whoa!' and trotting his tongue on the roof of his mouth.

It was the first time I had stayed in grandpa's house. The floorboards had squeaked like mice as I climbed into bed, and the mice between the walls had creaked like wood as though another visitor was walking on them. It was a mild summer night, but curtains had flapped and branches beaten against the window. I had pulled the sheets over my head, and soon was roaring and riding in a book.

'Whoa there, my beauties!' cried grandpa. His voice sounded very young and loud, and his tongue had powerful hooves, and he made his bedroom into a great meadow. I thought I would see if he was ill, or had set his bedclothes on fire, for my mother had said that he lit his pipe under the blankets, and had warned me to run to his help if I smelt smoke in the night. I went on tiptoe through the darkness to his bedroom door, brushing against the furniture and upsetting a candlestick with a thump. When I saw there was a light in the room I felt frightened, and as I opened the door I heard grandpa shout, 'Gee-up!' as loudly as a bull with a megaphone.

He was sitting straight up in bed and rocking from side to side as though the bed were on a rough road; the knotted edges of the counterpane were his reins; his invisible horse stood in a shadow beyond the bedside candle. Over a white flannel nightshirt he was wearing a red waistcoat with walnut-sized brass buttons. The over-filled bowl of his pipe smouldered among his whiskers like a little, burning hayrick on a stick. At the sight of me, his hands dropped from the reins and lay blue and quiet, the bed stopped still on a level road, he muffled his tongue into silence, and the horses drew softly up.

'Is there anything the matter, grandpa?' I asked, though the clothes were not on fire. His face in the candlelight looked like a ragged quilt pinned upright on the black air and patched all over with goat-beards.

He stared at me mildly. Then he blew down his pipe, scattering the sparks and making a high, wet dog-whistle of the stem, and shouted: 'Ask no questions.'

After a pause, he said slyly: 'Do you ever have nightmares, boy?'

'I said: 'No.'

'Oh, yes, you do,' he said.

I said I was woken by a voice that was shouting to horses.

'What did I tell you?' he said. 'You eat too much. Who ever heard of horses in a bedroom?'

He fumbled under his pillow, brought out a small tinkling bag, and carefully untied its strings. He put a sovereign in my hand, and said: 'Buy a cake.' I thanked him and wished him good night.

As I closed my bedroom door, I heard his voice crying loudly and gaily, 'Gee-up! gee-up!' and the rocking of the travelling bed.

In the morning I woke from a dream of fiery horses on a plain that was littered with furniture, and of large, cloudy men who rode six horses at a time and whipped them with burning bed-clothes. Grandpa was at breakfast, dressed in deep black. After breakfast he said, 'There was a terrible loud wind last night,' and sat in his arm-chair by the hearth to make clay balls for the fire. Later in the morning he took me for a walk, through Johnstown village and into the fields on the Llanstephan road.

A man with a whippet said, 'There's a nice morning, Mr Thomas,' and when he had gone, leanly as his dog, into the short-treed green wood he should not have entered because of the notices, grandpa said: 'There, do you hear what he called you? Mister!'

We passed by small cottages, and all the men who leant on the gates congratulated grandpa on the fine morning. We passed through the wood full of pigeons, and their wings broke the branches as they rushed to the tops of the trees. Among the soft, contented voices and the loud, timid flying, grandpa said, like a man calling across a field: 'If you heard those old birds in the night, you'd wake me up and say there were horses in the trees.'

We walked back slowly, for he was tired, and the lean man stalked out of the forbidden wood with a rabbit held as gently over his arm as a girl's arm in a warm sleeve.

On the last day but one of my visit I was taken to Llanstephan in a governess cart pulled by a short, weak pony. Grandpa might have been driving a bison, so tightly he held the reins, so ferociously cracked the long whip, so blasphemously shouted warning to boys who played in the road, so stoutly stood with his gaitered legs apart and cursed the demon strength and wilfulness of his tottering pony.

'Look out, boy!' he cried when we came to each corner, and pulled and tugged and jerked and sweated and waved his whip like a rubber sword. And when the pony had crept miserably round each corner, grandpa turned to me with a sighing smile: 'We weathered that one, boy.'

When we came to Llanstephan village at the top of the hill, he left the cart by the 'Edwinsford Arms' and patted the pony's muzzle and gave it sugar, saying: 'You're a weak little pony, Jim, to pull big men like us.'

He had strong beer and I had lemonade, and he paid Mrs Edwinsford with a sovereign out of the tinkling bag; she inquired after his health, and he said that Llangadock was better for the tubes. We went to look at the churchyard and the sea, and sat in the wood called the Sticks, and stood on the concert platform in the middle of the wood where visitors sang on midsummer nights and, year by year, the innocent of the village was elected mayor. Grandpa paused at the churchyard and pointed over the iron gate at the angelic headstones and the poor wooden crosses. 'There's no sense in lying there,' he said.

We journeyed back furiously: Jim was a bison again.

I woke late on my last morning, out of dreams where the Llanstephan sea carried bright sailing-boats as long as liners; and heavenly choirs in the Sticks, dressed in bards' robes and brass-buttoned waistcoats, sang in a strange Welsh to the departing sailors. Grandpa was not at breakfast; he rose early. I walked in the fields with a new sling, and shot at the Towy gulls and the rooks in the parsonage trees. A warm wind blew from the summer points of the weather; a morning mist climbed from the ground and floated among the trees and hid the noisy birds; in the mist and the wind my pebbles flew lightly up like hailstones in a world on its head. The morning passed without a bird falling.

I broke my sling and returned for the midday meal through the parson's orchard. Once, grandpa told me, the parson had bought three ducks at Carmarthen Fair and made a pond for them in the centre of the garden, but they waddled to the gutter under the crumbling doorsteps of the house, and swam and quacked there. When I reached the end of the orchard path, I looked through a hole in the hedge and saw that the parson had made a tunnel through the rockery that was between the gutter and the pond and had set up a notice in plain writing: 'This way to the pond.'

The ducks were still swimming under the steps.

Grandpa was not in the cottage. I went into the garden, but grandpa was not staring at the fruit-trees. I called across to a man who leant on a spade in the field beyond the garden hedge: 'Have you seen my grandpa this morning?'

He did not stop digging, and answered over his shoulder: 'I seen him in his fancy waistcoat.'

Griff, the barber, lived in the next cottage. I called to him through the open door: 'Mr Griff, have you seen my grandpa?'

The barber came out in his shirtsleeves.

I said: 'He's wearing his best waistcoat.' I did not know if it was important, but grandpa wore his waistcoat only in the night.

'Has grandpa been to Llanstephan?' asked Mr Griff anxiously.

'He went there yesterday in a little trap,' I said.

He hurried indoors and I heard him talking in Welsh, and he came out again with his white coat on, and he carried a striped and coloured walking-stick. He strode down the village street and I ran by his side.

When we stopped at the tailor's shop, he cried out, 'Dan!' and Dan Tailor stepped from his window where he sat like an Indian priest but wearing a derby hat. 'Dai Thomas has got his waistcoat on,' said Mr Griff, 'and he's been to Llanstephan.'

As Dan Tailor searched for his overcoat, Mr Griff was striding on. 'Will Evans,' he called outside the carpenter's shop, 'Dai Thomas has been to Llanstephan, and he's got his waistcoat on.'

'I'll tell Morgan now,' said the carpenter's wife out of the hammering, sawing darkness of the shop.

We called at the butcher's shop and Mr Price's house, and Mr Griff repeated his message like a town crier.

We gathered together in Johnstown square. Dan Tailor had his bicycle, Mr Price his pony trap. Mr Griff, the butcher, Morgan carpenter, and I climbed into the shaking trap, and we trotted off towards Carmarthen town. The tailor led the way, ringing his bell as though there were a fire or a robbery, and an old woman by the gate of a cottage at the end of the street ran inside like a pelted hen. Another woman waved a bright handkerchief.

'Where are we going?' I asked.

Grandpa's neighbours were as solemn as old men with black hats and jackets on the outskirts of a fair. Mr Griff shook his head and mourned: 'I didn't expect this again from Dai Thomas.'

'Not after last time,' said Mr Price sadly.

We trotted on, we crept up Constitution Hill, we rattled down into Lammas Street, and the tailor still rang his bell and a dog ran, squealing, in front of his wheels. As we clip-clopped over the cobbles that led down to the Towy bridge, I remembered grandpa's nightly noisy journeys that rocked the bed and shook the walls, and I saw his gay waistcoat in a vision and his patchwork head tufted and smiling in the candlelight. The tailor before us turned round on his saddle, his bicycle wobbled and skidded. 'I see Dai Thomas!' he cried.

The trap rattled on to the bridge, and I saw grandpa there: the buttons of his waistcoat shone in the sun, he wore his tight, black Sunday trousers and a tall, dusty hat I had seen in a cupboard in the attic, and he carried an ancient bag. He bowed to us. 'Good morning, Mr Price,' he said, 'and Mr Griff and Mr Morgan and Mr Evans.' To me he said: 'Good morning, boy.'

Mr Griff pointed his coloured stick at him.

'And what do you think you are doing on Carmarthen bridge in the middle of the afternoon,' he said sternly, 'with your best waistcoat and your old hat?'

Grandpa did not answer, but inclined his face to the river wind, so that his beard was set dancing and wagging as though he talked, and watched the coracle men move, like turtles, on the shore.

Mr Griff raised his stunted barber's pole. 'And where do you think you are going,' he said, 'with your old black bag?'

Grandpa said: 'I am going to Llangadock to be buried.' And he watched the coracle shells slip into the water lightly, and the gulls complain over the fish-filled water as bitterly as Mr Price complained:

'But you aren't dead yet, Dai Thomas.'

For a moment grandpa reflected, then: 'There's no sense in lying dead in Llanstephan,' he said. 'The ground is comfy in Llangadock; you can twitch your legs without putting them in the sea.'

His neighbours moved close to him. They said: 'You aren't dead, Mr Thomas.'

'How can you be buried, then?'

'Nobody's going to bury you in Llanstephan.'

'Come on home, Mr Thomas.'

'There's strong beer for tea.'

'And cake.'

But grandpa stood firmly on the bridge, and clutched his bag to his side, and stared at the flowing river and the sky, like a prophet who has no doubt.

Patricia, Edith, and Arnold

The small boy in his invisible engine, the Cwmdonkin Special, its wheels, polished to dazzle, crunching on the small back garden scattered with breadcrumbs for the birds and white with yesterday's snow, its smoke rising thin and pale as breath in the cold afternoon, hooted under the wash-line, kicked the dog's plate at the washhouse stop, and puffed and pistoned slower and slower while the servant girl lowered the pole, unpegged the swinging vests, showed the brown stains under her arms, and called over the wall; 'Edith, Edith, come here, I want you.'

Edith climbed on two tubs on the other side of the wall and called back: 'I'm here, Patricia.' Her head bobbed up above the broken glass.

He backed the Flying Welshman from the washhouse to the open door of the coal-hole and pulled hard on the brake that was a hammer in his pocket: assistants in uniform ran out with fuel; he spoke to a saluting fireman, and the engine shuffled off, round the barbed walls of China that kept the cats away, by the frozen rivers in the sink, in and out of the coal-hole tunnel. But he was listening carefully all the time, through the squeals and whistles, to Patricia and the next-door servant, who belonged to Mrs Lewis, talking when they should have been working, calling his mother Mrs T., being rude about Mrs L.

He heard Patricia say: 'Mrs T. won't be back till six.'

And Edith next door replied: 'Old Mrs L. has gone to Neath to look for Mr Robert.'

'He's on the randy again,' Patricia whispered.

'Randy, sandy, bandy!' cried the boy out of the coal-hole.

'You get your face dirty, I'll kill you,' Patricia said absent-mindedly.

She did not try to stop him when he climbed up the coal-heap. He stood quietly on the top, King of the Coal Castle, his head touching the roof, and listened to the worried voices of the girls. Patricia was almost in tears, Edith was sobbing and rocking on the unsteady tubs. 'I'm standing on top of the coal,' he said, and waited for Patricia's anger.

She said: 'I don't want to see him, you go alone.'

'We must, we must go together,' said Edith. 'I've got to know.'

'I don't want to know.'

'I can't stand it, Patricia, you must go with me.'

'You go alone, he's waiting for you.'

'Please, Patricia!'

'I'm lying on my face in the coal,' said the boy.

'No, it's your day with him. I don't want to know. I just want to think he loves me.'

'Oh, talk sense, Patricia, please! Will you come or no? I've got to hear what he says.'

'All right then, in half an hour. I'll shout over the wall.'

'You'd better come soon,' the boy said, 'I'm dirty as Christ knows what.'

Patricia ran to the coal-hole. 'The language! Come out of there at once!' she said.

The tubs began to slide and Edith vanished.

'Don't you dare use language like that again. Oh! your suit!' Patricia took him indoors.

She made him change his suit in front of her. 'Otherwise there's no telling.' He took off his trousers and danced around her, crying: 'Look at me, Patricia!'

'You be decent,' she said, 'or I won't take you to the park.'

'Am I going to the park, then?'

'Yes, we're all going to the park; you and me and Edith next door.'

He dressed himself neatly, not to annoy her, and spat on his hands before parting his hair. She appeared not to notice his silence and neatness. Her large hands were clasped together; she stared down at the white brooch on her chest. She was a tall, thick girl with awkward hands, her fingers were like toes, her shoulders were wide as a man's.

'Am I satisfactory?' he asked.

'There's a long word,' she said, and looked at him lovingly. She lifted him up and seated him on the top of the chest of drawers. 'Now you're as tall as I am.'

'But I'm not so old,' he said.

He knew that this was an afternoon on which anything might happen; it might snow enough for sliding on a tray; uncles from America, where he had no uncles, might arrive with revolvers and St Bernards; Ferguson's shop might catch on fire and all the piece-packets fall on the pavements; and he was not surprised when she put her black, straight-haired heavy head on his shoulder and whispered into his collar: 'Arnold, Arnold Matthews.'

'There, there,' he said, and rubbed her parting with his finger and winked at himself in the mirror behind her and looked down her dress at the back.

'Are you crying?'

'No.'

'Yes, you are, I can feel the wet.'

She dried her eyes on her sleeve. 'Don't you let on that I was crying.'

'I'll tell everybody, I'll tell Mrs T. and Mrs L., I'll tell the policeman and Edith and my dad and Mr Chapman, Patricia was crying on my shoulder like a nanny goat, she cried for two hours, she cried enough to fill a kettle. I won't really,' he said.

As soon as he and Patricia and Edith set off for the park, it began to snow. Big flakes unexpectedly fell on the rocky hill, and the sky grew dark as dusk though it was only three in the afternoon. Another boy, somewhere in the allotments behind the houses, shouted as the first flakes fell. Mrs Ocky Evans opened the top bay-windows of Springmead and thrust her head and hands out, as though to catch the snow. He waited, without revolt, for Patricia to say, 'Quick! hurry back, it's snowing!' and to pack him in out of the day before his feet were wet. Patricia can't have seen the snow, he thought at the top of the hill, though it was falling heavily, sweeping against her face, covering her black hat. He dared not speak for fear of waking her, as they turned the corner into the road that led down to the park. He lagged behind to take his cap off and catch the snow in his mouth.

'Put on your cap,' said Patricia, turning, 'Do you want to catch your death of cold?'

She tucked his muffler inside his coat, and said to Edith: 'Will he be there in the snow, do you think? He's bound to be there, isn't he? He was always there on my Wednesdays, wet or fine.' The tip of her nose was red, her cheeks glowed like coals, she looked handsomer in the snow than in the summer, when her hair would lie limp on her wet forehead and a warm patch spread on her back.

'He'll be there,' Edith said. 'One Friday it was pelting down and he was there. He hasn't got anywhere else to go, he's always there. Poor Arnold!' She looked white and tidy in a coat with a fur piece, and twice as small as Patricia; she stepped through the thick snow as though she were going shopping.

'Wonders will never cease,' he said aloud to himself. This was Patricia letting him walk in the snow, this was striding along in a storm with two big girls. He sat down in the road. 'I'm on a sledge,' he said, 'pull me, Patricia, pull me like an Eskimo.'

'Up you get, you moochin, or I'll take you home.'

He saw that she did not mean it. 'Lovely Patricia, beautiful Patricia,' he said, 'pull me along on my bottom.'

'Any more dirty words, and you know who I'll tell.'

'Arnold Matthews,' he said.

Patricia and Edith drew closer together.

'He notices everything,' Patricia whispered.

Edith said: 'I'm glad I haven't got your job.'

'Oh,' said Patricia, catching him by the hand and pressing it on her arm, 'I wouldn't change him for the world!'

He ran down the gravel path on to the upper walk of the park. 'I'm spoilt!' he shouted, 'I'm spoilt! Patricia spoils me!'

Soon the park would be white all over; already the trees were blurred round the reservoir and fountain, and the training college on the gorse hill was hidden in a cloud. Patricia and Edith took the steep path down to the shelter. Following on the forbidden grass, he slid past them straight into a bare bush, but the bump and the pricks left him shouting and unhurt. The girls gossiped sadly now. They shook their coats in the deserted shelter, scattering snow on the seats, and sat down, close together still, outside the bowling-club window.

'We're only just on time,' said Edith. 'It's hard to be punctual in the snow.'

'Can I play by here?'

Patricia nodded. 'Play quietly then; don't be rough with the snow.'

'Snow! snow! snow!' he said, and scooped it out of the gutter and made a small ball.

'Perhaps he's found a job,' Patricia said.

'Not Arnold.'

'What if he doesn't come at all?'

'He's bound to come, Patricia; don't say things like that.'

'Have you brought your letters?'

'They're in my bag. How many have you got?'

'No, how many have you got, Edith?'

'I haven't counted.'

'Show me one of yours,' Patricia said.

He was used to their talk by this time; they were old and cuckoo, sitting in the empty shelter sobbing over nothing. Patricia was reading a letter and moving her lips.

'He told me that, too,' she said, 'that I was his star.'

'Did he begin: "Dear Heart"?'

'Always: "Dear Heart".'

Edith broke into real loud tears. With a snowball in his hand, he watched her sway on the seat and hide her face in Patricia's snowy coat.

Patricia said, patting and calming Edith, rocking her head: 'I'll give him a piece of my mind when he comes!'

When who comes? He threw the snowball high into the silently driving fall. Edith's crying in the deadened park was clear and thin as a whistle, and, disowning the soft girls and standing away from them in case a stranger passed, a man with boots to his thighs, or a sneering, bigger boy from the Uplands, he piled the snow against the wire of the tennis court and thrust his hands into the snow like a baker making bread. As he delved and moulded the snow into loaves, saying under his breath, 'This is the way it is done, ladies and gentlemen,' Edith raised her head and said: 'Patricia, promise me, don't be cross with him. Let's all be quiet and friendly.'

'Writing, "Dear Heart" to us both,' said Patricia angrily. 'Did he ever take off your shoes and pull your toes and —'

'No, no, you mustn't, don't go on, you mustn't speak like that!' Edith put her fingers to her cheeks. 'Yes, he did,' she said.

'Somebody has been pulling Edith's toes,' he said to himself, and ran round the other side of the shelter, chuckling. 'Edith went to market,' he laughed aloud, and stopped at the sight of a young man without an overcoat sitting in the corner seat and cupping his hands and blowing into them. The young man wore a white muffler and a check cap. When he saw the boy, he pulled his cap down over his eyes. His hands were pale blue and the ends of his fingers yellow.

The boy ran back to Patricia. 'Patricia, there's a man!' he cried.

'Where's a man?'

'On the other side of the shelter; he hasn't got an overcoat and he's blowing in his hands like this.'

Edith jumped up. 'It's Arnold!'

'Arnold Matthews, Arnold Matthews, we know you're there!' Patricia called round the shelter, and, after a long minute, the young man, raising his cap and smiling, appeared at the corner and leant against a wooden pillar.

The trousers of his sleek blue suit were wide at the bottoms; the shoulders were high and hard, and sharp at the ends; his pointed patent shoes were shining; a red handkerchief stuck from his breast pocket; he had not been out in the snow.

'Fancy you two knowing each other,' he said loudly, facing the red-eyed girls and the motionless, open-mouthed boy who stood at Patricia's side with his pockets full of snowballs.

Patricia tossed her head and her hat fell over one eye. As she straightened her hat, 'You come and sit down here, Arnold Matthews, you've got some questions to answer!' she said in her washing-day voice.

Edith clutched at her arm: 'Oh! Patricia you promised.' She picked at the edge of her handkerchief. A tear rolled down her cheek.

Arnold said softly then: 'Tell the little boy to run away and play.'

The boy ran round the shelter once and returned to hear Edith saying: 'There's a hole in your elbow, Arnold,' and to see the young man kicking the snow at his feet and staring at the names and hearts cut on the wall behind the girls' heads.

'Who did you walk out with on Wednesdays?' Patricia asked. Her clumsy hands held Edith's letter close to the sprinkled folds of her chest.

'You, Patricia.'

'Who did you walk out with on Fridays?'

'With Edith, Patricia.'

He said to the boy: 'Here, son, can you roll a snowball as big as a football?'

'Yes, as big as two footballs.'

Arnold turned back to Edith, and said: 'How did you come to know Patricia Davies? You work in Brynmill.'

'I just started work in Cwmdonkin,' she said. 'I haven't seen you since, to tell you. I was going to tell you today, but I found out. How could you Arnold? Me on my afternoon off, and Patricia on Wednesdays.'

The snowball had turned into a short snow man with a lop-sided, dirty head and a face full of twigs, wearing a boy's cap and smoking a pencil.

'I didn't mean any harm,' said Arnold. 'I love you both.'

Edith screamed. The boy jumped forward and the snow man with a broken back collapsed.

'Don't tell your lies, how can you love two of us?' Edith cried, shaking her handbag at Arnold. The bag snapped open, and a bundle of letters fell on the snow.

'Don't you dare pick up those letters,' Patricia said.

Arnold had not moved. The boy was searching for his pencil in the snow man's ruins.

'You make your choice, Arnold Matthews, here and now.'

'Her or me,' said Edith.

Patricia turned her back to him. Edith, with her bag in her hand hanging open, stood still. The sweeping snow turned up the top page of a letter.

'You two,' he said, 'you go off the handle. Sit down and talk. Don't cry like that, Edith. Hundreds of men love more than one woman, you're always reading about it. Give us a chance, Edith, there's a girl.'

Patricia looked at the hearts and arrows and old names. Edith saw the letters curl.

'It's you, Patricia,' said Arnold.

Still Patricia stood turned away from him. Edith opened her mouth to cry, and he put a finger to his lips. He made the shape of a whisper, too soft for Patricia to hear. The boy watched him soothing and promising Edith, but she screamed again and ran out of the shelter and down the path, her handbag beating against her side.

'Patricia,' he said, 'turn round to me. I had to say it. It's you, Patricia.'

The boy bent down over the snow man and found his pencil driven through its head. When he stood up he saw Patricia and Arnold arm in arm.

Snow dripped through his pockets, snow melted in his shoes, snow trickled down his collar into his vest. 'Look at you now,' said Patricia, rushing to him and holding him by the hands, 'you're wringing wet.'

'Only a bit of snow,' said Arnold, suddenly alone in the shelter.

'A bit of snow indeed, he's as cold as ice and his feet are like sponges. Come on home at once!'

The three of them climbed the path to the upper walk, and Patricia's footprints were large as a horse's in the thickening snow.

'Look, you can see our house, it's got a white roof!'

'We'll be there, ducky, soon.'

'I'd rather stay out and make a snow man like Arnold Matthews.'

'Hush! hush! your mother'll be waiting. You must come home.'

'No she won't. She gone on a randy with Mr Robert. Randy, sandy, bandy!'

'You know very well she's shopping with Mrs Partridge, you mustn't tell wicked lies.'

'Well Arnold Matthews told lies. He said he loved you better than Edith, and he whispered behind your back to her.'

'I swear I didn't, Patricia, I don't love Edith at all!'

Patricia stopped walking. 'You don't love Edith?'

'No, I've told you, it's you. I don't love her at all,' he said. 'Oh! my God, what a day! Don't you believe me? It's you Patricia. Edith isn't anything. I just used to meet her; I'm always in the park.'

'But you told her you loved her.'

The boy stood bewildered between them. Why was Patricia so angry and serious? Her face was flushed and her eyes shone. Her chest moved up and down. He saw the long black hairs on her leg through a tear in her stockings. Her leg is as big as my middle, he thought. I'm cold; I want tea; I've got snow in my fly.

Arnold backed slowly down the path. 'I had to tell her that or she wouldn't have gone away. I had to, Patricia. You saw what she was like. I hate her. Cross my heart!'

'Bang! bang!' cried the boy.

Patricia was smacking Arnold, tugging at his muffler, knocking him with her elbows. She pummelled him down the path, and shouted at the top of her voice, 'I'll teach you to lie to Edith! You pig! you black! I'll teach you to break her heart!'

He shielded his face from her blows as he staggered back. 'Patricia, Patricia, don't hit me! There's people!'

As Arnold fell, two women with umbrellas up peered through the whirling snow from behind a bush.

Patricia stood over him. 'You lied to her and you'd lie to me,' she said. 'Get up, Arnold Matthews!'

He rose and set his muffler straight and wiped his eyes with the red handkerchief, and raised his cap and walked toward the shelter.

'And as for you,' Patricia said, turning to the watching women, 'you should be ashamed of yourselves! Two old women playing about in the snow.'

They dodged behind the bush.

Patricia and the boy climbed, hand in hand, back to the upper walk.

'I've left my cap by the snow man,' he remembered. 'It's my cap with the Tottenham colours.'

'Run back quickly,' she said, 'you can't get any wetter than you are.'

He found his cap half hidden under snow. In a corner of the shelter, Arnold sat reading the letters that Edith had dropped, turning the wet pages slowly. He did not see the boy, and the boy, behind a pillar, did not interrupt him. Arnold read every letter carefully.

'You've been a long time finding your cap,' Patricia said. 'Did you see the young man?'

'No,' he said, 'he was gone.'

At home, in the warm living-room, Patricia made him change his clothes again. He held his hands in front of the fire, and soon they began to hurt.

'My hands are on fire,' he told her, 'and my toes, and my face.'

After she had comforted him, she said: 'There, that's better. The hurting's gone. You won't call the king your uncle in a minute.' She was bustling about the room. 'Now we've all had a good cry to-day.'

The Fight

I was standing at the end of the lower playground and annoying Mr Samuels, who lived in the house just below the high railings. Mr Samuels complained once a week that boys from the school threw apples and stones and balls through his bedroom window. He sat in a deck chair in a small square of trim garden and tried to read the newspaper. I was only a few yards from him. I was staring him out. He pretended not to notice me, but I knew he knew I was standing there rudely and quietly. Every now and then he peeped at me from behind his newspaper, saw me still and serious and alone, with my eyes on his. As soon as he lost his temper I was going to go home. Already I was late for dinner. I had almost beaten him, the newspaper was trembling, he was breathing heavily, when a strange boy, whom I had not heard approach, pushed me down the bank.

I threw a stone at his face. He took off his spectacles, put them in his coat pocket, took off his coat, hung it neatly on the railings, and attacked. Turning round as we wrestled on the top of the bank, I saw that Mr Samuels had folded his newspaper on the deck chair and was standing up to watch us. It was a mistake to turn round. The strange boy rabbit-punched me twice. Mr Samuels hopped with excitement as I fell against the railings. I was down in the dust, hot and scratched and biting, then up and dancing, and I butted the boy in the belly and we tumbled in a heap. I saw through a closing eye that his nose was bleeding. I hit his nose. He tore at my collar and spun me round by the hair.

'Come on! come on!' I heard Mr Samuels cry.

We both turned towards him. He was shaking his fists and dodging about in the garden. He stopped then, and coughed, and set his panama straight, and avoided our eyes, and turned his back and walked slowly to the deck chair.

We both threw gravel at him.

'I'll give him "Come on!",' the boy said, as we ran along the playground away from the shouts of Mr Samuels and down the steps on to the hill.

We walked home together. I admired his bloody nose. He said that my eye was like a poached egg, only black.

'I've never seen such a lot of blood,' I said.

He said I had the best black eye in Wales, perhaps it was the best black eye in Europe; he bet Tunney never had a black eye like that.

'And there's blood all over your shirt.'

'Sometimes I bleed in dollops,' he said.

On Walter's Road we passed a group of high school girls, and I cocked my cap and hoped my eye was as big as a bluebag, and he walked with his coat flung open to show the bloodstains.

I was a hooligan all during dinner, and a bully, and as bad as a boy from the Sandbanks, and I should have more respect, and I sat silently, like Tunney, over the sago pudding. That afternoon I went to school with an eye-shade on. If I had had a black silk sling I would have been as gay and desperate as the wounded captain in the book that my sister used to read, and that I read under the bedclothes at night, secretly with a flash-lamp.

On the road, a boy from an inferior school, where the parents did not have to pay anything, called me 'One eye!' in a harsh, adult voice. I took no notice, but walked along whistling, my good eye on the summer clouds sailing, beyond insult, above Terrace Road.

The mathematics master said: 'I see that Mr Thomas at the back of the class has been straining his eyesight. But it isn't over his homework, is it, gentlemen?'

Gilbert Rees, next to me, laughed loudest.

'I'll break your leg after school!' I said.

He'd hobble, howling, up to the head master's study. A deep hush in the school. A message on a plate brought by the porter. 'The head master's compliments, sir, and will you come at once?' 'How did you happen to break this boy's leg?' 'Oh! damn and bottom, the agony!' cried Gilbert Rees. 'Just a little twist,' I would say. 'I don't know my own strength. I apologize. But there's nothing to worry about. Let me set the leg, sir.' A rapid manipulation, the click of a bone. 'Doctor Thomas, sir, at your service.' Mrs Rees was on her knees. 'How can I thank you?' 'It's nothing at all, dear lady. Wash his ears every morning. Throw away his rulers. Pour his red and green inks down the sink.'

In Mr Trotter's drawing class we drew naked girls inaccurately on sheets of paper under our drawings of a vase and passed them along under the desks. Some of the drawings were detailed strangely, others were tailed off like mermaids. Gilbert Rees drew the vase only.

'Sleep with your wife, sir?'

'What did you say?'

'Lend me a knife, sir?'

'What would you do if you had a million pounds?'

'I'd buy a Bugatti and a Rolls and a Bentley and I'd go two hundred miles an hour on Pendine sands.'

'I'd buy a harem and keep the girls in the gym.'

'I'd buy a house like Mrs Cotmore-Richard's, twice as big as hers, and a cricket field and a football field and a proper garage with mechanics and a lift.'

'And a lavatory as big as, as big as the Melba pavilion, with plush seats and a golden chain and . . .'

'And I'd smoke cigarettes with real gold tips, better than Morris's Blue Book.'

'I'd buy all the railway trains, and only 4A could travel in them.'

'And not Gilbert Rees either.'

'What's the longest you've been?'

'I went to Edinburgh.'

'My father went to Salonika in the War.'

'Where's that, Cyril?'

'Cyril, tell us about Mrs Pussie Edwards in Hanover Street.'

'Well, my brother says he can do anything.'

I drew a wild guess below the waist, and wrote Pussie Edwards in small letters at the foot of the page.

'Cave!'

'Hide your drawings.'

'I bet you a greyhound can go faster than a horse.'

Everybody liked the drawing class, except Mr Trotter.

In the evening, before calling on my new friend, I sat in my bedroom by the boiler and read through my exercise-books full of poems. There were Danger Don'ts on the backs. On my bedroom walls were pictures of Shakespeare, Walter de la Mare torn from my father's Christmas *Bookman*, Robert Browning, Stacy Aumonier, Rupert Brooke, a bearded man who I had discovered was Whittier, Watts's 'Hope', and a Sunday school certificate I was ashamed to want to pull down. A poem I had had printed in the 'Wales Day by Day' column of the *Western Mail* was pasted on the mirror to make me blush, but the shame of the poem had died. Across the poem I had written, with a stolen quill and in flourishes: 'Homer Nods.' I was always waiting for the opportunity to bring someone into my bedroom – 'Come into my den; excuse the untidiness; take a chair.

No! not that one, it's broken!' – and force him to see the poem accidentally. 'I put it there to make me blush.' But nobody ever came in except my mother.

Walking to his house in the early dusk through solid, deserted professional avenues lined with trees, I recited pieces of my poems and heard my voice, like a stranger's voice in Park Drive accompanied by the tap-tapping of nailed boots, rise very thinly up through the respectable autumn evening.

'My mind is fashioned
In the ways of intertissue;
Veiled and passioned
Are the thoughts that issue
From its well of furtive lust
Raptured by the devil's dust.'

If I looked through a window on to the road, I would see a scarlet-capped boy with big boots striding down the middle, and would wonder who it could be. If I were a young girl watching, my face like Mona Lisa's, my coal-black hair coiled in earphones, I'd see beneath the 'Boys' Department' suit a manly body with hair and sun tan, and call him and ask, 'Will you have tea or cocktails?' and hear his voice reciting the *Grass Blade's Psalm* in the half-dark of the heavily curtained and coloured drawing-room hung about with famous reproductions and glowing with books and wine bottles:

'The frost has lain,
Frost that is dark with flowered slain,
Fragilely strewn
With patches of illuminated moon,
About my lonely head in flagged unlovely red,

'The frost has spake,
Frost secretive and thrilled in silent flake,
With unseen lips of blue
Glass in the glaze stars threw,
Only to my ears, has spake in visionary tears.

'The frost has known,
From scattered conclave by the few winds blown,
That the lone genius in my roots,
Bare down there in a jungle of fruits,

Has planted a green year, for praise in the heart of my upgrowing days.

'The frost has filled
My heart with longing that the night's sleeve spilled,
Frost of celestial vapour fraught,
Frost that the columns of unfallen snow have sought,
With desire for the fields of space hovering about my single place.'

'Look! there's a strange boy, walking alone like a prince.'

'No, no, like a wolf! Look at his long stride!' Sketty church was shaking its bells for me.

'When I am strewn low
And all my ashes are
Dust in a dumb provoking show
Of minatory star...'

I recited. A young man and woman, arm in arm, suddenly appeared from a black lane between houses. I changed my recitation into a tune and hummed past them. They would be tittering together now, with their horrid bodies close. Cissy, moony, long hair. I whistled hard and loud, kicked a tradesmen's entrance, and glanced back over my shoulder. The couple were gone. Here's a kick at 'The Elms'. 'Where are the bleedy elms, mister?' Here's a handful of gravel, Mrs. 'The Croft', right at your window. One night I would paint 'Bum' all over the front gate of 'Kia-ora'.

A woman stood on 'Lyndhurst' steps with a hissing pom, and, stuffing my cap in my pocket, I was off down the road; and there was Dan's house, 'Warmley', with music coming loudly out of it.

He was a composer and a poet too; he had written seven historical novels before he was twelve, and he played the piano and the violin; his mother made wool pictures, his brother was a clerk at the docks and syncopated, his aunt kept a preparatory school on the first floor, and his father wrote music for the organ. All this he had told me as we walked home bleeding, strutting by the gym-frocks waving to boys in the trams.

My new friend's mother answered the door with a ball of wool in her hand. Dan, in the upstairs drawing-room, heard my arrival and played the piano faster.

'I didn't hear you come in,' he said when I found him. He finished on a grand chord, stretching all his fingers.

The room was splendidly untidy, full of wool and paper and open cupboards stacked with things you could never find; all the expensive furniture had been kicked; a waistcoat hung on the chandelier. I thought I could live for ever in that room, writing and fighting and spilling ink, having my friends for picnics there after midnight with Walker's rum-and-butter and charlottes russes from Eynon's, and Cydrax and Vino.

He showed me his books and his seven novels. All the novels were about battles, sieges, and kings. 'Just early stuff,' he said.

He let me take out his violin and make a cat noise.

We sat on a sofa in the window and talked as though we had always known each other. Would the 'Swans' beat the 'Spurs'? When could girls have babies? Was Arnott's average last year better than Clay's?

'That's my father outside there on the road,' he said, 'the tall one waving his arms.'

Two men were talking on the tram lines. Mr Jenkyn looked as if he were trying to swim down Eversley Road, he breast-stroked the air and beat on the ground with his feet, and then he limped and raised one shoulder higher than the other.

'Perhaps he's describing a fight,' I said.

'Or telling Mr Morris a story about cripples,' said Dan. 'Can you play the piano?'

'I can do chords, but not tunes,' I said.

We played a duet with crossed hands.

'Now who's that sonata by?'

We made a Dr Percy, who was the greatest composer for four hands in the world, and I was Paul America, the pianist, and Dan was Winter Vaux.

I read him an exercise-book full of poems. He listened wisely, like a boy aged a hundred, his head on one side and his spectacles shaking on his swollen nose. 'This is called *Warp*,' I said:

> 'Like suns red from running tears,
> Five suns in the glass,
> Together, separate yet, yet separately round,
> Red perhaps, but the glass is as pale as grass,
> Glide, without sound.
> In unity, five tears lid-awake, suns yet, but salt,
> Five inscrutable spears in the head,
> Each sun but an agony,
> Twist perhaps, pain bled of hate,

Five into one, the one made of five into one, early
Suns distorted to late.
All of them now, madly and desolate,
Spun with the cloth of the five, run
Widely and foaming, wildly and desolate,
Shoot through and dive. One of the five is the sun.'

The noise of the trams past the house clattered away as far as the sea or farther, into the dredgered bay. Nobody had ever listened like that before. The school had vanished, leaving on Mount Pleasant hill a deep hole that smelt of cloakrooms and locker mice, and 'Warmley' shone in the dark of a town I did not know. In the still room, that had never been strange to me, sitting in heaps of coloured wool, swollen-nosed and one-eyed, we acknowledged our gifts. The future spread out beyond the window, over Singleton Park crowded with lovers messing about, and into smoky London paved with poems.

Mrs Jenkyn peered round the door and switched the light on. 'There, that's more homely,' she said. 'You aren't cats.'

The future went out with the light, and we played a thumping piece by Dr Percy – 'Have you ever heard anything so beautiful? Louder, louder, America!' said Dan. 'Leave a bit of bass for me,' I said – until the next-door wall was rapped.

'That's the Careys. Mr Carey's a Cape Horner,' Dan said.

We played him one harsh, wailing piece before Mrs Jenkyn, with wool and needles, ran upstairs.

When she had gone, Dan said: 'Why is a man always ashamed of his mother?'

'Perhaps he isn't when he is older,' I said, but I doubted it. The week before I was walking down High Street with three boys after school, and I saw my mother with a Mrs Partridge outside the Kardomah. I knew she would stop me in front of the others and say, 'Now you be home early for tea,' and I wanted High Street to open and suck me down. I loved her and disowned her. 'Let's cross over,' I said, 'there's some sailor's boots in Griffith's window.' But there was only a dummy with a golf suit on, and a roll of tweed.

'Supper isn't for half an hour yet. What shall we do?'

'Let's see who can hold up that chair the longest,' I said.

'No, let's edit a paper: you do the literature, I'll do the music.'

'What shall we call it, then?'

He wrote, '*The* –, edited by D. Jenkyn and D. Thomas,' on the back of a hat-box from under the sofa. The rhythm was better with D. Thomas and D. Jenkyn, but it was his house.

'What about *The Maestersingers*?'

'No, that's too musical,' I said.

'*The Warmley Magazine*?'

'No,' I said, 'I live in "Glanrhyd".'

After the hat-box was covered, we wrote:

'*The Thunderer*, edited by D. <u>Jenkyn</u>,' in chalk on a piece of
Thomas
cardboard and pinned it on the wall.

'Would you like to see our maid's bedroom?' asked Dan. We whispered up to the attic.

'What's her name?'

'Hilda.'

'Is she young?'

'No, she's twenty or thirty.'

Her bed was untidy. 'My mother says you can always smell a maid.' We smelled the sheets. 'I can't smell anything.'

In her brass-bound box was a framed photograph of a young man wearing plus-fours.

'That's her boy.'

'Let's give him a moustache.'

Somebody moved downstairs, a voice called, 'Supper now!' and we hurried out, leaving the box open. 'One night we'll hide under her bed,' Dan said as we opened the dining-room door.

Mr Jenkyn, Mrs Jenkyn, Dan's aunt, and a Reverend Bevan and Mrs Bevan were seated at the table.

Mr Bevan said grace. When he stood up, it was just as though he were still sitting down, he was so short. 'Bless our repast this evening,' he said, as though he didn't like the food at all. But once 'Amen' was over, he went at the cold meat like a dog.

Mrs Bevan didn't look all there. She stared at the table-cloth and made hesitant movements with her knife and fork. She appeared to be wondering which to cut up first, the meat or the cloth.

Dan and I stared at her with delight; he kicked me under the table and I spilt the salt. In the commotion I managed to put some vinegar on his bread.

Mrs Jenkyn said, while everyone except Mr Bevan was watching Mrs Bevan moving her knife slowly along the edge of her plate: 'I do hope you like cold lamb.'

Mrs Bevan smiled at her, assured, and began to eat. She was grey-haired and grey-faced. Perhaps she was grey all over. I tried to undress her, but my mind grew frightened when it came to her short flannel petticoat and navy bloomers to the knees. I couldn't even dare unbutton her tall boots to see how grey her legs were. She looked up from her plate and gave me a wicked smile.

Blushing, I turned to answer Mr Jenkyn, who was asking me how old I was. I told him, but added one year. Why did I lie then? I wondered. If I lost my cap and found it in my bedroom, and my mother asked me where I had found it, I would say, 'In the attic,' or 'Under the hall stand.' It was exciting to have to keep wary all the time in case I contradicted myself, to make up the story of a film I pretended to have seen and put Jack Holt in Richard Dix's place.

'Fifteen and three-quarters,' said Mr Jenkyn, 'that's a very exact age. I see we have a mathematician with us. Now see if he can do this little sum.'

He finished his supper and laid out matches on the plate.

'That's an old one, Dad,' Dan said.

'Oh, I'd like to see it very much,' I said in my best voice. I wanted to come to the house again. This was better than home, and there was a woman off her head, too.

When I failed to place the matches rightly, Mr Jenkyn showed me how it was done, and, still not understanding, I thanked him and asked him for another one. It was almost as good being a hypocrite as being a liar; it made you warm and shameful.

'What were you talking to Mr Morris about in the street, Dad?' asked Dan. 'We saw you from upstairs.'

'I was telling him how the Swansea and District Male Voice did the *Messiah*, that's all. Why do you ask?'

Mr Bevan couldn't eat any more, he was full. For the first time since supper began, he looked round the table. He didn't seem to like what he saw. 'How are studies progressing, Daniel?'

'Listen to Mr Bevan, Dan, he's asking you a question.'

'Oh, so so.'

'So so?'

'I mean they're going very well, thank you, Mr Bevan.'

'Young people should attempt to say what they mean.'

Mrs Bevan giggled, and asked for more meat. 'More meat,' she said.

'And you, young man, have you a mathematical bent?'

'No, sir,' I said, 'I like English.'

'He's a poet,' said Dan, and looked uncomfortable.

'A brother poet,' Mr Bevan corrected, showing his teeth.

'Mr Bevan has published books,' said Mr Jenkyn. '*Proserpine, Psyche* –'

'*Orpheus*,' said Mr Bevan sharply.

'And *Orpheus*. You must show Mr Bevan some of your verses.'

'I haven't got anything with me, Mr Jenkyn.'

'A poet,' said Mr Bevan, 'should carry his verses in his head.'

'I remember them all right,' I said.

'Recite me your latest one; I'm always very interested.'

'What a gathering,' Mrs Jenkyn said, 'poets, musicians, preachers. We only want a painter now, don't we?'

'I don't think you'll like the very latest one,' I said.

'Perhaps,' said Mr Bevan, smiling, 'I am the best judge of that.'

'Frivolous is my hate,' I said, wanting to die, watching Mr Bevan's teeth.

'Singed with bestial remorse
Of unfulfilment of desired force,
And lust of tearing late;

'Now could I raise
Her dead, dark body to my own
And hear the joyous rustle of her bone
And in her eyes see deathly blaze;

'Now could I wake
To passion after death, and taste
The rapture of her hating, tear the waste
Of body. Break, her dead, dark body, break.'

Dan kicked my shins in the silence before Mr Bevan said 'The influence is obvious, of course. "Break, break, break, on thy cold, grey stones, O sea." '

'Hubert knows Tennyson backwards,' said Mrs Bevan, 'backwards.'

'Can we go upstairs now?' Dan asked.

'No annoying Mr Carey then.'

And we shut the door softly behind us and ran upstairs with our hands over our mouths.

'Damn! damn! damn!' said Dan. 'Did you see the reverend's face?'

We imitated him up and down the room, and had a short fight on the carpet. Dan's nose began to bleed again. 'That's nothing, it'll stop in a minute. I can bleed when I like.'

'Tell me about Mrs Bevan. Is she mad?'

'She's terribly mad, she doesn't know who she is. She tried to throw herself out of the window but he didn't take any notice, so she came up to our house and told mother all about it.'

Mrs Bevan knocked and walked in. 'I hope I'm not interrupting you.'

'No, of course not, Mrs Bevan.'

'I wanted a little change of air,' she said. She sat down in the wool on the sofa by the window.

'Isn't it a close night?' said Dan. 'Would you like the window open?'

She looked at the window.

'I can easily open it for you,' Dan said, and winked at me.

'Let me open it for you, Mrs Bevan,' I said.

'It's good to have the window open.'

'And this is a nice high window too.'

'Plenty of air from the sea.'

'Let it be, dear,' she said. 'I'll just sit here and wait for my husband.'

She played with the balls of wool, picked up a needle and tapped it gently on the palm of her hand.

'Is Mr Bevan going to be long?'

'I'll just sit and wait for my husband,' she said.

We talked to her some more about windows, but she only smiled and undid the wool, and once she put the blunt end of the long needle in her ear. Soon we grew tired of watching her, and Dan played the piano – 'My twentieth sonata,' he said, 'this one is *Homage to Beethoven*' – and at half-past nine I had to go home.

I said good night to Mrs Bevan, who waved the needle and bowed sitting down, and Mr Bevan downstairs gave me his cold hand to shake, and Mr and Mrs Jenkyn told me to come again, and the quiet aunt gave me a Mars bar.

'I'll send you a bit of the way,' said Dan.

Outside, on the pavement, in the warm night, we looked up at the lighted drawing-room window. It was the only light in the road.

'Look! there she is!'

Mrs Bevan's face was pressed against the glass, her hook nose flattened, her lips pressed tight, and we ran all the way down Eversley Road in case she jumped.

At the corner, Dan said: 'I must leave you now, I've got to finish a string trio tonight.'

'I'm working on a long poem,' I said, 'about the princes of Wales and the wizards and everybody.'

We both went home to bed.

Extraordinary little cough

One afternoon, in a particularly bright and glowing August, some years before I knew I was happy, George Hooping, whom we called Little Cough, Sidney Evans, Dan Davies, and I sat on the roof of a lorry travelling to the end of the Peninsula. It was a tall, six-wheeled lorry, from which we could spit on the roofs of the passing cars and throw our apple stumps at women on the pavement. One stump caught a man on a bicycle in the middle of the back, he swerved across the road, for a moment we sat quiet and George Hooping's face grew pale. And if the lorry runs him over, I thought calmly as the man on the bicycle swayed towards the hedge, he'll get killed and I'll be sick on my trousers and perhaps on Sidney's too, and we'll be arrested and hanged, except George Hooping who didn't have an apple.

But the lorry swept past; behind us, the bicycle drove into the hedge, the man stood up and waved his fist, and I waved my cap back at him.

'You shouldn't have waved your cap,' said Sidney Evans, 'he'll know what school we're in.' He was clever, dark, and careful, and had a purse and a wallet.

'We're not in school now.'

'Nobody can expel me,' said Dan Davies. He was leaving next term to serve in his father's fruit shop for a salary.

We all wore haversacks, except George Hooping whose mother had given him a brown-paper parcel that kept coming undone, and carried a suitcase each. I had placed a coat over my suitcase because the initials on it were 'N. T.' and everybody would know that it belonged to my sister. Inside the lorry were two tents, a box of food, a packing-case of kettles and saucepans and knives and forks, an oil lamp, a primus stove, ground sheets and blankets, a gramophone with three records, and a table-cloth from George Hooping's mother.

We were going to camp for a fortnight in Rhossilli, in a field above the sweeping five-mile beach. Sidney and Dan had stayed there last year, coming back brown and swearing, full of stories of campers' dances round the fires at midnight, and elderly girls from the training college who sun-bathed naked on ledges of rocks surrounded by laughing boys, and singing in bed that lasted until dawn. But George had never left home for more than a night; and then, he told me, one half-holiday when it was raining and there was nothing to do but stay in the wash-house racing his guineapigs giddily along the benches, it was only to stay in St Thomas, three miles from his house, with an aunt who could see through the walls and who knew what a Mrs Hoskin was doing in the kitchen.

'How much further?' asked George Hooping, clinging to his split parcel, trying in secret to push back socks and suspenders, enviously watching the solid green fields skim by as though the roof were a raft on an ocean with a motor in it. Anything upset his stomach, even liquorice and sherbet, but I alone knew that he wore long combinations in the summer with his name stitched in red on them.

'Miles and miles,' Dan said.

'Thousands of miles,' I said. 'It's Rhossilli, USA. We're going to camp on a bit of rock that wobbles in the wind.'

'And we have to tie the rock on to a tree.'

'Cough can use his suspenders,' Sidney said.

The lorry roared round a corner – 'Upsy-daisy! Did you feel it then, Cough? It was on one wheel' – and below us, beyond fields and farms, the sea, with a steamer puffing on its far edge, shimmered.

'Do you see the sea down there, it's shimmering, Dan,' I said.

George Hooping pretended to forget the lurch of the slippery roof and, from that height, the frightening smallness of the sea. Gripping the rail of the roof, he said: 'My father saw a killer whale.' The conviction in his voice died quickly as he began. He beat against the wind with his cracked, treble voice, trying to make us believe. I knew he wanted to find a boast so big it would make our hair stand up and stop the wild lorry.

'Your father's a herbalist.' But the smoke on the horizon was the white, curling fountain the whale blew through his nose, and its black nose was the bow of the poking ship.

'Where did he keep it, Cough, in the wash-house?'

'He saw it in Madagascar. It had tusks as long as from here to, from here to . . .'

'From here to Madagascar.'

All at once the threat of a steep hill disturbed him. No longer bothered about the adventures of his father, a small, dusty skullcapped and alpaca-coated man standing and mumbling all day in a shop full of herbs and curtained holes in the wall, where old men with backache and young girls in trouble waited for consultations in the half-dark, he stared at the hill swooping up and clung to Dan and me.

'She's doing fifty!'

'The brakes have gone, Cough!'

He twisted away from us, caught hard with both hands on the rail, pulled and trembled, pressed on a case behind him with his foot, and steered the lorry to safety round a stone-walled corner and up a gentler hill to a gate of a battered farm-house.

Leading down from the gate, there was a lane to the first beach. It was high tide, and we heard the sea dashing. Four boys on a roof – one tall, dark, regular-featured, precise of speech, in a good suit, a boy of the world; one squat, ungainly, red-haired, his red wrists fighting out of short, frayed sleeves; one heavily spectacled, small-paunched, with indoor shoulders and feet in always unlaced boots wanting to go different ways; one small, thin, indecisively active, quick to get dirty, curly – saw their field in front of them, a fortnight's new home that had thick, pricking hedges for walls, the sea for a front garden, a green gutter for a lavatory, and a wind-struck tree in the very middle.

I helped Dan unload the lorry while Sidney tipped the driver and George struggled with the farm-yard gate and looked at the ducks inside. The lorry drove away.

'Let's build our tents by the tree in the middle,' said George.

'Pitch!' Sidney said, unlatching the gate for him.

We pitched our tents in a corner, out of the wind.

'One of us must light the primus,' Sidney said, and, after George had burned his hand, we sat in a circle outside the sleeping-tent talking about motor-cars, content to be in the country, lazily easy in each other's company, thinking to ourselves as we talked, knowing always that the sea dashed on the rocks not far below us and rolled out into the world, and that tomorrow we would bathe and throw a ball on the sands and stone a bottle on a rock and perhaps meet three girls. The oldest would be for Sidney, the plainest for Dan, and the youngest for me. George broke his spectacles when he spoke to girls; he had to walk off, blind as a bat, and the next morning he would say: 'I'm sorry I had to leave you, but I remembered a message.'

It was past five o'clock. My father and mother would have finished tea; the plates with famous castles on them were cleared from the table; father with a newspaper, mother with socks, were far away in the blue haze to the left, up a hill, in a villa, hearing from the park the faint cries of children drift over the public tennis court, and wondering where I was and what I was doing. I was alone with my friends in a field, with a blade of grass in my mouth saying, 'Dempsey would hit him cold,' and thinking of the great whale that George's father never saw thrashing on the top of the sea, or plunging underneath, like a mountain.

'Bet you I can beat you to the end of the field.'

Dan and I raced among the cowpads, George thumping at our heels.

'Let's go down to the beach.'

Sidney led the way, running straight as a soldier in his khaki shorts, over a stile, down fields to another, into a wooded valley, up through heather on to a clearing near the edge of the cliff, where two broad boys were wrestling outside a tent. I saw one bite the other in the leg, they both struck expertly and savagely at the face, one struggled clear, and, with a leap, the other had him face to the ground. They were Brazell and Skully.

'Hallo, Brazell and Skully!' said Dan.

Skully had Brazell's arm in a policeman's grip; he gave it two quick twists and stood up, smiling.

'Hallo, boys! Hallo, Little Cough! How's your father?'

'He's very well, thank you.'

Brazell, on the grass, felt for broken bones. 'Hallo, boys! How are your fathers?'

They were the worst and biggest boys in school. Every day for a term they caught me before class began and wedged me in the wastepaper basket and then put the basket on the master's desk. Sometimes I could get out and sometimes not. Brazell was lean, Skully was fat.

'We're camping in Button's field,' said Sidney.

'We're taking a rest cure here,' said Brazell. 'And how is Little Cough these days? Father given him a pill?'

We wanted to run down to the beach, Dan and Sidney and George and I, to be alone together, to walk and shout by the sea in the country, throw stones at the waves, remember adventures and make more to remember.

'We'll come down to the beach with you,' said Skully.

He linked arms with Brazell, and they strolled behind us, imitating George's wayward walk and slashing the grass with switches.

Dan said hopefully: 'Are you camping here for long, Brazell and Skully?'

'For a whole nice fortnight, Davies and Thomas and Evans and Hooping.'

When we reached Mewslade beach and flung ourselves down, as I scooped up sand and it trickled, grain by grain through my fingers, as George peered at the sea through his double lenses and Sidney and Dan heaped sand over his legs, Brazell and Skully sat behind us like two warders.

'We thought of going to Nice for a fortnight,' said Brazell – he rhymed it with ice, dug Skully in the ribs, – 'but the air's nicer here for the complexion.'

'It's as good as a herb,' said Skully.

They shared an enormous joke, cuffing and biting and wrestling again, scattering sand in the eyes, until they fell back with laughter, and Brazell wiped the blood from his nose with a piece of picnic paper. George lay covered to the waist in sand. I watched the sea slipping out, with birds quarrelling over it, and the sun beginning to go down patiently.

'Look at Little Cough,' said Brazell. 'Isn't he extraordinary? He's growing out of the sand. Little Cough hasn't got any legs.'

'Poor Little Cough,' said Skully, 'he's the most extraordinary boy in the world.'

'Extraordinary Little Cough,' they said together, 'extraordinary, extraordinary, extraordinary.' They made a song out of it, and both conducted with their switches.

'He can't swim.'

'He can't run.'

'He can't learn.'

'He can't bowl.'

'He can't bat.'

'And I bet he can't make water.'

George kicked the sand from his legs. 'Yes, I can!'

'Can you swim?'

'Can you run?'

'Can you bowl?'

'Leave him alone,' Dan said.

They shuffled nearer to us. The sea was racing out now. Brazell said in a serious voice, wagging his finger: 'Now, quite truthfully, Cough, aren't you extraordinary? Very extraordinary? Say "Yes" or "No".'

'Categorically, "Yes" or "No".' said Skully.

'No,' George said. 'I can swim and I can run and I can play cricket. I'm not frightened of anybody.'

I said: 'He was second in the form last term.'

'Now isn't that extraordinary? If he can be second he can be first. But no, that's too extraordinary. Little Cough must be second.'

'The question is answered,' said Skully. 'Little Cough is extraordinary.' They began to sing again.

'He's a very good runner,' Dan said.

'Well, let him prove it. Skully and I ran the whole length of Rhossilli sands this morning, didn't we, Skull?'

'Every inch.'

'Can Little Cough do it?'

'Yes,' said George.

'Do it, then.'

'I don't want to.'

'Extraordinary Little Cough can't run,' they sang, 'can't run, can't run.'

Three girls, all fair, came down the cliff-side arm in arm, dressed in short, white trousers. Their arms and legs and throats were brown as berries; I could see when they laughed that their teeth were very white; they stepped on to the beach, and Brazell and Skully stopped singing. Sidney smoothed his hair back, rose casually, put his hands in his pockets, and walked towards the girls, who now stood close together, gold and brown, admiring the sunset with little attention, patting their scarves, turning smiles on each other. He stood in front of them, grinned, and saluted: 'Hallo, Gwyneth! do you remember me?'

'La-di-da!' whispered Dan at my side, and made a mock salute to George still peering at the retreating sea.

'Well, if this isn't a surprise!' said the tallest girl. With little studied movements of her hands, as though she were distributing flowers, she introduced Peggy and Jean.

Fat Peggy, I thought, too jolly for me, with hockey legs and tomboy crop, was the girl for Dan; Sidney's Gwyneth was a distinguished piece and quite sixteen, as immaculate and unapproachable as a girl in Ben Evans' stores; but Jean, shy and curly, with butter-coloured hair, was mine. Dan and I walked slowly to the girls.

I made up two remarks: 'Fair's fair, Sidney, no bigamy abroad,' and 'Sorry we couldn't arrange to have the sea in when you came.'

Jean smiled, wriggling her heel in the sand, and I raised my cap.

'Hallo!'

The cap dropped at her feet.

As I bent down, three lumps of sugar fell from my blazer pocket.

'I've been feeding a horse,' I said, and began to blush guiltily when all the girls laughed.

I could have swept the ground with my cap, kissed my hand gaily, called them señoritas, and made them smile without tolerance. Or I could have stayed at a distance, and this would have been better still, my hair blown in the wind, though there was no wind at all that evening, wrapped in mystery and staring at the sun, too aloof to speak to girls; but I knew that all the time my ears would have been burning, my stomach would have been as hollow and as full of voices as a shell. 'Speak to them quickly, before they go away!' a voice would have said insistently over the dramatic silence, as I stood like Valentino on the edge of the bright, invisible bull-ring of the sands. 'Isn't it lovely here!' I said.

I spoke to Jean alone; and this is love, I thought, as she nodded her head and swung her curls and said: 'It's nicer than Porthcawl.'

Brazell and Skully were two big bullies in a nightmare; I forgot them when Jean and I walked up the cliff, and, looking back to see if they were baiting George again or wrestling together, I saw that George had disappeared around the corner of the rocks and that they were talking at the foot of the cliff with Sidney and the two girls.

'What's your name?'

I told her.

'That's Welsh,' she said.

'You've got a beautiful name.'

'Oh, it's just ordinary.'

'Shall I see you again?'

'If you want to.'

'I want to all right! We can go and bathe in the morning. And we can try to get an eagle's egg. Did you know that there were eagles here?'

'No,' she said. 'Who was that handsome boy on the beach, the tall one with dirty trousers?'

'He's not handsome, that's Brazell. He never washes or combs his hair or anything. He's a bully and he cheats.'

'I think he's handsome.'

We walked into Button's field, and I showed her inside the tents and gave her one of George's apples. 'I'd like a cigarette,' she said.

It was nearly dark when the others came. Brazell and Skully were with Gwyneth, one each side of her holding her arms, Sidney was with Peggy, and Dan walked, whistling, behind with his hands in his pockets.

'There's a pair,' said Brazell, 'they've been here all alone and they aren't even holding hands. You want a pill,' he said to me.

'Build Britain's babies,' said Skully.

'Go on!' Gwyneth said. She pushed him away from her, but she was laughing, and she said nothing when he put his arm around her waist.

'What about a bit of fire?' said Brazell.

Jean clapped her hands like an actress. Although I knew I loved her, I didn't like anything she said or did.

'Who's going to make it?'

'He's the best, I'm sure,' she said, pointing at me.

Dan and I collected sticks, and by the time it was quite dark there was a fire crackling. Inside the sleeping-tent, Brazell and Jean sat close together; her golden head was on his shoulder; Skully, near them, whispered to Gwyneth; Sidney unhappily held Peggy's hand.

'Did you ever see such a sloppy lot?' I said, watching Jean smile in the fiery dark.

'Kiss me, Charley!' said Dan.

We sat by the fire in the corner of the field. The sea, far out, was still making a noise. We heard a few nightbirds. "Tu-whit! tu-whoo!' Listen! I don't like owls,' Dan said, 'they scratch your eyes out!' – and tried not to listen to the soft voices in the tent. Gwyneth's laughter floated out over the suddenly moonlit field, but Jean, with the beast, was smiling and silent in the covered warmth; I knew her little hand was in Brazell's hand.

'Women!' I said.

Dan spat in the fire.

We were old and alone, sitting beyond desire in the middle of the night, when George appeared, like a ghost, in the firelight and stood there trembling until I said: 'Where've you been? You've been gone hours. Why are you trembling like that?'

Brazell and Skully poked their heads out.

'Hallo, Cough my boy! How's your father? What have you been up to tonight?'

George Hooping could hardly stand. I put my hand on his shoulder to steady him, but he pushed it away.

'I've been running on Rhossilli sands! I ran every bit of it! You said I couldn't, and I did! I've been running and running!'

Someone inside the tent had put a record on the gramophone. It was a selection from *No, No, Nanette*.

'You've been running all the time in the dark, Little Cough?'

'And I bet I ran it quicker than you did, too!' George said.

'I bet you did,' said Brazell.

'Do you think we'd run five miles?' said Skully.

Now the tune was 'Tea for Two'.

'Did you ever hear anything so extraordinary? I told you Cough was extraordinary. Little Cough's been running all night.'

'Extraordinary, extraordinary, extraordinary Little Cough,' they said.

Laughing from the shelter of the tent into the darkness, they looked like a boy with two heads. And when I stared round at George again he was lying on his back fast asleep in the deep grass and his hair was touching the flames.

Just Like Little Dogs

Standing alone under a railway arch out of the wind, I was looking at the miles of sands, long and dirty in the early dark, with only a few boys on the edge of the sea and one or two hurrying couples with their mackintoshes blown around them like balloons, when two young men joined me, it seemed out of nowhere, and struck matches for their cigarettes and illuminated their faces under bright-checked caps.

One had a pleasant face; his eyebrows slanted comically towards his temples, his eyes were warm, brown, deep, and guileless, and his mouth was full and weak. The other man had a boxer's nose and a weighted chin ginger with bristles.

We watched the boys returning from the oily sea; they shouted under the echoing arch, then their voices faded. Soon there was not a single couple in sight; the lovers had disappeared among the sandhills and were lying down there with broken tins and bottles of the summer passed, old paper blowing by them, and nobody with any sense was about. The strangers, huddled against the wall, their hands deep in their pockets, their cigarettes sparkling, stared, I thought, at the thickening of the dark over the empty sands, but their eyes may have been closed. A train raced over us, and the arch shook. Over the shore, behind the vanishing train, smoke clouds flew together, rags of wings and hollow bodies of great birds black as tunnels, and broke up lazily; cinders fell through a sieve in the air, and the sparks were put out by the wet dark before they reached the sand. The night before, little quick scarecrows had bent and picked at the track-line and a solitary dignified scavenger wandered three miles by the edge with a crumpled coal sack and a park-keeper's steel-tipped stick. Now they were tucked up in sacks, asleep in a siding, their heads in bins, their beards in straw, in coal-trucks thinking of fires, or lying beyond pickings on Jack Stiff's slab near the pub in the Fishguard Alley, where the methylated-spirit drinkers danced into the policemen's arms and women like lumps of clothes in a pool waited, in doorways and holes in the soaking wall, for vampires or firemen. Night was properly down on us now. The wind changed. Thin rain began. The sands themselves went out. We stood in the scooped, windy room of the arch, listening to the noises from the muffled town, a goods train shunting, a siren in the docks, the hoarse trams in the streets far behind, one bark of a dog, unplaceable sounds, iron being beaten, the distant creaking of wood, doors slamming where there were no houses, an engine coughing like a sheep on a hill.

The two young men were statues smoking, tough-capped and collarless watchers and witnesses carved out of the stone of the blowing room where they stood at my side with nowhere to go, nothing to do, and all the raining, almost winter, night before them. I cupped a match to let them see my face in a dramatic shadow, my eyes mysteriously sunk, perhaps, in a startling white face, my young looks savage in the sudden flicker of light, to make them wonder who I was as I puffed my last butt and puzzled about them. Why was the soft-faced young man, with his tame devil's eyebrows, standing like a stone figure with a glow-worm in it? He should have a nice girl to bully him gently and take him to cry in the pictures, or kids to bounce in a kitchen in Rodney Street. There was no sense in standing silent for hours under a railway arch on a hell of a night at the end of a bad summer when girls were waiting, ready to be hot and friendly, in chip shops and shop doorways and Rabbiotti's all-night café, when the public bar of the 'Bay View' at the corner had a fire and skittles and a swarthy, sensuous girl with different coloured eyes, when the billiard saloons were open, except the one in High Street you couldn't go into without a collar and tie, when the closed parks had empty, covered bandstands and the railings were easy to climb.

A church clock somewhere struck a lot, faintly from the night on the right, but I didn't count.

The other young man, less than two feet from me, should be shouting with the boys, boasting in lanes, propping counters, prancing and clouting in the Mannesmann Hall, or whispering around a bucket in a ring corner. Why was he humped here with a moody man and myself, listening to our breathing, to the sea, the wind scattering sand through the archway, a chained dog and a foghorn and the rumble of trams a dozen streets away, watching a match strike, a boy's fresh face spying in a shadow, the lighthouse beams, the movement of a hand to a fag, when the sprawling town in a drizzle, the pubs and the clubs and the coffee-shops, the prowlers' streets, the arches near the promenade, were full of friends and enemies? He could be playing nap by a candle in a shed in a wood-yard.

Families sat down to supper in rows of short houses, the wireless sets were on, the daughters' young men sat in the front rooms. In neighbouring houses they read the news off the table-cloth, and the potatoes from dinner were fried up. Cards were played in the front rooms of houses on the hills. In the houses on tops of the hills families were entertaining friends, and the blinds of the front rooms were not quite drawn. I heard the sea in a cold bit of the cheery night.

One of the strangers said suddenly, in a high, clear voice: 'What are we all doing then?'

'Standing under a bloody arch,' said the other one.

'And it's cold,' I said.

'It isn't very cosy,' said the high voice of the young man with the pleasant face, now invisible. 'I've been in better hotels than this.'

'What about that night in the Majestic?' said the other voice.

There was a long silence.

'Do you often stand here?' said the pleasant man. His voice might never have broken.

'No, this is the first time here,' I said. 'Sometimes I stand in the Brynmill arch.'

'Ever tried the old pier?'

'It's no good in the rain, is it?'

'Underneath the pier, I mean, in the girders.'

'No, I haven't been there.'

'Tom spends every Sunday under the pier,' the pug-faced young man said bitterly. 'I got to take him his dinner in a piece of paper.'

'There's another train coming,' I said. It tore over us, the arch bellowed, the wheels screamed through our heads, we were deafened and spark-blinded and crushed under the fiery weight and we rose again, like battered black men, in the grave of the arch. No noise at all from the swallowed town. The trams had rattled themselves dumb. A pressure of the hidden sea rubbed away the smudge of the docks. Only three young men were alive.

One said: 'It's a sad life, without a home.'

'Haven't you got a home then?' I said.

'Oh, yes, I've got a home all right.

'I got one, too.'

'And I live near Cwmdonkin Park,' I said.

'That's another place Tom sits in in the dark. He says he listens to the owls.'

'I knew a chap once who lived in the country, near Bridgend,' said Tom, 'and they had a munition works there in the War and it spoiled all the birds. The chap I know says you can always tell a cuckoo from Bridgend, it goes: "Cuckbloodyoo! cuckbloodyoo!" '

'Cuckbloodyoo!' echoed the arch.

'Why are you standing under the arch, then?' asked Tom. 'It's warm at home. You can draw the curtains and sit by the fire, snug as a bug. Gracie's on the wireless tonight. No shananacking in the old moonlight.'

'I don't want to go home, I don't want to sit by the fire. I've got nothing to do when I'm in and I don't want to go to bed. I like standing about like this with nothing to do, in the dark all by myself,' I said.

And I did, too. I was a lonely nightwalker and a steady stander-at-corners. I liked to walk through the wet town after midnight, when the streets were deserted and the window lights out, alone and alive on the glistening tramlines in dead and empty High Street under the moon, gigantically sad in the damp streets by ghostly Ebenezer Chapel. And I never felt more a part of the remote and overpressing world, or more full of love and arrogance and pity and humility, not for myself alone, but for the living earth I suffered on and for the unfeeling systems in the upper air, Mars and Venus and Brazell and Skully, men in China and St Thomas, scorning girls and ready girls, soldiers and bullies and policemen and sharp, suspicious buyers of second-hand books, bad, ragged women who'd pretend against the museum wall for a cup of tea, and perfect, unapproachable women out of the fashion magazines, seven feet high, sailing slowly in their flat, glazed creations through steel and glass and velvet. I leant against the wall of a derelict house in the residential areas or wandered in the empty rooms, stood terrified on the stairs or gazing through the smashed windows at the sea or at nothing, and the lights going out one by one in the avenues. Or I mooched in a half-built house, with the sky stuck in the roof and cats on the ladders and a wind shaking through the bare bones of the bedrooms.

'And you can talk,' I said. 'Why aren't you at home?'

'I don't want to be home,' said Tom.

'I'm not particular,' said his friend.

When a match flared, their heads rocked and spread on the wall, and shapes of winged bulls and buckets grew bigger and smaller. Tom began to tell a story. I thought of a new stranger walking on the sands past the arch and hearing all of a sudden that high voice out of a hole.

I missed the beginning of the story as I thought of the man on the sands listening in a panic or dodging, like a footballer, in and out among the jumping dark towards the lights behind the railway line, and remembered Tom's voice in the middle of a sentence.

'... went up to them and said it was a lovely night. It wasn't a lovely night at all. The sands were empty. We asked them what their names were and they asked us what ours were. We were walking along by this time. Walter here was telling them about the glee party in the "Melba" and what went on in the ladies' cloakroom. You had to drag the tenors away like ferrets.'

'What were their names?' I asked.

'Doris and Norma,' Walter said.

'So we walked along the sands towards the dunes,' Tom said, 'and Walter was with Doris and I was with Norma. Norma worked in the steam laundry. We hadn't been walking and talking for more than a few minutes when, by God, I knew I was head over heels in love with the girl, and she wasn't the pretty one, either.'

He described her. I saw her clearly. Her plump, kind face, jolly brown eyes, warm wide mouth, thick bobbed hair, rough body, bottle legs, broad bum, grew from a few words right out of Tom's story, and I saw her ambling solidly along the sands in a spotted frock in a showering autumn evening with fancy gloves on her hard hands, a gold bangle, with a voile handkerchief tucked in it, round her wrist, and a navy-blue handbag with letters and outing snaps, a compact, a bus ticket, and a shilling.

'Doris was the pretty one,' said Tom, 'smart and touched up and sharp as a knife. I was twenty-six years old and I'd never been in love, and there I was, gawking at Norma in the middle of Tawe sands, too frightened to put my finger on her gloves. Walter had his arm round Doris then.'

They sheltered behind a dune. The night dropped down on them quickly. Walter was a caution with Doris, hugging and larking, and Tom sat close to Norma, brave enough to hold her hand in its cold glove and tell her all his secrets. He told her his age and his job. He liked staying in in the evenings with a good book. Norma liked dances. He liked dances, too. Norma and Doris were sisters. 'I'd never have thought that,' Tom said, 'you're beautiful, I love you.'

Now the story-telling thing in the arch gave place to the loving night in the dunes. The arch was as high as the sky. The faint town noises died. I lay like a pimp in a bush by Tom's side and squinted through to see him round his hands on Norma's breast. 'Don't you dare!' Walter and Doris lay quietly near them. You could have heard a safety-pin fall.

'And the curious thing was,' said Tom, 'that after a time we all sat up on the sand and smiled at each other. And then we all moved softly about on the sand in the dark, without saying a word. And Doris was lying with me, and Norma was with Walter.'

'But why did you change over, if you loved her?' I asked.

'I never understood why,' said Tom. 'I think about it every night.'

'That was in October,' Walter said.

And Tom continued: 'We didn't see much of the girls until July. I couldn't face Norma. Then they brought two paternity orders against us, and Mr Lewis, the magistrate, was eighty years old, and stone deaf, too. He put a little trumpet by his ear and Norma and Doris gave evidence. Then we gave evidence, and he couldn't decide whose was which. And at the end he shook his head back and fore and pointed his trumpet and said: "Just like little dogs!"'

All at once I remembered how cold it was. I rubbed my numb hands together. Fancy standing all night in the cold. Fancy listening, I thought, to a long, unsatisfactory story in the frost-bite night in a polar arch. 'What happened then?' I asked.

Walter answered. 'I married Norma,' he said 'and Tom married Doris. We had to do the right thing by them, didn't we? That's why Tom won't go home. He never goes home till the early morning. I've got to keep him company. He's my brother.'

It would take me ten minutes to run home. I put up my coat collar and pulled my cap down.

'And the curious thing is,' said Tom, 'that I love Norma and Walter doesn't love Norma or Doris. We've two nice little boys. I call mine Norman.'

We all shook hands.

'See you again,' said Walter.

'I'm always hanging about,' said Tom.

'Abyssinia!'

I walked out of the arch, crossed Trafalgar Square, and pelted up the steep streets.

Where Tawe Flows

Mr Humphries, Mr Roberts, and young Mr Thomas knocked on the front door of Mrs Emlyn Evans's small villa, 'Lavengro', punctually at nine o'clock in the evening. They waited, hidden behind a veronica bush, while Mr Evans shuffled in carpet slippers up the passage from the back room and had trouble with the bolts.

Mr Humphries was a school teacher, a tall, fair man with a stammer, who had written an unsuccessful novel.

Mr Roberts, a cheerful, disreputable man of middle age, was a collector for an insurance company; they called him in the trade a body-snatcher, and he was known among his friends as Burke and Hare, the Welsh Nationalist. He had once held a high position in a brewery office.

Young Mr Thomas was at the moment without employment, but it was understood that he would soon be leaving for London to make a career in Chelsea as a freelance journalist; he was penniless, and hoped, in a vague way, to live on women.

When Mr Evans opened the door and shone his torch down the narrow drive, lighting up the garage and hen-run but missing altogether the whispering bush, the three friends bounded out and cried in threatening voices: 'We're Ogpu men, let us in!'

'We're looking for seditious literature,' said Mr Humphries with difficulty, raising his hand in a salute.

'Heil, Saunders Lewis! and we know where to find it,' said Mr Roberts.

Mr Evans turned off his torch. 'Come in out of the night air, boys, and have a drop of something. It's only parsnip wine,' he added.

They removed their hats and coats, piled them on the end of the bannister, spoke softly for fear of waking up the twins, George and Celia, and followed Mr Evans into his den.

'Where's the trouble and strife, Mr Evans?' said Mr Roberts in a cockney accent. He warmed his hands in front of the fire and regarded with a smile of surprise, though he visited the house every Friday, the neat rows of books, the ornate roll-top desk that made the parlour into a study, the shining grandfather clock, the photographs of children staring stiffly at a dickybird, the still, delicious home-made wine, that had such an effect, in an old beer bottle, the sleeping tom on the frayed rug. 'At home with the *bourgeoisie*.'

He was himself a homeless bachelor with a past, much in debt, and nothing gave him more pleasure than to envy his friends their wives and comforts and to speak of them intimately and disparagingly.

'In the kitchen,' said Mr Evans, handing out glasses.

'A woman's only place,' said Mr Roberts heartily, 'with one exception.'

Mr Humphries and Mr Thomas arranged the chairs around the fire, and all four sat down, close and confidential and with full glasses in their hands. None of them spoke for a time. They gave one another sly looks, sipped and sighed, lit the cigarettes that Mr Evans produced from a draughts box, and once Mr Humphries glanced at the grandfather clock and winked and put his finger to his lips. Then, as the visitors grew warm and the wine worked and they forgot the bitter night outside, Mr Evans said with a little shudder of forbidden delight: 'The wife will be going to bed in half an hour. Then we can start the good work. Have you all got yours with you?'

'And the tools,' said Mr Roberts, smacking his side pocket.

'What's the word until then?' said young Mr Thomas.

Mr Humphries winked again. 'Mum!'

'I've been waiting for tonight to come round like I used to wait for Saturdays when I was a boy,' said Mr Evans, 'I got a penny then. And it all went on gob-stoppers and jelly-babies, too.'

He was a traveller in rubber, rubber toys and syringes and bath mats. Sometimes Mr Roberts called him the poor man's friend to make him blush. 'No! no! no!' he would say, 'you can look at my samples, there's nothing like that there.' He was a Socialist.

'I used to buy a packet of Cinderellas with my penny,' said Mr Roberts, 'and smoke them in the slaughter-house. The sweetest little smoke in the world. You don't see them now.'

'Do you remember old Jim, the caretaker, in the slaughter-house?' asked Mr Evans.

'He was after my time; I'm no chicken, like you boys.'

'You're not old, Mr Roberts, think of G.B.S.'

'No clean Shavianism for me, I'm an unrepentant eater of birds and beasts,' said Mr Roberts.

'Do you eat flowers, too?'

'Oh! oh! you literary men, don't you talk above my head now. I'm only a poor resurrectionist on the knocker.'

'He'd put his hand down in the guts-box and bring you out a rat with it's neck broken clean as a match for the price of a glass of beer.'

'And it was beer then.'

'Shop! shop!' Mr Humphries beat on the table with his glass, 'you mustn't waste stories, we'll need them all,' he said. 'Have you got the abattoir anecdote down in your memory book, Mr Thomas?'

'I'll remember it.'

'Don't forget, you can only talk at random now,' said Mr Humphries.

'Okay, Roderick!' Mr Thomas said quickly.

Mr Roberts put his hands over his ears. 'The conversation is getting esoteric,' he said. 'Excuse my French! Mr Evans, have you such a thing as a rook rifle? I want to scare the highbrows off. Did I ever tell you the time I lectured to the John O' London's Society on "The Utility of Uselessness"? That was a poser. I talked about Jack London all the time, and when they said at the end that it wasn't a lecture about what I said it was going to be, I said "Well, it was useless lecturing about that, wasn't it?" and they hadn't a word to say. Mrs Dr Davies was in the front row, you remember her? She gave that first lecture on W. J. Locke and got spoonered in the middle. Remember talking about the "Bevagged Loveabond", Mr Humphries?'

'Shop! Shop!' said Mr Humphries, groaning, 'keep it until after.'

'More parsnip?'

'It goes down the throat like silk, Mr Evans.'

'Like baby's milk.'

'Say when, Mr Roberts.'

'A word of four syllables denoting a period of time. Thank you! I read that on a matchbox.'

'Why don't they have serials on matchboxes? You'd buy the shop up to see what Daphne did next,' Mr Humphries said.

He stopped and looked round in embarrassment at the faces of his friends. Daphne was the name of the grass widow in Manselton for whom Mr Roberts had lost both his reputation and his position in the brewery. He had been in the habit of delivering bottles to her house, free of charge, and he had bought her a cocktail cabinet and given her a hundred pounds and his mother's rings. In return she held large parties and never invited him. Only Mr Thomas had noticed the name, and he was saying: 'No, Mr Humphries, on toilet rolls would be best.'

'When I was in London,' Mr Roberts said, 'I stayed with a couple called Armitage in Palmer's Green. He made curtains and blinds. They used to leave each other messages on the toilet paper every single day.'

'If you want to make a Venetian blind,' said Mr Evans, 'stick him in the eye with a hatpin.' He felt, always, a little left out of his evenings at home, and he was waiting for Mrs Evans to come in, disapprovingly, from the kitchen.

'I've often had to use, "Dear Tom, don't forget the Watkinses are coming to tea", or, "To Peggy, from Tom, in remembrance." Mr Armitage was a Mosleyite.'

'Thugs,' said Mr Humphries.

'Seriously, what are we going to do about this uniformication of the individual?' Mr Evans asked. Maud was in the kitchen still; he heard her beating the plates.

'Answering your question with another,' said Mr Roberts, putting one hand on Mr Evans's knee, 'what individuality is there left? The mass-age produces the mass-man. The machine produces the robot.'

'As its slave,' Mr Humphries articulated clearly, 'not, mark you, as its master.'

'There you have it. There it is. Tyrannic dominance by a sparking plug, Mr Humphries, and it's flesh and blood that always pays.'

'Any empty glasses?'

Mr Roberts turned his glass upside down. 'That used to mean, "I'll take on the best man in the room in a bout of fisticuffs," in Llanelly. But seriously, as Mr Evans says, the old-fashioned individualist is a square peg now in a round hole.'

'What a hole!' said Mr Thomas.

'Take our national – what did Onlooker say last week? – our national misleaders.'

'You take them, Mr Roberts, we've got rats already,' Mr Evans said with a nervous laugh. The kitchen was silent. Maud was ready.

'Onlooker is a *nom de plume* for Basil Gorse Williams,' said Mr Humphries. 'Did any one know that?'

'*Nom de guerre*. Did you see his article on Ramsay Mac? "A sheep in wolf's clothing."'

'Know him!' Mr Roberts said scornfully, 'I've been sick on him.'

Mrs Evans heard the last remark as she came into the room. She was a thin woman with bitter lines, tired hands, the ruins of fine brown eyes, and a superior nose. An unshockable woman, she had once listened to Mr Roberts's description of his haemorrhoids for over an hour on a New Year's Eve and had allowed him, without protest to call them the grapes of wrath. When sober, Mr Roberts addressed her as 'ma'am' and kept the talk to weather and colds. He sprang to his feet and offered her his chair.

'No, thank you, Mr Roberts,' she said in a clear, hard voice, 'I'm going to bed at once. The cold disagrees with me.'

Go to bed plain Maud, thought young Mr Thomas. 'Will you have a little warm, Mrs Evans, before you retire?' he said.

She shook her head, gave the friends a thin smile, and said to Mr Evans: 'Put the world right before you come to bed.'

'Good night, Mrs Evans.'

'It won't be after midnight this time, Maud, I promise. I'll put Sambo out in the back.'

'Good night, ma'am.'

Sleep tight, hoity.

'I won't disturb you gentlemen any more,' she said. 'What's left of the parsnip wine for Christmas is in the boot cupboard, Emlyn. Don't let it waste. Good night.'

Mr Evans raised his eyebrows and whistled. 'Whew! boys.' He pretended to fan his face with his tie. Then his hand stopped still in the air. 'She was used to a big house,' he said, 'with servants.'

Mr Roberts brought out pencils and fountain pens from his side pocket. 'Where's the priceless MS? Tempus is fugiting.'

Mr Humphries and Mr Thomas put notebooks on their knees, took a pencil each, and watched Mr Evans open the door of the grandfather clock. Beneath the swinging weights was a heap of papers tied in a blue bow. These Mr Evans placed on the desk.

'I call order,' said Mr Roberts. 'Let's see where we were. Have you got the minutes, Mr Thomas?'

'"*Where Tawe Flows*",' said Mr Thomas. '"a Novel of Provincial Life. Chapter One: a cross-section description of the town, Dockland, Slums, Suburbia, etc." We finished that. The title decided upon was: Chapter One, "The Public Town". Chapter Two is to be called "The Private Lives", and Mr Humphries has proposed the following: "Each of the collaborators take one character from each social sphere or stratum of the town and introduce him to the readers with a brief history of his life up to the point at which we commence the story, i.e. the winter of this very year. These introductions of the characters, hereafter to be regarded as the principal protagonists, and their biographical chronicles shall constitute the second chapter." Any questions, gentlemen?'

Mr Humphries agreed with all he had said. His character was a sensitive schoolmaster of advanced opinions, who was misjudged and badly treated.

'No questions,' said Mr Evans. He was in charge of Suburbia. He rustled his notes and waited to begin.

'I haven't written anything yet,' Mr Roberts said, 'it's all in my head.' He had chosen the Slums.

'Personally,' said Mr Thomas, 'I haven't made up my mind whether to have a barmaid or a harlot.'

'What about a barmaid who's a harlot too?' Mr Roberts suggested. 'Or perhaps we could have a couple of characters each? I'd like to do an alderman. And a gold-digger.'

'Who had a word for them, Mr Humphries?' said Mr Thomas.

'The Greeks.'

Mr Roberts nudged Mr Evans and whispered: 'I just thought of an opening sentence for my bit. Listen Emlyn. "On the rickety table in the corner of the crowded, dilapidated room, a stranger might have seen, by the light of the flickering candle in the gin-bottle, a broken cup, full of sick or custard." '

'Be serious, Ted,' said Mr Evans laughing. 'You wrote that sentence down.'

'No, I swear it came to me just like that!' He flicked his fingers. 'And who's been reading my notes?'

'Have you put anything on paper yourself, Mr Thomas?'

'Not yet, Mr Evans.' He had been writing, that week, the story of a cat who jumped over a woman the moment she died and turned her into a vampire. He had reached the part of the story where the woman was an undead children's governess, but he could not think how to fit it into the novel.

'There's no need, is there,' he asked, 'for us to avoid the fantastic altogether?'

'Wait a bit! wait a bit!' said Mr Humphries, 'let's get our realism straight. Mr Thomas will be making all the characters Blue Birds before we know where we are. One thing at a time. Has anyone got the history of his character ready?' He had his biography in his hand, written in red ink. The writing was scholarly and neat and small.

'I think my character is ready to take the stage,' said Mr Evans. 'But I haven't written it out. I'll have to refer to the notes and make the rest up out of my head. It's a very silly story.'

'Well, you must begin, of course,' said Mr Humphries with disappointment.

'Everybody's biography is silly,' Mr Roberts said. 'My own would make a cat laugh.'

Mr Humphries said: 'I must disagree there. The life of that mythical common denominator, the man in the street, is dull as ditchwater, Mr Roberts. Capitalist society has made him a mere bundle of repressions and useless habits under that symbol of middle-class divinity, the bowler.' He looked quickly away from the notes in the palm of his hand. 'The ceaseless toil for bread and butter, the ogres of unemployment, the pettifogging gods of gentility, the hollow lies of the marriage bed. Marriage,' he said, dropping his ash on the carpet, 'legal monogamous prostitution.'

'Whoa! whoa! there he goes!'

'Mr Humphries is on his hobby-horse again.'

'I'm afraid,' said Mr Evans, 'that I lack our friend's extensive vocabulary. Have pity on a poor amateur. You're shaming my little story before I begin.'

'I still think the life of the ordinary man is most extraordinary,' Mr Roberts said, 'take my own ...'

'As the secretary,' said Mr Thomas, 'I vote we take Mr Evans's story. We must try to get *Tawe* finished for the spring list.'

'My *Tomorrow and Tomorrow* was published in the summer in a heat wave,' Mr Humphries said.

Mr Evans coughed, looked into the fire, and began.

'Her name is Mary,' he said, 'but that's not her name really. I'm calling her that because she is a real woman and we don't want any libel. She lives in a house called "Bellevue", but that's not the proper name, of course. A villa by any other name, Mr Humphries. I chose her for my character because her life is a little tragedy, but it's not without its touches of humour either. It's almost Russian. Mary – Mary Morgan now but she was Mary Phillips before she was married and that comes later, that's the anti-climax – wasn't a suburbanite from birth, she didn't live under the shadow of the bowler, like you and me. Or like me, anyway. I was born in "The Poplars" and now I'm in "Lavengro". From bowler to bowler, though I must say, apropos of Mr Humphries' diatribe, and I'm the first to admire his point of view, that the everyday man's just as interesting a character as the neurotic poets of Bloomsbury.'

'Remind me to shake your hand,' said Mr Roberts.

'You've been reading the Sunday papers,' said Mr Humphries accusingly.

'You two argue the toss later on,' Mr Thomas said.

'"Is the Ordinary Man a Mouse?" Now, what about Mary?'

'Mary Phillips,' continued Mr Evans, '– and any more interruptions from the intelligentsia and I'll get Mr Roberts to tell you the story of his operation, no pardons granted – lived on a big farm in Carmarthenshire, I'm not going to tell you exactly where, and her father was a widower. He had any amount of what counts and he drank like a fish, but he was always a gentleman with it. Now, now! forget the class war, I could see it smouldering. He came of a very good, solid family, but he raised his elbow, that's all there is to it.'

Mr Roberts said: 'Huntin', fishin' and boozin'.'

'No, he wasn't quite county and he wasn't a *nouveau riche* either. No Philippstein about him, though I'm not anti-Semite. You've only got to think of Einstein and Freud. There are bad Christians, too. He was just what I'm telling you, if you'd only let me, a man of good farming stock who'd made his pile and now he was spending it.'

'Liquidating it.'

'He'd only got one child, and that was Mary, and she was so prim and proper she couldn't bear to see him the worse for drink. Every night he came home, and he was always the worse, she'd shut herself in her bedroom and hear him rolling about the house and calling for her and breaking the china sometimes. But only sometimes, and he wouldn't have hurt a hair of her head. She was about eighteen and a fine-looking girl, not a film star, mind, not Mr Roberts's type at all, and perhaps she had an Oedipus complex, but she hated her father and she was ashamed of him.'

'What's my type, Mr Evans?'

'Don't pretend not to know, Mr Roberts. Mr Evans means the sort you can take home and show her your stamp collection.'

'I will have hush,' said Mr Thomas.

''Ave 'ush, is the phrase,' Mr Roberts said. 'Mr Thomas, you're afraid we'll think you're patronizing the lower classes if you drop your aspirates.'

'No nasturtiums, Mr Roberts,' said Mr Humphries.

'Mary Phillips fell in love with a young man whom I shall call Marcus David,' Mr Evans went on, still staring at the fire, avoiding his friends' eyes, and speaking to the burning pictures, 'and she told her father: "Father, Marcus and I want to be engaged. I'm bringing him home one night for supper, and you must promise me that you'll be sober."'

'He said: "I'm always sober!" but he wasn't sober when he said it, and after a time he promised.'

'"If you break your word, I'll never forgive you," Mary said to him.'

'Marcus was a wealthy farmer's son from another district, a bit of a Valentino in a bucolic way, if you can imagine that. She invited him to supper, and he came, very handsome, with larded hair. The servants were out. Mr Phillips had gone to a mart that morning and hadn't returned. She answered the door herself. It was a winter's evening.

'Picture the scene. A prim, well-bred country girl, full of fixations and phobias, proud as a duchess, and blushing like a dairymaid, opening the door to her beloved and seeing him standing there on the pitch-black threshold, shy and handsome. This is from my notes.

'Her future hung on that evening as on a thread. "Come in," she insisted. They didn't kiss, but she wanted him to bow and print his lips on her hand. She took him over the house, which had been specially cleaned and polished, and showed him the case with Swansea china in it. There was a portrait gallery, so she showed him the snaps of her mother and the photograph of her father, tall and young and sober, in the suit he hunted otters in. And all the time she was proudly parading their possessions, attempting to prove to Marcus, whose father was a J. P., that her background was prosperous enough for her to be his bride, she was waiting fearfully the entrance of her father.

'"O God," she was praying, when they sat down to a cold supper, "that my father will arrive presentable." Call her a snob, if you will, but remember that the life of country gentry or near gentry, was bound and dedicated by the antiquated totems and fetishes of possession. Over supper she told him her family tree and hoped the supper was to his taste. It should have been a hot supper, but she didn't want him to see the servants who were old and dirty. Her father wouldn't change them because they'd always been with him, and there you see the Toryism of this particular society rampant. To cut a long story (this is only the gist, Mr Thomas). They were halfway through supper, and their conversation was becoming more intimate, and she had almost forgotten her father, when the front door burst open and Mr Phillips staggered into the passage, drunk as a judge. The dining-room door was ajar and they could see him plainly. I will not try to describe Mary's kaleidoscopic emotions as her father rocked and mumbled in a thick voice in the passage. He was a big man – I forgot to tell you – six foot and eighteen stone.

'"Quick! quick! under the table!" she whispered urgently, and she pulled Marcus by the hand and they crouched under the table. What bewilderment Marcus experienced we shall never know.

'Mr Phillips came in and saw nobody and sat down at the table and finished all the supper. He licked both plates clean, and under the table they heard him swearing and guzzling. Every time Marcus fidgeted, Mary said: "Shh!"

'When there was nothing left to eat, Mr Phillips wandered out of the room. They saw his legs. Then, somehow, he climbed upstairs, saying words that made Mary shudder under the table, words of three syllables.'

'Give us three guesses,' said Mr Roberts.

'And she heard him go into his bedroom. She and Marcus crept out of hiding and sat down in front of their empty plates.

' "I don't know how to apologise, Mr David," she said, and she was nearly crying.'

' "There's nothing the matter," he said, he was an amenable young man by all accounts, "he's only been to the mart at Carmarthen. I don't like t.t.s myself."

' "Drink makes men sodden beasts," she said.

'He said she had nothing to worry about and that he didn't mind, and she offered him fruit.

' "What will you think of us, Mr David? I've never seen him like that before."

'The little adventure brought them closer together, and soon they were smiling at one another and her wounded pride was almost healed again, but suddenly Mr Phillips opened his bedroom door and charged downstairs, eighteen stone of him, shaking the house.

' "Go away!" she cried softly to Marcus, "please go away before he comes in!"

'There wasn't time. Mr Phillips stood in the passage in the nude.

'She dragged Marcus under the table again, and she covered her eyes not to see her father. She could hear him fumbling in the hall-stand for an umbrella, and she knew what he was going to do. He was going outside to obey a call of nature. "O God," she prayed, "let him find an umbrella and go out. Not in the passage! Not in the passage!" They heard him shout for his umbrella. She uncovered her eyes and saw him pulling the front door down. He tore it off its hinges and held it flat above him and tottered out into the dark.

' "Hurry! please hurry!" she said. "Leave me now, Mr David." She drove him out from under the table.

' "Please, please go now," she said, "we'll never meet again. Leave me to my shame." She began to cry, and he ran out of the house. And she stayed under the table all night.'

'Is that all?' said Mr Roberts. 'A very moving incident, Emlyn. How did you come by it?'

'How can it be all?' said Mr Humphries. 'It doesn't explain how Mary Phillips reached "Bellevue". We've left her under a table in Carmarthenshire.'

'I think Marcus is a fellow to be despised,' Mr Thomas said. 'I'd never leave a girl like that, would you, Mr Humphries?'

'Under a table, too. That's the bit I like. That's a position. Perspectives were different,' said Mr Roberts, 'in those days. That narrow puritanism is a spent force. Imagine Mrs Evans under the table. And what happened afterwards? Did the girl die of cramp?'

Mr Evans turned from the fire to reprove him. 'Be as flippant as you will, but the fact remains that an incident like that has a lasting effect on a proud, sensitive girl like Mary. I'm not defending her sensitivity, the whole basis of her pride is outmoded. The social system, Mr Roberts, is not in the box. I'm telling you an incident that occurred. Its social implications are outside our concern.'

'I'm put in my place, Mr Evans.'

'What happened to Mary then?'

'Don't vex him, Mr Thomas, he'll bite your head off.'

Mr Evans went out for more parsnip wine, and returning, said:

'What happened next? Oh! Mary left her father, of course. She said she'd never forgive him, and she didn't, so she went to live with her uncle in Cardiganshire, a Dr Emyr Lloyd. He was a J. P. too, and rolling in it, about seventy-five – now, remember the age – with a big practice and influential friends. One of his oldest friends was John William Hughes – that's not his name – the London draper, who had a country house near his. Remember what the great Caradoc Evans says? The Cardies always go back to Wales to die when they've rooked the cockneys and made a packet.

'And the only son, Henry William Hughes, who was a nicely educated young man, fell in love with Mary as soon as he saw her and she forgot Marcus and her shame under the table and she fell in love with him. Now don't look disappointed before I begin, this isn't a love story. But they decided to get married, and John William Hughes gave his consent because Mary's uncle was one of the most respected men in the country and her father had money and it would come to her when he died and he was doing his best.

'They were to be married quietly in London. Everything was

arranged. Mr Phillips wasn't invited. Mary had her trousseau. Dr Lloyd was to give her away. Beatrice and Betti William Hughes were bridesmaids. Mary went up to London with Beatrice and Betti and stayed with a cousin, and Henry William Hughes stayed in the flat above his father's shop, and the day before the wedding Dr Lloyd arrived from the country, saw Mary for tea, and had dinner with John William Hughes. I wonder who paid for it, too. Then Dr Lloyd retired to his hotel. I'm giving you these trivial details so that you can see how orderly and ordinary everything was. There the actors were, safe and sure.

'Next day. Just before the ceremony was to begin, Mary and her cousin, whose name and character are extraneous, and the two sisters, they were both plain and thirty, waited impatiently for Dr Lloyd to call on them. The minutes passed by, Mary was crying, the sisters were sulking, the cousin was getting in everybody's way, but the doctor didn't come. The cousin telephoned the doctor's hotel, but she was told he hadn't spent the night there. Yes, the clerk in the hotel said, he knew the doctor was going to a wedding. No, his bed hadn't been slept in. The clerk suggested that perhaps he was waiting at the church.

'The taxi was ticking away, and that worried Beatrice and Betti, and at last the sisters and the cousin and Mary drove together to the church. A crowd had gathered outside. The cousin poked her head out of the taxi window and asked a policeman to call a churchwarden, and the warden said that Dr Lloyd wasn't there and the groom and the best man were waiting. You can imagine Mary Phillips's feelings when she saw a commotion at the church door and a policeman leading her father out. Mr Phillips had his pockets full of bottles, and how he ever got into the church in the first place no one knew.'

'That's the last straw,' said Mr Roberts.

'Beatrice and Betti said to her: "Don't cry, Mary, the policeman's taking him away. Look! he's fallen in the gutter! There's a splash! Don't take on, it'll be all over soon. You'll be Mrs Henry William Hughes." They were doing their best.

'"You can marry without Dr Lloyd," the cousin told her, and she brightened through her tears – anybody would be crying – and at that moment another policeman –'

'Another!' said Mr Roberts.

' – made his way through the crowd and walked up to the door of the church and sent a message inside. John William Hughes and

Henry William Hughes and the best man came out, and they all talked to the policeman, waving their arms and pointing to the taxi with Mary and the bridesmaids and the cousin in it.

'John William Hughes ran down the path to the taxi and shouted through the window: "Dr Lloyd is dead! We'll have to cancel the wedding."

'Henry William Hughes followed him and opened the taxi door and said: "You must drive home Mary. We've got to go to the police station."

' "And the mortuary," his father said.

'So the taxi drove the bride-to-be home, and the sisters cried worse than she did all the way.'

'That's a sad end,' said Mr Roberts with appreciation. He poured himself another drink.

'It isn't really the end,' Mr Evans said, 'because the wedding wasn't just cancelled. It never came off.'

'But why?' asked Mr Humphries, who had followed the story with a grave expression, even when Mr Phillips fell in the gutter. 'Why should the doctor's death stop everything? She could get someone else to give her away. I'd have done it myself.'

'It wasn't the doctor's death, but where and how he died,' said Mr Evans. 'He died in bed in a bed-sitting-room in the arms of a certain lady. A woman of the town.'

'Kiss me!' Mr Roberts said. 'Seventy-five years old. I'm glad you asked us to remember his age, Mr Evans.'

'But how did Mary Phillips come to live in "Bellevue"? You haven't told us that,' Mr Thomas said.

'The William Hugheses wouldn't have the niece of a man who died in those circumstances –'

'However complimentary to his manhood,' Mr Humphries said, stammering.

'– marry into their family, so she went back to live with her father and he reformed at once – oh! she had a temper those days – and one day she met a traveller in grain and pigs' food and she married him out of spite. They came to live in "Bellevue", and when Mr Phillips died he left his money to the chapel, so Mary got nothing after all.'

'Nor her husband either. What did you say he travelled in?' asked Mr Roberts.

'Grain and pigs' food.'

After that, Mr Humphries read his biography, which was long and sad and detailed and in good prose; and Mr Roberts told a story about the slums, which could not be included in the book.

Then Mr Evans looked at his watch. 'It's midnight. I promised Maud not after midnight. Where's the cat? I've got to put him out; he tears the cushions. Not that I mind. Sambo! Sambo!'

'There he is, Mr Evans, under the table.'

'Like poor Mary,' said Mr Roberts.

Mr Humphries, Mr Roberts, and young Mr Thomas collected their hats and coats from the bannister.

'Do you know what time it is, Emlyn?' Mrs Evans called from upstairs.

Mr Roberts opened the door and hurried out.

'I'm coming now, Maud, I'm just saying good night. Good night,' Mr Evans said in a loud voice. 'Next Friday, nine sharp,' he whispered. 'I'll polish my story up. We'll finish the second chapter and get going on the third. Good night, comrades.'

'Emlyn! Emlyn!' called Mrs Evans.

'Good night, Mary,' said Mr Roberts to the closed door.

The three friends walked down the drive.

Who Do You Wish Was With Us?

Birds in the Cresent trees were singing; boys on bicycles were ringing their bells and pedalling down the slight slope to make the whirrers in their wheels startle the women gabbing on the sunny doorsteps; small girls on the pavement, wheeling young brothers and sisters in prams, were dressed in their summer best and with coloured ribbons; on the circular swing in the public playground, children from the snot school spun themselves happy and sick, crying 'Swing us!' and 'Swing us!' and 'Ooh! I'm falling!'; the morning was as varied and bright as though it were an international or a jubilee when Raymond Price and I, flannelled and hatless, with sticks and haversacks, set out together to walk to the Worm's Head. Striding along, in step, through the square of the residential Uplands, we brushed by young men in knife-creased whites and showing-off blazers, and hockey-legged girls with towels round their necks and celluloid sun-glasses, and struck a letterbox with our sticks, and bullied our way through a crowd of day-trippers who waited at the stop of the Gower-bound buses, and stepped over luncheon baskets, not caring if we trod in them.

'Why can't those bus lizards walk?' Ray said.

'They were born too tired,' I said.

We went on up Sketty Road at a great speed, our haversacks jumping on our backs. We rapped on every gate to give a terrific walker's benediction to the people in the choking houses. Like a breath of fresh air we passed a man in office pin-stripes standing, with a dog-lead in his hand, whistling at a corner. Tossing the sounds and smells of the town from us with the swing of our shoulders and loose-limbed strides, half-way up the road we heard women on an outing call 'Mutt and Jeff!' for Ray was tall and thin and I was short. Streamers flew out of the charabanc. Ray, sucking hard at his bulldog pipe, walked too fast to wave and did not even smile. I wondered whom I had missed among the waving women bowling over the rise. My love to come, with a paper cap on, might have sat at the back of the outing, next to the barrel; but, once away from the familiar roads and swinging towards the coast, I forgot her face and voice, that had been made at night, and breathed the country air in.

'There's a different air here. You breathe, It's like the country,' Ray said, 'and a bit of the sea mixed. Draw it down; it'll blow off the nicotine.'

He spat in his hand. 'Still town grey,' he said.

He put back the spit in his mouth and we walked on with our heads high.

By this time we were three miles from the town. The semi-detached houses, with a tin-roofed garage each and a kennel in the back plot and a mowed lawn, with sometimes a hanging coconut on a pole, or a bird-bath, or a bush like a peacock, grew fewer when we reached the outskirts of the common.

Ray stopped and sighed and said: 'Wait half a sec, I want to fill the old pipe.' He held a match to it as though we were in a storm.

Hot-faced and wet-browed, we grinned at each other. Already the day had brought us close as truants; we were running away, or walking with pride and mischief, arrogantly from the streets that owned us into the unpredictable country. I thought it was against our fate to stride in the sun without the shop-windows dazzling or the music of mowers rising above the birds. A bird's dropping fell on a fence. It was one in the eye for the town. A sheep cried 'Baa!' out of sight, and that would show the Uplands. I did not know what it would show. 'A couple of wanderers in wild Wales,' Ray said, winking, and a lorry carrying cement drove past us towards the golf links. He slapped my haversack and straightened his shoulders. 'Come on. Let's be going.' We walked uphill faster than before.

A party of cyclists had pulled up on the roadside and were drinking dandelion and burdock from paper cups. I saw the empty bottles in a bush. All the boys wore singlets and shorts, and the girls wore open cricket shirts and boys' long grey trousers, with safety-pins for clips at the bottoms.

'There's room for one behind, sonny boy,' a girl on a tandem said to me.

'It won't be a stylish marriage,' Ray said.

'That was quick,' I told Ray as we walked away from them and the boys began to sing.

'God, I like this!' said Ray. On the first rise of the dusty road through the spreading heathered common, he shaded his eyes and looked all round him, smoking like a chimney and pointing with his Irish stick at the distant clumps of trees and sights of the sea between them. 'Down there is Oxwich, but you can't see it. That's a farm. See the roof? No, there, follow my finger. This is the life,' he said.

Side by side, thrashing the low banks, we marched down the very middle of the road, and Ray saw a rabbit running. 'You wouldn't think this was near town. It's wild.'

We pointed out the birds whose names we knew, and the rest of the names we made up. I saw gulls and crows, though the crows may have been rooks, and Ray said that thrushes and swallows and skylarks flew above us as we hurried and hummed.

He stopped to pull some blades of grass. 'They should be straws,' he said, and put them in his mouth next to his pipe. 'God, the sky's blue! Think of me, in the GWR when all this is about. Rabbits and fields and farms. You wouldn't think I'd suffered to look at me now. I could do anything, I could drive cows, I could plough a field.'

His father and sister and brother were dead, and his mother sat all day in a wheel-chair, crippled with arthritis. He was ten years older than I was. He had a lined and bony face and a tight, crooked mouth. His upper lip had vanished.

Alone on the long road, the common in the heat mist wasting for miles on either side, we walked on under the afternoon sun, growing thirsty and drowsy but never slowing our pace. Soon the cycling party rode by, three boys and three girls and the one girl on the tandem, all laughing and ringing.

'How's Shanks's pony?'

'We'll see you on the way back.'

'You'll be walking still.'

'Like a crutch?' They shouted.

Then they were gone. The dust settled again. Their bells rang faintly through the wood around the road before us. The wild common, six miles and a bit from the town, lay back without a figure on it, and, under the trees, smoking hard to keep the gnats away, we leant against a trunk and talked like men, on the edge of an untrodden place, who have not seen another man for years.

'Do you remember Curly Parry?'

I had seen him only two days ago in the snooker-room, but his dimpled face was fading, even as I thought of him, into the colours of our walk, the ash-white of the road, the common heathers, the green and blue of fields and fragmentary sea, and the memory of his silly voice was lost in the sounds of birds and unreasonably moving leaves in the lack of wind.

'I wonder what he's doing now? He should get out more in the open air, he's a proper town boy. Look at us here.' Ray waved his pipe at the trees and leafy sky. 'I wouldn't change this for High Street.'

I looked at us there; a boy and a young man, with faces, under the strange sunburn, pale from the cramped town, out of breath and hot-footed, pausing in the early afternoon on a road through a popular wood, and I could see the unaccustomed happiness in Ray's eyes and the impossible friendliness in mine, and Ray protested against his history each time he wondered or pointed in the country scene and I had more love in me than I could ever want or use.

'Yes, look at us here,' I said, 'dawdling about. Worm's Head is twelve miles off. Don't you want to hear a tramcar, Ray? That's a wood pigeon. See! The boys are out on the streets with the sports special now. Paper! paper! I bet you Curl's potting the red. Come on! come on!'

'Eyes right!' said Ray, 'I's b – d! Remember that story?'

Up the road and out of the wood, and a double-decker roared behind us.

'The Rhossilli bus is coming,' I said.

We both held up our sticks to stop it.

'Why did you stop the bus?' Ray said, when we were sitting upstairs. 'This was a walking holiday.'

'You stopped it as well.'

We sat in front like two more drivers.

'Can't you mind the ruts?' I said.

'You're wobbling,' said Ray.

We opened our haversacks and shared the sandwiches and hard-boiled eggs and meat paste and drank from the thermos in turns.

'When we get home don't say we took a bus,' I said. 'Pretend we walked all day. There goes Oxwich! It doesn't seem far, does it? We'd have had beards by now.'

The bus passed the cyclists crawling up a hill. 'Like a tow along?' I shouted, but they couldn't hear. The girl on the tandem was a long way behind the others.

We sat with our lunch on our laps, forgetting to steer, letting the driver in his box beneath drive where and how he liked on the switch-back road, and saw grey chapels and weather-worn angels; at the feet of the hills farthest from the sea, pretty, pink cottages – horrible, I thought, to live in, for grass and trees would imprison me more securely than any jungle of packed and swarming streets and chimney-roosting roofs – and petrol pumps and hayricks and a man on a cart-horse standing stock still in a ditch, surrounded by flies.

'This is the way to see the country.'

The bus, on a narrow hill, sent two haversacked walkers bounding to the shelter of the hedge, where they stretched out their arms and drew their bellies in.

'That might have been you and me.'

We looked back happily at the men against the hedge. They climbed on to the road, slow as snails continued walking, and grew smaller.

At the entrance to Rhossilli we pushed the conductor's bell and stopped the bus, and walked, with springing steps, the few hundred yards to the village.

'We've done it in pretty good time,' said Ray.

'I think it's a record,' I said.

Laughing on the cliff above the very long golden beach, we pointed out to each other, as though the other were blind, the great rock of the Worm's Head. The sea was out. We crossed over on slipping stones and stood, at last, triumphantly on the windy top. There was monstrous, thick grass there that made us spring-heeled, and we laughed and bounced on it, scaring the sheep who ran up and down the battered sides like goats. Even on this calmest day a wind blew along the Worm. At the end of the humped and serpentine body, more gulls than I had ever seen before cried over their new dead and the droppings of ages. On the point, the sound of my quiet voice was scooped and magnified into a hollow shout, as though the wind around me had made a shell or cave, with blue, intangible roof and sides, as tall and wide as all the arched sky, and the flapping gulls were made thunderous. Standing there, legs apart, one hand on my hip, shading my eyes like Raleigh in some picture, I thought myself alone in the epileptic moment near bad sleep, when the legs grow long and sprout into the night and the heart hammers to wake the neighbours and breath is a hurricane through the elastic room. Instead of becoming small on the great rock poised between sky and sea, I felt myself the size of a breathing building, and only Ray in the world could match my lovely bellow as I said: 'Why don't we live here always? Always and always. Build a bloody house and live like bloody kings!' The word bellowed among the squawking birds, they carried it off to the headland in the drums of their wings; like a tower, Ray pranced on the unsteady edge of a separate rock and beat about with his stick, which could turn into snakes or flames; and we sank to the ground, the rubbery, gull-limed grass, the sheep-piled stones, the pieces of bones and feathers, and crouched at the extreme point of the Peninsula. We were still for so long that the dirty-grey gulls calmed down, and some settled near us.

Then we finished our food.

'This isn't like any other place,' I said. I was almost my own size again, five feet five and eight stone, and my voice didn't sweep any longer up to the amplifying sky. 'It could be in the middle of the sea. You could think the Worm was moving, couldn't you? Guide it to Ireland, Ray. We'll see W. B. Yeats and you can kiss the Blarney. We'll have a fight in Belfast.'

Ray looked out of place on the end of the rock. He would not make himself easy and loll in the sun and roll on to his side to stare down a precipice into the sea, but tried to sit upright as though he were in a hard chair and had nothing to do with his hands. He fiddled with his tame stick and waited for the day to be orderly, for the Head to grow paths and for railings to shoot up on the scarred edges.

'It's too wild for a townee,' I said.

'Townee yourself! Who stopped the bus?'

'Aren't you glad we stopped it? We'd still be walking, like Felix. You're just pretending you don't like it here. You were dancing on the edge.'

'Only a couple of hops.'

'I know what it is, you don't like the furniture. There's not enough sofas and chairs,' I said.

'You think you're a country boy; you don't know a cow from a horse.'

We began to quarrel, and soon Ray felt at home again and forgot the monotonous out-of-doors. If snow had fallen suddenly he would not have noticed. He drew down into himself, and the rock, to him, became dark as a house with the blinds drawn. The sky-high shapes that had danced and bellowed at birds crept down to hide, two small town mutterers in a hollow.

I knew what was going to happen by the way Ray lowered his head and brought his shoulders up so that he looked like a man with no neck, and by the way he sucked his breath in between his teeth. He stared at his dusty white shoes and I knew what shapes his imagination made of them, they were the feet of a man dead in bed, and he was going to talk about his brother. Sometimes, leaning against a fence when we watched football, I caught him staring at his own thin hand; he was thinning it more and more, removing the flesh, seeing Harry's hand in front of him, with the bones appearing through the sensitive skin. If he lost the world around him for a moment, if I left him alone, if he cast his eyes down, if his hand lost its grip on the hard, real fence or the hot bowl of his pipe, he would be back in ghastly bedrooms, carrying cloths and basins and listening for handbells.

'I've never seen such a lot of gulls,' I said. 'Have you ever seen such a lot? Such a lot of gulls. You try and count them. Two of them are fighting up there; look, pecking each other like hens in the air. What'll you bet the big one wins? Old dirty beak! I wouldn't like to have had his dinner, a bit of sheep and dead gull.' I swore at myself for saying the word 'dead'. 'Wasn't it gay enough in town this morning?' I said.

Ray stared at his hand. Nothing could stop him now. 'Wasn't it gay in town this morning? Everybody laughing and smiling in their summer outfits. The kids were playing and everybody was happy; they almost had the band out. I used to hold my father down on the bed when he had fits. I had to change the sheets twice a day for my brother, there was blood on everything. I watched him getting thinner and thinner; in the end you could lift him up with one hand. And his wife wouldn't go to see him because he coughed in her face, Mother couldn't move, and I had to cook as well, cook and nurse and change the sheets and hold father down when he got mad. It's embittered my outlook,' he said.

'But you loved the walk, you enjoyed yourself on the common. It's a wonderful day, Ray. I'm sorry about your brother. Let's explore. Let's climb down to the sea. Perhaps there's a cave with prehistoric drawings, and we can write an article and make a fortune. Let's climb down.'

'My brother used to ring a bell for me; he could only whisper. He used to say: "Ray, look at my legs. Are they thinner today?" '

'The sun's going down. Let's climb.'

'Father thought I was trying to murder him when I held him on the bed. I was holding him down when he died, and he rattled. Mother was in the kitchen in her chair, but she knew he was dead and she started screaming for my sister. Brenda was in a sanatorium in Craigynos. Harry rang the bell in his bedroom when mother started, but I couldn't go to him, and father was dead in the bed.'

'I'm going to climb to the sea,' I said. 'Are you coming?'

He got up out of the hollow into the open world again and followed me slowly over the point and down the steep side; the gulls rose in a storm. I clung to dry, spiked bushes but the roots came out; a foothold crumbled, a crevice for the fingers broke as I groped in it; I scrambled on to a black, flat-backed rock whose head, like a little Worm's, curved out of the sea a few perilous steps away from me, and, drenched by flying water, I gazed up to see Ray and a shower of stones falling. He landed at my side.

'I thought I was done for,' he said, when he had stopped shaking. 'I could see all my past life in a flash.'

'All of it?'

'Well, nearly. I saw my brother's face clear as yours.'

We watched the sun set.

'Like an orange.'

'Like a tomato.'

'Like a goldfish bowl.'

We went one better than the other, describing the sun. The sea beat on our rock, soaked our trouser-legs, stung our cheeks. I took off my shoes and held Ray's hand and slid down the rock on my belly to trail my feet in the sea. Then Ray slid down, and I held him fast while he kicked up water.

'Come back now,' I said, pulling his hand.

'No, no,' he said, 'this is delicious. Let me keep my feet in a bit more. It's warm as the baths.' He kicked and grunted and slapped the rock in a frenzy with his other hand, pretending to drown. 'Don't save me!' he cried. 'I'm drowning! I'm drowning!'

I pulled him back, and in his struggles he brushed a shoe off the rock. We fished it out. It was full of water.

'Never mind, it was worth it. I haven't paddled since I was six. I can't tell you how much I enjoyed it.'

He had forgotten about his father and brother, but I knew that once his joy in the wild, warm water was over he would return to the painful house and see his brother growing thinner. I had heard Harry die so many times, and the mad father was as familiar to me as Ray himself. I knew every cough and cry, every clawing at the air.

'I'm going to paddle once a day from now on,' Ray said. 'I'm going to go down to the sands every evening and have a good paddle. I'm going to splash about and get wet up to my knees. I don't care who laughs.'

He sat still for a minute, thinking gravely of this. 'When I wake up in the mornings there's nothing to look forward to, except on Saturdays,' he said then, 'or when I come up to your house for Lexicon. I may as well be dead. But now I'll be able to wake up and think: "This evening I'm going to splash about in the sea." I'm going to do it again now.' He rolled up his wet trousers and slid down the rock. 'Don't let go.'

As he kicked his legs in the sea, I said: 'This is a rock at the world's end. We're all alone. It all belongs to us, Ray. We can have anybody we like here and keep everybody else away. Who do you wish was with us?'

He was too busy to answer, splashing and snorting, blowing as though his head were under, making circular commotions in the water or lazily skimming the surface with his toes.

'Who would you like to be here on the rock with us?'

He was stretched out like a dead man, his feet motionless in the sea, his mouth on the rim of a rock pool, his hand clutched round my foot.

'I wish George Gray was with us,' I said. 'He's the man from London who's come to live in Norfolk street. You don't know him. He's the most curious man I ever met, queerer than Oscar Thomas, and I thought nobody could ever be queerer than that. George Gray wears glasses, but there's no glass in them, only the frames. You wouldn't know until you came near him. He does all sorts of things. He's a cat's doctor and he goes to somewhere in Sketty every morning to help a woman put her clothes on. She's an old widow, he said, and she can't dress by herself. I don't know how he came to know her. He's only been in town for a month. He's a B.A., too. The things he's got in his pockets! Pincers, and scissors for cats, and lots of diaries. He read me some of the diaries, about the jobs he did in London. He used to go to bed with a policewoman and she used to pay him. She used to go to bed in her uniform. I've never met such a queer man. I wish he was here now. Who do you wish was with us, Ray?'

Ray began to move his feet again, kicking them out straight behind him and bringing them down hard on the water, and then stirring the water about.

'I wish Gwilym was here, too,' I said. 'I've told you about him, He could give a sermon to the sea. This is the very place, there isn't anywhere as lonely as this.' Oh, the beloved sunset! Oh, the terrible sea! Pity the sailors, pity the sinners, pity Raymond Price and me! Oh, the evening is coming like a cloud! Amen. Amen. 'Who do you wish, Ray?'

'I wish my brother was with us,' Ray said. He climbed on to the flat rock and dried his feet. 'I wish Harry was here. I wish he was here now, at this moment, on this rock.'

The sun was nearly right down, halved by the shadowed sea. Cold came up, spraying out of the sea, and I could make a body for it, icy antlers, a dripping tail, a rippling face with fishes passing across it. A wind, cornering the Head, chilled through our summer shirts, and the sea began to cover our rock quickly, our rock already covered with friends, with living and dead, racing against the darkness. We did not speak as we climbed. I thought: 'If we open our mouths we'll both say: "Too late, it's too late." ' We ran over the spring-board grass and the scraping rock needles, down the hollow in which Ray had talked about blood, up rustling humps, and along the ragged flat. We stood on the beginning of the Head and looked down, though both of us could have said, without looking: 'The sea is in.'

The sea was in. The slipping stepping-stones were gone. On the mainland, in the dusk, some little figures beckoned to us. Seven clear figures, jumping and calling. I thought they were the cyclists.

Old Garbo

Mr Farr trod delicately and disgustedly down the dark, narrow stairs like a man on ice. He knew, without looking or slipping, that vicious boys had littered the darkest corners with banana peel; and when he reached the lavatory, the basins would be choked and the chains snapped on purpose. He remembered 'Mr Farr, no father' scrawled in brown, and the day the sink was full of blood that nobody admitted having lost. A girl rushed past him up the stairs, knocked the papers out of his hand, did not apologize, and the loose meg of his cigarette burned his lower lip as he failed to open the lavatory door. I heard from inside his protest and rattlings, the sing-song whine of his voice, the stamping of his small patent-leather shoes, his favourite swear-words – he swore, violently and privately, like a collier used to thinking in the dark – and I let him in.

'Do you always lock the door?' he asked, scurrying to the tiled wall.

'It stuck,' I said.

He shivered, and buttoned.

He was the senior reporter, a great shorthand writer, a chain-smoker, a bitter drinker, very humorous, round-faced and round-bellied, with dart holes in his nose. Once, I thought as I stared at him then in the lavatory of the offices of the *Tawe News* he might have been a mincing-mannered man, with a strut and a cane to balance it, a watch-chain across the waistcoat, a gold tooth, even, perhaps a flower from his own garden in his buttonhole. But now each attempt at a precise gesture was caked and soaked before it began; when he placed the tips of his thumb and forefinger together, you saw only the cracked nails in mourning and the Woodbine stains. He gave me a cigarette and shook his coat to hear matches.

'Here's a light, Mr Farr,' I said.

It was good to keep in with him; he covered all the big stories, the occasional murder, such as when Thomas O'Connor used a bottle on his wife – but that was before my time – the strikes, the best fires. I wore my cigarette as he did, a hanging badge of bad habits.

'Look at that word on the wall,' he said. 'Now that's ugly. There's a time and a place.'

Winking at me, scratching his bald patch as though the thought came from there, he said: 'Mr Solomon wrote that.'

Mr Solomon was the news editor and a Wesleyan.

'Old Solomon,' said Mr Farr, 'he'd cut every baby in half just for pleasure.'

I smiled and said: 'I bet he would!' But I wished that I could have answered in such a way as to show for Mr Solomon the disrespect I did not feel. This was a great male moment, and the most enjoyable since I had begun work three weeks before: leaning against the cracked tiled wall, smoking and smiling, looking down at my shoe scraping circles on the wet floor, sharing a small wickedness with an old, important man. I should have been writing up last night's performance of the *The Crucifixion* or loitering, with my new hat on one side, through the Christmas-Saturday-crowded town in the hopes of an accident.

'You must come along with me one night,' Mr Farr said slowly. 'We'll go down the "Fishguard" on the docks; you can see the sailors knitting there in the public bar. Why not tonight? And there's shilling women in the "Lord Jersey". You stick to Woodbines, like me.'

He washed his hands as a young boy does, wiping the dirt on the roll-towel, stared in the mirror over the basin, twirled the ends of his moustache, and saw them droop again immediately after.

'Get to work,' he said.

I walked into the lobby, leaving him with his face pressed to the glass and one finger exploring his bushy nostrils.

It was nearly eleven o'clock, and time for a cocoa or a Russian tea in the Café Royal, above the tobacconist's in High Street, where junior clerks and shop assistants and young men working in their fathers' offices or articled to stock brokers and solicitors meet every morning for gossip and stories. I made my way through the crowds: the Valley men, up for the football; the country shoppers, the window gazers; the silent, shabby men at the corners of the packed streets, standing in isolation in the rain; the press of mothers and prams; old women in black, brooched dresses carrying frails, smart girls with shining mackintoshes and splashed stockings; little, dandy lascars, bewildered by the weather; business men with wet spats; through a mushroom forest of umbrellas; and all the time I thought of the paragraphs I would never write. I'll put you all in a story by and by.

Mrs Constable, laden and red with shopping, recognized me as she charged out of Woolworth's like a bull. 'I haven't seen your mother for ages! Oh! this Christmas rush! Remember me to Florrie. I'm going to have a cup of tea at the "Modern". There,' she said, 'I've lost a pan!'

I saw Percy Lewis, who put chewing gum in my hair at school.

A tall man stared at the doorway of a hat shop, resisting the crowds, standing hard and still. All the moving irrelevancies of good news grew and acted around me as I reached the café entrance and climbed the stairs.

'What's for you, Mr Swaffer?'

'The usual, please.' Cocoa and free biscuit.

Most of the boys were there already. Some wore the outlines of moustaches, others had sideboards and crimped hair, some smoked curved pipes and talked with them gripped between their teeth, there were pin-stripe trousers and hard collars, one daring bowler.

'Sit by here,' said Leslie Bird. He was in the boots at Dan Lewis's.

'Been to the flicks this week, Thomas?'

'Yes. The Regal. *White Lies*. Damned good show, too! Connie Bennett was great! Remember her in the foam-bath, Leslie?'

'Too much foam for me, old man.'

The broad vowels of the town were narrowed in, the rise and fall of the family accent was caught and pressed.

At the top window of the International Stores across the street a group of uniformed girls were standing with tea-cups in their hands. One of them waved a handkerchief. I wondered if she waved it to me. 'There's that dark piece again,' I said. 'She's got her eye on you.'

'They look all right in their working clothes,' he said. 'You catch them when they're all dolled up, they're awful. I knew a little nurse once, she looked a peach in her uniform, really refined; no, really, I mean. I picked her up on the prom one night. She was in her Sunday best. There's a difference; she looked like a bit of Marks and Spencer's.' As he talked he was looking through the window with the corners of his eyes.

The girl waved again, and turned away to giggle.

'Pretty cheap!' he said.

I said: 'And little Audrey laughed and laughed.'

He took out a plated cigarette case. 'Present,' he said. 'I bet my uncle with three balls has it in a week. Have a best Turkish.'

His matches were marked Allsopps. 'Got them from the "Carlton",' he said. 'Pretty girl behind the bar: knows her onions. You've never been there, have you? Why don't you drop in for one tonight? Gil

Morris'll be there, too. We usually sink a couple Saturdays. There's a hop at the "Melba".'

'Sorry,' I said. 'I'm going out with our senior reporter. Some other time, Leslie. So long!'

I paid my threepence.

'Good morning, Cassie.'

'Good morning, Hannen.'

The rain stopped and High Street shone. Walking on the tram-lines, a neat man held his banner high and prominently feared the Lord. I knew him as a Mr Matthews, who had been saved some years ago from British port and who now walked every night, in rubber shoes with a prayer book and a flashlight, through the lanes. There went Mr Evans the Produce through the side-door of the 'Bugle'. Three typists rushed by for lunch, poached egg and milk-shake, leaving a lavender scent. Should I take the long way through the Arcade, and stop to look at the old man with the broken, empty pram who always stood there, by the music store, and who would take off his cap and set his hair alight for a penny? It was only a trick to amuse boys, and I took the short cut down Chapel Street, on the edge of the slum called the Strand past the enticing Italian chip shop where young men who had noticing parents bought twopennyworth on late nights to hide their breath before the last tram home. Then up the narrow office stairs and into the reporters' room.

Mr Solomon was shouting down the telephone. I heard the last words: 'You're just a dreamer, Williams.' He put the receiver down. 'That boy's a buddy dreamer,' he said to no one. He never swore.

I finished my report of *The Crucifixion* and handed it to Mr Farr.

'Too much platitudinous verbosity.'

Half an hour later, Ted Williams, dressed to golf, sidled in, smiling, thumbed his nose at Mr Solomon's back, and sat quietly in a corner with a nail-file.

I whispered: 'What was he slanging you for?'

'I went out on a suicide, a tram conductor called Hopkins, and the widow made me stay and have a cup of tea. That's all.' He was very winning in his ways, more like a girl than a man who'd dreamed of Fleet Street and spent his summer fortnight walking up and down past the *Daily Express* and looking for celebrities in the pubs.

Saturday was my free afternoon. It was one o'clock and time to leave, but I stayed on; Mr Farr said nothing. I pretended to be busy scribbling words and caricaturing with no likeness Mr Solomon's toucan profile and the snub copy-boy who whistled out of tune behind the windows of the telephone box. I wrote my name, 'Reporters' Room, *Tawe News*, Tawe, South Wales, England, Europe, The Earth.' And a list of books I had not written: 'Land of My Fathers, a study of the Welsh Character in all its aspects'; 'Eighteen, a Provincial Autobiography'; 'The Merciless Ladies, a Novel'. Still Mr Farr did not look up. I wrote 'Hamlet'. Surely Mr Farr, stubbornly transcribing his council notes had not forgotten. I heard Mr Solomon mutter, leaning over his shoulder: 'To aitch with Alderman Daniels.' Half-past one. Ted was in a dream. I spent a long time putting on my overcoat, tied my Old Grammarian's scarf one way and then another.

'Some people are too lazy to take their half-days off,' said Mr Farr suddenly. 'Six o'clock in the "Lamps" back bar.' He did not turn round or stop writing.

'Going for a nice walk?' asked my mother.

'Yes, on the common. Don't keep tea waiting.'

I went to the Plaza. 'Press,' I said to the girl with the Tyrolean hat and skirt.

'There's been two reporters this week.'

'Special notice.'

She showed me to a seat. During the educational film, with the rude seeds hugging and sprouting in front of my eyes and plants like arms and legs, I thought of the bob women and the pansy sailors in the dives. There might be a quarrel with razors, and once Ted Williams found a lip outside the Mission to Seamen. It had a small moustache. The sinuous plants danced on the screen. If only Tawe were a larger sea-town, there would be curtained rooms underground with blue films. The potato's life came to an end. Then I entered an American college and danced with the president's daughter. The hero, called Lincoln, tall and dark with good teeth, I displaced quickly, and the girl spoke my name as she held his shadow, the singing college chorus in sailors' hats and bathing dresses called me big boy and king, Jack Oakie and I sped up the field, and on the shoulders of the crowd the president's daughter and I brought across the shifting-coloured curtain with a kiss that left me giddy and bright-eyed as I walked out of the cinema into the strong lamplight and the new rain.

A whole wet hour to waste in the crowds. I watched the queue outside the Empire and studied the posters of *Nuit de Paris*, and thought of the long legs and startling faces of the chorus girls I had seen walking arm in arm, earlier that week, up and down the streets in the winter sunshine, their mouths, I remembered remarking and treasuring for the first page of 'The Merciless Ladies' that was never begun, like crimson scars, their hair raven-black or silver; their scent and paint reminded me of the hot and chocolate-coloured East, their eyes were pools. Lola de Kenway, Babs Courcey, Ramona Day would be with me all my life. Until I died, of a wasting, painless disease, and spoke my prepared last words, they would always walk with me, recalling me to my dead youth in the vanished High Street nights when the shop windows were blazing, and singing came out of the pubs, and sirens from the Hafod sat in the steaming chip shops with their handbags on their knees and their ear-rings rattling. I stopped to look at the window of Dirty Black's, the Fancy Man, but it was innocent; there were only itching and sneezing powders, stink bombs, rubber pens, and Charlie masks; all the novelties were inside, but I dared not go in for fear a woman should serve me, Mrs Dirty Black with a moustache and knowing eyes, or a thin, dog-faced girl I saw there once, who winked and smelt of seaweed. In the market I bought pink cachous. You never knew.

The back room of 'The Three Lamps' was full of elderly men. Mr Farr had not arrived. I leant against the bar, between an alderman and a solicitor, drinking bitter, wishing that my father could see me now and glad, at the same time, that he was visiting Uncle A. in Aberavon. He could not fail to see that I was a boy no longer, not fail to be angry at the angle of my fag and my hat and the threat of the clutched tankard. I liked the taste of beer, its live, white lather, its brass-bright depths, the sudden world through the wet brown walls of the glass, the tilted rush to the lips and the slow swallowing down to the lapping belly, the salt on the tongue, the foam at the corners.

'Same again, miss.' She was middle-aged. 'One for you, miss?'

'Not during hours, ta all the same.'

'You're welcome.'

Was that an invitation to drink with her afterwards, to wait at the back door until she glided out, and then to walk through the night along the promenade and sands, on to a soft dune where couples lay loving under their coats and looking at the Mumbles lighthouse? She was plump and plain, her netted hair was auburn and wisped with grey. She gave me my change like a mother giving her boy pennies for the pictures, and I would not go out with her if she put cream on it.

Mr Farr hurried down High Street, savagely refusing laces and matches, averting his eyes from the shabby crowds. He knew that the poor and the sick and the ugly, unwanted people were so close around him that, with one look of recognition, one gesture of sympathy, he would be lost among them and the evening would be spoiled for ever.

'You're a pint man then,' he said at my elbow.

'Good evening, Mr Farr. Only now and then for a change. What's yours? Dirty night,' I said.

Safe in a prosperous house, out of the way of the rain and the unsettling streets, where the poor and the past could not touch him, he took his glass lazily in the company of business and professional men and raised it to the light. 'It's going to get dirtier,' he said. 'You wait till the "Fishguard". Here's health! You can see the sailors knitting there. And the old fish-girls in the "Jersey". Got to go to the w. for a breath of fresh air.'

Mr Evans the Producer came in quickly through a side door hidden by curtains, whispered his drink, shielded it with his overcoat, swallowed it in secrecy.

'Similar,' said Mr Farr, 'and half for his nibs.'

The bar was too high class to look like Christmas. A notice said 'No Ladies'.

We left Mr Evans gulping in his tent.

Children screamed in Goat Street, and one boy, out of season, pulled my sleeve, crying: 'Penny for the guy!' Big women in men's caps barricaded their doorways, and a posh girl gave us the wink at the corner of the green iron convenience opposite the Carlton Hotel. We entered to music, the bar was hung with ribbons and balloons, a tubercular tenor clung to the piano, behind the counter Leslie Bird's pretty barmaid was twitting a group of young men who leant far over and asked to see her garters and invited her to gins and limes and lonely midnight walks and moist adventures in the cinema. Mr Farr sneered down his glass as I watched the young men enviously and saw how much she liked their ways, how she slapped their hands lightly and wriggled back, in pride of her prettiness and gaiety, to pull the beer-handles.

'Toop little Twms from the Valleys. There'll be some puking to-night,' he said with pleasure.

Other young men, sleek-haired, pale, and stocky, with high cheek-bones and deep eyes, bright ties, double-breasted waistcoats and wide trousers, some pocked from the pits, their broad hands scarred and damaged, all exultantly half-drunk, stood singing round the piano, and the tenor with the fallen chest led in a clear voice. Oh! to be able to join in the suggestive play or the rocking choir, to shout *Bread of Heaven*, with my shoulders back and my arms linked with Little Moscow, or to be called 'saucy' and 'a one' as I joked and ogled at the counter, making innocent, dirty love that could come to nothing among the spilt beer and piling glasses.

'Let's get away from the bloody nightingales,' said Mr Farr.

'Too much bloody row,' I said.

'Now we're coming to somewhere.' We crawled down Strand alleys by the side of the mortuary, through a gas-lit lane where hidden babies cried together and reached the 'Fishguard' door as a man, muffled like Mr Evans, slid out in front of us with a bottle or a black-jack in one gloved hand. The bar was empty. An old man whose hands trembled sat behind the counter, staring at his turnip watch.

'Merry Christmas, Pa.'

'Good evening, Mr F.'

'Drop of rum, Pa.'

A red bottle shook over two glasses.

'Very special poison, son.'

'This'll make your eyes bulge,' said Mr Farr.

My iron head stood high and firm, no sailors' rum could rot the rock of my belly. Poor Leslie Bird the port-sipper, and little Gil Morris who marked dissipation under his eyes with a blacklead every Saturday night, I wished they could have seen me now, in the dark, stunted room with photographs of boxers peeling on the wall.

'More poison, Pa,' I said.

'Where's the company tonight? gone to the Riviera?'

'They're in the snuggery, Mr F., there's a party for Mrs Prothero's daughter.'

In the back room, under a damp royal family, a row of black-dressed women on a hard bench sat laughing and crying, short glasses lined by their Guinnesses. On an opposite bench two men in jerseys drank appreciatively, nodding at the emotions of the women. And on the one chair, in the middle of the room, an old woman, with a bonnet tied under her chins, a feather boa, and white gym-shoes, tittered and wept above the rest. We sat on the men's bench. One of the two touched his cap with a sore hand.

'What's the party, Jack?' asked Mr Farr. 'Meet my colleague, Mr Thomas; this is Jack Stiff, the mortuary keeper.'

Jack Stiff spoke from the side of his mouth. 'It's Mrs Prothero there. We call her Old Garbo because she isn't like her, see. She had a message from the hospital about an hour ago, Mrs Harris's Winifred brought it here, to say her second daughter's died in pod.'

'Baby girl dead, too,' said the man at his side.

'So all the old girls came round to sympathize, and they made a big collection for her, and now she's beginning to drink it up and treating round. We've had a couple of pints from her already.'

'Shameful!'

The rum burned and kicked in the hot room, but my head felt tough as a hill and I could write twelve books before morning and roll the 'Carlton' barmaid, like a barrel, the length of Tawe sands.

'Drinks for the troops!'

Before a new audience, the women cried louder, patting Mrs Prothero's knees and hands, adjusting her bonnet, praising her dead daughter.

'What'll you have, Mrs Prothero, dear?'

'No, have it with me, dear, best in the house.'

'Well, a Guinness tickles my fancy.'

'And a little something in it, dear.'

'Just for Margie's sake, then.'

'Think if she was here now, dear, singing *One of the Ruins* or *Cockles and Mussels*; she had a proper madam's voice.'

'Oh, don't, Mrs Harris!'

'There, we're only bucking you up. Grief killed the cat, Mrs Prothero. Let's have a song together, dear.'

'The pale moon was rising above the grey mountain,
The sun was declining beneath the blue sea,
When I strolled with my love to the pure crystal fountain,'

Mrs Prothero sang.

'It was her daughter's favourite song,' said Jack Stiff's friend.

Mr Farr tapped me on the shoulder; his hand fell slowly from a great height and his thin, bird's voice spoke from a whirring circle on the ceiling. 'A drop of out-of-doors for you and me.' The gamps and bonnets, the white gym-shoes, the bottles and the mildew king, the singing mortuary man, the *Rose of Tralee*, swam together in the snuggery; two small men, Mr Farr and his twin brother, led me on an ice-rink to the door, and the night air slapped me down. The evening happened suddenly. A wall slumped over and knocked off my trilby; Mr Farr's brother disappeared under the cobbles. Here came a wall like a buffalo; dodge him, son. Have a drop of angostura, have a drop of brandy, Fernet Branca, Polly, Ooo! the mother's darling! have a hair of the dog.

'Feeling better now?'

I sat in a plush chair I had never seen before, sipping a mothball drink and appreciating an argument between Ted Williams and Mr

Farr. Mr Farr was saying sternly: 'You came in here to look for sailors.'

'No, I didn't then,' said Ted. 'I came for local colour.'

The notices on the walls were: '"The Lord Jersey". Prop.: Titch Thomas'. 'No Betting'. 'No Swearing, B – you.' 'The Lord helps Himself, but you mustn't.' 'No Ladies allowed, except Ladies.'

'This is a funny pub,' I said. 'See the notices?'

'Okay now?'

'I'm feeling upsydaisy.'

'There's a pretty girl for you. Look, she's giving you the glad.'

'But she's got no nose.'

My drink, like winking, had turned itself into beer. A hammer tapped. 'Order! order!' At a sound in a new saloon a collarless chairman with a cigar called on Mr Jenkins to provide *The Lily of Laguna*.

'By request,' Said Mr Jenkins.

'Order! order! for Katie Sebastopol Street. What is it, Katie?'

She sang the National Anthem.

'Mr Fred Jones will supply his usual dirty one.'

A broken baritone voice spoiled the chorus: I recognised it as my own, and drowned it.

A girl of the Salvation Army avoided the arms of two firemen and sold them a *War Cry*.

A young man with a dazzling handkerchief round his head, black and white holiday shoes with holes for the toes, and no socks, danced until the bar cried: 'Mabel!'

Ted clapped at my side. 'That's style! "Nijinsky of the Nightworld", there's a story! Wonder if I can get an interview?'

'Half a crack,' said Mr Farr.

'Don't make me cross.'

A wind from the docks tore up the street, I heard the rowdy dredger in the bay and a boat blowing to come in, the gas-lamps bowed and bent, then again smoke closed about the stained walls with George and Mary dripping above the women's bench, and Jack Stiff whispered, holding his hand in front of him like the paw of an animal: 'Old Garbo's gone.'

The sad and jolly women huddled together.

'Mrs Harris's little girl got the message wrong. Old Garbo's daughter's right as rain, the baby was born dead. Now the old girls want their money back, but they can't find Garbo anywhere.' He licked his hand. 'I know where she's gone.'

His friend said: 'To a boozer over the bridge.'

In low voices the women reviled Mrs Prothero, liar adulteress, mother of bastards, thief.

'She got you know what.'

'Never cured it.'

'Got Charlie tattooed on her.'

'Three and eight she owes me.'

'Two and ten.'

'Money for my teeth.'

'One and a tanner out of my Old Age.'

Who kept filling my glass? Beer ran down my cheek and my collar. My mouth was full of saliva. The bench spun. The cabin of the 'Fishguard' tilted. Mr Farr retreated slowly; the telescope twisted, and his face, with wide and hairy nostrils, breathed against mine.

'Mr Thomas is going to get sick.'

'Mind your brolly, Mrs Arthur.'

'Take his head.'

The last tram clanked home. I did not have the penny for the fare. 'You get off here. Careful!' The revolving hill to my father's house reached to the sky. Nobody was up. I crept to a wild bed, and the wallpaper lakes converged and sucked me down.

Sunday was a quiet day, though St Mary's bells, a mile away, rang on, long after church time, in the holes of my head. Knowing that I would never drink again, I lay in bed until midday dinner and remembered the unsteady shapes and far-off voices of the ten o'clock town. I read the newspapers. All news was bad that morning, but an article called 'Our Lord was a Flower-lover' moved me to tears of bewilderment and contrition. I excused myself from the Sunday joint and three vegetables.

In the park in the afternoon I sat alone near the deserted bandstand. I caught a ball of waste paper that the wind blew down the gravel path towards the rockery, and, straightening it out and holding it on my knee, wrote the first three lines of a poem without hope. A dog nosed me out where I crouched, behind a bare tree in the cold, and rubbed its nose against my hand. 'My only friend,' I said. It stayed with me up to the early dusk, sniffing and scratching.

On Monday morning, with shame and hate, afraid to look at them again, I destroyed the article and the poem, throwing the pieces on to the top of the wardrobe, and I told Leslie Bird in the tram to the office: 'You should have been with us, Saturday, Christ!'

Early on Tuesday night, which was Christmas Eve, I walked, with a borrowed half-crown, into the back room of the 'Fishguard'. Jack Stiff was alone. The women's bench was covered with sheets of newspaper. A bunch of balloons hung from the lamp.

'Here's health!'

'Merry Christmas!'

'Where's Mrs Prothero?'

His hand was bandaged now. 'Oh! You haven't heard? She spent all the collection money. She took it over the bridge to the "Heart's Delight". She didn't let one of the old girls see her. It was over a pound. She'd spent a lot of it before they found her daughter wasn't dead. She couldn't face them then. Have this one with me. So she finished it up by stop-tap Monday. Then a couple of men from the banana boats saw her walking across the bridge, and she stopped half-way. But they weren't in time.'

'Merry Christmas!'

'We got a pair of gym-shoes on our slab.'

None of Old Garbo's friends came in that night.

When I showed this story a long time later to Mr Farr, he said: 'You got it all wrong. You got the people mixed. The boy with the handkerchief danced in the "Jersey". Fred Jones was singing in the "Fishguard". Never mind. Come and have one tonight in the "Nelson". There's a girl down there who'll show you where the sailor bit her. And there's a policeman who knew Jack Johnson.'

'I'll put them all in a story by and by,' I said.

One Warm Saturday

The young man in a sailor's jersey, sitting near the summer huts to see the brown and white women coming out and the groups of pretty-faced girls with pale vees and scorched backs who picked their way delicately on ugly, red-toed feet over the sharp stones to the sea, drew on the sand a large, indented woman's figure; and a naked child, just out of the sea, ran over it and shook water, marking on the figure two wide wet eyes and a hole in the footprinted middle. He rubbed the woman away and drew a paunched man; the child ran over it, tossing her hair, and shook a row of buttons down its belly and a line of drops, like piddle in a child's drawing, between the long legs stuck with shells.

In a huddle of picnicking women and their children, stretched out limp and damp in the sweltering sun or fussing over paper carriers or building castles that were at once destroyed by the tattered march of other picnickers to different pieces of the beach, among the ice-cream cries, the angrily happy shouts of boys playing ball, and the screams of girls as the sea rose to their waists, the young man sat alone with the shadows of his failure at his side. Some silent husbands, with rolled up trousers and suspenders dangling, padded slowly on the border of the sea, paddling women, in thick, black picnic dresses, laughed at their own legs, dogs chased stones, and one proud boy rode the water on a rubber seal. The young man, in his wilderness, saw the holiday Saturday set down before him, false and pretty, as a flat picture under the vulgar sun; the disporting families with paper bags, buckets and spades, parasols and bottles, the happy, hot, and aching girls with sunburn liniments in their bags, the bronzed young men with chests, and the envious, white young men in waistcoats, the thin, pale, hairy, pathetic legs of the husbands silently walking through the water, the plump and curly, shaven-headed and bowed-backed children up to no sense with unrepeatable delight in the dirty sand, moved him, he thought dramatically in his isolation, to an old shame and pity; outside all holiday, like a young man doomed for ever to the company of his maggots, beyond the high and ordinary, sweating, sun-awakened power and stupidity of the summer flesh on a day and a world out, he caught the ball that a small boy had whacked into the air with a tin tray, and rose to throw it back.

The boy invited him to play. A friendly family stood waiting some way off, the tousled women with their dresses tucked in their knickers, the bare-footed men in shirt-sleeves, a number of children in slips and cut-down underwear. He bowled bitterly to a father standing with a tray before the wicket of hats. 'The lone wolf playing ball,' he said to himself as the tray whirled. Chasing the ball towards the sea, passing undressing women with a rush and a wink, tripping over a castle into a coil of wet girls lying like snakes, soaking his shoes as he grabbed the ball off a wave, he felt his happiness return in a boast of the body, and, 'Look out, Duckworth, here's a fast one coming,' he cried to the mother behind the hats. The ball bounced on a boy's head. In and out of the scattered families, among the sandwiches and clothes, uncles and mothers fielded the bouncing ball. A bald man, with his shirt hanging out, returned it in the wrong direction, and a collie carried it into the sea. Now it was mother's turn with the tray. Tray and ball together flew over her head. An uncle in a panama smacked the ball to the dog, who swam with it out of reach. They offered the young man egg-and-cress sandwiches and warm stout, and he and an uncle and a father sat down on the *Evening Post* until the sea touched their feet.

Alone again, hot and unhappy, for the boasting minute when he ran among the unknown people lying and running loudly at peace was struck away, like a ball, he said, into the sea, he walked to a space on the beach where a hell-fire preacher on a box marked 'Mr Matthews' was talking to a congregation of expressionless women. Boys with pea-shooters sat quietly near him. A ragged man collected nothing in a cap. Mr Matthews shook his cold hands, stormed at the holiday, and cursed the summer from his shivering box. He cried for new warmth. The strong sun shone into his bones, and he buttoned his coat collar. Valley children, with sunken, impudent eyes, quick tongues and singing voices, chests thin as shells, gathered round the Punch and Judy and the Stop Me tricycles, and he denied them all. He contradicted the girls in the underclothes combing and powdering, and the modest girls cleverly dressing under tents of towels.

As Mr Matthews cast down the scarlet town, drove out the bare-bellied boys who danced around the ice-cream man, wound the girls' sunburnt thighs about with his black overcoat – 'Down! down!' he cried, 'the night is upon us' – the young man in dejection stood, with a shadow at his shoulder, and thought of Porthcawl's Coney beach, where his friends were rocking with girls on the Giant Racer or tearing in the Ghost Train down the skeletons' tunnel. Leslie Bird would have his arms full of coconuts. Brenda was with Herbert at the rifle-range. Gil Morris was buying Molly a cocktail with a cherry at the 'Esplanade'. Here he stood, listening to Mr Matthews, the retired drinker, crying darkness on the evening sands, with money hot in his pocket and Saturday burning away.

In his loneliness he had refused their invitations. Herbert, in his low, red sports car, GB at the back, a sea-blown nymph on the radiator, called at his father's house, but he said: 'I'm not in the mood, old man. I'm going to spend a quiet day. Enjoy yourselves. Don't take too much pop.' Only waiting for the sun to set, he stood in the sad circle with the pleasureless women who were staring at a point in the sky behind their prophet, and wished the morning back. Oh, boy! to be wasting his money now on the rings and ranges of the fair, to be sitting in the chromium lounge with a short worth one and six and a Turkish cigarette, telling the latest one to the girls, seeing the sun, through the palms in the lounge window, sink over the promenade, over the Bath chairs, the cripples and widows, the beach-trousered, kerchiefed, weekend wives, the smart, kiss-curled girls with plain and spectacled girl friends, the innocent, swaggering, loud bad boys, and the poms at the ankles, and the cycling sweet-men. Ronald had sailed to Ilfracombe on the *Lady Moira*, and, in the thick saloon, with a party from Brynhyfryd, he'd be knocking back nips without a thought that on the sands at home his friend was alone and pussyfoot at six o'clock, and the evening dull as a chapel. All his friends had vanished into their pleasures.

He thought: Poets live and walk with their poems; a man with visions needs no other company; Saturday is a crude day; I must go home and sit in my bedroom by the boiler. But he was not a poet living and walking, he was a young man in a sea town on a warm bank holiday, with two pounds to spend; he had no visions, only two pounds and a small body with its feet on the littered sand; serenity was for old men; and he moved away, over the railway points, on to the tramlined road.

He snarled at the flower clock in Victoria Gardens.

'And what shall a prig do now?' he said aloud, causing a young woman on a bench opposite the white-tiled urinal to smile and put her novel down.

She had chestnut hair arranged high on her head in an old-fashioned way, in loose coils and a bun, and a Woolworth's white rose grew out of it and drooped to touch her ear. She wore a white frock with a red paper flower pinned on the breast, and rings and bracelets that came from a fun-fair stall. Her eyes were small and quite green.

He remarked, carefully and coldly in one glance, all the unusual details of her appearance; it was the calm, unstartled certainty of her bearing before his glance from head to foot, the innocent knowledge, in her smile and the set of her head, that she was defended by her gentleness and accessible strangeness against all rude encounters and picking looks, that made his fingers tremble. Though her frock was long and the collar high, she could as well be naked there on the blistered bench. Her smile confessed her body bare and spotless and willing and warm under the cotton, and she waited without guilt.

How beautiful she is, he thought, with his mind on words and his eyes on her hair and red and white skin, how beautifully she waits for me, though she does not know she is waiting and I can never tell her.

He had stopped and was staring. Like a confident girl before a camera, she sat smiling, her hands folded, her head slightly to one side so that the rose brushed her neck. She accepted his admiration. The girl in a million took his long look to herself, and cherished his stupid love.

Midges flew into his mouth. He hurried on shamefully. At the gates of the gardens he turned to see her for the last time on earth. She had lost her calm with his abrupt and awkward going, and stared in confusion after him. One hand was raised as though to beckon him back. If he waited, she would call him. He walked round the corner and heard her voice, a hundred voices, and all hers, calling his name, and a hundred names that were all his, over the bushy walls.

And what shall the terrified prig of a love-mad young man do next? he asked his reflection silently in the distorting mirror of the empty 'Victoria' saloon. His ape-like hanging face, with 'Bass' across his forehead, gave back a cracked sneer.

If Venus came in on a plate, said the two red, melon-slice lips, I would ask for vinegar to put on her.

She could drive my guilt out; she could smooth away my shame; why didn't I stop to talk to her? he asked.

You saw a queer tart in a park, his reflection answered, she was a child of nature, oh my! oh my! Did you see the dewdrops in her hair? Stop talking to the mirror like a man in a magazine, I know you too well.

A new head, swollen and lop-jawed, wagged behind his shoulder. He spun round to hear the barman say:

'Has the one and only let you down? You look like death warmed up. Have this one on the house. Free beer today. Free X's.' He pulled the beer handle. 'Only the best served here. Straight from the rust. You do look queer,' he said, 'the only one saved from the wreck and the only wreck saved. Here's looking at you!' He drank the beer he had drawn.

'May I have a glass of beer, please?'

'What do you think this is, a public house?'

On the polished table in the middle of the saloon the young man drew, with a finger dipped in strong, the round head of a girl and piled a yellow froth of hair upon it.

'Ah! dirty, dirty!' said the barman, running round from behind the counter and rubbing the head away with a dry cloth.

Shielding the dirtiness with his hat, the young man wrote his name on the edge of the table and watched the letters dry and fade.

Through the open bay-window, across the useless railway covered with sand, he saw the black dots of bathers, the stunted huts, the jumping dwarfs round the Punch and Judy, and the tiny religious circle. Since he had walked and played down there in the crowded wilderness excusing his despair, searching for company though he refused it, he had found his own true happiness and lost her all in one bewildering and clumsy half a minute by the 'Gentlemen' and the flower clock. Older and wiser and no better, he would have looked in the mirror to see if his discovery and loss had marked themselves upon his face in shadows under the eyes or lines about the mouth, were it not for the answer he knew he would receive from the distorted reflection.

The barman came to sit near him, and said in a false voice; 'Now you tell me all about it, I'm a regular storehouse of secrets.'

'There isn't anything to tell. I saw a girl in Victoria Gardens and I was too shy to speak to her. She was a piece of God help us all right.'

Ashamed of his wish to be companionable, even in the depth of love and distress, with her calm face before his eyes and her smile reproving and forgiving him as he spoke, the young man defiled his girl on the bench, dragged her down into the spit and sawdust and dolled her up to make the barman say:

'I like them big myself. Once round Bessy, once round the gasworks. I missed the chance of a lifetime, too. Fifty lovelies in the nude and I'd left my Bunsen burner at home.'

'Give me the same, please.'

'You mean similar.'

The barman drew a glass of beer, drank it, and drew another.

'I always have one with the customers,' he said, 'it puts us on even terms. Now we're just two heart-broken bachelors together.' He sat down again.

'You can't tell me anything I don't know,' he said. 'I've seen over twenty chorines from the Empire in this bar, drunk as printers. Oh, les girls! les limbs!'

'Will they be in tonight?'

'There's only a fellow sawing a woman in half this week.'

'Keep a half for me.'

A drunk man walked in on an invisible white line, and the barman, reeling in sympathy across the room, served him with a pint. 'Free beer today,' he said. 'Free X's. You've been out in the sun.'

'I've been out in the sun all day,' said the man.

'I thought you looked sunburnt.'

'That's drink,' said the man. 'I've been drinking.'

'The holiday is drawing to an end,' the young man whispered into his glass. Bye-bye blackbird, the moment is lost, he thought, examining, with an interest he could not forgive, the comic coloured postcards of mountain-buttocked women on the beach and hen-pecked, pin-legged men with telescopes, pasted on the wall beneath the picture of a terrier drinking stout; and now, with a jolly barman and a drunk in a crushed cap, he was mopping the failing day down. He tipped his hat over his forehead, and a lock of hair that fell below the hat tickled his eyelid. He saw, with a stranger's darting eye that missed no single subtlety of the wry grin or the faintest gesture drawing the shape of his death on the air, an unruly-haired young man who coughed into his hand in the corner of a rotting room and puffed the smoke of his doped Weight.

But as the drunk man weaved towards him on wilful feet, carrying his dignity as a man might carry a full glass around a quaking ship, as the barman behind the counter clattered and whistled and dipped to drink, he shook off the truthless, secret tragedy with a sneer and a blush, straightened his melancholy hat into a hard-brimmed trilby, dismissed the affected stranger. In the safe centre of his own identity, the familiar world about him like another flesh, he sat sad and content in the plain room of the undistinguished hotel at the sea-end of the shabby, spreading town where everything was happening. He had no need of the dark interior world when Tawe pressed in upon him and the eccentric ordinary people came bursting and crawling, with noise and colours, out of their houses, out of the graceless buildings, the factories and avenues, the shining shops and blaspheming chapels, the terminuses and the meeting-halls, the falling alleys and brick lanes, from the arches and shelters and holes behind the hoardings, out of the common, wild intelligence of the town.

At last the drunk man had reached him. 'Put your hand here,' he said, and turned about and tapped himself on the bottom.

The barman whistled and rose from his drink to see the young man touch the drunk on the seat of the trousers.

'What can you feel there?'

'Nothing.'

'That's right. Nothing. Nothing. There's nothing there to feel.'

'How can you sit down then?' asked the barman.

'I just sit down on what the doctor left,' the man said angrily. 'I had as good a bottom as you've got once. I was working underground in Dowlais, and the end of the world came down on me. Do you know what I got for losing my bottom? Four and three! Two and three ha'pence a cheek. That's cheaper than a pig.'

The girl from Victoria gardens came into the bar with two friends; a blonde young girl almost as beautiful as she was, and a middle-aged woman dressed and made up to look young. The three of them sat at the table. The girl he loved ordered three ports and gins.

'Isn't it delicious weather?' said the middle-aged woman.

The barman said: 'Plenty of sky about.' With many bows and smiles he placed their drinks in front of them. 'I thought the princesses had gone to a better pub,' he said.

'What's a better pub without you, handsome?' said the blonde girl.

'This is the "Ritz" and the "Savoy", isn't it *garçon* darling?' the girl from the Gardens said, and kissed her hand to him.

The young man in the window seat, still bewildered by the first sudden sight of her entering the darkening room, caught the kiss to himself and blushed. He thought to run out of the room and through the miracle-making Gardens, to rush into his house and hide his head in the bed-clothes and lie all night there, dressed and trembling, her voice in his ears, her green eyes wide awake under his closed eyelids. But only a sick boy with tossed blood would run from his proper love into a dream, lie down in a bedroom that was full of his shames, and sob against the feathery, fat breast and face on the damp pillow. He remembered his age and poems, and would not move.

'Tanks a million, Lou,' said the barman.

Her name was Lou, Louise, Lousia. She must be Spanish or French or a gipsy, but he could tell the street that her voice came from; he knew where her friends lived by the rise and fall of their sharp voices, and the name of the middle-aged woman was Mrs Emerald Franklin. She was to be seen every night in the 'Jew's Harp', sipping and spying and watching the clock.

'We've been listening to Matthews Hellfire on the sands. Down with this and down with that, and he used to drink a pint of biddy before his breakfast,' Mrs Franklin said. 'Oh there's a nerve!'

'And his eye on the fluff all the time,' said the blonde girl. 'I wouldn't trust him any further than Ramon Navarro behind the counter.'

'Whoops! I've gone up in the world. Last week I was Charley Chase,' said the barman.

Mrs Franklin raised her empty glass in a gloved hand and shook it like a bell. 'Men are deceivers ever,' she said. 'And a drop of mother's ruin right around.'

'Especially Mr Franklin,' said the barman.

'But there's a lot in what the preacher says, mind,' Mrs Franklin said, 'about the carrying on. If you go for a constitutional after stop-tap along the sands you might as well be in Sodom and Gomorrah.'

The blonde girl laughed. 'Hark to Mrs Grundy! I see her with a black man last Wednesday, round by the museum.'

'He was an Indian,' said Mrs Franklin, 'from the university college, and I'd thank you to remember it. Every one's brothers under the skin, but there's no tarbrush in my family.'

'Oh, dear! oh dear!' said Lou. 'Lay off it, there's loves. This is my birthday. It's a holiday. Put a bit of fun in it. Miaow! miaow! Marjorie, kiss Emerald and be friends.' She smiled and laughed at them both. She winked at the barman, who was filling their glasses to the top. 'Here's to your blue eyes, *garçon*!' She had not noticed the young man in the corner. 'And one for grand-dad there,' she said, smiling at the swaying, drunk man. 'He's twenty-one today. There! I've made him smile.'

The drunk man made a deep, dangerous bow, lifted his hat, stumbled against the mantelpiece, and his full pint in his free hand was steady as a rock. 'The prettiest girl in Carmarthenshire,' he said.

'This is Glamorganshire, dad,' she said, 'where's your geography? Look at him waltzing! mind your glasses! He's got that Kruschen feeling. Come on, faster! give us the Charleston.'

The drunk man, with the pint held high, danced until he fell, and all the time he never spilt a drop. He lay at Lou's feet on the dusty floor and grinned up at her in confidence and affection. 'I fell,' he said. 'I could dance like a trooper when I had a beatyem.'

'He lost his bottom at the last trump,' the barman explained.

'When did he lose his bottom?' said Mrs Franklin.

'When Gabriel blew his whistle down in Dowlais.'

'You're pulling my leg.'

'It's a pleasure, Mrs Em. Hoi, you! get up from the vomitorium.'

The man wagged his end like a tail, and growled at Lou's feet.

'Put your head on my foot. Be comfy. Let him lie there,' she said.

He went to sleep at once.

'I can't have drunks on the premises.'

'You know where to go then.'

'Cru-el Mrs Franklin!'

'Go on, attend to your business. Serve the young man in the corner, his tongue's hanging out.'

'Cru-el lady!'

As Mrs Franklin called attention to the young man, Lou peered shortsightedly across the saloon and saw him sitting with his back to the window.

'I'll have to get glasses,' she said.

'You'll have plenty of glasses before the night's out.'

'No, honest, Marjorie, I didn't know anyone was there. I do beg your pardon, you in the corner,' she said.

The barman switched on the light. 'A bit of *lux in tenebris*.'

'Oh!' said Lou.

The young man dared not move for fear that he might break the long night of her scrutiny, the enchantment shining like a single line of light between them, or startle her into speaking; and he did not conceal the love in his eyes, for she could pierce through to it as easily as she could turn his heart in his chest and make it beat above the noises of the two friends' hurried conversation, the rattle of glasses behind the counter where the barman spat and polished and missed nothing, and the snores of the comfortable sleeper. Nothing can hurt me. Let the barman jeer. Giggle in your glass, our Em. I'm telling the world, I'm walking in clover, I'm staring at Lou like a fool, she's my girl, she's my lily. O love! O love! She's no lady, with her sing-song Tontine voice, she drinks like a deep-sea diver; but Lou, I'm yours, and Lou, you're mine. He refused to meditate on her calmness now and twist her beauty into words. She was nothing under the sun or moon but his. Unashamed and certain, he smiled at her; and, though he was prepared for all, her answering smile made his fingers tremble again, as they had trembled in the gardens, and reddened his cheeks and drove his heart to a gallop.

'Harold, fill the young man's glass up,' Mrs Franklin said.

The barman stood still, a duster in one hand and a dripping glass in the other.

'Have you got water in your ears? Fill the young man's glass!'

The barman put the duster to his eyes. He sobbed. He wiped away the mock tears.

'I thought I was attending a *première* and this was the royal box,' he said.

'He's got water on the brain, not in his earhole,' said Marjorie.

'I dreamt it was a beautiful tragi-comedy entitled "Love at First Sight, or, Another Good Man Gone Wrong". Act one in a boozer by the sea.'

The two women tapped their foreheads.

Lou said, still smiling: 'Where was the second act?'

Her voice was as gentle as he had imagined it to be before her gay and nervous playing with the over-familiar barman and the inferior women. He saw her as a wise, soft girl whom no hard company could spoil, for her soft self, bare to the heart, broke through every defence of her sensual falsifiers. As he thought this, phrasing her gentleness, faithlessly running to words away from the real room and his love in the middle, he woke with a start and saw her lively body six steps from him, no calm heart dressed in a sentence, but a pretty girl, to be got and kept. He must catch hold of her fast. He got up to cross to her.

'I woke before the second act came on,' said the barman. 'I'd sell my dear old mother to see that. Dim lights. Purple couches. Ecstatic bliss. Là, là chèrie!'

The young man sat down at the table, next to her.

Harold, the barman, leaned over the counter and cupped his hand to his ear.

The man on the floor rolled in his sleep, and his head lay in the spittoon.

'You should have come and sat here a long time ago,' Lou whispered. 'You should have stopped to talk to me in the Gardens. Were you shy?'

'I was too shy,' the young man whispered.

'Whispering isn't manners. I can't hear a word,' said the barman.

At a sign from the young man, a flick of the fingers that sent the waiters in evening dress bustling with oysters about the immense room, the barman filled the glasses with port, gin, and Nutbrown.

'We never drink with strangers,' Mrs Franklin said, laughing.

'He isn't a stranger,' said Lou, 'are you Jack?'

He threw a pound note on the table: 'Take the damage.'

The evening that had been over before it began raced along among the laughter of the charming women sharp as knives, and the stories of the barman, who should be on the stage, and Lou's delighted smiles and silences at his side. Now she is safe and sure, he thought, after her walking like my doubtful walking, around the lonely distances of the holiday. In the warm, spinning middle they were close and alike. The town and the sea and the last pleasure-makers drifted into the dark that had nothing to do with them, and left this one room burning.

One by one, some lost men from the dark shuffled into the bar, drank sadly, and went out. Mrs Franklin, flushed and dribbling waved her glass at their departures. Harold winked behind their backs. Marjorie showed them her long, white legs.

'Nobody loves us except ourselves,' said Harold. 'Shall I shut the bar and keep the riff-raff out?'

'Lou is expecting Mr O'Brien, but don't let that stop you,' Marjorie said. 'He's her sugar daddy from old Ireland.'

'Do you love Mr O'Brien?' the young man whispered.

'How could I, Jack?'

He could see Mr O'Brien as a witty, tall fellow of middle age, with waved greying hair and a clipped bit of dirt on his upper lip, a flash ring on his marriage finger, a pouched knowing eye, dummy dressed with a whalebone waist, a broth of a man about Cardiff, Lou's horrible lover tearing towards her now down the airless streets in the firm's car. The young man clenched his hand on the table covered with dead, and sheltered her in the warm strength of his fist. 'My round, my round,' he said, 'up again, plenty! Doubles, trebles, Mrs Franklin is a jibber.'

'My mother never had a jibber.'

'Oh, Lou!' he said, 'I am more than happy with you.'

'Coo! coo! hear the turtle doves.'

'Let them coo,' said Marjorie. 'I could coo, too.'

The barman looked around him in surprise. He raised his hands, palms up, and cocked his head.

'The bar is full of birds,' he said.

'Emerald's laying an egg,' he said, as Mrs Franklin rocked in her chair.

Soon the bar was full of customers. The drunk man woke up and ran out, leaving his cap in a brown pool. Sawdust dropped from his hair. A small, old, round, red-faced, cheery man sat facing the young man and Lou, who held hands under the table and rubbed their legs against each other.

'What a night for love!' said the old man. 'On such a night as this did Jessica steal from the wealthy Jew. Do you know where that comes from?'

'*The Merchant of Venice*,' Lou said. 'But you're an Irishman, Mr O'Brien.'

'I could have sworn you were a tall man with a little tish,' said the young man gravely.

'What's the weapons, Mr O'Brien?'

'Brandies at dawn, I should think, Mrs Franklin.'

'I never described Mr O'Brien to you at all. You're dreaming!' Lou whispered. 'I wish this night could go on for ever.'

'But not here. Not in the bar. In a room with a big bed.'

'A bed in a bar,' said the old man, 'if you'll pardon me hearing you, that's what I've always wanted. Think of it, Mrs Franklin.'

The barman bobbed up from behind the counter.

'Time, gentlemen and others!'

The sober strangers departed to Mrs Franklin's laughter.

The lights went out.

'Lou, don't you lose me.'

'I've got your hand.'

'Press it hard, hurt it.'

'Break his bloody neck,' Mrs Franklin said in the dark. 'No offence meant.'

'Marjorie smack hand,' said Marjorie. 'Let's get out of the dark. Harold's a rover in the dark.'

'And the girl guides.'

'Let's take a bottle each and go down to Lou's,' she said.

'I'll buy the bottles,' said Mr O'Brien.

'It's you don't lose me now,' Lou whispered. 'Hold on to me, Jack. The others won't stay long. Oh, Mr Christ, I wish it was just you and me!'

'Will it be just you and me?'

'You and me and Mr Moon.'

Mr O'Brien opened the saloon door. 'Pile into the Rolls, you ladies. The gentlemen are going to see to the medicine.'

The young man felt Lou's quick kiss on his mouth before she followed Marjorie and Mrs Franklin out.

'What do you say we split the drinks?' said Mr O'Brien.

'Look what I found in the lavatory,' said the barman, 'he was singing on the seat.' He appeared behind the counter with the drunk leaning on his arm.

They all climbed into the car.

'First stop, Lou's.'

The young man, on Lou's knee, saw the town in a daze spin by them, the funnelled and masted smoke-blue outline of the still, droning docks, the lightning lines of the poor streets growing longer, and the winking shops that were snapped out one by one. The car smelt of scent and powder and flesh. He struck with his elbow, by accident, Mrs Franklin's upholstered breast. Her thighs, like cushions, bore the drunk man's rolling weight. He was bumped and tossed on a lump of woman. Breasts, legs, bellies, hands, touched, warmed, and smothered him. On through the night, towards Lou's bed, towards the unbelievable end of the dying holiday, they tore past black houses and bridges, a station in a smoke cloud, and drove up a steep side street with one weak lamp in a circle of railings at the top, and swerved into a space where a tall tenement house stood surrounded by cranes, standing ladders, poles and girders, barrows, brick-heaps.

They climbed to Lou's room up many flights of dark, perilous stairs. Washing hung on the rails outside closed doors. Mrs Franklin, fumbling alone with the drunk man behind the others, trod in a bucket, and a lucky black cat ran over her foot. Lou led the young man by the hand through a passage marked with names and doors, lit a match, and whispered: 'It won't be very long. Be good and patient with Mr O'Brien. Here it is. Come in first. Welcome to you, Jack!' She kissed him again at the door of her room.

She turned on the lights, and he walked with her proudly into her own room, into the room that he would come to know, and saw a wide bed, a gramophone on a chair, a wash-basin half-hidden in a corner, a gas fire and a cooking ring, a closed cupboard, and her photograph in a cardboard frame on the chest of drawers with no handles. Here she slept and ate. In the double bed she lay all night, pale and curled, sleeping on her left side. When he lived with her always, he would not allow her to dream. No other men must lie and love in her head. He spread his fingers on her pillow.

'Why do you live at the top of the Eiffel Tower!' said the barman, coming in.

'What a climb!' said Mr O'Brien. 'But it's very nice and private when you get here.'

'If you get here!' said Mrs Franklin. 'I'm dead beat. This old nuisance weighs a ton. Lie down, lie down on the floor and go to sleep. The old nuisance!' she said fondly. 'What's your name?'

'Ernie,' the drunk man said, raising his arm to shield his face.

'Nobody's going to bite you, Ernie. Here, give him a nip of whiskey. Careful! Don't pour it on your waistcoat; you'll be squeezing your waistcoat in the morning. Pull the curtains, Lou, I can see the wicked old moon,' she said.

'Does it put ideas in your head?'

'I love the moon,' said Lou.

'There never was a young lover who didn't love the moon,' Mr O'Brien gave the young man a cheery smile, and patted his hand. His own hand was red and hairy. 'I could see at the flash of a glance that Lou and this nice young fellow were made for each other. I could see it in their eyes. Dear me, no! I'm not so old and blind I can't see love in front of my nose. Couldn't you see it, Mrs Franklin? Couldn't you see it, Marjorie?'

In the long silence, Lou collected glasses from the cupboard as though she had not heard Mr O Brien speak. She drew the curtains, shut out the moon, sat on the edge of her bed with her feet tucked under her, looked at her photograph as at a stranger, folded her hands as she folded them, on the first meeting, before the young man's worship in the Gardens.

'A host of angels must be passing by,' said Mr O'Brien. 'What a silence there is! Have I said anything out of place? Drink and be merry, tomorrow we die. What do you think I brought these lovely shining bottles for?'

The bottles were opened. The dead were lined on the mantelpiece. The whiskey went down. Harold the barman and Marjorie, her dress lifted, sat in the one armchair together. Mrs Franklin, with Ernie's head on her lap, sang in a sweet, trained contralto voice *The Shepherd's Lass*. Mr O'Brien kept rhythm with his foot.

I want Lou in my arms, the young man said to himself, watching Mr O'Brien tap and smile and the barman draw Marjorie down deep. Mrs Franklin's voice sang sweetly in the small bedroom where he and Lou should be lying in the white bed without any smiling company to see them drown. He and Lou could go down together, one cool body weighted with a boiling stone, onto the falling, blank white, entirely empty sea, and never rise. Sitting on their bridal bed, near enough to hear his breath, she was farther from him than before they met. Then he had everything but her body; now she had given him two kisses, and everything had vanished but that beginning. He must be good and patient with Mr O'Brien. He could wipe away the embracing, old smile with the iron back of his hand. Sink lower, lower, Harold and Marjorie, tumble like whales at Mr O'Brien's feet.

He wished that the light would fail. In the darkness he and Lou could creep beneath the clothes and imitate the dead. Who would look for them there, if they were dead still and soundless? The others would shout to them down the dizzy stairs or rummage in the silence about the narrow, obstacled corridors or stumble out into the night to search for them among the cranes and ladders in the desolation of the destroyed houses. He could hear, in the made-up dark, Mr O'Brien's voice cry, 'Lou, where are you? Answer! answer!' the hollow answer of the echo, 'answer!' and hear her lips in the cool pit of the bed secretly move around another name and feel them move.

'A fine piece of singing, Emerald, and very naughty words. That was a shepherd, that was,' Mr. O'Brien said.

Ernie, on the floor, began to sing in a thick, sulking voice, but Mrs Franklin placed her hand over his mouth and he sucked and nuzzled it.

'What about this young shepherd?' said Mr O'Brien, pointing his glass at the young man. 'Can he sing as well as make love? You ask him kindly, girlie,' he said to Lou, 'and he'll give us a song like a nightingale.'

'Can you sing, Jack?'

'Like a crow, Lou.'

'Can't he even talk poetry? What a young man to have who can't spout the poets to his lady!' Mr O'Brien said.

From the cupboard Lou brought out a red-bound book and gave it to the young man, saying: 'Can you read us a piece out of here? The second volume's in the hatbox. Read us a dreamy piece, Jack. It's nearly midnight.'

'Only a love poem, no other kind,' said Mr O'Brien. 'I won't hear anything but a love poem.'

'Soft and sweet,' Mrs Franklin said. She took her hand away from Ernie's mouth and looked at the ceiling.

The young man read, but not aloud, lingering on her name, the inscription on the fly-leaf of the first volume of the collected poems of Tennyson: 'To Louisa, from her Sunday School teacher, Miss Gwyneth Forbes. God's in His Heaven, all's right with the world.'

'Make it a love poem, don't forget.'

The young man read aloud closing one eye to steady the dancing print, *Come into the garden, Maud*. And when he reached the beginning of the fourth verse his voice grew louder:

> 'I said to the lily, "there is but one
> With whom she has heart to be gay.
> When will the dancers leave her alone?
> She is weary of dance and play."
>
> Now half to the setting moon are gone,
> And half to the rising day;
> Low on the sand and loud on the stone
> The last wheel echoes away.
>
> 'I said to the rose, "The brief night goes
> In babble and revel and wine.
> O young lord-lover, what sighs are those,
> For one that will never be thine?
> But mine, but mine," so I sware to the rose
> "For ever and ever, mine." '

At the end of the poem, Harold said, suddenly, his head hanging over the arm of the chair, his hair made wild, and his mouth red with lipstick: 'My grandfather remembers seeing Lord Tennyson, he was a little man with a hump.'

'No,' said the young man, 'he was tall and he had long hair and a beard.'

'Did you ever see him?'

'I wasn't born then.'

'My grandfather saw him. He had a hump.'

'Not Alfred Tennyson.'

'Lord Alfred Tennyson was a little man with a hump.'

'It couldn't have been the same Tennyson.'

'You've got the wrong Tennyson, this was the famous poet with a hump.'

Lou, on the wonderful bed, waiting for him alone of all the men, ugly or handsome, old or young, in the wide town and the small world that would be bound to fall, lowered her head and kissed her hand to him and held her hand in the river of light on the counterpane.

The hand, to him, became transparent, and the light on the counterpane glowed up steadily through it in the thin shape of her palm and fingers.

'Ask Mr O'Brien what Lord Tennyson was like,' said Mrs Franklin. 'We appeal to you, Mr O'Brien, did he have a hump or not?'

Nobody but the young man, for whom she lived and waited now, noticed Lou's little loving movements. She put her glowing hand to her left breast. She made a sign of secrecy on her lips.

'It depends,' Mr O'Brien said.

The young man closed one eye again, for the bed was pitching like a ship; a sickening, hot storm out of a cigarette cloud unsettled cupboard and chest. The motions of the sea-going bedroom were calmed with the cunning closing of his eye, but he longed for night air. On sailor's legs he walked to the door.

'You'll find the House of Commons on the second floor at the end of the passage,' said Mr O'Brien.

At the door, he turned to Lou and smiled with all his love, declaring it to the faces of the company and making her, before Mr O'Brien's envious regard, smile back and say: 'Don't be long, Jack, Please! You mustn't be long.'

Now every one knew. Love had grown up in an evening.

'One minute, my darling,' he said. 'I'll be here.'

The door closed behind him. He walked into the wall of the passage. He lit a match. He had three left. Down the stairs, clinging to the sticky, shaking rails, rocking on see-saw floorboards, bruising his shin on a bucket, past the noises of secret lives behind doors he slid and stumbled and swore and heard Lou's voice in a fresh fever drive him on, call him to return, speak to him with such passion and abandonment that even in the darkness and the pain of his haste he was dazzled and struck still. She spoke, there on the rotting stairs in the middle of the poor house, a frightening rush of love words; from her mouth, at his ear, endearments were burned out. Hurry! hurry! Every moment is being killed. Love, adored, dear, run back and whistle to me, open the door, shout my name, lay me down. Mr O'Brien has his hands on my side.

He ran into a cavern. A draught blew out his matches. He lurched into a room where two figures on a black heap on the floor lay whispering, and ran from there in a panic. He made water at the dead end of the passage and hurried back towards Lou's room, finding himself at last on a silent patch of stairway at the top of the house; he put out his hand, but the rail was broken and nothing there prevented a long drop to the ground down a twisted shaft that would echo and double his cry, bring out from their holes in the wall the sleeping or stirring families, the whispering figures, the blind startled turners of night into day. Lost in a tunnel near the roof, he fingered the damp walls for a door; he found a handle and gripped it hard, but it came off in his hand. Lou had led him down a longer passage than this. He remembered the number of doors: there were three on each side. He ran down the broken-railed flight into another passage and dragged his hand along the wall. Three doors, he counted. He opened the third door, walked into darkness, and groped for the switch on the left. He saw, in the sudden light, a bed and a cupboard and a chest of drawers with no handles, a gas fire, a wash-basin in the corner. No bottles. No glasses. No photograph of Lou. The red counterpane on the bed was smooth. He could not remember the colour of Lou's counterpane.

He left the light burning and opened the second door, but a strange woman's voice cried, half-asleep: 'Who is there? Is it you, Tom? Tom, put the light on.' He looked for a line of light at the foot of the next door, and stopped to listen for voices. The woman was still calling in the second room.

'Lou, where are you?' he cried. 'Answer! answer!'

'Lou, what Lou? There's no Lou here,' said a man's voice through the open door of the first dark room at the entrance to the passage.

He scampered down another flight and counted four doors with his scratched hand. One door opened and a woman in a nightdress put out her head. A child's head appeared below her.

'Where does Lou live? Do you know where Lou lives?'

The woman and the child stared without speaking.

'Lou! Lou! her name is Lou!' he heard himself shout. 'She lives here, in this house! Do you know where she lives?'

The woman caught the child by the hair and pulled her into the room. He clung to the edge of her door. The woman thrust her arm round the edge and brought down a bunch of keys sharply on his hands. The door slammed.

A young woman with a baby in a shawl stood at an open door on the opposite side of the passage, and caught his sleeve as he ran by. 'Lou who? You woke my baby.'

'I don't know her other name. She's with Mrs Franklin and Mr O'Brien.'

'You woke my baby.'

'Come in and find her in the bed,' a voice said from the darkness behind the young woman.

'He's woken my baby.'

He ran down the passage, holding his wet hand to his mouth. He fell against the rails of the last flight of stairs. He heard Lou's voice in his head once more whisper to him to return as the ground floor rose, like a lift full of dead, towards the rails. Hurry! hurry! I can't, I won't wait, the bridal night is being killed.

Up the rotten, bruising, mountainous stairs he climbed, in his sickness, to the passage where he had left the one light burning in an end room. The light was out. He tapped all the doors and whispered her name. He beat on the doors and shouted, and a woman, dressed in a vest and a hat, drove him out of the passage with a walking-stick.

For a long time he waited on the stairs, though there was no love now to wait for and no bed but his own too many miles away to lie in, and only the approaching day to remember his discovery. All round him the disturbed inhabitants of the house were falling back into sleep. Then he walked out of the house on to the waste space and under the leaning cranes and ladders. The light of the one weak lamp in a rusty circle fell across the brick-heaps and the broken wood and the dust that had been houses once, where the small and hardly known and never-to-be-forgotten people of the dirty town had lived and loved and died and, always, lost.

The Followers

It was six o'clock on a winter's evening. Thin, dingy rain spat and drizzled past the lighted street lamps. The pavements shone long and yellow. In squeaking goloshes, with mackintosh collars up and bowlers and trilbies weeping, youngish men from the offices bundled home against the thistly wind –

'Night, Mr Macey.'

'Going my way, Charlie?'

'Ooh, there's a pig of a night!'

'Good night, Mr Swan.' –

and older men, clinging on to the big, black circular birds of their umbrellas, were wafted back, up the gaslit hills, to safe, hot, slippered, weatherproof hearths, and wives called Mother, and old, fond, fleabag dogs, and the wireless babbling.

Young women from the offices, who smelt of scent and powder and wet pixie hoods and hair, scuttled, giggling, arm-in-arm, after the hissing trams, and screeched as they splashed their stockings in the puddles rainbowed with oil between the slippery lines.

In a shop window, two girls undressed the dummies:

'Where you going tonight?'

'Depends on Arthur. Up she comes.'

'Mind her cami-knicks, Edna...'

The blinds came down over another window.

A newsboy stood in a doorway, calling the news to nobody, very softly:

'Earthquake. Earthquake in Japan.'

Water from a chute dripped on to his sacking. He waited in his own pool of rain.

A flat, long girl drifted, snivelling into her hanky, out of a jeweller's shop, and slowly pulled the steel shutters down with a hooked pole. She looked, in the grey rain, as though she were crying from top to toe.

A silent man and woman, dressed in black, carried the wreaths away from the front of their flower shop into the scented deadly darkness behind the window lights. Then the lights went out.

A man with a balloon tied to his cap pushed a shrouded barrow up a dead end.

A baby with an ancient face sat in its pram outside the wine vaults, quiet, very wet, peering cautiously all round it.

It was the saddest evening I had ever known.

A young man, with his arm round his girl, passed by me, laughing; and she laughed back, right into his handsome, nasty face. That made the evening sadder still.

I met Leslie at the corner of Crimea Street. We were both about the same age: too young and too old. Leslie carried a rolled umbrella, which he never used, though sometimes he pressed doorbells with it. He was trying to grow a moustache. I wore a check, ratting cap at a Saturday angle. We greeted each other formally:

'Good evening, old man.'

'Evening, Leslie.'

'Right on the dot, boy.'

'That's right,' I said. 'Right on the dot.'

A plump, blonde girl, smelling of wet rabbits, self-conscious even in that dirty night, minced past on high-heeled shoes. The heels clicked, the soles squelched.

Leslie whistled after her, low and admiring.

'Business first,' I said.

'Oh, boy!' Leslie said.

'And she's too fat as well.'

'I like them corpulent,' Leslie said. 'Remember Penelope Bogan? a Mrs too.'

'Oh, come *on*. That old bird of Paradise Alley! How's the exchequer, Les?'

'One and a penny. How you fixed?'

'Tanner.'

'What'll it be, then? The Compasses?'

'Free cheese at the Marlborough.'

We walked towards the Marlborough, dodging umbrella spokes, smacked by our windy macs, stained by steaming lamplight, seeing the sodden, blown scourings and street-wash of the town, papers, rags, dregs, rinds, fag-ends, balls of fur, flap, float, and cringe along the gutters, hearing the sneeze and rattle of the bony trams and a ship hoot like a fog-ditched owl in the bay, and Leslie said:

'What'll we do after?'

'We'll follow someone,' I said.

'Remember following that old girl up Kitchener Street? The one who dropped her handbag?'

'You should have given it back.'

'There wasn't anything in it, only a piece of bread-and-jam.'

'Here we are,' I said.

The Marlborough saloon was cold and empty. There were notices on the damp walls: No Singing. No Dancing. No Gambling. No Peddlers.

'You sing,' I said to Leslie, 'and I'll dance, then we'll have a game of nap and I'll peddle my braces.'

The barmaid, with gold hair and two gold teeth in front, like a well-off rabbit's, was blowing on her nails and polishing them on her black marocain. She looked up as we came in, then blew on her nails again and polished them without hope.

'You can tell it isn't Saturday night,' I said. 'Evening, Miss. Two pints.'

'And a pound from the till,' Leslie said.

'Give us your one-and-a-penny, Les,' I whispered and then said aloud: 'Anybody can tell it isn't Saturday night. Nobody sick.'

'Nobody here to *be* sick,' Leslie said.

The peeling, liver-coloured room might never have been drunk in at all. Here, commercials told jokes and had Scotches and sodas with happy, dyed, port-and-lemon women; dejected regulars grew grand and muzzy in the corners, inventing their pasts, being rich, important, and loved; reprobate grannies in dustbin black cackled and nipped; influential nobodies revised the earth; a party, with earrings, called 'Frilly Willy' played the crippled piano, which sounded like a hurdy-gurdy playing under water, until the publican's nosy wife said, 'No.' Strangers came and went, but mostly went. Men from the valleys dropped in for nine or ten; sometimes there were fights; and always there was something doing, some argy-bargy, giggle and bluster, horror or folly, affection, explosion, nonsense, peace, some wild goose flying in the boozy air of that comfortless, humdrum nowhere in the dizzy, ditchwater town at the end of the railway lines. But that evening it was the saddest room I had ever known.

Leslie said, in a low voice: 'Think she'll let us have one on tick?'

'Wait a bit, boy,' I murmured. 'Wait for her to thaw.'

But the barmaid heard me, and looked up. She looked clean through me, back through my small history to the bed I was born in, then shook her gold head.

'I don't know what it is,' said Leslie as we walked up Crimea Street in the rain, 'but I feel kind of depressed tonight.'

'It's the saddest night in the world,' I said.

We stopped, soaked and alone, to look at the stills outside the cinema we called the Itch-pit. Week after week, for years and years, we had sat on the edges of the springless seats there, in the dank but snug, flickering dark, first with toffees and monkey-nuts that crackled for the dumb guns, and then with cigarettes: a cheap special kind that would make a fire-swallower cough up the cinders of his heart. 'Let's go in and see Lon Chaney,' I said, 'and Richard Talmadge and Milton Sills and ... and Noah Beery,' I said, 'and Richard Dix ... and Slim Summerville and Hoot Gibson.'

We both sighed.

'Oh, for our vanished youth,' I said.

We walked on heavily, with wilful feet, splashing the passers-by.

'Why don't you open your brolly?' I said.

'It won't open. You try.'

We both tried, and the umbrella suddenly bellied out, the spokes tore through the soaking cover; the wind danced its tatters; it wrangled above us in the wind like a ruined, mathematical bird. We tried to tug it down: an unseen, new spoke sprang through its ragged ribs. Leslie dragged it behind him, along the pavement, as though he had shot it.

A girl called Dulcie, scurrying to the Itch-pit, sniggered 'Hallo', and we stopped her.

'A rather terrible thing has happened,' I said to her. She was so silly that, even when she was fifteen, we had told her to eat soap to make her straw hair crinkle, and Les took a piece from the bathroom, and she did.

'I know,' she said, 'you broke your gamp.'

'No, you're wrong there,' Leslie said. 'It isn't *our* umbrella at all. It fell off the roof. *You* feel,' he said. 'You can feel it fell off the roof.' She took the umbrella gingerly by its handle.

'There's someone up there throwing umbrellas down,' I said. 'It may be serious.'

She began to titter, and then grew silent and anxious as Leslie said: 'You never know. It might be walking-sticks next.'

'Or sewing-machines,' I said.

'You wait here, Dulce, and we'll investigate,' Leslie said.

We hurried on down the street, turned a blowing corner and then ran.

Outside Rabiotti's café, Leslie said: 'It isn't fair on Dulcie.' We never mentioned it again.

A wet girl brushed by. Without a word, we followed her. She cantered, long-legged, down Inkerman Street and through Paradise Passage, and we were at her heels.

'I wonder what's the point in following people,' Leslie said, 'it's kind of daft. It never gets you anywhere. All you do is follow them home and then try to look through the window and see what they're doing and mostly there's curtains anyway. I bet nobody else does things like that.'

'You never know,' I said. The girl turned into St Augustus Crescent, which was a wide lamplit mist. 'People are always following people. What shall we call her?'

'Hermione Weatherby,' Leslie said. He was never wrong about names. Hermione was fey and stringy, and walked like a long gym-mistress, full of love, through the stinging rain.

'You never know. You never know what you'll find out. Perhaps she lives in a huge house with all her sisters – '

'How many?'

'Seven. All full of love. And when she gets home they all change into kimonos and lie on divans with music and whisper to each other and all they're doing is waiting for somebody like us to walk in, lost, and then they'll all chatter round us like starlings and put us in kimonos too, and we'll never leave the house until we die. Perhaps it's so beautiful and soft and noisy – like a warm bath full of birds . . .'

'I don't want birds in my bath,' said Leslie. 'Perhaps she'll slit her throat if they don't draw the blinds. I don't care what happens so long as it's interesting.'

She slip-slopped round a corner into an avenue where the neat trees were sighing and the cosy windows shone.

'I don't wand old feathers in the tub,' Leslie said.

Hermione turned in at number thirteen, Beach-view.

'You can see the beach all right,' Leslie said, 'if you got a periscope.'

We waited on the pavement opposite, under a bubbling lamp, as Hermione opened her door, and then we tiptoed across and down the gravel path and were at the back of the house, outside an uncurtained window.

Hermione's mother, a round, friendly, owlish woman in a pinafore, was shaking a chip-pan on the kitchen stove.

'I'm hungry,' I said.

'Ssh!'

We edged to the side of the window as Hermione came into the kitchen. She was old, nearly thirty, with a mouse-brown shingle and big earnest eyes. She wore horn-rimmed spectacles and a sensible, tweed costume, and a white shirt with a trim bow-tie. She looked as though she tried to look like a secretary in domestic films, who had only to remove her spectacles and have her hair cherished, and be dressed like a silk dog's dinner, to turn into a dazzler and make her employer Warner Baxter, gasp, woo, and marry her; but if Hermione took off her glasses, she wouldn't be able to tell if he was Warner Baxter or the man who read the meters.

We stood so near the window, we could hear the chips spitting.

'Have a nice day in the office, dear? There's weather,' Hermione's mother said, worrying the chip-pan.

'What's *her* name, Les?'

'Hetty.'

Everything there in the warm kitchen, from the tea-caddy and the grandmother clock, to the tabby that purred like a kettle, was good, dull, and sufficient.

'Mr Truscott was something awful,' Hermione said as she put on her slippers.

'Where's her kimono?' Leslie said.

'Here's a nice cup of tea,' said Hetty.

'Everything's nice in that old hole,' said Leslie, grumbling. 'Where's the seven sisters like starlings?'

It began to rain much more heavily. It bucketed down on the black back yard, and the little comfy kennel of a house, and us, and the hidden, hushed town, where, even now, in the haven of the Marlborough, the submarine piano would be tinning 'Daisy', and the happy henna'd women squealing into their port.

Hetty and Hermione had their supper. Two drowned boys watched them enviously.

'Put a drop of Worcester on the chips,' Leslie whispered; and by God she did.

'Doesn't anything happen anywhere?' I said, 'in the whole wide world? I think the *News of the World* is all made up. Nobody murders no one. There isn't any sin any more, or love, or death, or pearls and divorces and mink-coats or anything, or putting arsenic in the cocoa . . .'

'Why don't they put on some music for us,' Leslie said, 'and do a dance? It isn't every night they got two fellows watching them in the rain. Not *every* night, anyway!'

All over the dripping town, small lost people with nowhere to go and nothing to spend were gooseberrying in the rain outside wet windows, but nothing happened.

'I'm getting pneumonia,' Leslie said.

The cat and the fire were purring, grandmother time tick-tocked our lives away. The supper was cleared, and Hetty and Hermione, who had not spoken for many minutes, they were so confident and close in their little lighted box, looked at one another and slowly smiled.

They stood still in the decent, purring kitchen, facing one another.

'There's something funny going to happen,' I whispered very softly.

'It's going to begin,' Leslie said.

We did not notice the sour, racing rain any more.

The smiles stayed on the faces of the two still, silent women.

'It's going to begin.'

And we heard Hetty say in a small secret voice: 'Bring out the album, dear.'

Hermione opened a cupboard and brought out a big, stiff-coloured photograph album, and put it in the middle of the table. Then she and Hetty sat down at the table, side by side, and Hermione opened the album.

'That's Uncle Eliot who died in Porthcawl, the one who had the cramp,' said Hetty.

They looked with affection at Uncle Eliot, but we could not see him.

'That's Martha-the-woolshop, you wouldn't remember her, dear, it was wool, wool, wool, with her all the time; she wanted to be buried in her jumper, the mauve one, but her husband put his foot down. He'd been in India. That's your Uncle Morgan,' Hetty said, 'one of the Kidwelly Morgans, remember him in the snow?'

Hermione turned a page. 'And that's Myfanwy, she got queer all of a sudden, remember. It was when she was milking. That's your cousin Jim, the Minister, until they found out. And that's our Beryl,' Hetty said.

But she spoke all the time like somebody repeating a lesson: a well-loved lesson she knew by heart.

We knew that she and Hermione were only waiting.

Then Hermione turned another page. And we knew, by their secret smiles, that this was what they had been waiting for.

'My sister Katinka,' Hetty said.

'Auntie Katinka,' Hermione said. They bent over the photograph.

'Remember that day in Aberystwyth, Katinka?' Hetty said softly. 'The day we went on the choir outing.'

'I wore my new white dress,' a new voice said.

Leslie clutched at my hand.

'And a straw hat with birds,' said the clear, new voice.

Hermione and Hetty were not moving their lips.

'I was always a one for birds on my hat. Just the plumes of course. It was August the third, and I was twenty-three.'

'Twenty-three come October, Katinka,' Hetty said.

'That's right, love,' the voice said. 'Scorpio I was. And we met Douglas Pugh on the Prom and he said: "You look like a queen today, Katinka," he said, "You look like a queen, Katinka," he said. Why are those two boys looking in at the window?'

We ran up the gravel drive, and around the corner of the house, and into the avenue and out on to St Augustus Crescent. The rain roared down to drown the town. There we stopped for breath. We did not speak or look at each other. Then we walked on through the rain. At Victoria corner, we stopped again.

'Good night, old man,' Leslie said.

'Good night,' I said.

And we went our different ways.

A Story

If you can call it a story. There's no real beginning or end and there's very little in the middle. It is all about a day's outing, by charabanc, to Porthcawl, which, of course, the charabanc never reached, and it happened when I was so high and much nicer.

I was staying at the time with my uncle and his wife. Although she was my aunt, I never thought of her as anything but the wife of my uncle, partly because he was so big and trumpeting and red-hairy and used to fill every inch of the hot little house like an old buffalo squeezed into an airing cupboard, and partly because she was so small and silk and quick and made no noise at all as she whisked about on padded paws, dusting the china dogs, feeding the buffalo, setting the mousetraps that never caught her; and once she sneaked out of the room, to squeak in a nook or nibble in the hayloft, you forgot she had ever been there.

But there he was, always, a steaming hulk of an uncle, his braces straining like hawsers, crammed behind the counter of the tiny shop at the front of the house, and breathing like a brass band; or guzzling and blustery in the kitchen over his gutsy supper, too big for everything except the great black boats of his boots. As he ate, the house grew smaller; he billowed out over the furniture, the loud check meadow of his waistcoat littered, as though after a picnic, with cigarette ends, peelings, cabbage stalks, birds' bones, gravy; and the forest fire of his hair crackled among the hooked hams from the ceiling. She was so small she could hit him only if she stood on a chair, and every Saturday night at half past ten he would lift her up, under his arm, on to a chair in the kitchen so that she could hit him on the head with whatever was handy, which was always a china dog. On Sundays, and when pickled, he sang high tenor, and had won many cups.

The first I heard of the annual outing was when I was sitting one evening on a bag of rice behind the counter, under one of my uncle's stomachs, reading an advertisement for sheep-dip, which was all there was to read. The shop was full of my uncle, and when Mr Benjamin

Franklyn, Mr Weazley, Noah Bowen, and Will Sentry came in, I thought it would burst. It was like all being together in a drawer that smelt of cheese and turps, and twist tobacco and sweet biscuits and snuff and waistcoat. Mr Benjamin Franklyn said that he had collected enough money for the charabanc and twenty cases of pale ale and a pound apiece over that he would distribute among the members of the outing when they first stopped for refreshment, and he was about sick and tired, he said, of being followed by Will Sentry.

'All day long, wherever I go,' he said, 'he's after me like a collie with one eye. I got a shadow of my own *and* a dog. I don't need no Tom, Dick, or Harry pursuing me with his dirty muffler on.'

Will Sentry blushed, and said: 'It's only oily. I got a bicycle.'

'A man has no privacy at all,' Mr Franklyn went on. 'I tell you he sticks so close I'm afraid to go out the back in case I sit in his lap. It's a wonder to me,' he said, 'he don't follow me into bed at night.'

'Wife won't let,' Will Sentry said.

And that started Mr Franklyn off again, and they tried to soothe him down by saying: 'Don't you mind Will Sentry' ... 'No harm in old Will' ... 'He's only keeping an eye on the money, Benjie.'

'Aren't I honest?' asked Mr Franklyn in surprise. There was no answer for some time, then Noah Bowen said: 'You know what the committee is. Ever since Bob the Fiddle they don't feel safe with a new treasurer.'

'Do you think *I'm* going to drink the outing funds, like Bob the Fiddle did?' said Mr Franklyn.

'You *might*,' said my uncle slowly.

'I resign,' said Mr Franklyn.

'Not with our money you won't,' Will Sentry said.

'Who put dynamite in the salmon pool?' said Mr Weazley, but nobody took any notice of him. And, after a time, they all began to play cards in the thickening dusk of the hot, cheesy shop, and my uncle blew and bugled whenever he won, and Mr Weazley grumbled like a dredger, and I fell to sleep on the gravy-scented mountain meadow of uncle's waistcoat.

On Sunday evening, after Bethesda, Mr Franklyn walked into the kitchen where my uncle and I were eating sardines with spoons from the tin because it was Sunday and his wife would not let us play draughts. She was somewhere in the kitchen, too. Perhaps she was inside the grandmother clock, hanging from the weights and breathing. Then, a second later, the door opened again and Will Sentry edged into the room, twiddling his hard, round hat. He and Mr

Franklyn sat down on the settee, stiff and moth-balled and black in their chapel and funeral suits.

'I brought the list,' said Mr Franklyn. 'Every member fully paid. You ask Will Sentry.'

My uncle put on his spectacles, wiped his whiskery mouth with a handkerchief big as a Union Jack, laid down his spoon of sardines, took Mr Franklyn's list of names, removed the spectacles so that he could read, and then ticked the names off one by one.

'Enoch Davies. Aye. He's good with his fists. You never know. Little Gerwain. Very melodious bass. Mr Cadwalladwr. That's right. He can tell opening time better than my watch. Mr Weazley. Of course. He's been to Paris. Pity he suffers so much in the charabanc. Stopped us nine times last year between the Beehive and the Red Dragon. Noah Bowen, ah, very peaceable. He's got a tongue like a turtle-dove. Never a argument with Noah Bowen. Jenkins Loughor. Keep him off economics. It cost us a plate-glass window. And ten pints for the Sergeant. Mr Jervis. Very tidy.'

'He tried to put a pig in the charra,' Will Sentry said.

'Live and let live,' said my uncle.

Will Sentry blushed.

'Sinbad the Sailor's Arms. Got to keep in with him. Old O. Jones.'

'Why old O. Jones?' said Will Sentry.

'Old O. Jones always goes,' said my uncle.

I looked down at the kitchen table. The tin of sardines was gone. By Gee, I said to myself, Uncle's wife is quick as a flash.

'Cuthbert Johnny Fortnight. Now there's a card,' said my uncle.

'He whistles after women,' Will Sentry said.

'So do you,' said Mr Benjamin Franklyn, 'in your mind.'

My uncle at last approved the whole list, pausing only to say, when he came across one name: 'If we weren't a Christian community, we'd chuck that Bob the Fiddle in the sea.'

'We can do that in Porthcawl,' said Mr Franklyn, and soon after that he went, Will Sentry no more than an inch behind him, their Sunday-bright boots squeaking on the kitchen cobbles.

And then, suddenly, there was my uncle's wife standing in front of the dresser, with a china dog in one hand. By Gee, I said to myself again, did you ever see such a woman, if that's what she is. The lamps were not lit yet in the kitchen and she stood in a wood of shadows, with the plates on the dresser behind her shining – like pink-and-white eyes.

'If you go on that outing on Saturday, Mr Thomas,' she said to my uncle in her small, silk voice, 'I'm going home to my mother's.'

Holy Mo, I thought, she's got a mother. Now that's one old bald mouse of a hundred and five I won't be wanting to meet in a dark lane.

'It's me or the outing, Mr Thomas.'

I would have made my choice at once, but it was almost half a minute before my uncle said: 'Well, then, Sarah, it's the outing, my love.' He lifted her up, under his arm, on to a chair in the kitchen, and she hit him on the head with the china dog. Then he lifted her down again, and then I said good night.

For the rest of the week my uncle's wife whisked quiet and quick round the house with her darting duster, my uncle blew and bugled and swore, and I kept myself busy all the time being up to no good. And then at breakfast time on Saturday morning, the morning of the outing, I found a note on the kitchen table. It said: 'There's some eggs in the pantry. Take your boots off before you go to bed.' My uncle's wife had gone, as quick as a flash.

When my uncle saw the note, he tugged out the flag of his handkerchief and blew such a hubbub of trumpets that the plates on the dresser shook. 'It's the same every year,' he said. And then he looked at me. 'But this year it's different. *You*'ll have to come on the outing, too, and what the members will say I dare not think.'

The charabanc drew up outside, and when the members of the outing saw my uncle and me squeeze out of the shop together, both of us cat-licked and brushed in our Sunday best, they snarled like a zoo.

'Are you bringing a *boy*?' asked Mr Benjamin Franklyn as we climbed into the charabanc. He looked at me with horror.

'Boys is nasty,' said Mr Weazley.

'He hasn't paid his contributions,' Will Sentry said.

'No room for boys. Boys get sick in charabancs.'

'So do you, Enoch Davies,' said my uncle.

'Might as well bring *women*.'

The way they said it, women were worse than boys.

'Better than bringing grandfathers.'

'Grandfathers is nasty too,' said Mr Weazley.

'What can we do with him when we stop for refreshments?'

'I'm a grandfather,' said Mr Weazley.

'Twenty-six minutes to opening time,' shouted an old man in a panama hat, not looking at a watch. They forgot me at once.

'Good old Mr Cadwalladwr,' they cried, and the charabanc started off down the village street.

A few cold women stood at their doorways, grimly watching us go. A very small boy waved good-bye, and his mother boxed his ears. It was a beautiful August morning.

We were out of the village, and over the bridge, and up the hill towards Steeplehat Wood when Mr Franklyn, with his list of names in his hand, called out loud: 'Where's old O. Jones?'

'Where's old O?'

'We've left old O behind.'

'Can't go without old O.'

And though Mr Weazley hissed all the way, we turned and drove back to the village, where, outside the Prince of Wales, old O. Jones was waiting patiently and alone with a canvas bag.

'I didn't want to come at all,' old O. Jones said as they hoisted him into the charabanc and clapped him on the back and pushed him on a seat and stuck a bottle in his hand, 'but I always go.' And over the bridge and up the hill and under the deep green wood and along the dusty road we wove, slow cows and ducks flying by, until 'Stop the bus!' Mr Weazley cried. 'I left my teeth on the mantelpiece.'

'Never you mind,' they said, 'you're not going to bite nobody,' and they gave him a bottle with a straw.

'I might want to smile,' he said.

'Not you,' they said.

'What's the time, Mr Cadwalladwr?'

'Twelve minutes to go,' shouted back the old man in the panama, and they all began to curse him.

The charabanc pulled up outside the Mountain Sheep, a small, unhappy public-house with a thatched roof like a wig with ringworm. From a flagpole by the Gents fluttered the flag of Siam. I knew it was the flag of Siam because of cigarette cards. The landlord stood at the door to welcome us, simpering like a wolf. He was a long, lean, blackfanged man with a greased love-curl and pouncing eyes. 'What a beautiful August day!' he said, and touched his love-curl with a claw. That was the way he must have welcomed the Mountain Sheep before he ate it, I said to myself. The members rushed out, bleating, and into the bar.

'You keep an eye on the charra,' my uncle said, 'see nobody steals it now.'

'There's nobody to steal it,' I said, 'except some cows,' but my uncle was gustily blowing his bugle in the bar. I looked at the cows opposite, and they looked at me. There was nothing else for us to do. Forty-five minutes passed, like a very slow cloud. The sun shone down on the lonely road, the lost, unwanted boy, and the lake-eyed cows. In the dark bar they were so happy they were breaking glasses. A Shoni-Onion Breton man, with a beret and a necklace of onions, bicycled down the road and stopped at the door.

'Quelle un grand matin, monsieur,' I said.

'There's French, boy bach!' he said.

I followed him down the passage, and peered into the bar. I could hardly recognize the members of the outing. They had all changed colour. Beetroot, rhubarb, and puce, they hollered and rollicked in that dark, damp hole like enormous ancient bad boys, and my uncle surged in the middle, all red whiskers and bellies. On the floor was broken glass and Mr Weazley.

'Drinks all round,' cried Bob the Fiddle, a small, absconding man with bright blue eyes and a plump smile.

'Who's been robbing the orphans?'

'Who sold his little babby to the gyppoes?'

'Trust old Bob, he'll let you down.'

'You will have your little joke,' said Bob the Fiddle, smiling like a razor, 'but I forgive you, boys.'

Out of the fug and babel I heard: 'Come out and fight.'

'No, not now, later.'

'No, now when I'm in a temper.'

'Look at Will Sentry, he's proper snobbled.'

'Look at his wilful feet.'

'Look at Mr Weazley lording it on the floor.'

Mr Weazley got up, hissing like a gander. 'That boy pushed me down deliberate,' he said, pointing to me at the door, and I slunk away down the passage and out to the mild, good cows. Time clouded over, the cows wondered, I threw a stone at them and they wandered, wondering, away. Then out blew my uncle, ballooning, and one by one the members lumbered after him in a grizzle. They had drunk the Mountain Sheep dry. Mr Weazley had won a string of onions that the Shoni-Onion man raffled in the bar. 'What's the good of onions if you left your teeth on the mantelpiece?' he said. And when I looked through the back window of the thundering charabanc, I saw the pub grow smaller in the distance. And the flag of Siam, from the flagpole by the Gents, fluttered now at half-mast.

The Blue Bull, the Dragon, the Star of Wales, the Twll in the Wall, the Sour Grapes, the Shepherd's Arms, the Bells of Aberdovey: I had nothing to do in the whole, wild August world but remember the names where the outing stopped and keep an eye on the charabanc. And whenever it passed a public-house, Mr Weazley would cough like a billygoat and cry: 'Stop the bus, I'm dying of breath!' And back we would all have to go.

Closing time meant nothing to the members of that outing. Behind locked doors, they hymned and rumpused all the beautiful afternoon. And, when a policeman entered the Druid's Tap by the back door, and found them all choral with beer, 'Sssh!' said Noah Bowen, 'the pub is shut.'

'Where do you come from?' he said in his buttoned, blue voice.

They told him.

'I got a auntie there,' the policeman said. And very soon he was singing 'Asleep in the Deep'.

Off we drove again at last, the charabanc bouncing with tenors and flagons, and came to a river that rushed along among willows.

'Water!' they shouted.

'Porthcawl!' sang my uncle.

'Where's the donkeys?' said Mr Weazley.

And out they lurched, to paddle and whoop in the cool, white, winding water. Mr Franklyn, trying to polka on the slippery stones, fell in twice. 'Nothing is simple,' he said with dignity as he oozed up the bank.

'It's cold!' they cried.

'It's lovely!'

'It's smooth as a moth's nose!'

'It's *better* than Porthcawl!'

And dusk came down warm and gentle on thirty wild, wet, pickled, splashing men without a care in the world at the end of the world in the west of Wales. And, 'Who goes there?' called Will Sentry to a wild duck flying.

They stopped at the Hermit's Nest for a rum to keep out the cold. 'I played for Aberavon in 1898,' said a stranger to Enoch Davies.

'Liar,' said Enoch Davies.

'I can show you photos,' said the stranger.

'Forged,' said Enoch Davies.

'And I'll show you my cap at home.'

'Stolen.'

'I got friends to prove it,' the stranger said in a fury.

'Bribed,' said Enoch Davies.

On the way home, through the simmering moon-splashed dark,

old O. Jones began to cook his supper on a primus stove in the middle of the charabanc. Mr Weazley coughed himself blue in the smoke. 'Stop the bus,' he cried, 'I'm dying of breath!' We all climbed down into the moonlight. There was not a public-house in sight. So they carried out the remaining cases, and the primus stove, and old O. Jones himself, and took them into a field, and sat down in a circle in the field and drank and sang while old O. Jones cooked sausage and mash and the moon flew above us. And there I drifted to sleep against my uncle's mountainous waistcoat, and, as I slept, 'Who goes there?' called out Will Sentry to the flying moon.

BROADCASTS

Memories of Christmas

One Christmas was so much like another, in those years, around the sea-town corner now, and out of all sound except the distant speaking of the voices I sometimes hear a moment before sleep, that I can never remember whether it snowed for six days and six nights when I was twelve or whether it snowed for twelve days and twelve nights when I was six; or whether the ice broke and the skating grocer vanished like a snowman through a white trap-door on that same Christmas Day that the mincepies finished Uncle Arnold and we tobogganed down the seaward hill, all the afternoon, on the best tea-tray, and Mrs Griffiths complained, and we threw a snowball at her niece, and my hands burned so, with the heat and the cold, when I held them in front of the fire, that I cried for twenty minutes and then had some jelly.

All the Christmases roll down the hill towards the Welsh-speaking sea, like a snowball growing whiter and bigger and rounder, like a cold and headlong moon bundling down the sky that was our street; and they stop at the rim of the ice-edged, fish-freezing waves, and I plunge my hands in the snow and bring out whatever I can find; holly or robins or pudding, squabbles and carols and oranges and tin whistles, and the fire in the front room, and bang go the crackers, and holy, holy, holy, ring the bells, and the glass bells shaking on the tree, and Mother Goose, and Struwelpeter – oh! the baby-burning flames and the clacking scissorman! – Billy Bunter and Black Beauty, Little Women and boys who have three helpings, Alice and Mrs Potter's badgers, penknives, teddy-bears – named after a Mr Theodore Bear, their inventor, or father, who died recently in the United States – mouth-organs, tin-soldiers, and blancmange, and Auntie Bessie playing 'Pop Goes the Weasel' and 'Nuts in May' and 'Oranges and Lemons' on the untuned piano in the parlour all through the thimble-hiding musical-chairing blind-man's-buffing party at the end of the never-to-be-forgotten day at the end of the unremembered year.

In goes my hand into that wool-white bell-tongued ball of holidays resting at the margin of the carol-singing sea, and out come Mrs Prothero and the firemen.

It was on the afternoon of the day of Christmas Eve, and I was in Mrs Prothero's garden, waiting for cats, with her son Jim. It was snowing. It was always snowing at Christmas; December, in my memory, is white as Lapland, though there were no reindeers. But there were cats. Patient, cold, and callous, our hands wrapped in socks, we waited to snowball the cats. Sleek and long as jaguars and terrible-whiskered, spitting and snarling they would slink and sidle over the white back-garden walls, and the lynx-eyed hunters, Jim and I, furcapped and moccasined trappers from Hudson's Bay off Eversley Road, would hurl our deadly snowballs at the green of their eyes. The wise cats never appeared. We were so still, Eskimo-footed arctic marksmen in the muffling silence of the eternal snows – eternal, ever since Wednesday – that we never heard Mrs Prothero's first cry from her igloo at the bottom of the garden. Or, if we heard it at all, it was, to us, like the far-off challenge of our enemy and prey, the neighbour's Polar Cat. But soon the voice grew louder. 'Fire!' cried Mrs Prothero, and she beat the dinner-gong. And we ran down the garden, with the snowballs in our arms, towards the house, and smoke, indeed, was pouring out of the dining-room, and the gong was bombilating, and Mrs Prothero was announcing ruin like a towncrier in Pompeii. This was better than all the cats in Wales standing on the walls in a row. We bounded into the house, laden with snowballs, and stopped at the open door of the smoke-filled room. Something was burning all right; perhaps it was Mr Prothero, who always slept there after midday dinner with a newspaper over his face; but he was standing in the middle of the room, saying 'A fine Christmas!' and smacking at the smoke with a slipper.

'Call the fire-brigade,' cried Mrs Prothero as she beat the gong.

'They won't be there,' said Mr Prothero, 'it's Christmas.'

There was no fire to be seen, only clouds of smoke and Mr Prothero standing in the middle of them, waving his slipper as though he were conducting.

'Do something,' he said.

And we threw all our snowballs into the smoke – I think we missed Mr Prothero – and ran out of the house to the telephone box.

'Let's call the police as well,' Jim said.

'And the ambulance.'

'And Ernie Jenkins, he likes fires.'

But we only called the fire-brigade, and soon the fire-engine came and three tall men in helmets brought a hose into the house and Mr Prothero got out just in time before they turned it on. Nobody could have had a noisier Christmas Eve. And when the firemen turned off the hose and were standing in the wet and smoky room, Jim's aunt, Miss Prothero, came downstairs and peered in at them. Jim and I waited, very quietly, to hear what she would say to them. She said the right thing, always. She looked at the three tall firemen in their shining helmets, standing among the smoke and cinders and dissolving snowballs, and she said: 'Would you like something to read?'

Now out of that bright white snowball of Christmas gone comes the stocking, the stocking of stockings, that hung at the foot of the bed with the arm of a golliwog dangling over the top and small bells ringing in the toes. There was a company, gallant and scarlet but never nice to taste though I always tried when very young, of belted and busbied and musketed lead soldiers so soon to lose their heads and legs in the wars on the kitchen table after the tea-things, the mincepies, and the cakes that I helped to make by stoning the raisins and eating them, had been cleared away; and a bag of moist and many-coloured jelly-babies and a folded flag and a false nose and a tram-conductor's cap and a machine that punched tickets and rang a bell; never a catapult; once, by a mistake that no one could explain, a little hatchet; and a rubber buffalo, or it may have been a horse, with a yellow head and haphazard legs; and a celluloid duck that made, when you pressed it, a most unducklike noise, a mewing moo that an ambitious cat might make who wishes to be a cow; and a painting-book in which I could make the grass, the trees, the sea, and the animals any colour I pleased; and still the dazzling sky-blue sheep are grazing in the red field under a flight of rainbow-beaked and peagreen birds.

Christmas morning was always over before you could say Jack Frost. And look! suddenly the pudding was burning! Bang the gong and call the fire brigade and the book-loving firemen! Someone found the silver three-penny-bit with a currant on it; and the someone was always Uncle Arnold. The motto in my cracker read:

> Let's all have fun this Christmas Day,
> Let's play and sing and shout hooray!

and the grown-ups turned their eyes towards the ceiling, and Auntie Bessie, who had already been frightened, twice, by a clockwork mouse, whimpered at the sideboard and had some elderberry wine.

And someone put a glass bowl full of nuts on the littered table, and my uncle said, as he said once every year: 'I've got a shoe-nut here. Fetch me a shoe-horn to open it, boy.'

And dinner was ended.

And I remember that on the afternoon of Christmas Day, when the others sat around the fire and told each other that this was nothing, no, nothing, to the great snowbound and turkey-proud yule-log-crackling holly-berry-bedizined and kissing-under-the-mistletoe Christmas when *they* were children, I would go out, school-capped and gloved and mufflered, with my bright new boots squeaking, into the white world on to the seaward hill, to call Jim and Dan and Jack and to walk with them through the silent snowscape of our town.

We went padding through the streets, leaving huge deep footprints in the snow, on the hidden pavements.

'I bet people'll think there's been hippoes.'

'What would you do if you saw a hippo coming down Terrace Road?'

'I'd go like this, bang! I'd throw him over the railings and roll him down the hill and then I'd tickle him under the ear and he'd wag his tail . . .'

'What would you do if you saw *two* hippoes . . .?'

Iron-flanked and bellowed he-hippoes clanked and blundered and battered through the scudding snow towards us as we passed by Mr Daniel's house.

'Let's post Mr Daniel a snowball through his letter-box.'

'Let's write things in the snow.'

'Let's write "Mr Daniel looks like a spaniel" all over his lawn.'

'Look,' Jack said, 'I'm eating snow-pie.'

'What's it taste like?'

'Like snow-pie,' Jack said.

Or we walked on the white shore.

'Can the fishes see it's snowing?'

'They think it's the sky falling down.'

The silent one-clouded heavens drifted on to the sea.

'All the old dogs have gone.'

Dogs of a hundred mingled makes yapped in the summer at the sea-rim and yelped at the trespassing mountains of the waves.

'I bet St Bernards would like it now.'

And we were snowblind travellers lost on the north hills, and the great dewlapped dogs, with brandy-flasks round their necks, ambled and shambled up to us, baying 'Excelsior'.

We returned home through the desolate poor sea-facing streets where only a few children fumbled with bare red fingers in the thick wheel-rutted snow and cat-called after us, their voices fading away, as we trudged uphill, into the cries of the dock-birds and the hooters of ships out in the white and whirling bay.

Bring out the tall tales now that we told by the fire as we roasted chestnuts and the gaslight bubbled low. Ghosts with their heads under their arms trailed their chains and said 'whooo' like owls in the long nights when I dared not look over my shoulder; wild beasts lurked in the cubby-hole under the stairs where the gas-meter ticked. 'Once upon a time,' Jim said, 'there were three boys, just like us, who got lost in the dark in the snow, near Bethesda Chapel, and this is what happened to them. . . .' It was the most dreadful happening I had ever heard.

And I remember that we went singing carols once, a night or two before Christmas Eve, when there wasn't the shaving of a moon to light the secret, white-flying streets. At the end of a long road was a drive that led to a large house, and we stumbled up the darkness of the drive that night, each one of us afraid, each one holding a stone in his hand in case, and all of us too brave to say a word. The wind made through the drive-trees noises as of old and unpleasant and maybe web-footed men wheezing in caves. We reached the black bulk of the house.

'What shall we give them?' Dan whispered.

' "Hark the Herald"? "Christmas comes but Once a Year"?'

'No,' Jack said: 'We'll sing "Good King Wenceslas", I'll count three.'

One, two, three, and we began to sing, our voices high and seemingly distant in the snow-felted darkness round the house that was occupied by nobody we knew. We stood close together, near the dark door.

Good King Wenceslas looked out
On the Feast of Stephen.

And then a small, dry voice, like the voice of someone who has not spoken for a long time, suddenly joined our singing: a small, dry voice from the other side of the door: a small, dry voice through the keyhole. And when we stopped running we were outside *our* house; the front room was lovely and bright; the gramophone was playing; we saw the red and white balloons hanging from the gas-bracket; uncles and aunts sat by the fire; I thought I smelt our supper being fried in the kitchen. Everything was good again, and Christmas shone through all the familiar town.

'Perhaps it was a ghost,' Jim said.

'Perhaps it was trolls,' Dan said, who was always reading.

'Let's go in and see if there's any jelly left,' Jack said. And we did that.

Holiday Memory

August Bank Holiday. A tune on an ice-cream cornet. A slap of sea and a tickle of sand. A fanfare of sunshades opening. A wince and whinny of bathers dancing into deceptive water. A tuck of dresses. A rolling of trousers. A compromise of paddlers. A sunburn of girls and a lark of boys. A silent hullabaloo of balloons.

I remember the sea telling lies in a shell held to my ear for a whole harmonious, hollow minute by a small, wet girl in an enormous bathing-suit marked 'Corporation Property'.

I remember sharing the last of my moist buns with a boy and a lion. Tawny and savage, with cruel nails and capacious mouth, the little boy tore and devoured. Wild as seed-cake, ferocious as a hearth-rug, the depressed and verminous lion nibbled like a mouse at his half a bun, and hiccupped in the sad dusk of his cage.

I remember a man like an alderman or a bailiff, bowlered and collarless, with a bag of monkey-nuts in his hand, crying 'Ride 'em, cowboy!' time and again as he whirled in his chairoplane giddily above the upturned laughing faces of the town girls bold as brass and the boys with padded shoulders and shoes sharp as knives; and the monkey-nuts flew through the air like salty hail.

Children all day capered or squealed by the glazed or bashing sea, and the steam-organ wheezed its waltzes in the threadbare playground and the waste lot, where the dodgems dodged, behind the pickle factory.

And mothers loudly warned their proud pink daughters or sons to put that jellyfish down; and fathers spread newspapers over their faces; and sand-fleas hopped on the picnic lettuce; and someone had forgotten the salt.

In those always radiant, rainless, lazily rowdy and sky-blue summers departed, I remember August Monday from the rising of the sun over the stained and royal town to the dusky hushing of the roundabout music and the dowsing of the naphtha jets in the seaside fair: from bubble-and-squeak to the last of the sandy sandwiches.

There was no need, that holiday morning, for the sluggardly boys to be shouted down to breakfast; out of their jumbled beds they tumbled, scrambled into their rumpled clothes; quickly at the bathroom basin they catlicked their hands and faces, but never forgot to run the water loud and long as though they washed like colliers; in front of the cracked looking-glass bordered with cigarette-cards, in their treasure-trove bedrooms, they whisked a gap-tooth comb through their surly hair; and with shining cheeks and noses and tide-marked necks, they took the stairs three at a time.

But for all their scramble and scamper, clamour on the landing, catlick and toothbrush flick, hair-whisk and stair-jump, their sisters were always there before them. Up with the lady lark, they had prinked and frizzed and hot-ironed; and smug in their blossoming dresses, ribboned for the sun, in gym-shoes white as the blanco'd snow, neat and silly with doilies and tomatoes they helped in the higgledy kitchen. They were calm; they were virtuous; they had washed their necks; they did not romp, or fidget; and only the smallest sister put out her tongue at the noisy boys.

And the woman who lived next door came into the kitchen and said that her mother, an ancient uncertain body who wore a hat with cherries, was having 'one of her days' and had insisted, that very holiday morning, in carrying all the way to the tram-stop a photograph album and the cut-glass fruit-bowl from the front room.

This was the morning when father, mending one hole in the thermos-flask, made three; when the sun declared war on the butter, and the butter ran; when dogs, with all the sweet-binned backyards to wag and sniff and bicker in, chased their tails in the jostling kitchen, worried sandshoes, snapped at flies, writhed between legs, scratched among towels, sat smiling on hampers.

And if you could have listened at some of the open doors of some of the houses in the street you might have heard:

'Uncle Owen says he can't find the bottle-opener ...'

'Has he looked under the hall-stand?'

'Willy's cut his finger ...'

'Got your spade?'

'If somebody doesn't kill that dog ...'

'Uncle Owen says why should the bottle-opener be under the hall-stand?'

'Never again, never again ...'

'I know I put the pepper somewhere ...'

'Willy's bleeding ...'

'Look, there's a bootlace in my bucket ...'

'Oh come *on,* come on ...'

'Let's have a look at the bootlace in your bucket ...'

'If I lay my hands on that dog ...'

'Uncle Owen's found the bottle-opener ...'

'Willy's bleeding over the cheese ...'

And the trams that hissed like ganders took us all to the beautiful beach.

There was cricket on the sand, and sand in the sponge cake, sandflies in the watercress, and foolish, mulish, religious donkeys on the unwilling trot. Girls undressed in slipping tents of propriety; under invisible umbrellas, stout ladies dressed for the male and immoral sea. Little naked navvies dug canals; children with spades and no ambition built fleeting castles; wispy young men, outside the bathing-huts, whistled at substantial young women and dogs who desired thrown stones more than the bones of elephants. Recalcitrant uncles huddled over luke ale in the tiger-striped marquees. Mothers in black, like wobbling mountains, gasped under the discarded dresses of daughters who shrilly braved the goblin waves. And fathers, in the once-a-year sun, took fifty winks. Oh, think of all the fifty winks along the paper-bagged sand.

Liquorice Allsorts, and Welsh hearts, were melting, and the sticks of rock, that we all sucked, were like barbers' poles made of rhubarb.

In the distance, surrounded by disappointed theoreticians and an ironmonger with a drum, a cross man on an orange-box shouted that holidays were wrong.

And the waves rolled in, with rubber ducks and clerks upon them.

I remember the patient, laborious, and enamouring hobby, or profession, of burying relatives in sand.

I remember the princely pastime of pouring sand, from cupped hands or buckets, down collars and tops of dresses; the shriek, the shake, the slap.

I can remember the boy by himself, the beachcombing lone-wolf, hungrily waiting at the edge of family cricket; the friendless fielder, the boy uninvited to bat or to tea.

I remember the smell of sea and seaweed, wet flesh, wet hair, wet bathing-dresses, the warm smell as of a rabbity field after rain, the smell of pop and splashed sunshades and toffee, the stable-and-straw smell of hot, tossed, tumbled, dug, and trodden sand, the swill-and-gaslamp smell of Saturday night, though the sun shone strong, from the bellying beer-tents, the smell of the vinegar on shelled cockles, winkle-smell, shrimp-smell, the dripping-oily backstreet winter-smell of chips in newspapers, the smell of ships from the sun-dazed docks round the corner of the sand-hills, the smell of the known and paddled-in sea moving, full of the drowned and herrings, out and away and beyond and further still towards the antipodes that hung their koala-bears and Maoris, kangaroos, and boomerangs, upside down over the backs of the stars.

And the noise of pummelling Punch, and Judy falling, and a clock tolling or telling no time in the tenantless town; now and again a bell from a lost tower or a train on the lines behind us clearing its throat, and always the hopeless, ravenous swearing and pleading of the gulls, donkey-bray and hawker-cry, harmonicas and toy trumpets, shouting and laughing and singing, hooting of tugs and tramps, the clip of the chair-attendant's puncher, the motor-boat coughing in the bay, and the same hymn and washing of the sea that was heard in the Bible.

'If it could only just, if it could only just?' your lips said again and again as you scooped, in the hob-hot sand, dungeons, garages, torture-chambers, train tunnels, arsenals, hangars for zeppelins, witches' kitchens, vampires' parlours, smugglers' cellars, trolls' grog-shops, sewers, under a ponderous and cracking castle, 'If it could only just be like this for ever and ever amen.' August Monday all over the earth, from Mumbles where the aunties grew like ladies on a seaside tree to brown, bear-hugging Henty-land and the turtled Ballantyne Islands.

'Could donkeys go on the ice?'

'Only if they got snowshoes.'

We snowshoed a meek, complaining donkey and galloped him off in the wake of the ten-foot-tall and Atlas-muscled Mounties, rifled and pemmicanned, who always, in the white Gold Rush wastes, got their black-oathed-and-bearded Man.

'Are there donkeys on desert islands?'

'Only sort-of-donkeys.'

'What d'you mean, sort-of-donkeys?'

'Native donkeys. They hunt things on them!'

'Sort-of walruses and seals and things?'

'Donkeys can't swim!'

'These donkeys can. They swim like whales, they swim like anything, they swim like –'

'Liar.'

'Liar yourself.'

And two small boys fought fiercely and silently in the sand, rolling together in a ball of legs and bottoms.

Then they went and saw the pierrots, or bought vanilla ices.

Lolling or larrikin that unsoiled, boiling beauty of a common day, great gods with their braces over their vests sang, spat pips, puffed smoke at wasps, gulped and ogled, forgot the rent, embraced, posed for the dicky-bird, were coarse, had rainbow-coloured armpits, winked, belched, blamed the radishes, looked at Ilfracombe, played hymns on paper-and-comb, peeled bananas, scratched, found seaweed in their panamas, blew up paper-bags and banged them, wished for nothing.

But over all the beautiful beach I remember most the children playing, boys and girls tumbling, moving jewels, who might never be happy again. And 'happy as a sandboy' is true as the heat of the sun.

Dusk came down; or grew up out of the sands and the sea; or curled around us from the calling docks and the bloodily smoking sun. The day was done, the sands brushed and ruffled suddenly with a sea-broom of cold wind.

And we gathered together all the spades and buckets and towels, empty hampers and bottles, umbrellas and fish-frails, bats and balls and knitting, and went – oh, listen, Dad! – to the fair in the dusk on the bald seaside field.

Fairs were no good in the day; then they were shoddy and tired; the voices of hoop-la girls were crimped as elocutionists; no cannon-ball could shake the roosting coconuts; the gondolas mechanically repeated their sober lurch; the Wall of Death was safe as a governess cart; the wooden animals were waiting for the night.

But in the night, the hoop-la girls, like operatic crows, croaked at the coming moon; whizz, whirl, and ten for a tanner, the coconuts rained from their sawdust like grouse from the Highland sky; tipsy the griffin-prowed gondolas weaved on dizzy rails and the Wall of Death was a spinning rim of ruin, and the neighing wooden horses took, to a haunting hunting tune, a thousand Becher's Brooks as easily and breezily as hooved swallows.

Approaching, at dusk, the fair-field from the beach, we scorched and gritty boys heard above the belabouring of the batherless sea the siren voices of the raucous, horsy barkers.

'Roll up, roll up!'

In her tent and her rolls of flesh the Fattest Woman in the World sat sewing her winter frock, another tent, and fixed her little eyes, blackcurrants in blancmange, on the skeletons who filed and sniggered by.

'Roll up, roll up, roll up to see the Largest Rat on Earth, the Rover or Bonzo of vermin.'

Here scampered the smallest pony, like a Shetland shrew. And here 'The Most Intelligent Fleas', trained, reined, bridled, and bitted, minutely cavorted in their glass corral.

Round galleries and shies and stalls, pennies were burning holes in a hundred pockets.

Pale young men with larded hair and Valentino-black side-whiskers, fags struck to their lower lips, squinted along their swivel-sighted rifles and aimed at ping-pong balls dancing on fountains.

In knife-creased, silver-grey, skirt-like Oxford bags, and a sleeveless, scarlet, zip-fastened shirt with yellow horizontal stripes, a collier at the strength-machine spat on his hands, raised the hammer, and brought it Thor-ing down. The bell rang for Blaina.

Outside his booth stood a bitten-eared and barndoor-chested pug with a nose like a twisted swede and hair that started from his eyebrows and three teeth yellow as a camel's inviting any sportsman to a sudden and sickening basting in the sandy ring or a quid if he lasted a round; and, wiry, cocky, bow-legged, coal-scarred, boozed, sportsmen by the dozen strutted in and reeled out; and still those three teeth remained, chipped and camel-yellow in the bored, teak face.

Draggled and stout-wanting mothers, with haphazard hats, hostile hatpins, buns awry, bursting bags, and children at their skirts like pop-filled and jam-smeared limpets, screamed before distorting mirrors, at their suddenly tapering or tubular bodies and huge ballooning heads, and the children gaily bellowed at their own reflected bogies withering and bulging in the glass.

Old men, smelling of Milford Haven in the rain, shuffled, badgering and cadging, round the edges of the swaggering crowd, their only wares a handful of damp confetti.

A daring dash of schoolboys, safely, shoulder to shoulder, with their father's trilbies cocked at a desperate angle over one eye, winked at and whistled after the procession past the swings of two girls arm-in-arm: always one pert and pretty, and always one with glasses.

Girls in skulled and cross-boned tunnels shrieked, and were comforted.

Young men, heroic after pints, stood up on the flying chairoplanes, tousled, crimson, and against the rules.

Jaunty girls gave sailors sauce.

All the fun of the fair in the hot, bubbling night. The Man in the sand-yellow moon over the hurdy of gurdies. The swingboats swimming to and fro like slices of the moon. Dragons and hippogriffs at the prows of the gondolas breathing fire and Sousa. Midnight roundabout riders tantivying under the fairy-lights, huntsmen on billygoats and zebras hallooing under a circle of glow-worms.

And as we climbed home, up the gas-lit hill, to the still homes over the mumbling bay, we heard the music die and the voices drift like sand. And we saw the lights of the fair fade. And, at the far end of the seaside field, they lit their lamps, one by one, in the caravans.

The Festival Exhibition, 1951

The extent of the site of the exhibition on the South Bank of the Thames in the heart of London is four and a half acres. There are twenty-two pavilions in the exhibition, and thirteen restaurants, cafés, bars, and buffets.

Some people visit the twenty-two pavilions first, then glazed and crippled, windless, rudderless, and a little out of their minds, teeter, weeping, to one of the thirteen restaurants, cafés, bars, and buffets to find it packed to the dazzlingly painted and, possibly, levitating doors.

Other people visit all thirteen restaurants, cafés, bars, and buffets before attacking the pavilions, and rarely get further than the Dome of Discovery, which they find confusing, full, as it is, of totem poles, real dogs in snow, locusts, stars, the sun, the moon, things bubbling, thunder and lightning machines, chemical and physical surprises. And some never return.

Most people who wish, at the beginning, anyway, to make sense of the exhibition, follow the course indicated in the official guide-book – a series of conflicting arrows which lead many visitors who cannot understand these things slap-splash into the Thames – and work their way dutifully right through the land of Britain, the glaciers of twenty thousand years ago, and the inferno of blown desert sand which is now Birmingham, out at last into the Pavilion of Health – where, perhaps, they stop for an envious moment at the sign that says 'Euthanasia' – and on to the netted and capstaned, bollarded, buoyed, sea-shelled pebbly beautiful seaside of summer childhood gone.

And other visitors begin, of course, at the end. They are the people without whom the exhibition could not exist, nor the country it trombones and floats in with its lions and unicorns made of ears of wheat, its birds that sing to the push of a button, its flaming water, and its raspberry fountains. They are the suspicious people over whose eyes no coloured Festival wool can possibly be pulled, the great undiddleable; they are the women who 'will not queue on any account' and who smuggle in dyspeptic dogs; the strangely calculating men who think that the last pavilion must be first because it is number twenty-two; the people who believe they are somewhere else, and never find out they are not; sharp people who have been there before, who know the ropes, who chuckle to their country cousins: 'You get double your money's worth this way'; vaguely persecuted people, always losing their gloves, who know that the only way they could *ever* get around would be to begin at the end, which they do not want to; people of militant individuality who proclaim their right, as Englishmen, to look at the damfool place however they willynilly will; people nervously affected by all such occasions, who want to know only, 'Where's the place?'; timid people who want to be as far from the skylon as possible, because 'you never know'; foreigners, who have been directed this way by a school of irresponsible wits; glassy benighted men who are trying to remember they must see something of the exhibition to remember before they go home and try to describe it to their families; young people, hand-in-love, who will giggle at whatever they see, at a goldfish in a pond, a model of the *Queen Elizabeth*, or a flint hammer; people too bored to yawn, long and rich as borzois, who, before they have seen it, have seen better shows in Copenhagen and San Francisco; eccentric people: men with their deerstalker caps tied with rope to their lapels, who carry dried nut sandwiches and little containers of yoghurt in hairy green knapsacks labelled 'glass with care'; fat, flustered women in as many layers of coats as an onion or a cab-driver, hunting in a fever through fifty fluffed pockets to find a lost packet of bird-seed they are going to give to the parrots who are not there; old scaly sneezing men, born of lizards in a snuff-bin, who read, wherever they go, from books in tiny print, and who never look up, even at the tureen-lid of the just-tethered dome or the shining skylon, the skygoing nylon, the cylindrical leg-of-the-future jetting, almost, to the exhibition of stars; *real* eccentrics: people who have come to the South Bank to study the growth and development of Britain from the Iron Age till now. Here they will find no braying pageantry, no taxidermal museum of Culture, no cold and echoing inhuman hygienic barracks of technical information, no shoddily cajoling emporium of tasteless Empire wares, but something very odd indeed, magical and parochial: a parish-pump made of flying glass and thistledown gauze-thin steel, a rolypoly pudding full of luminous, melodious bells, wheels, coils, engines and organs, alembics and jorums in a palace in thunderland sizzling with scientific witches' brews, a place of trains, bones, planes, ships, sheep, shapes, snipe, mobiles, marbles, brass bands, and cheese, a place painted regardless, and by hand.

Perhaps you'll think I'm shovelling the colour on too thickly; that I am, as it were, speaking under the influence of strong pink. (And what a lot of pink – rose, raspberry, strawberry, peach, flesh, blush, lobster, salmon, tally-ho – there is, plastered and doodled all over this four-acre gay and soon-to-be-gone Festival City in sprawling London.) London: to many of us who live in the country, the Capital punishment. Perhaps you will go on a cool, dull day, sane as a biscuit, and find that the exhibition does, indeed, tell the story 'of British contributions to world civilization in the arts of peace'; that, and nothing else. But I'm pleased to doubt it. Of *course* it is instructive; of *course* there is behind it an articulate and comprehensive plan; it can show you, unless you are an expert, more about, say, mineralogy or the ionosphere than you may want to know. It's bursting its buttons, in an orderly manner, with knowledge. But what everyone I know, and have observed, seems to like most in it is the gay, absurd, irrelevant, delighting imagination that flies and booms and spurts and trickles out of the whole bright boiling; the small stone oddity that squints at you round a sharp, daubed corner; the sexless abstract sculptures serenely and secretly existing out of time in old cold worlds of their own in places that appear, but only for one struck second, inappropriate; the linked terra-cotta man and woman fly-defying gravity and elegantly hurrying up a w.c. wall; the sudden design of hands on another wall, as though the painter had said: 'Oh, to the daft devil with what I'm doing,' and just slap-slap-slapped all over the ochre his spread-out fingers and thumbs, ten blunt arrows, or as though large convict-birds, if there are any such, had waddled up the wall and webbed it as they went. You see people go along briskly down the wide white avenues towards the pavilion of their fancy – 'Our Humbert's dead keen on seeing the milk-separators' – and suddenly stop: another fancy swings or bubbles in front of their eyes. What is it they see? Indigo water waltzing to music. Row after row of rosy rolling balls spread on tall screens like the counting beads of Wellsian children fed on the food of the gods. Sheets of asbestos tied on to nowhere, by nothing, for nothing is anchored here and at the clap of hands the whole gallimaufry could take off to Sousa and zoom up the flagged sky. Small childbook-painted mobiles along the bridges that, at a flick of wind, become windmills and thrum round at night like rainbows with arms. Or the steel-and-platinum figure – created by the Welsh engineer and architect, Richard Huws – of maybe a mer-woman standing, if that is the word for one who grows out of it, in arc-light water; she weeps as she is wept on; first her glinting breast, then another plane of her, tips, slides, shoots, shelves, swings and sidles out to take, from the lake of her birth, one tone of water at a time to Handel's *Water Music*, absorbs it, inhales it through dripping steel, then casts and cascades it off and out again. Or even the hundreds of little vivid steel chairs that look like hundreds of little vivid steel people sitting down.

In the pavilion called 'The Natural Scene', see the seals and eagles, the foxes and wild cats, of these still wild islands, and the natural history of owled and cuckooed, ottered, unlikely London. A great naked tree climbs in the middle of all, with prodigious butterflies and beetles on it. A blackbird lights up, and the aviary's full of his singing; a thrush, a curlew, a skylark.

And, in the 'Country', see all the sculpted and woven loaves, in the shape of sheaves of wheat, in curls, plaits, and whirls. And men are thatching the roofs of cottages; and – what could be more natural? – the men are made of straw. And what a pleasure of baskets! Trugs, creels, pottles and punnets, heppers, dorsers and mounds, wiskets and whiskets. And if these are not the proper words, they should be.

In 'The Lion and the Unicorn' is celebrated, under flights of birds, the 'British Character', that stubborn, stupid seabound, lyrical, paradoxical dark farrago of uppishness, derring-do, and midsummer moonshine all fluting, snug, and copper-bottomed. Justice, for some reason, looms in the midst of the Hall, its two big wigs back to back, its black and scarlet robes falling below. The body of justice is shelves of law books. The black spaces beneath the white wigs looks like the profiles of eagles. The white knight rides there too, too much a Don Quixote for my looking-glass land, and very potless and panless. A bravo-ing hand pats his plaster back, and tells him good night. There is a machine for, I believe, grinding smoke. And a tea-set, I failed to see, of salmon bones. But, in all this authentically eccentric exhibition, it is the Eccentrics' Corner that is the most insipid. Some of the dullest exhibits in the pavilion are relieved by surrounding extravagance; but the department devoted to the rhapsodic inspirations of extravagance is by far the dullest. Why was not the exquisite talent utilized of the warlock who, offering his services to the Festival authorities, assured them he would, to order, throw a rainbow over the Thames? I wish he would throw a rainbow over me as I walk through the grey days. 'Yes, we can tell it's him coming,' the envious neighbours would murmur, 'we recognize his rainbow.' And, on the balcony, there is a row of tiny theatres; in each, the stage is set for a Shakespearian play; and out of the theatres come the words of the players. If you're in luck, something may go wrong with the works and Hamlet rant from Dunsinane.

In 'Homes and Gardens', blink at the grievous furniture, ugly as sin and less comfy.

In the 'Transport Pavilions', goggle at the wizard diesels and the smashing, unpuffing streamlines and the miracle model railway for dwarf nabobs.

Then, if there are by this time no spots in front of your eyes, go to the Telecinema and see them astonishingly all around you: spots with scarlet tadpole tails, and spottedly sinuous tintacks dancing with dissolving zebra heads, and blobs and nubbins and rubbery squirls receding, to zig-zag blasts of brass, down nasty polychrome corridors, a St Vitus's gala of abstract shapes and shades in a St Swithin's day of torrential dazzling darning needles. Sit still in the startling cinema and be kissed by a giraffe, who stretches his neck right out of the screen for you. Follow the deliberately coloured course of the Thames, the Royal River; the whispering water's more like water than water ever was; closer, closer, comes the slow kingfisher – blue water and suddenly it ripples all over you: that'll be the day when film stars do the same.

Go to the South Bank first by day; the rest of your times at night. Sit at a café table in the night of musical lights, by the radiant river, the glittering skylon above you rearing to be off, the lit pavilion, white, black, and silver in sweeps of stone and feathery steel, transplendent round you as you sip and think:

This is the first time I have ever truly seen that London whose sweet Thames runs softly; that minstrel mermaid of a town, the water-streeted eight-million-headed village in a blaze. *This* is London, not the huge petty misshaped nightmare I used to know as I hum-drummed along its graceless streets through fog and smoke and past the anonymous unhappy bodies lively as wet brollies. This Festival is London. The arches of the bridges leap into light; the moon clocks glow; the river sings; the harmonious pavilions are happy. And this is what London should always be like, till St Paul's falls down and the sea slides over the Strand.

A Visit to America

Across the United States of America, from New York to California and back, glazed, again, for many months of the year there streams and sings for its heady supper a dazed and prejudiced procession of European lecturers, scholars, sociologists, economists, writers, authorities on this and that and even, in theory, on the United States of America. And, breathlessly between addresses and receptions, in planes and trains and boiling hotel bedroom ovens, many of these attempt to keep journals and diaries. At first, confused and shocked by shameless profusion and almost shamed by generosity, unaccustomed to such importance as they are assumed, by their hosts, to possess, and up against the barrier of a common language, they write their note-books like demons, generalizing away, on character and culture and the American political scene. But, towards the middle of their middle-aged whisk through middle-western clubs and universities, the fury of the writing flags; their spirits are lowered by the spirit with which they are everywhere strongly greeted and which, in ever-increasing doses, they themselves lower; and they begin to mistrust themselves, and their reputations – for they have found, too often, that an audience will receive a lantern-lecture on, say, ceramics, with the same uninhibited enthusiasm that it accorded the very week before to a paper on the Modern Turkish Novel. And, in their diaries, more and more do such entries appear as, 'No way of escape!' or 'Buffalo!' or 'I am beaten', until at last they cannot write a word. And, twittering all over, old before their time, with eyes like rissoles in the sand, they are helped up the gangway of the home-bound liner by kind bosom friends (of all kinds and bosoms) who boister them on the back, pick them up again, thrust bottles, sonnets, cigars, addresses into their pockets, have a farewell party in their cabin, pick them up again, and, snickering and yelping, are gone: to wait at the dockside for another boat from Europe and another batch of fresh, green lecturers.

There they go, every spring, from New York to Los Angeles:

exhibitionists, polemicists, histrionic publicists, theological rhetoricians, historical hoddy-doddies, balletomanes, ulterior decorators, windbags, and bigwigs and humbugs, men in love with stamps, men in love with steaks, men after millionaires' widows, men with elephantiasis of the reputation (huge trunks and teeny minds), authorities on gas, bishops, best sellers, editors looking for writers, writers looking for publishers, publishers looking for dollars, existentialists, serious physicists with nuclear missions, men from the B.B.C. who speak as though they had the Elgin Marbles in their mouths, potboiling philosophers, professional Irishmen (very lepri-corny), and I am afraid, fat poets with slim volumes. And see, too, in that linguaceous stream, the tall monocled men, smelling of saddle soap and club armchairs, their breath a nice blending of whisky and fox's blood, with big protruding upper-class tusks and county moustaches, presumably invented in England and sent abroad to advertise *Punch*, who lecture to women's clubs on such unlikely subjects as 'The History of Etching in the Shetland Islands'. And the brassy-bossy men-women, with corrugated-iron perms, and hippo hides, who come, self-announced, as 'ordinary British housewives', to talk to rich minked chunks of American matronhood about the iniquity of the Health Services, the criminal sloth of the miners, the *visible* tail and horns of Mr Aneurin Bevan, and the fear of everyone in England to go out alone at night because of the organized legions of cosh boys against whom the police are powerless owing to the refusal of those in power to equip them with revolvers and to flog to ribbons every adolescent offender on any charge at all. And there shiver and teeter also, meek and driven, those British authors unfortunate enough to have written, after years of unadventurous forgotten work, one bad novel which became enormously popular on both sides of the Atlantic. At home, when success first hit them, they were mildly delighted; a couple of literary luncheons went sugar-tipsy to their heads, like the washing sherry served before those luncheons; and perhaps, as the lovely money rolled lushly in, they began to dream in their moony writers' way, of being able to retire to the country, keep wasps (or was it bees?), and never write another lousy word. But in come the literary agent's triggermen and the publisher's armed narks: 'You must go to the States and make a Personal Appearance. Your novel is *killing* them over there, and we're not surprised either. You must go round the States lecturing to women.' And the inoffensive writers, who've never dared lecture anyone, let alone women – they are frightened of women, they do not understand women, they write about women as creatures that never existed, and the women lap it up – these sensitive plants cry out: 'But what shall we lecture about?'

'The English Novel.'

'I don't read novels.'

'Great Women in Fiction.'

'I don't like fiction *or* women.'

But off they're wafted, first class, in the plush bowels of the *Queen Victoria* with a list of engagements long as a New York menu or a half-hour with a book by Charles Morgan, and soon they are losing their little cold-as-goldfish paw in the great general glutinous handshake of a clutch of enveloping hostesses. I think, by the way, that it was Ernest Raymond, the author of *Tell England*, who once made a journey round the American women's clubs, being housed and entertained at each small town he stopped at by the richest and largest and furriest lady available. On one occasion he stopped at some little station, and was met, as usual, by an enormous motor-car full of a large hornrimmed business man, looking *exactly* like a large hornrimmed business man on the films – and his roly-poly pearly wife. Mr Raymond sat with her in the back of the car, and off they went, the husband driving. At once, she began to say how utterly delighted she and her husband and the committee were to have him at their Women's Literary and Social Guild, and to compliment him on his books. 'I don't think I've ever, in all my life, enjoyed a book so much as *Sorrel and Son*,' she said. 'What you don't know about human nature! I think Sorrel is one of the most beautiful characters ever portrayed.'

Ernest Raymond let her talk on, while he stared, embarrassed, in front of him. All he could see were the three double chins that her husband wore at the back of his neck. On and on she gushed in praise of *Sorrel and Son* until he could stand it no longer. 'I quite agree with you,' he said. 'A beautiful book indeed. But I'm afraid I didn't write *Sorrel and Son*. It was written by an old friend of mine, Mr Warwick Deeping.'

And the large hornrimmed double-chinned husband at the wheel said without turning: 'Caught again, Emily.'

See the garrulous others, also gabbing and garlanded from one nest of culture-vultures to another: people selling the English way of life and condemning the American way as they swig and guzzle through it; people resurrecting the theories of surrealism for the benefit of remote parochial female audiences who did not know it was dead, not having ever known it had been alive; people talking about

Etruscan pots and pans to a bunch of dead pans and wealthy pots in Boston. And there, too, in the sticky thick of lecturers moving across the continent black with clubs, go to foreign poets, catarrhal troubadours, lyrical one-night-standers, dollar-mad nightingales, remittance-bards from at home, myself among them booming with the worst.

Did we pass one another, *en route*, I wonder, one of us, spry-eyed, with clean, white lectures and a soul he could call his own, going buoyantly west to his remunerative doom in the great State University factories, another returning dog-eared as his clutch of poems and his carefully typed impromptu asides? I ache for us both. There one goes, unsullied as yet, in his Pullman pride, toying, oh boy, with a blunderbuss bourbon, being smoked by a large cigar, riding out to the wide open spaces of the faces of his waiting audience. He carries, besides his literary baggage, a new, dynamic razor, just on the market, bought in New York, which operates at the flick of a thumb, but cuts the thumb to the bone; a tin of new shaving-lather which is worked with the other, unbleeding, thumb and covers not only the face but the whole bath-room and, instantly freezing, makes an arctic, icicled cave from which it takes two sneering bell-boys to extract him; and, of course, a nylon shirt. This, he dearly believed from the advertisements, he could himself wash in his hotel, hang to dry overnight, and put on, without ironing, in the morning. (In my case, no ironing *was* needed, for, as someone cruelly pointed out in print, I looked, anyway, like an unmade bed.)

He is vigorously welcomed at the station by an earnest crew-cut platoon of giant collegiates, all chasing the butterfly culture with net, note-book, poison-bottle, pin, and label, each with at least thirty-six terribly white teeth, and is nursed away, as heavily gently as though he were an imbecile rich aunt with a short prospect of life, into a motor-car in which, for a mere fifty miles or so travelled at poet-breaking speed, he assures them of the correctness of their assumption that he is half-witted by stammering inconsequential answers in an over-British accent to their genial questions about what international conference Stephen Spender might be attending at the moment or the reactions of British poets to the work of a famous American whose name he did not know or catch. He is then taken to a small party of only a few hundred people all of whom hold the belief that what a visiting lecturer needs before he trips on to the platform is just enough martinis so that he can trip *off* the platform as well. And, clutching his explosive glass, he is soon contemptuously dismissing, in a flush of ignorance and fluency, the poetry of those androgynous literary ladies with three names who produce a kind of verbal ectoplasm to order as a waiter dishes up spaghetti – only to find that the fiercest of these, a wealthy huntress of small, seedy lions (such as himself), who stalks the middle-western bush with ears and rifle cocked, is his hostess for the evening. Of the lecture he remembers little but the applause and maybe two questions: 'Is it true that the young English intellectuals are *really* psychological?' or, 'I always carry Kierkegaard in my pocket. What do you carry?'

Late at night, in his room, he fills a page of his journal with a confused, but scathing, account of his first engagement; summarizes American advanced education in a paragraph that will be meaningless tomorrow, and falls to sleep where he is immediately chased through long, dark thickets by a Mrs Mabel Frankincense Mehaffey, with a tray of martinis and lyrics.

And there goes the other happy poet bedraggedly back to New York which struck him all of a sheepish never-sleeping heap at first but which seems to him now, after the ulcerous rigours of a lecturer's spring, a haven cosy as toast, cool as an icebox, and safe as skyscrapers.

Return Journey

NARRATOR

It was a cold white day in High Street, and nothing to stop the wind slicing up from the docks, for where the squat and tall shops had shielded the town from the sea lay their blitzed flat graves marbled with snow and headstoned with fences. Dogs, delicate as cats on water, as though they had gloves on their paws, padded over the vanished buildings. Boys romped, calling high and clear, on top of a levelled chemist's and a shoe-shop, and a little girl, wearing a man's cap, threw a snowball in a chill deserted garden that had once been the Jug and Bottle of the Prince of Wales. The wind cut up the street with a soft sea-noise hanging on its arm, like a hooter in a muffler. I could see the swathed hill stepping up out of the town, which you never could see properly before, and the powdered fields of the roofs of Milton Terrace and Watkin Street and Fullers Row. Fish-frailed, netbagged, umbrella'd, pixie-capped, fur-shoed, blue-nosed, puce-lipped, blinkered like dray-horses, scarved, mittened, galoshed, wearing everything but the cat's blanket, crushes of shopping-women crunched in the little Lapland of the once grey drab street, blew and queued and yearned for hot tea, as I began my search through Swansea town cold and early on that wicked February morning. I went into the hotel. 'Good morning.'

The hall-porter did not answer. I was just another snowman to him. He did not know that I was looking for someone after fourteen years, and he did not care. He stood and shuddered, staring through the glass of the hotel door at the snowflakes sailing down the sky, like Siberian confetti. The bar was just opening, but already one customer puffed and shook at the counter with a full pint of half-frozen Tawe water in his wrapped-up hand. I said Good morning, and the barmaid, polishing the counter vigorously as though it were a rare and valuable piece of Swansea china, said to her first customer:

BARMAID

Seen the film at the Elysium Mr Griffiths there's snow isn't it did you come up on your bicycle our pipes burst Monday ...

NARRATOR

A pint of bitter, please.

BARMAID

Proper little lake in the kitchen got to wear your Wellingtons when you boil a egg one and four please ...

CUSTOMER

The cold gets me just here ...

BARMAID

... and eightpence change that's your liver Mr Griffiths you been on the cocoa again ...

NARRATOR

I wonder whether you remember a friend of mine? He always used to come to this bar, some years ago. Every morning, about this time.

CUSTOMER

Just by here it gets me. I don't know what'd happen if I didn't wear a band ...

BARMAID

What's his name?

NARRATOR

Young Thomas.

BARMAID

Lots of Thomases come here it's a kind of home from home for Thomases isn't it Mr Griffiths what's he look like?

NARRATOR

He'd be about seventeen or eighteen ... (*Slowly*)

BARMAID

... I was seventeen once ...

NARRATOR

... and above medium height. Above medium height for Wales, I mean, he's five foot six and a half. Thick blubber lips; snub nose; curly mousebrown hair; one front tooth broken after playing a game called Cats and Dogs, in the Mermaid, Mumbles; speaks rather fancy; truculent; plausible; a bit of a shower-off; plus-fours and no breakfast, you know; used to have poems printed in the *Herald of Wales*; there was one about an open-air performance of *Electra* in Mrs Bertie Perkins's garden in Sketty; lived up the Uplands; a bombastic adolescent provincial Bohemian with a thick-knotted artist's tie made out of his sister's scarf, she never knew where it had gone, and a cricket-shirt dyed bottle-green; a gabbing, ambitious, mock-tough, pretentious young man; and mole-y, too.

BARMAID

There's words what d'you want to find *him* for I wouldn't touch him with a barge-pole ... would you, Mr Griffiths? Mind, you can never tell. I remember a man came here with a monkey. Called for 'alf for himself and a pint for the monkey. And he wasn't Italian at all. Spoke Welsh like a preacher.

NARRATOR

The bar was filling up. Snowy business bellies pressed their watch-chains against the counter; black business bowlers, damp and white now as Christmas puddings in their cloths, bobbed in front of the misty mirrors. The voice of commerce rang sternly through the lounge.

FIRST VOICE

Cold enough for you?

SECOND VOICE

How's your pipes, Mr Lewis?

THIRD VOICE

Another winter like this'll put paid to me, Mr Evans.

FOURTH VOICE

I got the 'flu ...

FIRST VOICE

Make it a double ...

SECOND VOICE

Similar ...

BARMAID

Okay, baby ...

CUSTOMER

I seem to remember a chap like you described. There couldn't be two like him let's hope. He used to work as a reporter. Down the Three Lamps I used to see him. Lifting his ikkle elbow.

(Confidentially)

NARRATOR

What's the Three Lamps like now?

CUSTOMER

It isn't like anything. It isn't there. It's nothing mun. You remember Ben Evans's stores? It's right next door to that. Ben Evans isn't there either ...

(Fade)

NARRATOR

I went out of the hotel into the snow and walked down High Street, past the flat white wastes where all the shops had been. Eddershaw Furnishers, Curry's Bicycles, Donegal Clothing Company, Doctor Scholl's, Burton Tailors, W. H. Smith, Boots Cash Chemists, Leslie's Stores, Upson's Shoes, Prince of Wales, Tucker's Fish, Stead & Simpson – all the shops bombed and vanished. Past the hole in space where Hodges & Clothiers had been, down Castle Street, past the remembered, invisible shops, Price's Fifty Shilling, and Crouch the Jeweller, Potter Gilmore Gowns, Evans Jeweller, Master's Outfitters, Style and Mantle, Lennard's Boots, True Form, Kardomah, R. E. Jones, Dean's tailor, David Evans, Gregory Confectioners, Bovega, Burton's, Lloyd's Bank, and nothing. And into Temple Street. There the Three Lamps had stood, old Mac magisterial in his corner. And there the Young Thomas whom I was searching for used to stand at the counter on Friday paynights with Freddie Farr Half Hook, Bill Latham, Cliff Williams, Gareth Hughes, Eric Hughes, Glyn Lowry, a man among men, his hat at a rakish angle, in that snug, smug, select, Edwardian holy of best-bitter holies . . .

(Bar noises in background)

OLD REPORTER

Remember when I took you down the mortuary for the first time, Young Thomas? He'd never seen a corpse before, boys, except old Ron on a Saturday night. 'If you want to be a proper newspaperman,' I said, 'you got to be well known in the right circles. You got to be *persona grata* in the mortuary, see.' He went pale green, mun.

FIRST YOUNG REPORTER

Look, he's blushing now . . .

OLD REPORTER

And when we got there what d'you think? The decorators were in at the mortuary, giving the old home a bit of a re-do like. Up on ladders having a slap at the roof. Young Thomas didn't see 'em, he had his pop eyes glued on the slab, and when one of the painters up the ladder said 'Good morning, gents' in a deep voice he upped in the air and out of the place like a ferret. Laugh!

BARMAID

(Off) You've had enough, Mr Roberts.
You heard what I said. *(Noise of a gentle scuffle)*

SECOND YOUNG REPORTER

(Casually) There goes Mr Roberts.

OLD REPORTER

Well fair do's they throw you out very genteel in this pub . . .

FIRST YOUNG REPORTER

Ever seen Young Thomas covering a soccer match down the Vetch and working it out in tries?

SECOND YOUNG REPORTER

And up the Mannesman Hall shouting 'Good footwork, sir,' and a couple of punch-drunk colliers galumphing about like jumbos.

FIRST YOUNG REPORTER

What you been reporting today, Young Thomas?

SECOND YOUNG REPORTER

Two typewriter Thomas the ace news-dick ...

OLD REPORTER

Let's have a dekko at your note-book. 'Called at British Legion: Nothing. Called at Hospital: One broken leg. Auction at the Metropole. Ring Mr Beynon *re* Gymanfa Ganu. Lunch: Pint and pasty at the Singleton with Mrs Giles. Bazaar at Bethesda Chapel. Chimney on fire at Tontine Street. Walters Road Sunday School Outing. Rehearsal of the *Mikado* at Skewen' – all front page stuff ... *(Fade)*

NARRATOR

The voices of fourteen years ago hung silent in the snow and ruin, and in the falling winter morning I walked on through the white havoc'd centre where once a very young man I knew had mucked about as chirpy as a sparrow after the sips and titbits and small change of the town. Near the *Evening Post* building and the fragment of the Castle I stopped a man whose face I thought I recognized from a long time ago. I said: I wonder if you can tell me ...

PASSER-BY

Yes?

NARRATOR

He peered out of his blanketing scarves and from under his snowballed Balaclava like an Eskimo with a bad conscience. I said: If you can tell me whether you used to know a chap called Young Thomas. He worked on the *Post* and used to wear an overcoat sometimes with the check lining inside out so that you could play giant draughts on him. He wore a conscious woodbine, too ...

PASSER-BY

What d'you mean, conscious woodbine?

NARRATOR

... and a perched pork pie with a peacock feather and he tried to slouch like a newshawk even when he was attending a meeting of the Gorseinon Buffalos . . .

PASSER-BY

Oh, *him*! he owes me half a crown. I haven't seen him since the old Kardomah days. He wasn't a reporter then, he'd just left the grammar school. Him and Charlie Fisher – Charlie's got whiskers now – and Tom Warner and Fred Janes, drinking coffee-dashes and arguing the toss.

NARRATOR

What about?

PASSER-BY

Music and poetry and painting and politics. Einstein and Epstein, Stravinsky and Greta Garbo, death and religion, Picasso and girls . . .

NARRATOR

And then?

PASSER-BY

Communism, symbolism, Bradman, Braque, the Watch Committee, free love, free beer, murder, Michelangelo, ping-pong, ambition, Sibelius, and girls . . .

NARRATOR

Is that all?

PASSER-BY

How Dan Jones was going to compose the most prodigious symphony, Fred Janes paint the most miraculously meticulous picture, Charlie Fisher catch the poshest trout, Vernon Watkins and Young Thomas write the most boiling poems, how they would ring the bells of London and paint it like a tart . . .

NARRATOR

And after that?

PASSER-BY

Oh the hissing of the butt-ends in the drains of the coffee-dashes and the tinkle and the gibble-gabble of the morning young lounge lizards as they talked about Augustus John, Emil Jannings, Carnera, Dracula, Amy Johnson, trial marriage, pocket-money, the Welsh sea, the London stars, King Kong, anarchy, darts, T. S. Eliot, and girls.... Duw, it's cold!

NARRATOR

And he hurried on, into the dervish snow, without a good morning or goodbye, swaddled in his winter woollens like a man in the island of his deafness, and I felt that perhaps he had never stopped at all to tell me of one more departed stage in the progress of the boy I was pursuing. The Kardomah Café was razed to the snow, the voices of the coffee-drinkers – poets, painters, and musicians in their beginnings – lost in the willynilly flying of the years and the flakes.

Down College Street I walked then, past the remembered invisible shops, Langley's, Castle Cigar Co., T. B. Brown, Pullar's, Aubrey Jeremiah, Goddard Jones, Richards, Hornes, Marles, Pleasance & Harper, Star Supply, Sidney Heath, Wesley Chapel, and nothing. ... My search was leading me back, through pub and job and café, to the School.

(Fade) (School bell)

SCHOOLMASTER

Oh yes, yes, I remember him well,
though I do not know if I would recognize him now:
nobody grows any younger, or better,
and boys grow into much the sort of men one would suppose
though sometimes the moustaches bewilder
and one finds it hard to reconcile one's memory for a small
none-too-clean urchin lying his way unsuccessfully out of his homework
with a fierce and many-medalled sergeant-major with three children or a divorced chartered accountant;
and it is hard to realize
that some little tousled rebellious youth whose only claim
to fame among his contemporaries was his undisputed right
to the championship of the spitting contest
is now perhaps one's own bank manager.
Oh yes, I remember him well, the boy you are searching for:
he looked like most boys, no better, brighter, or more respectful;
he cribbed, mitched, spilt ink, rattled his desk and
garbled his lessons with the worst of them;
he could smudge, hedge, smirk, wriggle, wince,

whimper, blarney, badger, blush, deceive, be
devious, stammer, improvise, assume
offended dignity or righteous indignation as though to the manner born;
sullenly and reluctantly he drilled, for some small
crime, under Sergeant Bird, so wittily nicknamed
Oiseau, on Wednesday half-holidays,
appeared regularly in detention classes,
hid in the cloakroom during algebra,
was, when a newcomer, thrown into the bushes of the
Lower Playground by bigger boys,
and threw newcomers into the bushes of the Lower
Playground when *he* was a bigger boy;
he scuffled at prayers,
he interpolated, smugly, the time-honoured wrong
irreverent words into the morning hymns,
he helped to damage the headmaster's rhubarb,
was thirty-third in trigonometry,
and, as might be expected, edited the School Magazine *(Fade)*

NARRATOR

The Hall is shattered, the echoing corridors charred where he scribbled and smudged and yawned in the long green days, waiting for the bell and the scamper into the Yard: the School on Mount Pleasant Hill has changed its face and its ways. Soon, they say, it may be no longer the School at all he knew and loved when he was a boy up to no good but the beat of his blood: the names are havoc'd from the Hall and the carved initials burned from the broken wood. But the names remain. What names did he know of the dead? Who of the honoured dead did he know such a long time ago? The names of the dead in the living heart and head remain for ever. Of all the dead whom did he know? *(Funeral bell)*

VOICE

Evans, K. J.
Haines, G. C.
Roberts, I. L.
Moxham, J.
Thomas, H.
Baines, W.
Bazzard, F. H.

Beer, L. J.
Bucknell, R.
Tywford, G.
Vagg, E. A.
Wright, G. *(Fade)*

NARRATOR

Then I tacked down the snowblind hill, a cat-o'-nine-gales whipping from the sea, and, white and eiderdowned in the smothering flurry, people padded past me up and down like prowling featherbeds. And I plodded through the ankle-high one cloud that foamed the town, into flat Gower Street, its buildings melted, and along long Helen's Road. Now my search was leading me back to the seashore.

(Noise of sea, softly)

NARRATOR

Only two living creatures stood on the promenade, near the cenotaph, facing the tossed crystal sea: a man in a chewed muffler and a ratting cap, and an angry dog of a mixed make. The man dithered in the cold, beat his bare blue hands together, waited for some sign from sea or snow; the dog shouted at the weather, and fixed his bloodshot eyes on Mumbles Head. But when the man and I talked together, the dog piped down and fixed his eyes on me, blaming me for the snow. The man spoke towards the sea. He knew all the dogs and boys and old men who came to see the sea, who ran or gambolled on the sand or stooped at the edge of the waves as though over a wild, wide, rolling ash-can. He knew the lovers who went to lie in the sandhills, the striding masculine women who roared at their terriers like tiger tamers, the loafing men whose work it was in the world to observe the great employment of the sea. He said:

PROMENADE-MAN

Oh yes, yes, I remember him well, but I didn't know what was his name. I don't know the names of none of the sandboys. They don't know mine. About fourteen or fifteen years old, you said, with a little red cap. And he used to play by Vivian's Stream. He used to dawdle in the arches, you said, and lark about on the railway-lines and holler at the old sea. He'd mooch about the dunes and watch the tankers and the tugs and the banana boats come out of the docks. He was going to run away to sea, he said. *I* know. On Saturday afternoon he'd go down to the sea when it was a long way out, and hear the foghorns though he couldn't see the ships. And on Sunday nights, after chapel, he'd be a swaggering with his pals along the prom, whistling after the girls.

(Titter)

GIRL

Does your mother know you're out? Go away now. Stop following us. *(Another girl titters)*

GIRL

Don't you say nothing, Hetty, you're only encouraging. No thank *you*, Mr Cheeky, with your cut-glass accent and your father's trilby! I don't want *no* walk on *no* sands. What d'you say? Ooh listen to him, Het, he's swallowed a dictionary. No, I don't want to go with nobody up no lane in the moonlight, see, and I'm not a baby-snatcher neither. I seen you going to school along Terrace Road, Mr Glad-Eye, with your little satchel and wearing your red cap and all. You seen me wearing my... no you never. Hetty, mind your glasses! Hetty Harris, you're as bad as them. Oh go away and do your homework, you. No I'm not then. I'm nobody's homework, see. Cheek! Hetty Harris, don't you let him! Oooh, there's brazen! Well, just to the end of the prom, if you like. No further, mind ...

PROMENADE-MAN

Oh yes, I knew him well. I've known him by the thousands ...

NARRATOR

Even now, on the frozen foreshore, a high, far cry of boys all like the boy I sought, slid on the glass of the streams and snowballed each other and the sky. Then I went on my way from the sea, up Brynmill Terrace and into Glanbrydan Avenue where Bert Trick had kept a grocer's shop and, in the kitchen, threatening the annihilation of the ruling classes over sandwiches and jelly and blancmange. And I came to the shops and houses of the Uplands. Here and around here it was that the journey had begun of the one I was pursuing through his past. *(Old piano cinema-music in background)*

FIRST VOICE

Here was once the flea-pit picture-house where he whooped for the scalping Indians with Jack Basset and banged for the rustlers' guns.

NARRATOR

Jackie Basset, killed.

THIRD VOICE

Here once was Mrs Ferguson's, who sold the best gob-stoppers and penny packets full of surprises and a sweet kind of glue.

FIRST VOICE

In the fields behind Cwmdonkin Drive, the Murrays chased him and all cats.

SECOND VOICE

No fires now where the outlaws' fires burned and the paradisiacal potatoes roasted in the embers.

THIRD VOICE

In the Graig beneath Town Hill he was a lonely killer hunting the wolves (or rabbits) and the red Sioux tribe (or Mitchell brothers).

(Fade cinema-music into background of children's voices reciting, in unison, the names of the counties of Wales)

FIRST VOICE

In Mirador School he learned to read and count. Who made the worst raffia doilies? Who put water in Joyce's galoshes, every morning prompt as prompt? In the afternoons, when the children were good, they read aloud from Struwelpeter. And when they were bad, they sat alone in the empty classroom, hearing, from above them, the distant, terrible, sad music of the late piano lesson.

(The children's voices fade. The piano lesson continues in background)

NARRATOR

And I went up, through the white Grove, into Cwmdonkin Park, the snow still sailing and the childish, lonely, remembered music fingering on in the suddenly gentle wind. Dusk was folding the Park around, like another, darker snow. Soon the bell would ring for the closing of the gates, though the Park was empty. The park-keeper walked by the reservoir, where swans had glided, on his white rounds. I walked by his side and asked him my questions, up the swathed drives past buried beds and loaded utterly still furred and birdless trees towards the last gate. He said:

PARK-KEEPER

Oh yes, yes, I knew him well. He used to climb the reservoir railings and pelt the old swans. Run like a billygoat over the grass you should keep off of. Cut branches off the trees. Carve words on the benches. Pull up moss in the rockery, go snip through the dahlias. Fight in the bandstand. Climb the elms and moon up the top like a owl. Light fires in the bushes. Play on the green bank. Oh yes, I knew him well. I think he was happy all the time. I've known him by the thousands.

NARRATOR

We had reached the last gate. Dusk drew around us and the town. I said: What has become of him now?

PARK-KEEPER

Dead.

NARRATOR

The Park-keeper said:

(The park bell rings)

PARK-KEEPER

Dead . . . Dead . . . Dead . . . Dead . . . Dead . . . Dead.

UNDER MILK WOOD

A Play for Voices

[Silence]

FIRST VOICE [Very softly]

To begin at the beginning:

It is spring, moonless night in the small town, starless and bible-black, the cobblestreets silent and the hunched, courters'-and-rabbits' wood limping invisible down to the sloeblack, slow, black, crowblack, fishingboat-bobbing sea. The houses are blind as moles (though moles see fine tonight in the snouting, velvet dingles) or blind as Captain Cat there in the muffled middle by the pump and the town clock, the shops in mourning, the Welfare Hall in widows' weeds. And all the people of the lulled and dumbfound town are sleeping now.

Hush, the babies are sleeping, the farmers, the fishers, the tradesmen and pensioners, cobbler, schoolteacher, postman and publican, the undertaker and the fancy woman, drunkard, dressmaker, preacher, policeman, the webfoot cocklewomen and the tidy wives. Young girls lie bedded soft or glide in their dreams, with rings and trousseaux, bridesmaided by glow-worms down the aisles of the organplaying wood. The boys are dreaming wicked or of the bucking ranches of the night and the jolly, rodgered sea. And the anthracite statues of the horses sleep in the fields, and the cows in the byres, and the dogs in the wetnosed yards; and the cats nap in the slant corners or lope sly, streaking and needling, on the one cloud of the roofs.

You can hear the dew falling, and the hushed town breathing.

Only your eyes are unclosed, to see the black and folded town fast, and slow, asleep.

And you alone can hear the invisible starfall, the darkest-before-dawn minutely dewgrazed stir of the black, dab-filled sea where the Arethusa, the Curlew and the Skylark, Zanzibar, Rhiannon, the Rover, the Cormorant, and the Star of Wales tilt and ride.

Listen. It is night moving in the streets, the processional salt slow musical wind in Coronation Street and Cockle Row, it is the grass growing on Llareggub Hill, dewfall, starfall, the sleep of birds in Milk Wood.

Listen. It is night in the chill, squat chapel, hymning, in bonnet and brooch and bombazine black, butterfly choker and bootlace bow, coughing like nannygoats, sucking mintoes, fortywinking hallelujah; night in the four-ale, quiet as a domino; in Ocky Milkman's loft like a mouse with gloves; in Dai Bread's bakery flying like black flour. It is tonight in Donkey Street, trotting silent, with seaweed on its hooves, along the cockled cobbles, past curtained fernpot, text and trinket, harmonium, holy dresser, watercolours done by hand, china dog and rosy tin teacaddy. It is night neddying among the snuggeries of babies.

Look. It is night, dumbly, royally winding through the Coronation cherry trees; going through the graveyard of Bethesda with winds gloved and folded, and dew doffed; tumbling by the Sailors' Arms.

Time passes. Listen. Time passes.

Come closer now.

Only you can hear the houses sleeping in the streets in the slow deep salt and silent black, bandaged night. Only you can see, in the blinded bedrooms, the coms and petticoats over the chairs, the jugs and basins, the glasses of teeth, Thou Shalt Not on the wall, and the yellowing dickybird-watching pictures of the dead. Only you can hear and see, behind the eyes of the sleepers, the movements and countries and mazes and colours and dismays and rainbows and tunes and wishes and flight and fall and despairs and big seas of their dreams.

From where you are, you can hear their dreams.

Captain Cat, the retired blind seacaptain, asleep in his bunk in the seashelled, ship-in-bottled, shipshape best cabin of Schooner House dreams of

never such seas as any that swamped the decks of his S.S. Kidwelly bellying over the bedclothes and jellyfish-slippery sucking him down salt deep into the Davy dark where the fish come biting out and nibble him down to his wishbone and the long drowned nuzzle up to him...

FIRST DROWNED

Remember me, Captain?

CAPTAIN CAT

You're Dancing Williams!

FIRST DROWNED

I lost my step in Nantucket.

SECOND DROWNED

Do you see me, Captain? the white bone talking? I'm Tom-Fred the donkeyman... We shared the same girl once... Her name was Mrs Probert...

WOMAN'S VOICE

Rosie Probert, thirty three Duck Lane. Come on up, boys, I'm dead.

THIRD DROWNED

Hold me, Captain, I'm Jonah Jarvis, come to a bad end, very enjoyable...

FOURTH DROWNED

Alfred Pomeroy Jones, sealawyer, born in Mumbles, sung like a linnet, crowned you with a flagon, tattooed with mermaids, thirst like a dredger, died of blisters...

FIRST DROWNED

This skull at your earhole is

FIFTH DROWNED

Curly Bevan. Tell my auntie it was me that pawned the ormolu clock...

CAPTAIN CAT

Aye, aye, Curly.

SECOND DROWNED

Tell my missus no my never

THIRD DROWNED

I never done what she said I never...

FOURTH DROWNED

Yes, they did.

FIFTH DROWNED

And who brings cocoanuts and shawls and parrots to *my* Gwen now?

FIRST DROWNED

How's it above?

SECOND DROWNED

Is there rum and lavabread?

THIRD DROWNED

Bosoms and robins?

FOURTH DROWNED

Concertinas?

FIFTH DROWNED

Ebenezer's bell?

FIRST DROWNED

Fighting and onions?

SECOND DROWNED

And sparrows and daisies?

THIRD DROWNED

Tiddlers in a jamjar?

FOURTH DROWNED

Buttermilk and whippets?

FIFTH DROWNED

Rock-a-bye baby?

FIRST DROWNED

Washing on the line?

SECOND DROWNED

And old girls in the snug?

THIRD DROWNED

How's the tenors in Dowlais?

FOURTH DROWNED

Who milks the cows in Maesgwyn?

FIFTH DROWNED

When she smiles, is there dimples?

FIRST DROWNED

What's the smell of parsley?

CAPTAIN CAT

Oh, my dead dears!

From where you are, you can hear, in Cockle Row in the spring, moonless night, Miss Price, dressmaker and sweetshop-keeper, dream of her lover, tall as the town clock tower, Samson-syrup-gold-maned, whacking thighed and piping hot, thunderbolt-bass'd and barnacle-breasted flailing up the cockles with his eyes like blowlamps and scooping low over her lonely loving hotwaterbottled body...

MR EDWARDS

Myfanwy Price!

MISS PRICE

Mr Mog Edwards!

MR EDWARDS

I am a draper mad with love. I love you more than all the flannelette and calico, candlewick, dimity, crash and merino, tussore, cretonne, crepon, muslin, poplin, ticking and twill in the whole Cloth Hall of the world. I have come to take you away to my Emporium on the hill, where the change hums on wires. Throw away your little bedsocks and your Welsh wool knitted jacket, I will warm the sheets like an electric toaster, I will lie by your side like the Sunday roast...

MISS PRICE

I will knit you a wallet of forget-me-not blue, for the money to be comfy. I will warm your heart by the fire so that you can slip it in under your vest when the shop is closed...

MR EDWARDS

Myfanwy, Myfanwy, before the mice gnaw at your bottom drawer will you say

MISS PRICE

Yes, Mog, yes, Mog, yes, yes, yes...

MR EDWARDS

And all the bells of the tills of the town shall ring for our wedding.

[Noise of money-tills and chapel bells.]

Come now, drift up the dark, come up the drifting sea-dark street now in the dark night seesawing like the sea, to the bible-black airless attic over Jack Black the cobbler's shop where alone and savagely Jack Black sleeps in a nightshirt tied to his ankles with elastic and dreams of

chasing the naughty couples down the grassgreen gooseberried double bed of the wood, flogging the tosspots in the spit-and-sawdust, driving out the bare, bold girls from the sixpenny hops of his nightmares . . .

JACK BLACK [Loudly]

Ach y fi!
Ach y fi!

Evans the Death, the undertaker,

EVANS THE DEATH

laughs high and aloud in his sleep and curls up his toes as he sees, upon waking fifty years ago, snow lie deep on the goosefield behind the sleeping house; and he runs out into the field where his mother is making Welshcakes in the snow, and steals a fistfull of snowflakes and currants and climbs back to bed to eat them cold and sweet under the warm, white clothes while his mother dances in the snow kitchen crying out for her lost currants.

And in the little pink-eyed cottage next to the undertaker's, lie, alone, the seventeen snoring gentle stone of Mister Waldo, rabbitcatcher, barber, herbalist, catdoctor, quack, his fat, pink hands, palms up, over the edge of the patchwork quilt, his black boots neat and tidy in the washing basin, his bowler on a nail above the bed, a milk stout and a slice of cold bread pudding under the pillow; and, dripping in the dark, he dreams of

MOTHER

This little piggy went to market
This little piggy stayed at home
This little piggy had roast beef
This little piggy had none
And this little piggy went

LITTLE BOY

wee wee wee wee wee

MOTHER
all the way home to

WIFE [Screaming]
Waldo! Wal-do!

MR WALDO
Yes, Blodwen love?

WIFE
Oh, what'll the neighbours say, what'll the neighbours...

FIRST NEIGHBOUR
Poor Mrs Waldo

SECOND NEIGHBOUR
What she puts up with

FIRST NEIGHBOUR
Never should of married

SECOND NEIGHBOUR
If she didn't had to

FIRST NEIGHBOUR
Same as her mother.

SECOND NEIGHBOUR
There's a husband for you

FIRST NEIGHBOUR
Bad as his father

SECOND NEIGHBOUR
And you know where he ended

FIRST NEIGHBOUR
Up in the asylum

SECOND NEIGHBOUR
Crying for his ma.

FIRST NEIGHBOUR
Every Saturday

SECOND NEIGHBOUR
He hasn't got a leg

FIRST NEIGHBOUR
And carrying on

SECOND NEIGHBOUR
With that Mrs Beattie Morris

FIRST NEIGHBOUR
Up in the quarry

SECOND NEIGHBOUR
And seen her baby

FIRST NEIGHBOUR
It's got his nose.

SECOND NEIGHBOUR
Oh, it makes my heart bleed

FIRST NEIGHBOUR
What he'll do for drink

SECOND NEIGHBOUR
He sold the pianola

FIRST NEIGHBOUR
And her sewing machine

SECOND NEIGHBOUR
Falling in the gutter

FIRST NEIGHBOUR
Talking to the lamp-post

SECOND NEIGHBOUR
Using language

FIRST NEIGHBOUR
Singing in the w.

SECOND NEIGHBOUR
Poor Mrs Waldo.

WIFE [Tearfully]
Oh, Waldo, Waldo!

MR WALDO
Hush, love, hush. I'm widower Waldo now.

MOTHER [Screaming]
Waldo, Wal-do!

LITTLE BOY
Yes, our mum?

MOTHER
Oh, what'll the neighbours say, what'll the neighbours...

THIRD NEIGHBOUR
Black as a chimbley

FOURTH NEIGHBOUR
Ringing doorbells

THIRD NEIGHBOUR
Breaking windows

FOURTH NEIGHBOUR
Making mudpies

THIRD NEIGHBOUR
Stealing currants

FOURTH NEIGHBOUR
Chalking words

THIRD NEIGHBOUR
Saw him in the bushes

FOURTH NEIGHBOUR
Playing moochins

THIRD NEIGHBOUR
Send him to bed without any supper

FOURTH NEIGHBOUR
Give him sennapods and lock him in the dark

THIRD NEIGHBOUR
Off to the reformatory

FOURTH NEIGHBOUR
Off to the reformatory

TOGETHER
Learn him with a slipper on his b.t.m.

ANOTHER MOTHER [Screaming]
Waldo, Wal-do! what you doing with our Matti?

LITTLE BOY
Give us a kiss, Matti Richards.

LITTLE GIRL
Give us a penny then.

MR WALDO
I only got a halfpenny.

FIRST WOMAN
Lips is a penny.

PREACHER
Will you take this woman Matti Richards

SECOND WOMAN
Dulcie Prothero

THIRD WOMAN
Effie Bevan

FOURTH WOMAN
Lil the Gluepot

FIFTH WOMAN
Mrs Flusher

WIFE
Blodwen Bowen

PREACHER
to be your awful wedded wife

LITTLE BOY [Screaming]
No, no, no!

Now, in her iceberg-white, holily laundered crinoline nightgown, under virtuous polar sheets, in her spruced and scoured dust-defying bedroom in trig and trim Bay View, a house for paying guests, at the top of the town, Mrs Ogmore-Pritchard, widow, twice, of Mr Ogmore, linoleum, retired, and Mr Pritchard, failed bookmaker, who, maddened by besoming, swabbing and scrubbing, the voice of the vacuum-cleaner and the fume of polish, ironically swallowed disinfectant, fidgets in her rinsed sleep, wakes in a dream, and nudges in the ribs dead Mr Ogmore, dead Mr Pritchard, ghostly on either side.

MRS OGMORE-PRITCHARD

Mr Ogmore!
Mr Pritchard!
It is time to inhale your balsam.

MR OGMORE

Oh, Mrs Ogmore!

MR PRITCHARD

Oh, Mrs Pritchard!

MRS OGMORE-PRITCHARD

Soon it will be time to get up.
Tell me your tasks, in order.

MR OGMORE

I must put my pyjamas in the drawer marked pyjamas.

MR PRITCHARD

I must take my cold bath which is good for me.

MR OGMORE

I must wear my flannel band to ward off sciatica.

MR PRITCHARD

I must dress behind the curtain and put on my apron.

MR OGMORE

I must blow my nose

MRS OGMORE-PRITCHARD

in the garden, if you please

MR OGMORE

in a piece of tissue-paper which I afterwards burn.

MR PRITCHARD

I must take my salts which are nature's friend.

MR OGMORE

I must boil the drinking water because of germs.

MR PRITCHARD

I must make my herb tea which is free from tannin

MR OGMORE

and have a charcoal biscuit which is good for me.

MR PRITCHARD

I may smoke one pipe of asthma mixture

MRS OGMORE-PRITCHARD

in the woodshed, if you please

MR PRITCHARD

and dust the parlour and spray the canary.

MR OGMORE

I must put on rubber gloves and search the peke for fleas.

MR PRITCHARD

I must dust the blinds and then I must raise them.

MRS OGMORE-PRITCHARD

And before you let the sun in, mind it wipes its shoes.

In Butcher Beynon's, Gossamer Beynon, daughter, schoolteacher, dreaming deep, daintily ferrets under a fluttering hummock of chicken's feathers in a slaughterhouse that has chintz curtains and a three-piece suite, and finds, with no surprise, a small rough ready man with a bushy tail winking in a paper carrier.

ORGAN MORGAN

Help,

cries Organ Morgan, the organist, in his dream,

there is perturbation and music in Coronation Street! All the spouses are honking like geese and the babies singing opera. P.C. Atilla Rees has got his truncheon out and is playing cadenzas by the pump, the cows from Sunday Meadow ring like reindeer, and on the roof of Handel Villa see the Women's Welfare hoofing, bloomered, in the moon.

GOSSAMER BEYNON

At last, my love,

sighs Gossamer Beynon. And the bushy tail wags rude and ginger.

At the sea-end of town, Mr and Mrs Floyd, the cocklers, are sleeping as quiet as death, side by wrinkled side, toothless, salt, and brown, like two old kippers in a box.

And high above, in Salt Lake Farm, Mr Utah Watkins counts, all night, the wife-faced sheep as they leap the fences on the hill, smiling and knitting and bleating just like Mrs Utah Watkins.

UTAH WATKINS [Yawning]
Thirty four, thirty five, thirty six, forty eight, eighty nine...

MRS UTAH WATKINS
Knit one slip one
Knit two together
Pass the slipstich over...
[Mrs Utah Watkins bleats.]

Ocky Milkman, drowned asleep in Cockle Street, is emptying his churns into the Dewi River,

OCKY MILKMAN [Whispering]
regardless of expense,

and weeping like a funeral.

Cherry Owen, next door, lifts a tankard to his lips but nothing flows out of it. He shakes the tankard. It turns into a fish. He drinks the fish.

P.C. Atilla Rees

ATILLA REES
lumps out of bed, dead to the dark, and still foghorning, and drags out his helmet from under the bed; but deep in the backyard lock-up of his sleep a mean voice murmurs,

A VOICE [Murmuring]
You'll be sorry for this in the morning,

ATILLA REES
and he heave-ho's back to bed. His helmet swashes in the dark.

Willy Nilly, postman, asleep up street, walks fourteen miles to deliver the post as he does every day of the night, and rat-a-tats hard and sharp on Mrs Willy Nilly.

MRS WILLY NILLY

Don't spank me, please, teacher,

whimpers his wife at his side, but every night of her married life she has been late for school.

Sinbad Sailors, over the taproom of the Sailors' Arms, hugs his damp pillow whose secret name is Gossamer Beynon.

A mogul catches Lily Smalls in the wash-house.

LILY SMALLS

Ooh, you old mogul!

Mrs Rose-Cottage's eldest, Mae, peels off her pink-and-white skin in a furnace in a tower in a cave in a waterfall in a wood and waits there raw as an onion for Mister Right to leap up the burning tall hollow splashes of leaves like a brilliantined trout.

MAE ROSE-COTTAGE

[Very close and softly, drawing out the words.]

Call me Dolores
Like they do in the stories.

Alone until she dies, Bessie Bighead, hired help, born in the workhouse, smelling of the cowshed, snores bass and gruff on a couch of straw in a loft in Salt Lake Farm and picks a posy of daisies in Sunday Meadow to put on the grave of Gomer Owen who kissed her once by the pig-sty when she wasn't looking and never kissed her again although she was looking all the time.

And the Inspectors of Cruelty fly down into Mrs Butcher Beynon's dream to persecute Mr Beynon for selling

BUTCHER BEYNON

owl meat, dogs' eyes, manchop.

Mr Beynon, in butcher's bloodied apron, springheels down Coronation Street, a finger, not his own, in his mouth. Straightfaced in his cunning sleep he pulls the legs of his dreams and

BUTCHER BEYNON

hunting on pigback shoots down the wild giblets.

ORGAN MORGAN [High and softly]

Help!

GOSSAMER BEYNON [Softly]

my foxy darling.

Now behind the eyes and secrets of the dreamers in the streets rocked to sleep by the sea, see the titbits and topsyturvies, bobs and buttontops, bags and bones, ash and rind and dandruff and nailparings, saliva and snowflakes and moulted feathers of dreams, the wrecks and sprats and shells and fishbones, whalejuice and moonshine and small salt fry dished up by the hidden sea...

The owls are hunting. Look, over Bethesda gravestones one hoots and swoops and catches a mouse by Hannah Rees, Belovèd Wife. And in Coronation Street, which you alone can see it is so dark under the chapel in the skies, the Reverend Eli Jenkins, poet, preacher, turns in his deep towards-dawn sleep and dreams of

REV. ELI JENKINS

Eisteddfodau.

He intricately rhymes, to the music of crwth and pibgorn, all night long in his druid's seedy nightie in a beer-tent black with parchs.

Mr Pugh, schoolmaster, fast asleep, pretends to be sleeping, spies foxy round the droop of his nightcap and

MR PUGH

Pssst!

whistles up

Murder.

Mrs Organ Morgan, groceress, coiled grey like a dormouse, her paws to her ears, conjures

MRS ORGAN MORGAN

Silence.

She sleeps very dulcet in a cove of wool, and trumpeting Organ Morgan at her side snores no louder than a spider.

Mary Ann the Sailors dreams of

MARY ANN THE SAILORS

The Garden of Eden.

She comes in her smock-frock and clogs

MARY ANN THE SAILORS

away from the cool scrubbed cobbled kitchen with the Sunday-school pictures on the whitewashed wall and the farmers' almanac hung above the settle and the sides of bacon on the ceiling hooks, and goes down the cockleshelled paths of that applepie kitchen garden, ducking under the gippo's clothespegs, catching her apron on the blackcurrant bushes, past beanrows and onion-bed and tomatoes ripening on the wall towards the old man playing the harmonium in the orchard, and sits down on the grass at his side and shells the green peas that grow up through the lap of her frock that brushes the dew.

In Donkey Street, so furred with sleep, Dai Bread, Polly Garter, Nogood Boyo, and Lord Cut-Glass sigh before the dawn that is about to be and dream of

DAI BREAD

Turkish girls. Horizontal.

POLLY GARTER

Babies.

NOGOOD BOYO

Nothing.

LORD CUT-GLASS

Tick tock tick tock tick tock tick tock.

Time passes. Listen. Time passes.
An owl flies home past Bethesda, to a chapel in an oak.
And the dawn inches up.

[One distant bell-note, faintly reverberating on.]

Stand on this hill. This is Llareggub Hill, old as the hills, high, cool, and green, and from this small circle of stones, made not by druids but by Mrs Beynon's Billy, you can see all the town below you sleeping in the first of the dawn.

You can hear the love-sick woodpigeons mooning in bed. A dog barks in his sleep, farmyards away. The town ripples like a lake in the waking haze.

VOICE OF A GUIDE-BOOK

Less than five hundred souls inhabit the three quaint streets and the few narrow bylanes and scattered farmsteads that constitute this small, decaying watering-place which may, indeed, be called a 'backwater of life' without disrespect to its natives who possess, to this day, a salty individuality of their own. The main street, Coronation Street, consists, for the most part, of humble, two-storied houses many of which attempt to achieve some measure of gaiety by prinking themselves out in crude colours and by the liberal use of pinkwash, though there are remaining a few eighteenth-century houses of more pretension, if, on the whole, in a sad state of disrepair. Though there is little to attract the hillclimber, the healthseeker, the sportsman, or the weekending motorist, the contemplative may, if sufficiently attracted to spare it some leisurely hours, find, in its cobbled streets and its little fishing harbour, in its several curious customs, and in the conversation of its local 'characters,' some of that picturesque sense of the past so frequently lacking in towns and villages which have kept more abreast of the times. The river Dewi is said to abound in trout, but is much poached. The one place of worship, with its neglected graveyard, is of no architectural interest.

[A cock crows.]

The principality of the sky lightens now, over our green hill, into spring morning larked and crowed and belling.

[Slow bell notes.]

Who pulls the townhall bellrope but blind Captain Cat? One by one, the sleepers are rung out of sleep this one morning as every morning. And soon you shall see the chimneys' slow upflying snow as Captain Cat, in sailor's cap and seaboots, announces today with his loud get-out-of-bed bell.

The Reverend Eli Jenkins, in Bethesda House, gropes out of bed into his preacher's black, combs back his bard's white hair, forgets to wash, pads barefoot downstairs, opens the front door, stands in the doorway and, looking out at the day and up at the eternal hill, and hearing the sea break and the gab of birds, remembers his own verses and tells them, softly, to empty Coronation Street that is rising and raising its blinds.

REV. ELI JENKINS

Dear Gwalia! I know there are
Towns lovelier than ours,
And fairer hills and loftier far,
And groves more full of flowers,

And boskier woods more blithe with spring
And bright with birds' adorning,
And sweeter bards than I to sing
Their praise this beauteous morning.

By Cader Idris, tempest-torn,
Or Moel y Wyddfa's glory,
Carnedd Llewelyn beauty born,
Plinlimmon old in story,

By mountains where King Arthur dreams,
By Penmaen Mawr defiant,
Llareggub Hill a molehill seems,
A pygmy to a giant.

By Sawdde, Senni, Dovey, Dee,
Edw, Eden, Aled, all,
Taff and Towy broad and free,
Llyfnant with its waterfall,

Claerwen, Cleddau, Dulas, Daw,
Ely, Gwili, Ogwr, Nedd,
Small is our *River Dewi*, Lord,
A baby on a rushy bed.

By Carreg Cennen, King of time,
Our *Heron Head* is only
A bit of stone with seaweed spread
Where gulls come to be lonely.

A tiny dingle is *Milk Wood*
By golden Grove 'neath Grongar,
But let me choose and oh! I should
Love all my life and longer

To stroll among our trees and stray
In Goosegog Lane, on Donkey Down,
And hear the Dewi sing all day,
And never, never leave the town.

The Reverend Jenkins closes the front door. His morning service is over.

[Slow bell notes.]

Now, woken at last by the out-of-bed-sleepy-head-Polly-put-the-kettle-on townhall bell, Lily Smalls, Mrs Beynon's treasure, comes downstairs from a dream of royalty who all night long went larking with her full of sauce in the Milk Wood dark, and puts the kettle on the primus ring in Mrs Beynon's kitchen, and looks at herself in Mr Beynon's shaving-glass over the sink, and sees:

LILY SMALLS

Oh, there's a face!
Where you get that hair from?
Got it from a old tom cat.
Give it back then, love.
Oh, there's a perm!

Where you get that nose from, Lily?
Got it from my father, silly.
You've got it on upside down!
Oh, there's a conk!

Look at your complexion!
Oh, no, *you* look.
Needs a bit of make-up.
Needs a veil.
Oh, there's glamour!

Where you get that smile, Lil?
Never you mind, girl.
Nobody loves you.
That's what *you* think.

Who is it loves you?
Shan't tell.
Come on, Lily.
Cross your heart, then?
Cross my heart.

And very softly, her lips almost touching her reflection, she breathes the name and clouds the shaving-glass.

MRS BEYNON [Loudly, from above]

Lily!

LILY SMALLS [Loudly]

Yes, mum...

MRS BEYNON

Where's my tea, girl?

LILY SMALLS

[Softly] Where d'you think? In the cat-box?
[Loudly] Coming up, mum...

Mr Pugh, in the School House opposite, takes up the morning tea to Mrs Pugh, and whispers on the stairs:

MR PUGH

Here's your arsenic, dear.
And your weedkiller biscuit.
I've throttled your parakeet.
I've spat in the vases.
I've put cheese in the mouseholes.
Here's your...
[Door creaks open]
... nice tea, dear.

MRS PUGH

Too much sugar.

MR PUGH

You haven't tasted it yet, dear.

MRS PUGH

Too much milk, then. Has Mr Jenkins said his poetry?

MR PUGH

Yes, dear.

MRS PUGH

Then it's time to get up. Give me my glasses. No, not my *reading* glasses, I want to look *out*. I want to see

Lily Smalls the treasure down on her red knees washing the front step.

She's tucked her dress in her bloomers – oh, the baggage!

P.C. Atilla Rees, ox-broad, barge-booted, stomping out of Handcuff House in a heavy beef-red huff, black-browed under his damp helmet...

He's going to arrest Polly Garter, mark my words.

MR PUGH

What for, my dear?

MRS PUGH

For having babies.

... and lumbering down towards the strand to see that the sea is still there.

Mary Ann the Sailors, opening her bedroom window above the taproom and calling out to the heavens:

MARY ANN THE SAILORS

I'm eighty-five years three months and a day!

MRS PUGH

I will say this for her, she never makes a mistake.

Organ Morgan at his bedroom window playing chords on the sill to the morning fishwife gulls who, heckling over Donkey Street, observe:

DAI BREAD

Me, Dai Bread, hurrying to the bakery, pushing in my shirt-tails, buttoning my waistcoat, ping goes a button, why can't they sew them, no time for breakfast, nothing for breakfast, there's wives for you...

MRS DAI BREAD ONE

Me, Mrs Dai Bread One, capped and shawled and no old corset, nice to be comfy, nice to be nice, clogging on the cobbles to stir up a neighbour. Oh, Mrs Sarah, can you spare a loaf, love? Dai Bread forgot the bread. There's a lovely morning! How's your boils this morning? Isn't that good news now, it's a change to sit down. Ta, Mrs Sarah.

MRS DAI BREAD TWO

Me, Mrs Dai Bread Two, gypsied to kill in a silky scarlet petticoat above my knees, dirty pretty knees, see my body through my petticoat brown as a berry, high heel shoes with one heel missing, tortoiseshell comb in my bright black slinky hair, nothing else at all on but a dab of scent, lolling gaudy at the doorway, tell your fortune in the tea-leaves, scowling at the sunshine, lighting up my pipe.

LORD CUT-GLASS

Me, Lord Cut-Glass, in an old frock-coat belonged to Eli Jenkins and a pair of postman's trousers from Bethesda Jumble, running out of doors to empty slops – mind there, Rover! – and then running in again, tick tock.

NOGOOD BOYO

Me, Nogood Boyo, up to no good in the wash-house.

MISS PRICE

Me, Miss Price, in my pretty print housecoat, deft at the clothesline, natty as a jenny-wren, then pit-pat back to my egg in its cosy, my crisp toast-fingers, my homemade plum and butterpat.

POLLY GARTER

Me, Polly Garter, under the washing line, giving the breast in the garden to my bonny new baby. Nothing grows in our garden, only washing. And babies. And where's their fathers live, my love? Over the hills and far away. You're looking up at me now. I know what you're thinking, you poor little milky creature. You're thinking, you're no better than you should be, Polly, and that's good enough for me. Oh, isn't life a terrible thing, thank God?

[Single long note held by Welsh male voices.]

Now frying-pans spit, kettles and cats purr in the kitchens. The town smells of seaweed and breakfast all the way down from Bay View, where Mrs Ogmore-Pritchard, in smock and turban, big-besomed to engage the dust, picks at her starchless bread and sips lemonrind tea, to Bottom

Cottage, where Mr Waldo, in bowler and bib, gobbles his bubble-and-squeak and kippers and swigs from the saucebottle. Mary Ann the Sailors

MARY ANN THE SAILORS

praises the Lord who made porridge.

Mr Pugh

MR PUGH

remembers ground glass as he juggles his omelette.

Mrs Pugh

MRS PUGH

nags the salt-cellar.

Willy Nilly postman

WILLY NILLY

downs his last bucket of black brackish tea and rumbles out bandy to the clucking back where the hens twitch and grieve for their tea-soaked sops.

Mrs Willy Nilly

MRS WILLY NILLY

full of tea to her double-chinned brim broods and bubbles over her coven of kettles on the hissing hot range always ready to steam open the mail.

The Reverend Eli Jenkins

REV. ELI JENKINS

finds a rhyme and dips his pen in his cocoa.

Lord Cut-Glass in his ticking kitchen

LORD CUT-GLASS

scampers from clock to clock, a bunch of clock-keys in one hand, a fish-head in the other.

Captain Cat in his galley

CAPTAIN CAT

blind and fine-fingered savours his sea-fry.

Mr and Mrs Cherry Owen, in their Donkey Street room that is bedroom, parlour, kitchen, and scullery, sit down to last night's supper of onions boiled in their overcoats and broth of spuds and baconrind and leeks and bones.

MRS CHERRY OWEN

See that smudge on the wall by the picture of Auntie Blossom? That's where you threw the sago.

[Cherry Owen laughs with delight.]

You only missed me by a inch.

CHERRY OWEN

I always miss Auntie Blossom too.

MRS CHERRY OWEN

Remember last night? In you reeled, my boy, as drunk as a deacon with a big wet bucket and a fish-frail full of stout and you looked at me and you said, 'God has come home!' you said, and then over the bucket you went, sprawling and bawling, and the floor was all flagons and eels.

CHERRY OWEN

Was I wounded?

MRS CHERRY OWEN

And then you took off your trousers and you said, 'Does anybody want a fight?' Oh, you old baboon.

CHERRY OWEN

Give us a kiss.

MRS CHERRY OWEN

And then you sang 'Aberystwyth', tenor *and* bass.

CHERRY OWEN

I *always* sing 'Aberystwyth'.

MRS CHERRY OWEN

And then you did a little dance on the table.

CHERRY OWEN

I did?

MRS CHERRY OWEN

Drop dead!

CHERRY OWEN

And then what did I do?

MRS CHERRY OWEN

Then you cried like a baby and said you were a poor drunk orphan with nowhere to go but the grave.

CHERRY OWEN

And what did I do next, my dear?

MRS CHERRY OWEN

Then you danced on the table all over again and said you were King Solomon Owen and I was your Mrs Sheba.

CHERRY OWEN [Softly]

And then?

MRS CHERRY OWEN

And then I got you into bed and you breathed all night like a brewery.

[Mr and Mrs Cherry Owen laugh delightedly together.]

From Beynon Butchers in Coronation Street, the smell of fried liver sidles out with onions on its breath. And listen! In the dark breakfast-room behind the shop, Mr and Mrs Beynon, waited upon by their treasure, enjoy, between bites, their everymorning hullabaloo, and Mrs Beynon slips the gristly bits under the tasselled tablecloth to her fat cat.

[Cat purrs.]

MRS BEYNON

She likes the liver, Ben.

MR BEYNON

She ought to do, Bess. It's her brother's.

MRS BEYNON [Screaming]

Oh, d'you hear that, Lily?

LILY SMALLS

Yes, mum.

MRS BEYNON

We're eating pusscat.

LILY SMALLS

Yes, mum.

MRS BEYNON
Oh, you cat-butcher!

MR BEYNON
It was doctored, mind.

MRS BEYNON [Hysterical]
What's that got to do with it?

MR BEYNON
Yesterday, we had mole.

MRS BEYNON
Oh, Lily, Lily!

MR BEYNON
Monday, otter. Tuesday, shrews.

[Mrs Beynon screams.]

LILY SMALLS
Go on, Mrs Beynon. He's the biggest liar in town.

MRS BEYNON
Don't you dare say that about Mr Beynon.

LILY SMALLS
Everybody knows it, mum.

MRS BEYNON
Mr Beynon never tells a lie. Do you, Ben?

MR BEYNON
No, Bess. And now I am going out after the corgis, with my little cleaver.

MRS BEYNON
Oh, Lily, Lily!

Up the street, in the Sailors' Arms, Sinbad Sailors, grandson of Mary Ann the Sailors, draws a pint in the sunlit bar. The ship's clock in the bar says half past eleven. Half past eleven is opening time. The hands of the clock have stayed still at half past eleven for fifty years. It is always opening time in the Sailors' Arms.

SINBAD
Here's to me, Sinbad.

All over the town, babies and old men are cleaned and put into their broken prams and wheeled on to the sunlit cockled cobbles or out into the backyards under the dancing vests, and left. A baby cries.

OLD MAN
I want my pipe and he wants his bottle.

[School bell rings.]

Noses are wiped, heads picked, hair combed, paws scrubbed, ears boxed, and the children shrilled off to school.

[Children's voices, up and out.]

Fishermen grumble to their nets. Nogood Boyo goes out in the dinghy Zanzibar, ships the oars, drifts slowly in the dab-filled bay, and, lying on his back in the unbaled water, among crabs' legs and tangled lines, looks up at the spring sky.

NOGOOD BOYO [Softly, lazily]
I don't know who's up there and I don't care.

He turns his head and looks up at Llareggub Hill, and sees, among green lathered trees, the white houses of the strewn away farms, where farmboys whistle, dogs shout, cows low, but all too far away for him, or you, to hear. And in the town, the shops squeak open. Mr Edwards, in butterfly-collar and straw-hat at the doorway of Manchester House, measures, with his eye, the dawdlers by, for striped flannel shirts and shrouds and flowery blouses, and bellows to himself, in the darkness behind his eye:

MR EDWARDS [whispers]
I love Miss Price.

Syrup is sold in the post-office. A car drives to market, full of fowls and a farmer. Milk churns stand at Coronation Corner like short, silver policemen. And, sitting at the open window of Schooner House, blind Captain Cat hears all the morning of the town. He hears the voices of children and the noise of children's feet on the cobbles.

CAPTAIN CAT [Softly, to himself]
Maggie Richards, Ricky Rhys, Tommy Powell, our Sal, little Gerwain, Billy Swansea with the dog's voice, one of Mr Waldo's, nasty Humphrey, Jackie with the sniff... Where's Dicky's Albie? and the

boys from Ty-pant? Perhaps they got the rash again.

[A sudden cry among the children's voices.]

Somebody's hit Maggie Richards. Two to one it's Billy Swansea. Never trust a boy who barks.

[A burst of yelping crying.]

Right again! That's Billy.

And the children's voices cry away.

[Postman's rat-a-tat on door. Distant.]

That's Willy Nilly knocking at Bay View. Rat-a-tat, very soft. The knocker's got a kid glove on. Who's sent a letter to Mrs Ogmore-Pritchard?

[Rat-a-tat. Distant again.]

Careful now, she swabs the front glassy. Every step's like a bar of soap. Mind your size twelveses. That old Bessie would beeswax the lawn to make the birds slip.

WILLY NILLY
Morning, Mrs Ogmore-Pritchard.

MRS OGMORE-PRITCHARD
Good morning, postman.

WILLY NILLY
Here's a letter for you with stamped and addressed envelope enclosed, all the way from Builth Wells. A gentleman wants to study birds and can he have accommodation for two weeks and a bath vegetarian.

MRS OGMORE-PRITCHARD
No.

WILLY NILLY [Persuasively]
You wouldn't know he was in the house, Mrs Ogmore-Pritchard. He'd be out in the mornings at the bang of dawn with his bag of breadcrumbs and his little telescope...

MRS OGMORE-PRITCHARD

And come home at all hours covered with feathers. I don't want persons in my *nice clean* rooms breathing all over the chairs...

WILLY NILLY

Cross my heart, he won't breathe...

MRS OGMORE-PRITCHARD

and putting their feet on my carpets and sneezing on my china and sleeping in my sheets...

WILLY NILLY

He only wants a *single* bed, Mrs Ogmore-Pritchard.

[Door slams.]

CAPTAIN CAT [Softly]

And back she goes to the kitchen, to polish the potatoes.

Captain Cat hears Willy Nilly's feet heavy on the distant cobbles...

One, two, three, four, five... That's Mrs Rose-Cottage. What's today? Today she gets the letter from her sister in Gorslas. How's the twins' teeth?

He's stopping at School House.

WILLY NILLY

Morning, Mrs Pugh. Mrs Ogmore-Pritchard won't have a gentleman in from Builth Wells because he'll sleep in her sheets, Mrs Rose-Cottage's sister in Gorslas's twins have got to have them out...

MRS PUGH

Give me the parcel.

WILLY NILLY

It's for *Mr* Pugh, Mrs Pugh.

MRS PUGH

Never you mind. What's inside it?

WILLY NILLY

A book called 'Lives of the Great Poisoners'.

CAPTAIN CAT

That's Manchester House.

WILLY NILLY

Morning, Mr Edwards. Very small news. Mrs Ogmore-Pritchard won't have birds in the house, and Mr Pugh's bought a book now on how to do in Mrs Pugh.

MR EDWARDS

Have you got a letter from *her*?

WILLY NILLY

Miss Price loves you with all her heart. Smelling of lavender today. She's down to the last of the elderflower wine but the quince jam's bearing up and she's knitting roses on the doilies. Last week she sold three jars of boiled sweets, pound of humbugs, half a box of jellybabies and six coloured photos of Llareggub. Yours for ever. Then twenty-one X's.

MR EDWARDS

Oh, Willy Nilly, she's a ruby! Here's my letter. Put it into her hands now.

Down the street comes Willy Nilly. And Captain Cat hears other steps approaching.

CAPTAIN CAT

Mr Waldo hurrying to the Sailors' Arms. Pint of stout with an egg in it.
[Softly] There's a letter for him.

WILLY NILLY

It's another paternity summons, Mr Waldo.

The quick footsteps hurry on along the cobbles and up three steps to the Sailors' Arms.

MR WALDO [Calling out]

Quick, Sinbad. Pint of stout. And no egg in.

People are moving now, up and down the cobbled street.

CAPTAIN CAT

All the women are out this morning, in the sun. You can tell it's Spring. There goes Mrs Cherry, you can tell her by her trotters, off she trots new as a daisy. Who's that talking by the pump? Mrs Floyd and Boyo, talking flatfish. What can you talk about flatfish? That's Mrs Dai Bread One, waltzing up the street like a jelly, every time she shakes it's slap slap slap. Who's that? Mrs Butcher Beynon with her pet black cat, it follows her everywhere, miaow and all. There goes Mrs Twenty Three, important, the sun gets up and goes down in her dewlap, when she shuts her eyes, it's night. High heels now, in the morning too, Mrs Rose-Cottage's eldest, Mae, seventeen and never been kissed ho ho, going young and milking under my window to the field with the nannygoats, she reminds me all the way. Can't hear what the women are gabbing round the pump. Same as ever. Who's having a baby, who blacked whose eye, seen Polly Garter giving her belly an airing, there should be a law, seen Mrs Beynon's new mauve jumper it's her old grey jumper dyed, who's dead, who's dying, there's a lovely day, oh the cost of soapflakes!

[Organ music distant.]

Organ Morgan's at it early. You can *tell* it's Spring.

And he hears the noise of milk-cans.

Ocky Milkman on his round. I will say this, his milk's as fresh as the dew. Half dew it is. Snuffle on, Ocky, watering the town.

Somebody's coming. Now the voices round the pump can see somebody coming. Hush, there's a hush! You can tell by the noise of the hush, it's Polly Garter. [Louder] Hullo, Polly, who's there?

POLLY GARTER [Off]

Me, love.

CAPTAIN CAT

That's Polly Garter. [Softly] Hullo, Polly, my love.

Can you hear the dumb goose-hiss of the wives as they huddle and peck or flounce at a waddle away? Who cuddled you when? Which of their gandering hubbies moaned in Milk Wood for your naughty mothering arms and body like a wardrobe, love? Scrub the floors of the Welfare Hall for the Mothers' Union Social Dance, you're one mother won't wriggle her roly poly bum or pat her fat little buttery foot in that wedding-ringed holy tonight though the waltzing breadwinners snatched from the cosy smoke of the Sailors' Arms will grizzle and mope.

[A cock crows.]

CAPTAIN CAT

Too late, cock, too late,

for the town's half over with its morning. The morning's busy as bees.

[Out background organ music.]

There's the clip clop of horses on the sunhoneyed cobbles of the humming streets, hammering of horseshoes, gobble quack and cackle, tomtit twitter from the bird-ounced boughs, braying on Donkey Down. Bread is baking, pigs are grunting, chop goes the butcher, milk churns bell, tills ring, sheep cough, dogs shout, saws sing. Oh, the Spring whinny and morning moo from the clog dancing farms, the gulls' gab and rabble on the boat bobbing river and sea and the cockles bubbling in the sand, scamper of sanderlings, curlew cry, crow caw, pigeon coo, clock strike, bull bellow, and the ragged gabble of the beargarden school as the women scratch and babble in Mrs Organ Morgan's general shop where everything is sold: custard, buckets, henna, rat-traps, shrimp nets, sugar, stamps, confetti, paraffin, hatchets, whistles.

FIRST WOMAN

Mrs Ogmore-Pritchard

SECOND WOMAN

la di da

FIRST WOMAN

got a man in Builth Wells

THIRD WOMAN

and he got a little telescope to look at birds

SECOND WOMAN
Willy Nilly said

THIRD WOMAN
Remember her first husband? He didn't need a telescope

FIRST WOMAN
he looked at them undressing through the keyhole

THIRD WOMAN
and he used to shout Tallyho

SECOND WOMAN
but Mr Ogmore was a proper gentleman

FIRST WOMAN
even though he hanged his collie

THIRD WOMAN
Seen Mrs Butcher Beynon?

SECOND WOMAN
She said Butcher Beynon put dogs in the mincer

FIRST WOMAN
Go on he's pulling her leg

THIRD WOMAN
Now don't you dare tell her that, there's a dear

SECOND WOMAN
or she'll think he's trying to pull it off and eat it –

FOURTH WOMAN
There's a nasty lot live here when you come to think.

FIRST WOMAN
Look at that Nogood Boyo now

SECOND WOMAN
too lazy to wipe his snout

THIRD WOMAN
and going out fishing every day and all he ever brought back was a Mrs Samuels

FIRST WOMAN

been in the water a week

SECOND WOMAN

And look at Ocky Milkman's wife that nobody's ever seen

FIRST WOMAN

he keeps her in the cupboard with the empties

THIRD WOMAN

and think of Dai Bread with two wives

SECOND WOMAN

one for the daytime one for the night

FOURTH WOMAN

Men are brutes on the quiet

THIRD WOMAN

And how's Organ Morgan, Mrs Morgan

FIRST WOMAN

you look dead beat

SECOND WOMAN

it's organ organ all the time with him

THIRD WOMAN

up every night until midnight playing the organ

MRS ORGAN MORGAN

Oh, I'm a martyr to music.

Outside, the sun springs down on the rough and tumbling town. It runs through the hedges of Goosegog Lane, cuffing the birds to sing. Spring whips green down Cockle Row, and the shells ring out. Llareggub this snip of a morning is wildfruit and warm, the streets, fields, sands and waters springing in the young sun.

Evans the Death presses hard, with black gloves, on the coffin of his breast, in case his heart jumps out.

EVANS THE DEATH [Harsh]

Where's your dignity. Lie down.

Spring stirs Gossamer Beynon schoolmistress like a spoon.

GOSSAMER BEYNON [Tearful]
Oh, what can I do? I'll *never* be refined if I twitch.

Spring this strong morning foams in a flame in Jack Black as he cobbles a high-heeled shoe for Mrs Dai Bread Two the gypsy, but he hammers it sternly out.

JACK BLACK [To a hammer rhythm]
There is *no leg* belonging to the foot that belongs to this shoe.

The sun and the green breeze ship Captain Cat sea-memory again.

CAPTAIN CAT
No, *I'll* take the mulatto, by God, who's captain here? Parlez-vous jig jig, Madam?

Mary Ann the Sailors says very softly to herself as she looks out at Llareggub Hill from the bedroom where she was born,

MARY ANN THE SAILORS [Loudly]
It is Spring in Llareggub in the sun in my old age, and this is the Chosen Land.

[A choir of children's voices suddenly cries out on one, high, glad, long, sighing note.]

And in Willy Nilly the Postman's dark and sizzling damp tea-coated misty pygmy kitchen where the spittingcat kettles throb and hop on the range, Mrs Willy Nilly steams open Mr Mog Edwards' letter to Miss Myfanwy Price and reads it aloud to Willy Nilly by the squint of the Spring sun through the one sealed window running with tears, while the drugged, bedraggled hens at the back door whimper and snivel for the lickerish bog-black tea.

MRS WILLY NILLY
From Manchester House, Llareggub. Sole Prop: Mr Mog Edwards (late of Twll), Linendraper, Haberdasher, Master Tailor, Costumier. For West End Negligee, Lingerie, Teagowns, Evening Dress, Trousseaux, Layettes. Also Ready to Wear for All Occasions. Economical Outfitting for Agricultural Employment Our Speciality. Wardrobes Bought. Among Our Satisfied Customers Ministers of Religion and J.P.'s. Fittings by Appointment. Adver-

tising Weekly in the Twll Bugle. Beloved Myfanwy Price my Bride in Heaven,

MOG EDWARDS

I love you until Death do us part and then we shall be together for ever and ever. A new parcel of ribbons has come from Carmarthen today all the colours in the rainbow. I wish I could tie a ribbon in your hair a white one but it cannot be. I dreamed last night you were all dripping wet and you sat on my lap as the Reverend Jenkins went down the street. I see you got a mermaid in your lap he said and he lifted his hat. He is a proper Christian. Not like Cherry Owen who said you should have thrown her back he said. Business is very poorly. Polly Garter bought two garters with roses but she never got stockings so what is the use I say. Mr Waldo tried to sell me a woman's nightie outsize he said he found it and we know where. I sold a packet of pins to Tom the Sailors to pick his teeth. If this goes on I shall be in the Workhouse. My heart is in your bosom and yours is in mine. God be with you always Myfanwy Price and keep you lovely for me in His Heavenly Mansion. I must stop now and remain, Your Eternal, Mog Edwards.

MRS WILLY NILLY

And then a little message with a rubber stamp. Shop at Mog's!!!

And Willy Nilly, rumbling, jockeys out again to the three-seated shack called the House of Commons in the back where the hens weep, and sees, in sudden Springshine,

herring gulls heckling down to the harbour where the fishermen spit and prop the morning up and eye the fishy sea smooth to the sea's end as it lulls in blue. Green and gold money, tobacco, tinned salmon, hats with feathers, pots of fish-paste, warmth for the winter-to-be, weave and leap in it rich and slippery in the flash and shapes of fishes through the cold sea-streets. But with blue lazy eyes the fishermen gaze at that milk-mild whispering water with no ruck or ripple as though it blew great guns and serpents and typhooned the town.

FISHERMAN

Too rough for fishing today.

And they thank God, and gob at a gull for luck, and moss-slow and silent make their way uphill, from the still still sea, towards the Sailors' Arms as the children

[School bell.]

spank and scamper rough and singing out of school into the draggletail yard. And Captain Cat at his window says soft to himself the words of their song.

CAPTAIN CAT [Keeping to the beat of the singing]

Johnnie Crack and Flossie Snail
Kept their baby in a milking pail
Flossie Snail and Johnnie Crack
One would pull it out and one would put it back
O it's my turn now said Flossie Snail
To take the baby from the milking pail
And it's my turn now said Johnnie Crack
To smack it on the head and put it back

Johnnie Crack and Flossie Snail
Kept their baby in a milking pail
One would put it back and one would pull it out
And all it had to drink was ale and stout
For Johnnie Crack and Flossie Snail
Always used to say that stout and ale
Was *good* for a baby in a milking pail.

[Pause.]

The music of the spheres is heard distinctly over Milk Wood. It is 'The Rustle of Spring'.

A glee-party sings in Bethesda Graveyard, gay but muffled.

Vegetables make love above the tenors.

And dogs bark blue in the face.

Mrs Ogmore-Pritchard belches in a teeny hanky and chases the sunlight with a flywhisk, but even she cannot drive out the Spring: from one of her fingerbowls, a primrose grows.

Mrs Dai Bread One and Mrs Dai Bread Two are sitting outside their house in Donkey Lane, one darkly one plumply blooming in the quick, dewy sun. Mrs Dai Bread Two is looking into a crystal ball which she holds in the lap of her dirty scarlet petticoat, hard against her hard dark thighs.

MRS DAI BREAD TWO

Cross my palm with silver. Out of our housekeeping money. Aah!

MRS DAI BREAD ONE

What d'you see, lovie?

MRS DAI BREAD TWO

I see a featherbed. With three pillows on it. And a text above the bed. I can't read what it says, there's great clouds blowing. Now they have blown away. God is love, the text says.

MRS DAI BREAD ONE [Delighted]

That's *our* bed.

MRS DAI BREAD TWO

And now it's vanished. The sun's spinning like a top. Who's this coming out of the sun? It's a hairy little man with big pink lips. He got a wall eye.

MRS DAI BREAD ONE

It's Dai, it's Dai Bread!

MRS DAI BREAD TWO

Ssh! The featherbed's floating back. The little man's taking his boots off. He's pulling his shirt over his head. He's beating his chest with his fists. He's climbing into bed.

MRS DAI BREAD ONE

Go on, go on.

MRS DAI BREAD TWO

There's *two* women in bed. He looks at them both, with his head cocked on one side. He's whistling through his teeth. Now he grips his little arms round one of the women.

MRS DAI BREAD ONE

Which one, which one?

MRS DAI BREAD TWO

I can't see any more. There's great clouds blowing again.

MRS DAI BREAD ONE

Ach, the mean old clouds!

The morning is all singing. The Reverend Eli Jenkins, busy on his morning calls, stops outside the Welfare Hall to hear Polly Garter as she scrubs the floors for the Mothers' Union Dance tonight.

POLLY GARTER [Singing]

I loved a man whose name was Tom
He was strong as a bear and two yards long
I loved a man whose name was Dick
He was big as a barrel and three feet thick
And I loved a man whose name was Harry
Six feet tall and sweet as a cherry
But the one I loved best awake or asleep
Was little Willy Wee and he's six feet deep.

Oh Tom Dick and Harry were three fine men
And I'll never have such loving again
But little Willy Wee who took me on his knee
Little Willy Weazel is the man for me.

Now men from every parish round
Run after me and roll me on the ground
But whenever I love another man back
Johnnie from the Hill or Sailing Jack
I always think as they do what they please
Of Tom Dick and Harry who were tall as trees
And most I think when I'm by their side
Of little Willy Wee who downed and died.

Oh Tom Dick and Harry were three fine men
And I'll never have such loving again
But little Willy Wee who took me on his knee
Little Willy Weazel is the man for me.

REV. ELI JENKINS

Praise the Lord! We are a musical nation.

And the Reverend Jenkins hurries on through the town, to visit the sick with jelly and poems.

The town's as full as a lovebird's egg.

MR WALDO

There goes the Reverend,

says Mr Waldo at the smoked herring brown window of the unwashed Sailors' Arms

with his brolly and
his odes. Fill 'em up, Sinbad, I'm on the
treacle today.

The silent fishermen flush down their pints.

SINBAD

Oh, Mr Waldo,

sighs Sinbad Sailors,

I dote on that Gossamer Beynon.

Love, sings the Spring. The bedspring grass bounces under birds' bums and lambs.

And Gossamer Beynon, schoolteacher, spoonstirred and quivering, teaches her slubberdegullion class

CHILDREN'S VOICES

It was a luvver and his lars
With a a and a o and a a nonino...

GOSSAMER BEYNON

Naow, naow, naow, your eccents, children!
It was a lover and his less
With a hey and a hao and a hey nonino...

SINBAD

Oh, Mr Waldo,

says Sinbad Sailors,

she's a lady all over.

And Mr Waldo, who is thinking of a woman soft as Eve and sharp as sciatica to share his bread-pudding bed, answers,

MR WALDO

No lady that I know is.

SINBAD

And if only grandma'd die, cross my heart I'd go

down on my knees Mr Waldo and I'd say Miss Gossamer I'd say

CHILDREN'S VOICES

When birds do sing a ding a ding a ding
Sweet luvvers luv the Spring...

Polly Garter sings, still on her knees,

POLLY GARTER

Tom Dick and Harry were three fine men
And I'll never have such

CHILDREN

Ding a ding

POLLY GARTER

again.

And the morning school is over, and Captain Cat at his curtained schooner's porthole open to the Spring sun tides hears the naughty forfeiting children tumble and rhyme on the cobbles...

GIRLS' VOICES

Gwennie call the boys
They make such a noise.

GIRL

Boys boys boys
Come along to me.

GIRLS' VOICES

Boys boys boys
Kiss Gwennie where she says
Or give her a penny.
Go on, Gwennie.

GIRL

Kiss me in Goosegog Lane
Or give me a penny.
What's your name?

FIRST BOY

Billy.

GIRL

Kiss me in Goosegog Lane Billy
Or give me a penny silly.

FIRST BOY

Gwennie Gwennie
I kiss you in Goosegog Lane
Now I haven't got to give you a penny.

GIRLS' VOICES

Boys boys boys
Kiss Gwennie where she says
Or give her a penny
Go on, Gwennie.

GIRL

Kiss me on Llareggub Hill
Or give me a penny
What's your name?

SECOND BOY

Johnnie Cristo.

GIRL

Kiss me on Llareggub Hill Johnnie Cristo
Or give me a penny, mister.

SECOND BOY

Gwennie Gwennie
I kiss you on Llareggub Hill.
Now I haven't got to give you a penny.

GIRLS' VOICES

Boys boys boys
Kiss Gwennie where she says
Or give her a penny.
Go on, Gwennie.

GIRL

Kiss me in Milk Wood
Or give me a penny.
What's your name?

THIRD BOY

Dicky.

GIRL

Kiss me in Milk Wood Dicky
Or give me a penny quickly.

THIRD BOY

Gwennie Gwennie
I can't kiss you in Milk Wood.

GIRLS' VOICES

Gwennie ask him why.

GIRL

Why?

THIRD BOY

Because my mother said I mustn't.

GIRLS' VOICES

Cowardy cowardy custard
Give Gwennie a penny.

GIRL

Give me a penny.

THIRD BOY

I haven't got any.

GIRLS' VOICES

Put him in the river
Up to his liver
Quick quick Dirty Dick
Beat him on the bum
With a rhubarb stick.
Aiee!
Hush!

And the shrill girls giggle and master around him and squeal as they clutch and thrash, and he blubbers away downhill with his patched pants falling, and his tear-splashed blush burns all the way as the triumphant bird-like sisters scream with buttons in their claws and the bully brothers hoot after him his little nickname and his mother's shame and his father's wickedness with the loose wild barefoot women of the hovels of the hills. It all means nothing at all, and, howling for his milky mum, for her cawl and buttermilk and cowbreath and Welshcakes and the fat birth-smelling bed and moonlit kitchen of her arms, he'll never forget as he paddles blind home through the weeping end of the world. Then his tormentors tussle and run to the Cockle Street sweet-shop, their pennies sticky as honey, to buy from Miss Myfanwy Price, who is cocky and neat as a puff-bosomed robin and her small round buttocks tight as ticks, gobstoppers big as wens that rainbow as you suck, brandyballs, winegums, hundreds and thousands, liquorice sweet as sick, nugget to tug and ribbon out like another red rubbery tongue, gum to glue in girls' curls, crimson coughdrops to spit blood, ice-cream cornets, dandelion-and-burdock, raspberry and cherryade, pop goes the weasel and the wind.

Gossamer Beynon high-heels out of school. The sun hums down through the cotton flowers of her dress into the bell of her heart and buzzes in the honey there and couches and kisses, lazy-loving and boozed, in her red-berried breast. Eyes run from the trees and windows of the street steaming, 'Gossamer', and strip her to the nipples and the bees. She blazes naked past the Sailors' Arms, the only woman on the Dai-Adamed earth. Sinbad Sailors places on her thighs still dewdamp from the first mangrowing cockcrow garden his reverent goat-bearded hands.

GOSSAMER BEYNON

I don't care if he *is* common,

she whispers to her salad-day deep self,

I want to gobble him up.

I don't care if he *does* drop his aitches,

she tells the stripped and mother-of-the-world big-beamed and Eve-hipped spring of her self,

so long as

he's all cucumber and hooves.

Sinbad Sailors watches her go by, demure and proud and schoolmarm in her crisp flower dress and sun-defying hat, with never a look or lilt or wriggle, the butcher's unmelting icemaiden daughter veiled forever from the hungry hug of his eyes.

SINBAD SAILORS

Oh, Gossamer Beynon, why are you so proud?

He grieves to his Guinness.

Oh, beautiful beautiful Gossamer B., I wish I wish

that you were for me. I wish you were not so educated.

She feels his goatbeard tickle her in the middle of the world like a tuft of wiry fire, and she turns, in a terror of delight, away from his whips and whiskery conflagration and sits down in the kitchen to a plate heaped high with chips and the kidneys of lambs.

In the blind-drawn dark dining-room of School House, dusty and echoing as a dining room in a vault, Mr and Mrs Pugh are silent over cold grey cottage pie. Mr Pugh reads, as he forks the shroud meat in, from 'Lives of the Great Poisoners'. He has bound a plain brown-paper cover round the book. Slyly, between slow mouthfuls, he sidespies up at Mrs Pugh, poisons her with his eye, then goes on reading. He underlines certain passages and smiles in secret.

MRS PUGH

Persons with manners do not read at table,

says Mrs Pugh. She swallows a digestive tablet as big as a horse-pill, washing it down with clouded peasoup water.

[Pause.]

Some persons were brought up in pigsties.

MR PUGH

Pigs don't read at table, dear.

Bitterly she flicks dust from the broken cruet. It settles on the pie in a thin gnat-rain.

MR PUGH

Pigs can't read, my dear.

MRS PUGH

I know one who can.

Alone in the hissing laboratory of his wishes, Mr Pugh minces among bad vats and jeroboams, tiptoes through spinneys of murdering herbs, agony dancing in his crucibles, and mixes especially for Mrs Pugh a venomous porridge unknown to toxologists which will scald and viper through her until her ears fall off like figs, her toes grow big and black as balloons, and steam comes screaming out of her navel.

You know best, dear,

says Mr Pugh, and quick as a flash he ducks her in rat soup.

MRS PUGH

What's that book by your trough, Mr Pugh?

MR PUGH

It's a theological work, my dear. 'Lives of the Great Saints.'

Mrs Pugh smiles. An icicle forms in the cold air of the dining vault.

MRS PUGH

I saw you talking to a saint this morning. Saint Polly Garter. She was martyred again last night in Milk Wood. Mrs Organ Morgan saw her with Mr Waldo.

MRS ORGAN MORGAN

And when they saw me they pretended they were looking for nests,

said Mrs Organ Morgan to her husband, with her mouth full of fish as a pelican's.

But you don't go nesting in long combinations, I said to myself, like Mr Waldo was wearing, and your dress nearly over your head like Polly Garter's. Oh, they didn't fool me.

One big bird gulp, and the flounder's gone. She licks her lips and goes stabbing again.

And when you think of all those babies she's got, then all I can say is she'd better give up bird nesting that's all I can say, it isn't the right kind of hobby at all for a woman that can't say No even to midgets. Remember Tom Spit? He wasn't any bigger than a baby and he gave her two. But they're two nice boys, I will say that, Fred Spit and Arthur. Sometimes I like Fred best and sometimes I like Arthur. Who do you like best, Organ?

ORGAN MORGAN

Oh, Bach without any doubt. Bach every time for me.

MRS ORGAN MORGAN

Organ Morgan, you haven't been listening to a word
I said. It's organ organ all the time with you...

And she bursts into tears, and, in the middle of her salty howling, nimbly spears a small flat fish and pelicans it whole.

ORGAN MORGAN

And then Palestrina,

says Organ Morgan.

Lord Cut-Glass, in his kitchen full of time, squats down alone to a dogdish, marked Fido, of peppery fish-scraps and listens to the voices of his sixty-six clocks – (one for each year of his loony age) – and watches, with love, their black-and-white moony loudlipped faces tocking the earth away: slow clocks, quick clocks, pendulumed heart-knocks, china, alarm, grandfather, cuckoo; clocks shaped like Noah's whirring Ark, clocks that bicker in marble ships, clocks in the wombs of glass women, hourglass chimers, tu-wit-tu-woo clocks, clocks that pluck tunes, Vesuvius clocks all black bells and lava, Niagara clocks that cataract their ticks, old time-weeping clocks with ebony beards, clocks with no hands forever drumming out time without ever knowing what time it is. His sixty-six singers are all set at different hours. Lord Cut-Glass lives in a house and a life at siege. Any minute or dark day now, the unknown enemy will loot and savage downhill, but they will not catch him napping. Sixty-six different times in his fish-slimy kitchen ping, strike, tick, chime and tock.

The lust and lilt and lather and emerald breeze and crackle of the bird-praise and body of Spring with its breasts full of rivering May-milk, means, to that lordly fish-head nibbler, nothing but another nearness to the tribes and navies of the Last Black Day who'll sear and pillage down Armageddon Hill to his double-locked rusty-shuttered tick tock dust-scrabbled shack at the bottom of the town that has fallen head over bells in love.

POLLY GARTER

And I'll never have such loving again,

pretty Polly hums and longs.

POLLY GARTER [Sings]

Now when farmers' boys on the first fair day
Come down from the hills to drink and be gay,

Before the sun sinks I'll lie there in their arms –
For they're *good* bad boys from the lonely farms,

But I always think as we tumble into bed
Of little Willy Wee who is dead, dead, dead...

[A long silence.]

The sunny slow lulling afternoon yawns and moons through the dozy town. The sea lolls, laps and idles in, with fishes sleeping in its lap. The meadows still as Sunday, the shut-eye tasselled bulls, the goat-and-daisy dingles, nap happy and lazy. The dumb duck-ponds snooze. Clouds sag and pillow on Llareggub Hill. Pigs grunt in a wet wallow-bath, and smile as they snort and dream. They dream of the acorned swill of the world, the rooting for pig-fruit, the bagpipe dugs of the mother sow, the squeal and snuffle of yesses of the women pigs in rut. They mud-bask and snout in the pig-loving sun; their tails curl; they rollick and slobber and snore to deep, smug, after-swill sleep. Donkeys angelically drowse on Donkey Down.

MRS PUGH

Persons with manners,

snaps Mrs cold Pugh,

do not nod at table.

Mr Pugh cringes awake. He puts on a soft-soaping smile: it is sad and grey under his nicotine-eggyellow weeping walrus Victorian moustache worn thick and long in memory of Doctor Crippen.

You should wait until you retire to your sty,

says Mrs Pugh, sweet as a razor. His fawning measly quarter-smile freezes. Sly and silent, he foxes into his chemist's den and there, in a hiss and prussic circle of cauldrons and phials brimful with pox and the Black Death, cooks up a fricassee of deadly nightshade, nicotine, hot frog, cyanide and bat-spit for his needling stalactite hag and bednag of a pokerbacked nutcracker wife.

MR PUGH

I beg your pardon, my dear,

he murmurs with a wheedle.

Captain Cat, at his window thrown wide to the sun and the clippered seas he sailed long ago when his eyes were blue and bright, slumbers and voyages; ear-ringed and rolling, I Love You Rosie Probert tattooed on his belly, he brawls with broken bottles in the fug and babel of the dark dock bars, roves with a herd of short and good time cows in every naughty port and twines and souses with the drowned and blowsy-breasted dead. He weeps as he sleeps and sails, and the tears run down his grog-blossomed nose.

One voice of all he remembers most dearly as his dream buckets down. Lazy early Rosie with the flaxen thatch, whom he shared with Tom-Fred the donkeyman and many another seaman, clearly and near to him speaks from the bedroom of her dust. In that gulf and haven, fleets by the dozen have anchored for the little heaven of the night; but she speaks to Captain napping Cat alone. Mrs Probert –

ROSIE PROBERT

From Duck Lane, Jack. Quack twice and ask for Rosie –

is the one love of his sea-life that was sardined with women.

ROSIE PROBERT [Softly]

What seas did you see,
Tom Cat, Tom Cat,
In your sailoring days
Long long ago?
What sea beasts were
In the wavery green
When you were my master?

CAPTAIN CAT

I'll tell you the truth.
Seas barking like seals,
Blue seas and green,
Seas covered with eels
And mermen and whales.

ROSIE PROBERT

What seas did you sail
Old whaler when
On the blubbery waves
Between Frisco and Wales
You were my bosun?

CAPTAIN CAT

As true as I'm here dear
You Tom Cat's tart
You landlubber Rosie
You cosy love
My easy as easy
My true sweetheart,
Seas green as a bean
Seas gliding with swans
In the seal-barking moon.

ROSIE PROBERT

What seas were rocking
My little deck hand
My favourite husband
In your seaboots and hunger
My duck my whaler
My honey my daddy
My pretty sugar sailor
With my name on your belly
When you were a boy
Long long ago?

CAPTAIN CAT

I'll tell you no lies.
The only sea I saw
Was the seesaw sea
With you riding on it.
Lie down, lie easy.
Let me shipwreck in your thighs.

ROSIE PROBERT

Knock twice, Jack,
At the door of my grave
And ask for Rosie.

CAPTAIN CAT

Rosie Probert.

ROSIE PROBERT

Remember her.
She is forgetting.
The earth which filled her mouth

Is vanishing from her.
Remember me.
I have forgotten you.
I am going into the darkness of the darkness for ever.
I have forgotten that I was ever born.

CHILD

Look,

says a child to her mother as they pass by the window of Schooner House,

Captain Cat is crying.

Captain Cat is crying,

CAPTAIN CAT

Come back come back,

up the silences and echoes of the passages of the eternal night.

CHILD

He's crying all over his nose,

says the child. Mother and child move on down the street.

He's got a nose like strawberries,

the child says; and then she forgets him too. She sees in the still middle of the bluebagged bay Nogood Boyo fishing from the Zanzibar.

Nogood Boyo gave me three pennies yesterday but I wouldn't,

the child tells her mother.

Boyo catches a whalebone corset. It is all he has caught all day.

NOGOOD BOYO

Bloody funny fish!

Mrs Dai Bread Two gypsies up his mind's slow eye, dressed only in a bangle.

She's wearing her nightgown.
[Pleadingly] Would you like this nice wet corset, Mrs Dai Bread Two?

MRS DAI BREAD TWO

No, I *won't*!

NOGOOD BOYO

And a bite of my little apple?

he offers with no hope.

She shakes her brass nightgown, and he chases her out of his mind; and when he comes gusting back, there in the bloodshot centre of his eye a geisha girl grins and bows in a kimono of ricepaper.

I want to be *good* Boyo, but nobody'll let me,

he sighs as she writhes politely. The land fades, the sea flocks silently away; and through the warm white cloud where he lies silky, tingling uneasy Eastern music undoes him in a Japanese minute.

The afternoon buzzes like lazy bees round the flowers round Mae Rose-Cottage. Nearly asleep in the field of nannygoats who hum and gently butt the sun, she blows love on a puffball.

MAE ROSE-COTTAGE [Lazily]

He loves me
He loves me not
He loves me
He loves me not
He *loves* me! – the dirty old fool.

Lazy she lies alone in clover and sweet-grass, seventeen and never been sweet in the grass, ho ho.

The Reverend Eli Jenkins inky in his cool front parlour or poem-room tells only the truth in his Lifework: the Population, Main Industry, Shipping, History, Topography, Flora and Fauna of the town he worships in: the White Book of Llareggub. Portraits of famous bards and preachers, all fur and wool from the squint to the kneecaps, hang over him heavy as sheep, next to faint lady watercolours of pale green Milk Wood like a lettuce salad dying. His mother, propped against a pot in a palm, with her wedding-ring waist and bust like a blackcloth diningtable, suffers in her stays.

REV. ELI JENKINS

Oh, angels be careful there with your knives and forks,

he prays. There is no known likeness of his father Esau, who, undog-

collared because of his little weakness, was scythed to the bone one harvest by mistake when sleeping with his weakness in the corn. He lost all ambition and died, with one leg.

Poor Dad,

grieved the Reverend Eli,

to die of drink and agriculture.

Farmer Watkins in Salt Lake Farm hates his cattle on the hill as he ho's them in to milking.

UTAH WATKINS [In a fury]
Damn you, you damned dairies!

A cow kisses him.

Bite her to death!

he shouts to his deaf dog who smiles and licks his hand.

Gore him, sit on him, Daisy!

he bawls to the cow who barbed him with her tongue, and she moos gentle words as he raves-and-dances among his summerbreath'd slaves walking delicately to the farm. The coming of the end of the Spring day is already reflected in the lakes of their great eyes. Bessie Bighead greets them by the names she gave them when they were maidens:

BESSIE BIGHEAD
Peg, Meg, Buttercup, Moll,
Fan from the Castle,
Theodosia and Daisy.

They bow their heads.

Look up Bessie Bighead in the White Book of Llareggub and you will find the few haggard rags and the one poor glittering thread of her history laid out in pages there with as much love and care as the lock of hair of a first lost love. Conceived in Milk Wood, born in a barn, wrapped in paper, left on a doorstep, big-headed and bass-voiced she grew in the dark until long-dead Gomer Owen kissed her when she wasn't looking because he was dared. Now in the light she'll work, sing, milk, say the cows' sweet names and sleep until the night sucks out her soul and spits it into the sky. In her life-long love-light, holily Bessie milks the fond lake-eyed cows as dusk showers slowly down over byre, sea and town.

Utah Watkins curses through the farmyard on a carthorse.

UTAH WATKINS

Gallop, you bleeding cripple! –

and the huge horse neighs softly as though he had given it a lump of sugar.

Now the town is dusk. Each cobble, donkey, goose and gooseberry street is a thoroughfare of dusk; and dusk and ceremonial dust, and night's first darkening snow, and the sleep of birds, drift under and through the live dusk of this place of love. Llareggub is the capital of dusk.

Mrs Ogmore-Pritchard, at the first drop of the dusk-shower, seals all her Sea View doors, draws the germ-free blinds, sits, erect as a dry dream on a highbacked hygienic chair and wills herself to cold, quick sleep. At once, at twice, Mr Ogmore and Mr Pritchard, who all dead day long have been gossiping like ghosts in the woodshed, planning the loveless destruction of their glass widow, reluctantly sigh and sidle into her clean house.

MR PRITCHARD

You first, Mr Ogmore.

MR OGMORE

After you, Mr Pritchard.

MR PRITCHARD

No, no, Mr Ogmore. You widowed her first.

And in through the keyhole, with tears where their eyes once were, they ooze and grumble.

MRS OGMORE-PRITCHARD

Husbands,

she says in her sleep. There is acid love in her voice for one of the two shambling phantoms. Mr Ogmore hopes that it is not for him. So does Mr Pritchard.

I love you both.

MR OGMORE [With terror]

Oh, Mrs Ogmore.

MR PRITCHARD [With horror]

Oh, Mrs Pritchard.

MRS OGMORE-PRITCHARD
Soon it will be time to go to bed. Tell me your tasks in order.

MR OGMORE & MR PRITCHARD
We must take our pyjamas from the drawer marked pyjamas.

MRS OGMORE-PRITCHARD [Coldly]
And then you must take them off.

Down in the dusking town, Mae Rose-Cottage, still lying in clover, listening to the nannygoats chew, draws circles of lipstick round her nipples.

MAE ROSE-COTTAGE
I'm *fast*. I'm a bad lot. God will strike me dead. I'm seventeen. I'll go to hell,

she tells the goats.

You just wait. I'll sin till I blow up!

She lies deep, waiting for the worst to happen; the goats champ and sneer.

And at the doorway of Bethesda House, the Reverend Jenkins recites to Llareggub Hill his sunset poem.

REV. ELI JENKINS
Every morning, when I wake,
Dear Lord, a little prayer I make,
O please to keep Thy lovely eye
On all poor creatures born to die.

And every evening at sun-down
I ask a blessing on the town,
For whether we last the night or no
I'm sure is always touch-and-go.

We are not wholly bad or good
Who live our lives under Milk Wood,
And Thou, I know, wilt be the first
To see our best side, not our worst.

O let us see another day!
Bless us this holy night, I pray,

And to the sun we all will bow
And say goodbye – but just for now!

Jack Black prepares once more to meet his Satan in the Wood. He grinds his night-teeth, closes his eyes, climbs into his religious trousers, their flies sewn up with cobbler's thread, and pads out, torched and bibled, grimly, joyfully, into the already sinning dusk.

JACK BLACK
Off to Gomorrah!

And Lily Smalls is up to Nogood Boyo in the wash-house.

Cherry Owen, sober as Sunday as he is every day of the week, goes off happy as Saturday to get drunk as a deacon as he does every night.

CHERRY OWEN
I always say she's got two husbands,

says Cherry Owen,

one drunk

and one sober.

And Mrs Cherry simply says

MRS CHERRY OWEN
And aren't I a lucky woman? Because I love them both.

SINBAD
Evening, Cherry.

CHERRY OWEN
Evening, Sinbad.

SINBAD
What'll you have?

CHERRY OWEN
Too much.

SINBAD
The *Sailors'* Arms is always open,

Sinbad suffers to himself, heartbroken,

Oh, Gossamer,
open yours!

Dusk is drowned for ever until tomorrow. It is all at once night now. The windy town is a hill of windows, and from the larrupped waves, the lights of the lamps in the windows call back the day and the dead that have run away to sea. All over the calling dark, babies and old men are bribed and lullabied to sleep.

FIRST WOMAN'S VOICE
Hushabye, baby, the sandman is coming...

SECOND WOMAN'S VOICE
Rockabye, grandpa, in the treetop,
When the wind blows, the cradle will rock,
When the bough breaks, the cradle will fall,
Down will come grandpa, whiskers and all.

Or their daughters cover up the old unwinking men like parrots, and in their little dark in the lit and bustling young kitchen corners, all night long they watch, beady-eyed, the long night through in case death catches them asleep.

Unmarried girls, alone in their privately bridal bedrooms, powder and curl for the Dance of the World.

[Accordion music – dim.]

They make, in front of their looking-glasses, haughty or come-hithering faces for the young men in the street outside, at the lamplit leaning corners, who wait in the all-at-once wind to wolve and whistle.

[Accordion music up and down and continuing dim.]

The drinkers in the Sailors' Arms drink to the failure of the dance.

FIRST DRINKER
Down with the waltzing and skipping.

SECOND DRINKER
Dancing isn't natural,

righteously says Cherry Owen who has just downed seventeen pints of flat, warm, thin, Welsh, bitter beer.

A farmer's lantern glimmers, a spark on Llareggub hillside.

Llareggub Hill, writes the Reverend Jenkins in his poem-room, that mystic tumulus, the memorial of peoples that dwelt in the region of

Llareggub before the Celts left the Land of Summer and where the old wizards made themselves a wife out of flowers.

[Accordion music out.]

Mr Waldo, in his corner of the Sailors' Arms, sings:

MR WALDO

In Pembroke City when I was young
I lived by the Castle Keep
Sixpence a week was my wages
For working for the chimbley sweep.

Six cold pennies he gave me
Not a farthing more or less
And all the fare I could afford
Was parsnip gin and watercress.

I did not need a knife and fork
Or a bib up to my chin
To dine on a dish of watercress
And a jug of parsnip gin.

Did you ever hear a growing boy
To live so cruel cheap
On grub that has no flesh and bones
And liquor that makes you weep?

Sweep sweep chimbley sweep,
I wept through Pembroke City
Poor and barefoot in the snow
Till a kind young woman took pity.

Poor little chimbley sweep she said
Black as the ace of spades
Oh nobody's swept my chimbley
Since my husband went his ways.

Come and sweep my chimbley
Come and sweep my chimbley
She sighed to me with a blush
Come and sweep my chimbley
Come and sweep my chimbley
Bring along your chimbley brush!

Blind Captain Cat climbs into his bunk. Like a cat, he sees in the dark. Through the voyages of his tears, he sails to see the dead.

CAPTAIN CAT
Dancing Williams!

FIRST DROWNED
Still dancing.

CAPTAIN CAT
Jonah Jarvis

THIRD DROWNED
Still.

Curly Bevan's skull.

ROSIE PROBERT
Rosie, with God. She has forgotten dying.

The dead come out in their Sunday best.

Listen to the night breaking.

Organ Morgan goes to chapel to play the organ. He plays alone at night to anyone who will listen: lovers, revellers, the silent dead, tramps or sheep. He sees Bach lying on a tombstone.

ORGAN MORGAN
Johann Sebastian!

CHERRY OWEN [Drunkenly]
Who?

ORGAN MORGAN
Johann Sebastian mighty Bach. Oh, Bach, fach.

CHERRY OWEN
To hell with you,

says Cherry Owen who is resting on the tombstone on his way home.

Mr Mog Edwards and Miss Myfanwy Price happily apart from one another at the top and the sea-end of the town write their everynight letters of love and desire. In the warm White Book of Llareggub you will find the little maps of the islands of their contentment.

MYFANWY PRICE
Oh, my Mog, I am yours for ever.

And she looks around with pleasure at her own neat neverdull room which Mr Mog Edwards will never enter.

MOG EDWARDS

Come to my arms, Myfanwy.

And he hugs his lovely money to his own *heart.*

And Mr Waldo drunk in Milk Wood hugs his lovely Polly Garter under the eyes and rattling tongues of the neighbours and the birds, and he does not care. He smacks his live red lips.

But it is not his *name that Polly Garter whispers as she lies under the oak and loves him back. Six feet deep that name sings in the cold earth.*

POLLY GARTER [Sings]

But I always think as we tumble into bed
Of little Willy Wee who is dead, dead, dead.

The thin night darkens. A breeze from the creased water sighs the streets close under Milk waking Wood. The Wood, whose every treefoot's cloven in the black glad sight of the hunters of lovers, that is a God-built garden to Mary Ann the Sailors who knows there is Heaven on earth and the chosen people of His kind fire in Llareggub's land, that is the fairday farmhands' wantoning ignorant chapel of bridebeds, and, to the Reverend Eli Jenkins, a greenleaved sermon on the innocence of men, the suddenly wind-shaken wood springs awake for the second dark time this one Spring day.